3Souls

an ancient uptown love triangle

By John Heers

3Souls

an ancient uptown love triangle

By John Heers

To my wife who reminds me
that I am much more than the paltry conceptions of my fallen mind.

PROLOGUE

As from a broken blister the words bleed from my mouth.

"Why, Mitkin?"

Mitkin looks at me, his eyes so blue I long for a second look.

"Is that really why you're here, David?"

I drum my fingers on the table and grind my teeth. Mitkin is reaching out from the past and poking me again with his bony mind. I can't take it. I ask again louder.

"Why, Mitkin?"

"David, I never intended, in my heart I never—"

"Never what?"

Mitkin turns melancholy. "There's so much to say. First you, David. Tell me why you're here."

Why am I here? Why am I in this dank, piss-beige waiting room with greasy tables and hulking vending machines stocked full of day-old cuisine sold by the box, special treats bought by doleful relatives who plug away with plastic tokens because real money isn't allowed here? Why have I come to this human meat locker to visit this half-man, a man I've avoided for nearly fourteen years?

An enormous pile of rubble rises in my soul and against it I feel myself lean, resigned again to use it as a crutch, not willing to take it apart as Mitkin is now asking me to do. No, this heap is too large and too dirty for mortal men like myself, the answers buried within too disquieting.

An otherworldly dynamite is what I need, a terrible explosive I don't own and never have. But Mitkin cares little for my mealy silence. He just keeps staring, waiting for me to take apart the junk heap, saying he'll tell all if only I do the same. And somewhere inside, I feel a compulsion that makes me want to comply, to make the deal, to let it all go and revisit the past entirely so that finally I can move on with my life. Isn't that why I've come? Isn't that the whole point?

I start to feel sticky and sweaty, I start to feel dirty. I desperately want to move, leave, walk away, but I stay. As I sit here now, writing about this first day with Mitkin, only ten days removed, I realize that all of it has been like a locomotive.

This moment has been looming for a long time, thundering down the tracks, once a long way off, but now whistling and roaring out of my soul. And what makes it all unbearable is that Mitkin seems to be driving this crap heap of a train. Mitkin is the goddamned conductor.

"I'm asking the questions, Mitkin. Why did you do it?"

"David," he pleads.

"Why?"

He dumps his words in a raw lump. "I didn't know love."

I've heard these words before but not from him. I've heard this from Raphaella, spoken with the same sorrowful tone, the same resignation and the same gentle humility. In his mouth, the words rattle me and cut me and stir me about. Laden as they are with the burden of lost love and the still unvarnished memories of beauty and separation, his words bring me to the brink of tears.

Then from a perch behind an elevated desk, a guard wearing the tag *Sgt. Rigliano* announces that visiting hours are over. Over? I rub my eyes to clear my mind. Mitkin stands up and I follow his lead, hoping he will yell to the guard that we need more time. Instead Mitkin says to me, "You coming back?"

"What?" I manage.

The guard thunders "Let's go!" and people start to hug and say their farewells.

Mitkin peers up. "Rocky, how about a couple more minutes?"

"Can't do it, Mitkin."

I ask suddenly, "Is the warden in?" A host of visitors turn and look as I ask again. "Is Warden Riley in right now?"

Sergeant Rigliano checks his watch. "First of all, relax. Second, yeah, the Warden's in. Where else he gonna be?" With an encumbered wave of his big tattooed arm, Rocky Rigliano ushers everyone out. We line up and shuffle toward the door, Mitkin and I side by side.

"So, you'll come back then?"

For fourteen years I've been stalling, running from this day, and now, as if shackled, I can't get loose. All of this is making me physically tired. "Uh, yeah," I say. "I'll come back… yeah. I'll come."

I leave Mitkin and pull myself across a well-kept courtyard, through three sliding steel doors and into the administrative offices of the prison. I know this complex well because this is where I have waited while my beloved daughter spent entire afternoons chatting with the man who catapulted New York City into an infamous inferno, and the city that is my soul into ruins. The secretary ushers me in immediately.

"I've got to see him again," I say to the warden. "Mitkin," I say, louder. "I've got to see him so I can finish my story." I nearly say *life* instead of *story*. Life. Story.

"What story, David?"

"Mine, and it's long."

"Your daughter never mentioned that you were a writer, you write?" The warden looked at me over his smudged reading glasses.

"Yeah, I do, I mean I am."

And then I think about how I haven't written anything for years, how I've been broken by a hell-hewn writer's block that has crushed my career. And then I think, nearly aloud, *writing career?* And that thought makes me feel very lazy and very wry, and in a weird way, soiled too.

"Well, of course you can see him again then," says the warden. "Given all that you've been through, Dana's visits here and their relationship, sure." He smiles. "How is your daughter by the way? Such a sweet thing."

I breathe and begin to think of Dana. She is my daughter, the fruit of my union with Raphaella Hurston and the one who, inexplicably, has devoted herself to visiting Mitchell Mitkin. She started coming to Saginaw State Prison at thirteen, maybe four times a year, and then more often as she got old enough to drive, borrowing my car and leaving very early to make the drive north. We had many arguments over these visits, especially when his letters would show up in our mailbox. I told her she was consorting with an evil man and she told me I was resentful and that I didn't know love.

I didn't know love. Inevitably, remembering her mother, I would relent, but until today I hated her trips to the state prison. Until today, I was wracked by them.

"David?" The warden plumbs my daydream. "How much time do you need?"

I know he is asking me how much time I need with Mitkin, but my mind drifts, still picturing Dana and how I hated her for coming here. Something cosmic, I think to myself, something her mother would call metanoia. "A week." I ask for one entire week out of my life. For him.

The warden is astounded too. "With Mitkin? What do you mean a week?"

"I need to see him every day for a week, every day for three or four hours or as many as I need to finish, uh, the book." I pause. "Please, Warden Riley, a week and then I'll forget about Mitkin."

He laughs and his meaty jowls jiggle, reminding me of Santa Claus. "You've become like your daughter, David, her time up here has rubbed off on you."

I hold a plastic smile. "A week then?"

Watching the warden, I can see him go from irritation to incomprehension to resignation. It's as if he realizes this is not for him. "I'll clear it."

And that is that.

I rent a hotel room just up the road, a mud-brown Motel 6 room. This is where I've been for the last ten days, gutting and disgorging my story, our story, under the glow of a little yellow lamp. It is from here that I call my department chair back in New York and let him know that I need the rest of the week off, telling him and now believing I have a family emergency. I've begun my personal transformation, my journey back to my soul, to my daughter and to her mother, to the very people who have confounded and captivated me for my entire adult life.

***

It is the next day and I've been given a little side room adjacent to the main visiting area. To my surprise, Warden Riley has provided me with pen and paper, long yellow legal pads that stretch out in front of me, my only comfort now, the only thing left between him and me. I startle when the door clicks and slides open, revealing like a Broadway curtain the man who'd become the improbable lead in my very own Greek tragedy. I get up to face him. Standing, I clear my throat but do not speak. I can't speak, actually. I search my mind for a good place to start, but it's a roiling, glaring, polychromatic mess. I dart from thoughts of Raphaella and her Transylvanian father to the manic, makeshift homeless shelter and dumb Andy Seever. I bound between bullet holes and arson and the overthrow of the New York City public school system. I entertain flash images of Mitkin's ugly friend and cult leader, a guy the world would come to know as Ed Taughtauer, juxtaposed a dour Dostoevsky who is bear hugging me and kissing me cheek to cheek, a million dollars piled cartoonishly in a brown oak bucket at our feet. And still I can't find anything to say. This is really stupid, I think, but then Mitkin speaks sheepishly.

"Dana told me this would happen. That you'd come to me."

"Is that right?" I say.

"She said you were a good man."

I waggle and roll my eyes. "Well, meeting with you hardly makes me a good man, besides, maybe this isn't about you at all." I look down. "Maybe it's about something else."

He nods. "Maybe, maybe so."

There is an awkward silence until finally he says, "Shall we sit?"

I nod and we sit. Another awkward silence. I scribble the words *calm* and *creepy* on a legal pad.

"Where shall we begin?" he asks.

"At the beginning."

He leans back in his chair, twines his fingers together just under his chin and sighs a peaceful sigh. Another long pause makes me think I should be saying something, but looking again I see he is meditating, or praying maybe. Really? This is not the same man I knew before, not the same man at all.

"David, when you write all this down and turn it into your memoir, could you do one thing?" Mitkin leans forward. "It won't be easy, this thing, it will be almost impossible." His eyes burn. "Could you tell the truth?"

"The truth?" It sort of slides out of my mouth.

"For her, perfectly?"

For her, he says. Like he loves her, like he cares for her. How odd, how sickening it sounds. I hate him. Then into my silent rage, his hand. He takes mine in his and says, softly, "Forgive me, David."

I am confused and defused all in the same moment. I don't know how long we sit before he asks, "Do you remember the day I moved in?" I nod. "Can we start there?"

"Yes. Start there."

CHAPTER I

Mitchell Mitkin

Damn, I thought. What time is it?

The doorbell was making a pit, pit, paaaat, paaaat and hurry up sound. Raphaella jumped up first and walked naked to the intercom. I rolled over into the warmth she'd left.

"Who is it?" she asked.

"Mitkin, Mitchell, your new neighbor. Please open the door, thank you." He said all of this quickly and orderly.

"Mitchell?" repeated Raphaella.

Neither of us knew Mitkin was moving in this day, and neither of us expected him to ring if he did. He had no reason to; his father owned the building.

"Hello? It's Martin Mitkin's son, Mitchell. I'm the heir to this building, the building that you live in for four hundred dollars a month. The lease, by the way, runs out in October. Open the door please. Thank you." Some static came through the intercom. I dragged myself out of the bed and pulled Raphaella's hand off the two-way talk button.

"Let me go down there and deal with this guy. I mean, what's his deal?"

She looked plainly at me. "His deal is his father owns the building."

I blinked. "And I own a bed and want to be in it…"

"No," she snapped, "that's my bed, and you sleep too much as it is." Then under her breath she whispered something cruel, or at least it sounded cruel, and then she rolled her eyes. She put her finger back on the intercom but it wouldn't buzz. There was no sound. She sucked air through her clenched teeth. "Go and let him in, and tell him his father needs to fix the buzzer, it hasn't worked right for a week." She opened the door and stared me out. I cowered and left, but not before a parcel of thought tumbled through my mind: Daybreak with Raphaella was never as good as nightfall. Never.

I descended three flights of stairs and could hear Mitkin ring the bell two more times. There were two front doors, one opening into a tiny foyer, the second into the building itself. Mitkin had already come through the first door and was doggedly waiting, peeking around a little curtain that covered the window on the inside, pushing his face against the glass and gawking.

He was switching from one eye and one vantage point to the other, back and forth, like a mad sleuth. Against the thick, heavy glass his face looked distorted. It was aquiline to be sure, and it was stern. I opened the door and immediately he walked in, resolutely studying every nook and corner, bouncing questions and answers back and forth between his eyes and his mind. And then he rested on me. He stood about six feet tall, his eyes sky blue, his face long and sharp and dominated by a strong, imposing nose. Forcefully, like a cop directing traffic, he stuck out his hand.

"Hello, I'm Mitchell Mitkin." I just stared. He extended his hand an extra inch, imploring me to take it and shake it. I didn't. "You must be a visitor because my father rents to Raphaella Hurston, and she's a woman." He dropped his outstretched hand. "You are?" I wanted to laugh because he was so stiff like a bad actor, and so old for his age.

"David."

"Just David?" he said.

"Yeah, just David."

He waited for me to add more and when I didn't he briskly looked away. Then after a short pause he nodded. He walked past me and up the stairs. Turning around, he stopped and looked down on me.

"David, if you are angry because I woke you up early, well I didn't plan to. Someone vandalized the lock last night and I was not able to use my key. My guess is, your key, Ms. Hurston's key that is, will not work either. I have already arranged to have a locksmith come, in fact he is on the way. When he is finished I will provide Raphaella Hurston with a new set of keys and I will also, of course, supply myself. This means it is unlikely that I will ever wake either of you up early on a Saturday morning again." He paused ceremoniously. "If Ms. Hurston is interested in greeting her new neighbor she can find him in the U-Haul truck outside, in the hall here, or in the apartment upstairs." He turned away quickly, took one step forward up the staircase, and looked back. "I trust you know how it is to move into a new apartment, things happen." With this he jerked himself back around and ascended the steps to the second floor.

"What a little wank," I said under my breath.

I took a peek outside and saw his truck. It sat trailer first, halfway up the sidewalk. I fought the sleep still in my muscles and trudged to the third floor where Raphaella was making tea. The kettle sang to a boil.

"This guy is crazy, Raphie!"

With no response I stuck my head around the corner to hear her say, "These things are a pain in my ass. Crap." And then in the bathroom, I heard the teeming tin-tapping of scattering pills. "Come on! What the…" I pulled the tea off the stove and headed down the hall toward the bathroom.

Raphaella emerged, her face a receding red. "Can you believe these damn things? How's a woman like me supposed to have the patience for this? Look." She thrust an empty bottle in my face. "Every last one of them on the floor." I nodded and she sauntered past me into the kitchen. She opened and then slammed shut a cupboard door. I scooped up the scattered pills and followed her into the kitchen.

"You met Mitkin?"

"Downstairs. He's crazy you know. He's—"

"Like nobody you've ever met? I know. I've spoken to him on the phone. He thinks he knows everything and I'm not so sure he doesn't." She pulled out a teacup with one hand while clutching the toaster in the other. "He's a little nerd. Reminds me of his father." Wearing only her bra, I noticed her bulbous belly. It stopped me.

"Look at that. Look at my baby, he's going to be a solid, fat baby." I walked over to rub her belly but she took my hand and put it to my head.

"If he's fat, it's your genes, the fat genes you got in your fat head." And with a little inglorious laugh she snatched her mug and headed down the long hall to the living room. I watched her go and fought the urge to curse her. I should have fought the next urge too, but I didn't. Nope, I followed her down that hall in search of her approval, not sure what I'd say or why. In the living room she ensconced herself in the only comfortable chair in the apartment, sprawling unbridled despite her near nakedness. This was nothing new; she often walked around naked, defiantly passing in front of windows, nonchalantly exposing her beautiful brown body. With her skin supping on the recliner's lush leather she clicked on the television and slurped from her cup.

I slithered up and leaned against the wall, my head dangling into the room, not altogether invited, but in, nonetheless. "Seriously Raphie, this guy is intense.

I think he wants us to come down and help him move in, I had to kind of make him know he was rude. I think he realized it."

"No he didn't," she quipped, still staring at the television.

"How do you know?"

"Because he doesn't realize things like that. He doesn't care about being polite, or normal behavior, he's more like a machine." She stopped to sip her tea and a bloated pause stilled the room. "I kind of like the way he is, actually. It gets rid of all the crap most people spend their whole life wading through. You know? I mean you're familiar with that?" She waited. "Right?"

There was a thud and then some hammering. I looked contemptuously at Raphaella. "Yeah, wow, he sounds really, really great." She didn't look at me, and instead paged through the *Daily News*. More than a few silent moments passed as page by page she turned my stomach and boiled my blood. Like the newspaper, I'd become a distraction.

There was another bang and some more hammering. Raphaella looked at me.

"Why don't you go help him," she said. "It's his first time living on his own for God's sake. Help him out. You'll probably learn something. He's on his way to Columbia you know, wants to study biology."

I was amazed. "That guy's only just now going to college? He looks like he's forty-five."

"I know. I think it's his eyes. Did you notice how blue they were?"

Her tone was a little too tender, so I lied. "Nah, I didn't notice."

"You will, you will." With that Raphaella got up, went to the bathroom and sat heavily on the toilet. She sighed. I imagined her saying something like, "Could you please leave me alone or is the toilet the only place I can get some peace?" Was it the hormones or was it just me, just us? I turned around and marched out the front door.

Mitkin's door gently knocked open and I peeked inside. He had already carried up a large box and a drawer full of clothes. Tightly tucked balls of cotton socks lay all over. He had dumped a gunnysack full of bricks against the wall that probably accounted for the thud. What does he want with a big bag of bricks? I went in a few more steps and saw a large box of books. I grabbed one. It was David Hume's *Treatise of Human Nature*. I put it back and grabbed another, this one entitled *Ethics Without God*. Another was exceptionally fat and looked like a biology textbook. I put that one back too; its width made me nervous. I left the books and turned to leave when Mitkin walked in carrying an armful of plastic crates filled to capacity.

"So she made you come down and help me move in, huh?" He peeked around his load. "Women." He kept talking as he moved away from me, stepping over boxes and making his way to the kitchen. I imagined that he never stood still.

"I stuck a nickel between the door and the frame so you can come and go as you please. The truck is open too. Thanks." He moved tactically, reminding me of a highly skilled, highly efficient Roman soldier, or maybe an Army Corps engineer. He gave me the creeps, yet his confident, calculated cadence was hypnotic. I succumbed to it involuntarily.

Mitkin's father, Martin Mitkin, was a respected professor at Columbia and had only recently bought this building at 102 E.103rd Street. He had negotiated a good deal on it from a trustee with whom he had worked on some project. The elder Mitkin was the department chair of biology and a retired physician renowned for his work on organ transplants. And he was a philanthropist. He had donated millions to public schools and their science programs, and as the chief executive of a multimillion dollar foundation called *Science Now,* he was renowned. Mitchell Mitkin had grown up in Martin's suburban household an only child, an exceptional only child, whose welfare was closely monitored by Martin himself. Both parents doted. Mitchell's mother worked in real estate after her son was old enough to go to school, but she never got over not being his full-time mother and indulged him even at the age of nineteen, especially at the age of nineteen. The thought of him living alone in this Manhattan apartment terrified her. Her fear had less to do with the big city and more to do with his outlook on life. She agonized about his inability to relate to youthful things; the simple, soft and loving things his mother had spent so much time trying to give him.

"She's far too emotional," he told me as he stood in the foyer. I had taken a seat on a box of books while he robotically divulged a matter-of-fact monologue of his life to date. "My mother doesn't always get it, if you know what I mean."

"What about your dad?" I said. "How's he with you moving in?"

"He only charges me half the rent. I feel like that's acceptable for now, but when I am able to make more I will pay more. It should be soon. School won't be so hard."

"But why pay? I mean your pops sounds willing to pay."

"He is willing to pay but I am not willing to be a millstone around his neck. Millstones are heavy—the Rolling Rock millstone upstate weighed nearly eleven thousand pounds, large for its day." He looked me dead in the eye waiting for a response, but how does one respond to uninvited information about colonial millstones? "Look," he snapped, "I don't want to burden my father. First high school, then college, then grad school, then teaching and then research. This is a long process. Expensive. I can't just expect payments, I look at it like the, the... the disentanglement of the self." He paused as I silently mouthed his word *disentanglement*. "Not accepting his money is a move toward monetary and intellectual independence, you know, taking care of my own business, my own self. If I do, one day I become like him and if I don't, I become a waste of skin, a nothing."

Looking at him, his eyes breathing a cold blue and his sandy hair a bit disheveled, I wondered how a kid comes to act like this, think like this. This guy was consumed with his ideas, the first among them the idea of intellectual independence, not exactly a chart-topper for most beer-swilling college freshmen. His deep, penetrating eyes, almost always furrowed, pointed to a boy driven to know something greater than childhood.

But Mitkin's intensity wasn't entirely offensive, in fact, it was contagious at times, and standing there I wondered if maybe I should try harder to know what he knows, be like him. But then there was the other thing there in that room with us, with him. I sensed that he protested too much, as if he were burying something, something ugly and sad. The thought crossed my mind that he'd been cocooned, and that maybe this excessive sheltering drove him to crave control. I imagined a dark night and a young owl raised in a zoo, and I imagined that young owl being let loose into the night. Weird, I know, but so was Mitkin.

I laughed, "Well, if you won't take his money, I will." He chuckled too, but only a bit.

"Do you need money?" he asked, looking at me.

I floundered, "No, no, not really, I was just joking." But I did need money. I always needed money in those days before the birth of our child. In fact, I always needed money, period.

"If you need money I can get it for you, just let me know."

"I will," I said, thinking to myself how odd it was that this rigid, rather rude guy also had a generous side. The door-buzz sounded and ended our little conversation. At the front door stood a locksmith with a thick, unshaven face and mussed hair. Mitkin opened the front door and immodestly shook his hand, just as he had wanted to shake mine.

"Mitchell Mitkin, I am the one who called. This lock has been tampered with and we need a new one. You do sell locks on site, don't you?" By "on site" I took him to mean here, standing in front of the apartment, at 7:45 a.m., on a Saturday morning. I knew the answer.

"You'll have to go to the shop when it opens at nine. Here's my card. But maybe you don't need a new lock. Let me take a look." The locksmith walked by Mitkin and into the foyer. He assumed it was an interior lock, not the front door, and Mitkin let him go but not without giving me this saturated look, the kind he'd flashed me earlier, a look that bled arrogance.

"Excuse me, locksmith," he said, "the lock is right here. And no, you won't be able to fix it unless you have a method for drying cyanoacrylate." He paused with a sarcastic smile. "Though I doubt you do, the sun and thousands of years is about the only method for drying super glue, and you won't get much sun in that little hole, will you?" He pointed at the door. The tubby locksmith returned and bent over.

"Yep, you're right kid. Gonna need a new one." Mitkin gave me another saturated smile, holding it uncharitably. The locksmith, guileless, replied with a straight face, "You're gonna want a—"

"Medeco, deadbolt. Nonretractable. Seventy-nine ninety-nine. We'll be in by 9:30. We need keys too." He poked a glance my way.

"We make keys," said the locksmith.

"Really? Oh perfect, we'll be by."

The locksmith left and I waited for Mitkin to laugh at the locksmith, smugly. He didn't. I watched as he just turned and occupied himself with keeping the door open. "You know a lot about locks, man."

The sun was breaking through the rows of trees that lined the street and the clear, crisp morning air intimated a more sweltering afternoon. I wanted to get the moving over so I could go about the business of enjoying my Saturday. I got the feeling he expected me to go with him to the hardware store so I began to invent stories in my head. *I need to paint my house. I have matinee tickets for Cats. I have to swing by the heliport. I hate moving things that are heavy, especially other people's heavy things.* He spoke before I could think of a good one.

"Do you drink beer?"

"Sure."

"Which?"

"Guinness," I said.

"How about going with me to get a cold beer and the keys in a couple hours. We'll toast to new neighbors, new keys and newborn babies. How about it?"

"Babies? Raphaella and I are having a baby." I smiled at him but his pursed lips told me he knew this already, and that, well, that was the reason he'd brought it up, idiot. I felt like the locksmith must have felt. "How did you know?" I asked.

"My father told me. I guessed you were the father, and you are."

"How does your father know?"

"She told him."

Why? I thought.

"Does your father talk to her often?" I tried to sound compliant, but inside a sea of jealousy swelled. And yes, it is utterly absurd that I could feel jealousy in this situation, but I did, and it was real, and really annoying.

"You sound resentful," said Mitkin, as if on cue.

"About what?"

"That's what I'm asking you. Why are you jealous that your girlfriend's landlord knows your girlfriend is pregnant?" He sort of rolled his eyes. "Who worries about that?"

Put this way sure, it sounded pretty silly, but not silly enough to stem the rolling tide. "Look, I'm not jealous, I was just wondering how you knew. Besides, who are you anyway?"

He looked at me, perplexed. It was as if I had been a toy whose head he'd made pop off. He just stared at me, a little dejected that I was so mad. A stilted silence lingered and it struck me that I was in a fight with a guy I barely knew, a guy who was indisputably odd, and incontrovertibly compelling. He was also a neighbor now, and the landlord's son, and I wasn't even on the lease. Any lease. Anywhere.

"Look," I said. "Sorry for that. I'm oversensitive maybe. Sorry." The whole scene was pathetic, and it made me despise the thought of sharing a beer with him. We got upstairs with the last of the boxes and needed only to move a couch, a television and his bed. I began to realize that without me he couldn't move in at all. Where was his help? Was he just always alone? Possible, I thought. Sitting in his apartment, amid boxes and boxes of books, I asked about his father.

"He couldn't make it." His voice trembled slightly. "He has small cell carcinoma."

Small cell carcinoma? "What?" I said.

"Small cell carcinoma of the lungs. But he'll be okay."

"I'm sorry," I said, thinking that I'd better be.

"Why?" he intoned. "Don't be sorry. If you think about it then you won't be sorry. It's simple, not sorry. His body has a flat and the repairmen are going to fix it. I go and see him once a day. He's on his way back, he's doing just fine."

"Well, I hope they fix him up."

"They will. They will. There's no doubt. It's amazing the things we have learned about our bodies since getting rid of the irrational beliefs of the past." I nodded incompletely, tentatively. Sitting on the same box I'd perused earlier, I was reminded of the *Treatise of Human Nature* and the *Ethics Without God*, two books that now dug like tridents into my thigh. They, I thought, are leaving a mark on me. "With the new medicines," he continued, "and new ways of thinking, well, we'll get my father fixed right up."

"Did you learn that from these books," I pointed between my legs.

"From those books? Oh, yeah, from some of those books anyway. The ones in that box help us make sense of the world. Especially Hume. Hume's in there right?" I nodded and he looked at me suspiciously. "How did you know that?"

"I... I saw it just now when I sat down."

He gazed and then continued, "Anyway, Hume makes sense because he admits." I must have cocked my head or raised an eyebrow, like a dog teased by a squeaky toy. "Admits knowing nothing, nothing but what is given to him through his five senses." His hand showed five outstretched fingers. "Sight. Sound. Taste. Smell. Touch. We are just a bundle of perceptions. Anyone who tells you anything else is deluded." He settled onto a box too. "My father reads Hume. He says Hume helped lead mankind through all the feces that piled up under the rule of kings and bishops. He says now all we have to do is wipe ourselves clean, lick ourselves like cats. I like that idea, don't you?" He stood up, grabbed his orange juice, sipped it, and then pretended to lick the top. It was unnerving and borderline creepy. He grinned and took two steps toward me, motioning that I get up. "Hummph," he muttered, still swallowing, but now pointing. I hopped up, afraid I was breaking something or acting foolish. He had that effect on people. He hooked Hume's heavy book and fished it out.

"Take it. Read the part about the slave to passions. Hume explains why there is no morality, only the mind. In a nutshell it's all about choice, or the lack thereof." He held the book up near his shoulder, wiggling it. "Our choices of right and wrong are not really choices at all, just the intellect following up on the flesh, mind to body, taking clues and hints from physical experiences and turning them into 'right' choices, or like I said once in class, navigable paths. Hume," he said, as if eating a delectable treat, "was the first real philosopher. Without him there's no modern science." He stuck the book out and I got the urge to wag my head in disbelief. A little, scraggly nineteen-year-old hand dangled 200-year-old prose nonchalantly in my face, handing it over like the latest from Stephen King. I grabbed it, after all, who wouldn't want to find out about "navigable paths" and the origins of modern science? Besides, Raphaella said something about philosophy and wanting to learn at the laundromat the day before.

"Yeah, thanks," I said.

We both got up to begin the last of his move. Soon we would have his bed, his television and his couch in the apartment. The job complete, it was surely too early for a Guinness.

"Now we go get that beer." Period. A done deal. Not too early. Like a serf I headed upstairs to tell Raphaella his plans. I met her in the hallway.

"He's all moved in," I said. "What time is it?"

"Around eleven I'd guess. Is he still around?" She peered over the banister looking toward Mitkin's front door. "His father called and left a message."

"He's inside. His father called you?"

"Yeah." She started down the stairs and around the banister toward the middle of the landing and Mitkin's front door. I let her pass and followed her into Mitkin's apartment. She tapped on the door before entering.

"Come on in, David, I'm ready to go," yelled Mitkin from his bedroom. Raphie waited in the foyer, facing Mitkin's room and waiting for him to emerge. He started out and immediately stopped.

"Raphaella?" He started again, this time a bit quicker. The whole scene made the ocean in me swell again. It just didn't seem like two strangers greeting each other. Or did it? I kept an eagle's eye on both of them.

"So this is what you look like? How many times have we spoken on the phone, three now? It is so good to finally meet you." He walked so close I thought he would kiss her. And his voice changed. He now sounded nearly normal, not excruciatingly clever and ridiculously officious. Normal, like a man with a thick mustache or a guy waiting in line to buy a hotdog at a Mets game. Almost cool normal. Raphaella gave him a peck on the cheek. A tiny, airy sound escaped from my dropping jowls.

"Mitchell Mitkin, it's nice to finally meet you, too. How you like this place?"

"You know I've seen it, Raphaella, it's just I've never seen you in it." He looked at her intensely, and there was a good deal to look at. She was beautiful. She stood straighter than he, and her posture made her seem just as tall. Her hair was thick and jet-black and cochlear, like a million ebony ropes. And it was long, past her shoulders long. Her skin was a burnished chestnut, her eyes emerald green. But more than anything—her lips. Underneath her Mediterranean nose, they rest like deep purple pillows, one on top of the other, but even, and pouty, and perfect. She was exotic, a woman of perfectly mixed blood.

"Show me the baby," said Mitkin.

Raphaella lifted her T-shirt and the little bulge that was my baby availed itself. He touched it. I was dumbstruck. He touched it again. None of his touches were in any way sensual; everything he did with her belly was purely clinical and cold. Still, I thought, this is all far too familiar. He held one hand against her and tapped with the other. He used his thumb to push gently into the flank of her abdominal area. He acted as if he knew what he was doing and I know it seems unlikely, but he hypnotized me into complacency and obedience. He called me over.

"Now, David. Here," he pointed to just below Raphaella's pant-line and just above her groin area, "is the actual resting place of the child. As it grows this is the best place to listen for signs of life. It's so perfect the way our bodies function. We are fine machines. Fine, fine machines." He tapped twice on her stomach as he finished the sentence. Raphaella did not seem to care at all. She was always like this when it came to her body, she had progressive notions about sex and self, sometimes too progressive.

"Well Mitchell," I said, "I say we get that beer. Let's go. You buy." I moved backwards as if to get everyone rolling in the same direction. "Shall we?"

Raphaella spoke up. "Wait Mitchell, your father called. He said to visit him before one. Says he's got tests after one. He called about twenty minutes ago." Mitkin seemed startled.

"Tests?"

"Yes."

"Was he on the phone or a nurse?"

"It was him. He sounded fine. I hope I didn't wait too long to tell you. Is everything all right?" Mitkin no longer seemed nervous.

"Yes, yes, no problem. It's just that I was scheduled to visit him later this afternoon and Father never postpones or preempts anything. For him to change plans, well, he must have asked for some exploratory work." Then he wondered aloud, "But if it's a liver function test then…" He trailed off and came back again. "Anyway, no problem. I think I'll skip the beer David. Later, that's a promise." I guessed that if it were a promise, it would undoubtedly happen. He darted back to his jumbled room and grabbed his running shoes and fanny pack. He tied his shoes in front of us.

"I'll see you later. I'm running to the hospital, it's faster. Plus, I'm getting a belly like yours, Raphaella. No good." Of course, he had no belly, and it was hard to imagine any fat on this man, be it on his body or in his mind or as a part of his life. Everything was streamlined and ordered and pertinent. We stepped aside as he locked up while jogging in place. It was annoying. "I'll bring back keys and a new lock for us all, no need to worry. Bye."

CHAPTER II
Raphaella and Me

I was born in Pittsburg, California, the back side of the bay, the California where cities bleed together, amalgamate; where low flat malls serve as land markers and cars are modified to bounce up and down. We moved twice when I was growing up, to San Francisco and back again. I remember the hills of San Francisco because I used to walk them on my way to grammar school, a little private school with red doors and blue window shutters. My mother said it used to be Lutheran, a Lutheran church, but now it was just a school. She said that even if they still taught Lutheran doctrine there it was okay. Her mother, after all, was an Episcopalian, and so were we, and well, Lutherans and Episcopalians are pretty much the same thing anyway, and anyone who tells you differently is probably just unsure that God even exists. She'd say nobody needs to go to church to love God and nobody was ever saved from talking to the gossips in the pews of Christ the Savior Concord. She said it like that too, flat, forcefully. My mother runs the English department at De La Rue, the high school I attended. I remember seeing her stand outside the B building, under the rain runners, herding kids in and out of their classes, saying things like, "I love you, Tom Ellis, but you're still late for math class," or, "Who wants to fail today, I've got to fail somebody, who's it gonna be?"

She was pretty standing there, my mother. Blond, brownish blond, tall and stylish. She always spoke her mind, and that, my father always said, is what made her beautiful. My school friends thought she was beautiful too, but not for the same reason as my father. They told me they liked her style, her stockings, her skirt. They wanted to say she was sexy but they thought I'd fight them if they did, if they said "nice legs" and "sexy" in the same sentence. I did fight a kid once who said "nice legs" and *your mother* in the same sentence, a sentence that ended with me pounding him with a furious fist to the forehead. I was suspended for two weeks instead of one because the kid's stitches wouldn't close over his eye and he had to wear a big gauze bandage with a little red blotch the shape of New Jersey continuously bleeding through. He looked like a veteran of the Civil War. My mother didn't think he looked so interesting however, and she recommended that a week be added to my sentence. So, that didn't help my cause much either. My mother was just that way.

John Higgins is my father. He is a very good lawyer. In fact, my mother says he's the best lawyer in the Bay Area. He works in San Francisco for Roberts, Higgins and Such, a job that has landed him in his big black Mercedes every morning and every evening for fifteen years, an hour and a half each way. When I was a kid my father told me San Francisco was a friendly city for gay men, and that more people should be friendly to gay men like the city was friendly. My sister and I would always laugh when he said this because we never knew how a city could be friendly to anybody.

I look up to my big sister Ella. She is pretty like my mother, with long black hair that curls at the end. It's black because she dyes it, but it doesn't look like she dyes it; it looks like she is a chic model type from *Cosmopolitan* or *Mademoiselle*, two magazines she hooked me on when I was still in high school. We'd read them together, she asking me which girls I thought were prettiest or stylish and I asking her which clothes she preferred, which cut, which colors. These conversations were always private and I'd make her promise not to tell anyone on the track team that I'd looked at *Cosmo* with her. I ran track because I was fast and I played lacrosse because I was agile and the coach told me I could be as good as I chose to be. But what I enjoyed most was *Cosmo*, and fashion, and reading and listening to my mother tell me why Hemingway was a revolutionary and why he'd be the one we'd all remember in the end, even if he were a boor.

My mother loved to read to me. The first good book she ever read to me was *Zorba the Greek*. She'd read to me when I'd come home from running the 400-meter relay at track practice, in the car while I learned to drive and while I wrote poetry on the computer. It was her way of killing two birds with one stone: She re-reading for her classes, me listening to great literature, to great movements in the soul of Nikos Kazantzakis. She would point out how his words glide through the mind; the effluvium of their flight gently licking and lapping at the subconscious of the reader, kissing and tickling them in places they did not know existed. And she taught me how words could be like drums in the night, how they could sound out tears and emotions and colors and the hemlines of a beautiful woman's beautiful skirt. She and Nikos are why I still write poetry, why I ever wrote poetry at all.

And because my mother loved men, and their books, I loved women. Very much. When I was twelve, turning thirteen, I fell in love with the daughter of my father's secretary. I saw her at one of my father's parties, leaving. I saw her turn and look at me as she closed the door, her gold hair switching from one side of her face to the other, her smile spreading out white, and her skirt, pure *Cosmo*, her skirt. I didn't know her name when I bought the tulips from my father's favorite florist, the florist right around the corner from his office in the city, the city I was forbidden to travel to alone. I trudged up the big hill and gave them, yellow and red and white, to my maiden's mother, a bead of sweat rolling down my cheek. And then I read my poem, aloud, with my father standing at the door, half sheepish, half peeved.

> *San Francisco is kind to gay men*
> *It is filled with hills and bad car clutches*
> *It is home to Roberts, Higgins and Such*
> *And now it is home to the girl I love*
> *And her mother too*
> *What is your daughter's name?*
> *My name is David Higgins*

Her mother told me that Carol was her name, her daughter's name. My father told me I'd get grounded if I ever came to the city alone again, and then he laughed, uncontrollably. I kissed Carol three months later at her fourteenth birthday party. She told me I was cute and a good kisser. I told her I loved her and she blushed. Her blush was deep crimson and innocent and I loved looking at it, watching it come and go with each *I love you* I could muster. Carol moved out of the Bay Area when her mother divorced her father and moved in with a volleyball player from Ventura. When she left I told her I loved her again, and I really did; I really, really loved her.

And then a girl named Heather invited me to her house so that I could lose my virginity. She was older than I was, a college girl, and I didn't like that she didn't blush when I told her I loved her. I did like that she was so pretty, strong pretty. So I went to her house—what would Zorba do after all? We made love and my head spun, and I sweated, and I shook and we laughed. I found my underwear in odd places all night, but put them on again in the morning. My father never knew

I wasn't at Jim's house and my mother never bothered to ask. My sister did though, and when she asked what Heather looked like I told her she looked like page 126.

When I was eighteen I got a job working for a publishing company in the city. It was more like an internship really, my mother arranging it with a former colleague of hers. I'd just finished my senior year and would go to college, a top flight graduate, at least in the humanities. I'd gotten straight A's in English and History and my mother had talked me into attending NYU, my sister's school now and my mother's alma mater. Going away meant I'd have to break it off with my girlfriend, the lovely and talented Lisa Sutherland, cheerleader supreme and popular girl ad nauseam. We started our short-lived affair when I saw her crying at a boring party one rainy Friday night. It was Al Almonte's party, the one he had every three months when his parents went on a cruise to some Caribbean island. It was the kind of party where people turn in unison and watch TV whenever an overexposed and utterly talentless pop star appears in a glossy music video. And why didn't anyone ever dance at Al's parties? I mean there was dancing, but only if you count the grisly couple making out to their own rhythm in a shadowy corner. Al always had enough liquor for everyone, including the real angry muscle-bound guys who inevitably showed up after boring conversation with one another, on the strip, in their cars, or in the mall parking lot.

Lisa Sutherland sort of sobbed over a coffee table full of empty beer cups, her hands on her brow, breasts heaving. I watched her. Her head bobbled. What could it be? I looked at her eyes, mahogany almonds glittering in their sea salt sadness. Beautiful. Beautiful, because for a moment they weren't hers. Not cheerleader eyes, not popular eyes, not student body chairwoman eyes, just marvelous, miraculous, wet, round orbs into which a man falls amorous, through which the male world accounts for itself, knows itself. They were Lisa Sutherland's eyes but I loved them because they were everything not male, not man, and not me. *Cosmo.* I took her hand and we danced a slow dance. For a long time we danced and she never asked me to explain why. We danced until she became my girlfriend and I her boyfriend. And things went on like that, until I decided to ship off for NYU where I'd find other girlfriends, other dances, and I told her as much. She understood because, well, she cried. We hugged and I left for New York, a new life, a new metaphor.

My father is the kind of man who measures his paternal love by calendar. First day of kindergarten. First big lacrosse tryout. First day of high school. First day behind the wheel. The Junior Prom, the Senior Ball, graduation, and of course, move-in day, freshman year in college. Is he current, was he there, has he shown that he cares enough to be my father? That's the barometer. He was there dammit, and he would be there for moving-in day, too. I'd hoped my mother would come to New York as well; after all, she had made me for this day, the first day of manhood, the first day out on my own, a poet, a New Yorker. But she would defer to my father. I think he told her he wanted to pat me on the back, share a beer at the college pub, tell me a story concerning drunken coeds, introduce me to an old partner of his, Bill Bert. Bill Bert took us both to lunch and that is when I learned that his daughter would be living not more than two blocks from me. With that, my father had found his reason to pat me on the back, and to wink the fatherly wink. I swigged and smiled back.

"Call her, Son," he said.

Bill Bert nodded.

And I did.

I loved Tabatha Bert. She was tall, handsome and sleek. Her hair was black as crow. She was the first girl I loved who had short hair, shorter than my own, and I wrote this down. She said she liked my soft eyes, but I think she liked the way we made love. She was gregarious and often held my hand in public, even in front of her father, Bill. We went to Central Park and walked her dog Frankie, we studied together and wrote poetry together. I wrote her a poem that I thought was the best poem ever written. I read it in my English class one day, in the small seminar section where our professor was, in fact, a graduate student.

Capsize! Capsize good doubt
Find the bottom of the sea
Where the cold will still you
the dark will keep you
Capsize good doubt
That lovers may live unencumbered
Alive, willing to do what lovers do
Love

No one clapped. Nobody even did that little finger snapping thing, but I still loved that poem. Tabatha said she loved it too, but looking back, I think she loved my muscles when we made love.

My sister hated Tabatha Bert. She said she was "overdone" and that if I dated her for a while I'd know what that meant. My sister would come over during that freshman year, to my dorm, my apartment on 5th Avenue and chat. She and I would laugh together while Tabatha brought us fancy coffees made with a cappuccino machine she'd given me. She gave me lots of gifts, expensive gifts, and I always said thank you. She was good to me, but Ella never relented. Ella was two years older than we were, and she made sure Tabatha knew it. She talked about internships that she'd planned for her senior year and she talked about her boyfriend, a musician with a goatee and a penchant for flunking classes. I'd tell her how Mom wouldn't approve and she'd say how not everyone needs to be an A student and then look at me as if I knew that already, as if I knew that Tabatha was dumb like an ox. And she was dumb, but her hair, with its black sheen and velvety lines, well, she wasn't *that* dumb. However, in the end, my sister was right. When I told Tabatha Bert, she cried and we went our separate ways, but I loved her then. I really, really loved her.

It went like this for two years. My mother calling, my father patting me on the back, girlfriends coming and going. I wrote. I had books filled with poems and half-written novels, short stories that always won fourth prize and essays filled with sentimental notions about world politics, disease, people in love. I had good friends with good looks like me, athletic types who didn't try out for the team, guys whose loyalties lie with bands that nobody else liked, lead singer types who didn't articulate; in short, borderline artists who did school because they didn't know how to risk their art, really risk being an artist. We took refuge knowing we'd make it one day. Cool, chic, relevant.

Then I became irrelevant. Raphaella. She would make me forget my piddling dreams, she would make me doubt myself, make me look in the mirror and change my clothes, make me wander about thinking of how I looked wandering about. I met her in the night, at a bar known for its good music and lack of accommodations, an alley with a roof. She was alone, standing there, and we all knew it. We'd been watching her all night, wondering how one woman could be so beautiful. I stared, oh yes I stared, because I couldn't help myself. I was writing poetry like a jazz musician, riffs staring through the air, sent manic in the hope they would reach her,

her lips, her hair, her beauty. She did nothing, just stood there, watching the lead singer, a friend of mine, as he mumbled through a set:

How you gonna know when knowing ain't seeing
   No more
What you gonna do when being ain't breathing
   No more
How you gonna live when life ain't worth living
   No more

Not real romantic I thought. And dumb, sure. A friend tapped me on the elbow and shouted. "Bro, you're looking like a stalker. Just go on over there." I smiled and nodded, but I didn't go. This was not Tabatha Bert, I wanted to tell him, this was a whole new world. She was older for one thing. Or was she? She was smart as hell, clearly. I could just tell. It was in her brow and her taught, trim posture, it was the way she listened as if digging through the sandbox for a lost toy, or a golden earring. She seemed like she'd been burned, ruined by bad love. I liked thinking that because, I thought, I could offer her something for that, something pure and light and easy. I almost waved at one point, but my wave collapsed when the music stopped. She applauded airily. I looked at my friend, the lead singer. He looked at her and then at me, and then he winked. I needed that microphone that he held like a miter, the king's miter that he tried to make into a sex wand, a magic sex wand. He'd done it before, and now I could see he was trying it again. He bowed. The whole band gave that little nod all bands give at the end of a set and I wondered what would come next. She stood still, still.

Poetry
Love
Beauty

I went to the stage where another friend was fiddling with the microphone, getting ready to introduce the band members. I grabbed the microphone and squinted out into the little crowd, then quickly at my friend. "Hey, Andrew, you look good in my shirt, bro." I looked at the band. "Nice job fellas," and then I looked at her. "I wonder if we could end the set with a little muse?" My friends wondered if I'd drank too much. "Great then," I said, responding to no one in particular, smiling a lost smile. With my palms still sweaty I recited the first real poem of my life, sent with the hint of fear and a swath of desire for the woman who'd become the mother of my child:

Why are we given beauty? How do we know what it is?
This is beautiful. This is not. How do we know?
What happens within that moment when
we are touched by it?
Why are we given the ability to know?
Beauty.
When we see it what should we do?
Fall down and cry, remain still, afraid
Timid? I don't know. I need help to know.
Why are we given beauty?

I let the microphone go limp in my hand as one of my friends yelled, "It's the sex stupid!" Another shouted, "My mommy said it's so we can see God!" Laughter. The beautiful woman just smiled. My emcee friend took the microphone and said, "Poetry night's tomorrow Dave, but thanks anyways." I got down to mock applause and looks of discomfort.

Then she came over. She, to me. I waited with sweat now staining my armpits. A mess.

"That was a good one," she said.

"Yeah?"

"Yep, it sounded like a confused nursery rhyme. What'd your baby brother write it?"

"Yeah, he's two. A genius, huh?"

She snickered, one side of her mouth curled invitingly.

"So what'ya want me to do now, lick your boots?"

"That's a start," I said.

"Yeah," she looked at me, head, toe, head. "That's a start."

We danced. The palm of her hand stayed in the small of my back even as I began to perspire. She led, all night long she led. The next morning, I had no regrets, none. She smiled too but this was all very wise, different from anything

I'd ever experienced and in the light of morning my poetry seemed pithy and cheap. I told her as much as she buttoned her blouse.

"Well, at least you wrote it." She grinned, "You did write it, didn't you?"

"Yeah, I wrote it."

"You believe it? I mean do you care about beauty and all that shit?"

"Yeah," I said looking away. "I care."

"Then I'll see you tomorrow. Lunch."

And we began.

One month into it all I took her to a restaurant called Carmine's, an Italian place with giant oak tables and a young, yuppy clientele. At least six of my friends joined us. "Everyone," I announced standing, "I want you to meet my girlfriend, Raphaella."

Under the table I felt a crack on my shin and a tug at my shirtwaist. I looked over and saw my "girlfriend" nodding and smiling a broad smile while stabbing at the ground with her index finger, all out of sight of the others. I couldn't decipher the motion, which was short and agitated and real quick, too quick, ticked-off quick. I must have looked at it too long, because I got another whack on my shin. It became clear she wanted me to get up, *now*.

"My boyfriend," she said, emphasizing the boy part while wagging her head, "forgot to order the right cake for all of us so I'm going to go and show him which one would be best, excuse us for a minute." She simpered and pulled me up by my bicep, walking me like this to the dessert counter. Like a child waiting to get spanked, I dreaded the coming moment. Not looking at her and instead fixing a fearful stare on the cakes, I felt her spittle while getting an earful of short, choppy, baleful words. "You know the deal, David. I don't have boyfriends. And if I did, you wouldn't be one of them. Commitment starts with a big C David, and I don't like when people use it for me, like I was a coward. Capiche?" She made a hard coughing C sound when she said coward and capiche. I was humiliated but I didn't leave her. Leaving her would be like quitting ice cream or getting rid of DirectTV. I was too young, undisciplined and too dependent on the image of me with a sexy, tough, uptown woman. She didn't leave me either. I always thought how she kept me around for a sense of normalcy. I thought about how I was that glint of common suburban sense that every girl from the city longs for. But when I asked her why she never left me, her answer was always the same: "Well I haven't decided yet,

David. It's either one, you're a good fuck, or two, you're just a really good man without a clue."

And what do you say to that?

We went on, repeating similar scenes, one or both of us blowing our tops in public, but never totally splitting. We subsisted, sometimes happy, sometimes miserable, often just confused, together, breathing.

As time went on I learned about her past. Mostly I learned while watching paid programming in the darkest hours of the night. She'd start talking then, a little trickle of pain slowly turning into a river of stories about things past. I'd listen, laying on the rug, on my back, while she sat on the couch above me, looking down into my eyes only now and then, mostly watching big-haired people sell kitchen equipment to insomniacs.

"He hit her with an open fist at first, a bitch slap. Then after a year he ended up just beatin' her regular, like a boxer." That was Tommy I learned, her mother's first man. "Momma was never too willing to call the cops, or anyone really." Still looking at the television, she went on as if far away, "One time I held on to the biggest, meanest of them all, a red-haired Indian black who they called Freck. When he felt me on his back, scratching and wailing, he laughed and said, 'You skinny little stupid bitch,' and then my ear bled for whole day after he cuffed me upside my head."

I asked her if she hated her mother for being so weak and she said, "Well, I just couldn't tolerate my mother's beatings as well as she could." When I asked her if she hated men, she said, "My momma said they loved her, and besides us, I never knew anyone that loved my mother, so what was there to hate?" Down on the rug I'd lose sight of her when she'd sit back to explain. When this would happen I'd put my head in my hand, prop it up on my elbow, catch a glimpse again, and keep on listening. "You know I said I never hated my mother when I was a kid, but now I wonder if I didn't hate her weakness, you know, her willingness to turn the cheek and all?"

There were also the little bits about her love life before us. "Loveless life," she'd say. "Loveless except for Jimmy in tenth grade. Jimmy never wanted to have sex and that made me feel weird, but not bad, just weird. I was afraid for the longest that he had some sort of problem, like a parts problem and that's why he didn't ever try anything with me. But turns out he was just shy. He was cute. I loved Jimmy." When I sat up and asked her what happened she just said, "His aunt sent him to Arkansas, then the army. Jimmy was southern and simple, and she figured he belonged back down south. He wrote me once and said he was learning to throw hand grenades," she wavered. "He was good to me." She told me about a man who said he loved her, at least until she got pregnant. She was fifteen. "He sent a letter with two hundred bucks in it, and signed it, *Good luck, Jarel*." She snickered, "I wasn't even old enough to go on my own so my mother took me to get it done. I got it done alright, and with his money. That was the worst part. I used his punk-ass money." On the way home Raphaella asked her mother if she should start taking the pill and her mother said, "That'll just make you more willing, more rabbitty. Stay away from that, hear?" She paused and then added, "And that's all she ever said to me ever again about that day. It. The end."

One night, the two of us covered in the blue, muted glow of late night television, I learned about her father. She'd gone into her jewelry box and brought me a business card that lay wrapped in red velvet beneath a coiled mess of rings and necklaces. "See, says right here he was a baker, from Romania. See?" She pointed to the card, "Adrian Cristescu, right there. How would you pronounce that last name, my last name?" I tried once or twice but it came out sounding French somehow. "He left the card after their big weekend together, said he'd call soon and that she should write him at this address. Ever heard of Transylvania?" I nodded and she said, "Well there you go, now you know about as much as I do. Next."

What came next, well, it was the biggest news of all. Sitting on the windowsill sipping coffee, she said, "I figure you should know something about me that I haven't told you yet."

I sat up. "What?"

"I'm divorced."

"Divorced?"

"Yep, it was finalized about six months before I met you. It's over. Completely, and thank God." She sipped. "He was an asshole." She paused and looked at me. "No, he was worse than that. This guy had serious problems, but of course, like they say, I picked sickness, so doesn't that make me sick too?"

I just sat there, nodding. In time I managed to speak. "Divorced, huh? At twenty-two years old. Wow." I gathered myself. "Why are you telling me this now?"

"Well, what if I end up really liking you, you know, a lot? You are a gentle man, I wouldn't want to hurt you." She paused and averted her eyes, "What can I say, I'm a divorcee."

His name was Dan, he was a graduate student at City College, and he was ten years older than Raphaella. "Ten years?" I said and she didn't flinch. His field was Zoology and he came to New York from Los Angeles, citing something about how City College offered fieldwork at the Bronx Zoo.

"He was sort of a hippie, a grungy guy before it was cool to be grungy," she said. They met at a City College house party in Hamilton Heights, a party Raphie had crashed with her crew of high school miscreants. Her friends were asked to leave soon after their arrival, but this guy Dan made sure Raphaella got to stay. And she did stay, not caring a damn that she was alone with an older crowd, people she didn't know, people that could hurt her. She liked being different, and she liked being noticed by the right people, and Dan apparently was right people. Anyway, as she told it to me that day, they fell madly in love. They married the day after her graduation from high school, in front of a city judge, Dan having met her family just the day before at graduation. She showed me pictures and sure enough, there he was, wearing a casual seersucker jacket, jeans, leather loafers and long hair. She wore a white graduation gown and I thought how ironic that was, a two-for-one wedding picture. When they got married the next day everyone was in total dismay, "Pissed off," she said pointedly. "They thought I'd at least marry a black man, and maybe actually introduce him to the family. I wasn't having it though."

They lived together just off campus in a married residence hall. Right away it began.

"He changed, or maybe he just got tired of me not listening to every little thing he said." She shifted in her seat. "David, he tried to control everything I did. Coming and going, everything. He was always complaining that we didn't have enough sex and, David, believe me, we had plenty of it. He was very fussy, very clean in ways that weren't normal." She spoke with a hint of shame. "He changed toothbrushes every week, every Sunday he'd throw one brush out and get another from this giant box of brushes he kept under the sink. He was nuts and he was my husband." Suddenly she burst out laughing. "Mrs. Daniel Duncan was in some real shit."

I simpered an incredulous, "Yeah, how 'bout that."

"Anyway, I got pregnant in less than three months and, oh shit, I thought, can we do this? He, of course, wanted me to have an abortion. But hell, no, that wasn't happening, I was tired of that road and plus, shit, I was married now. I mean, what is that? I told him no and he got up on me, real close, and said 'Yes'. 'Yes,' he said, real flat and short. 'Yes.' It was creepy. Then I had the miscarriage," she paused. "Well, he sort of helped with that one."

Oh boy, I thought. She *was* a piece of work with one helluva story to tell. In a boy's voice I plunked out a, "Helped how?"

"He was rough with me, you know, during sex, and I know he did that on purpose. Over and over, I hated it, throwing me around like that and just being nasty, trying to beat me so I'd lose the baby." Her lip curled, involuntarily. "And I did, I lost the baby."

Her mix of sorrow and anger evoked the same emotions in me. But I was also amazed at how nasty and loveless *her marriage* had been. I was seized by how brutal this man was, and how scary it was that Raphaella had chosen him. Amid these thoughts all I managed that morning was to sort of play along. "Dang, that's a rough story, Raphie." She concurred with a nod and a sip of her cool coffee, and that was the last thing I heard about Dan for a while. It wasn't until the winter of that year that I was reminded of this past. We were walking together in Central Park and she leaned over and kissed my cheek, clenched my hand and said, "I love you David, you're so gentle. So gentle." Then she burrowed her head in my chest as we walked. I felt warmth and hope for us, and I remembered Dan.

And there was her book.

One night instead of a little chat she went and dug out a thick, glossy, voluminous book scattered with rich pictures, hundreds of photos of paintings from every age. "My senior year I got an internship working at the Met." She opened the book. "Just a stupid little internship for my senior work credit. But that's where I met Ms. Wells." I asked her and she told me that Ms. Wells was the most wonderful woman she'd ever met, filled with life and an insatiable, infectious love for the classics. The book had been a gift from Ms. Wells to Raphaella. It was a homemade history of art scrapbook. A magnificent leathery thing, with pages and pages of pasted-in reproductions and short blurbs of interesting information on each. "Now I have a hobby. It's my own little hobby, my little love, and I don't tell too many people about it, so..." She put her forefinger to her lips and I nodded, putting my finger to my lips as well, only without the aplomb and style. Grinning slightly she called me off the floor and up to the couch where we sat close and took in her book, together, just like my sister and I used to do with *Cosmo*. Laughing. Carefree. Home. She knew every inch of her book, and soon I would, too. I loved how she got lost in the paintings, how her book suspended her anger and suspiciousness. "Let's get the book," I'd say sometimes in the middle of an argument. "Let's just get the book." And sometimes she would, sometimes she did.

***

Mitkin is tired, but not irritated. It is the end of our first day together and I've managed to keep him for almost three hours. The prison hierarchs like me for some reason. Mitkin looks directly at me and says, "Did you hate me?"

"Hate you," I say. "No, I didn't hate you. I was enthralled with you."

"That seems stupid," he says.

I think about it.

"Did you think I was going to steal your girlfriend?"

"Yes," I say. "But maybe she'd already been stolen. Or maybe she was never mine."

He looks at the ground. I think that he is embarrassed for me, but he is not. He is remembering.

CHAPTER III

Stirrings

Mitkin ran fast. Knowing the West Side best, he immediately headed for Riverside Drive and the comfort of the Hudson River. He picked it up after traversing the north end of Central Park and its dying brownstones with their massive granite stoops and crumbling tracery. As he ran, he thought. His mind did not flutter from one image to the next; he did not, for example, see a homeless person and immediately contemplate the plight of the poor, American power politics and encroaching, enraged individualism. He did not run by the Harlem Meer and think about fish heads or the *Creature from the Black Lagoon* as, let's say, I would do. His mind was steady. As he ran he focused on his father and specifically their life together.

Mitkin had always been in love with his father. In ninth grade his father showed him how to make a perfect fit for his physics project. It was a great project, one that tested his ability to construct the perfect causal relationship. Mitkin's was a mishmash of falling rocks, flittering balloons and flying helicopters. The whole ramshackle thing was built on a big, twelve by fifteen feet piece of plywood—twice the size of any competitors'. Two towers of bolted-down tennis ball cans rose higher than a man, making the project dreadfully imposing. The point of it all was inertia, and Mitkin's study was indubitable. He knew he was the winner when the last of his fourteen sequences sent a large, toy helicopter into the sky, landing softly on his teacher's desk. His father had given him the idea for the helicopter; in fact his father had given him all his ideas.

Martin Mitkin would often bring his son into the operating room, into his classrooms, into his board meetings, into every aspect of his adult life. Most of all, Martin Mitkin exposed his son to medicine and life lived inside a hospital. And Mitchell loved it. As a child he had walked among the patients, eaten lunch with his favorite doctors, giggled with his favorite nurses. He had traveled with his father too. By the time he was ten Mitchell had been to Jerusalem, Calcutta, Istanbul and Caracas. He'd accompanied his father wherever he went, and his father accompanied him whenever he thought, wherever he thought, whatever he thought. On this day, jogging alongside the gray-blue Hudson, Mitkin stayed focused on these good things. Just beyond these thoughts, however, lay the imposing matter of death, a matter that Mitkin had not yet decided to entertain.

"Hello Francine. Did they move my father?" Mitkin was topless, having removed his sweat-soaked T-shirt during his run. Standing in the hospital's atrium, a giant room with budding greens and distant echoes, Mitkin's nakedness was not unnoticed.

"Not that I know of," said Francine, a candy striper. "I saw your mom hanging around earlier. She told me she'd been here all night. I was looking for you. How are you, Mitchell?" She smiled.

"Me, well, you know…"

"Actually, I don't know," she replied flashing a look. Mitkin smiled insouciantly and resumed a brisk walk. Near the elevators he turned and walked backward raising his voice so the girl could hear over the din. "I'll be better when I find out why my mother was here all night."

He didn't take the elevator but instead ran up the stairs, lunging two steps at a time, like a kid at play. When he reached the second floor he saw an old friend of the family, the doctor who was supervising his father's treatment. Doctor Jim Wagner was a tall man with plenty of folds on his face. He had soft eyes and well-kept gray hair, big teeth and big hands. His voice was a melodious baritone. Wagner had studied with Martin Mitkin at Columbia and then worked with him overseas. Now he was together again with his old friend, treating him and worrying about him. He had known Mitchell as a baby, and since the onset of Martin Mitkin's cancer had dedicated himself to seeing Mitchell Mitkin once a week. He loved Mitchell, but spared him nothing. He would often tell Martin that the only thing tougher than finding a cure for cancer would be finding his son a wife. "Mitch," Doctor Wagner would joke, "is already married to his mind, a wife he'll never be able to divorce, or even take a business trip away from." Doctor Wagner saw Mitchell in the hall and opened his arms invitingly.

"The prodigal son is here to see his daddy take tests, and only twelve hours late." They hugged. Wagner looked Mitchell up and down and said, "Put your shirt on, you're making the visitors sick and the patients sicker."

"Not Francine," said Mitkin.

"Is it true? Have you really given up your one true love for a woman?"

"You are senile," said Mitkin. Wagner laughed and put his arm around him. Walking through the sterile hall, the sounds of vapid midday television and squeaky chrome carry carts all around, Mitkin felt at home. The big arms of Doctor Wagner and the caress of hospital sterility affirmed Mitkin. He was as far from doubt in this environment as one could be. He celebrated life most when he walked through this house for the dying, and the irony of it eluded him, or perhaps it is better to say, he eluded it.

Room 232 was bleach white, and it smelled that color too. It contrasted greatly with the glowering face of Mitchell's mother, Cassie Mitkin. Her eyes were gray with worry, and her face was a pewter hued dusk. Her hand gripped her husband's forearm as he sat upright in his bed, seemingly unperturbed. Glimpsing this as he came in, Mitchell thought how his father must be at least a little irritated with a doting wife so suffocatingly close.

"Hello Father, what have you done to yourself? I told you not to eat the cancer cantaloupe." Mitchell laughed at his own joke. Doctor Wagner laughed too, but Mitkin's mother only laughed halfheartedly. She smiled peculiarly at the end of her laugh. Everyone in the room felt her angst and there was silence.

Mitkin plowed in, "Mom, what's with the staring? Dad's going to be fine. Right, Doc?"

"Well—" Doctor Wagner began but was cut off by Martin Mitkin.

"Mitchell, that was cruel. Greet your mother properly."

Mitkin sighed, "Hello, Mom. You look tired. Francine told me you were here all night. Are you panicking again, Mom?" He tried to sound comical, but it just came out as penurious. An embarrassing noiselessness sat between mother and son. Cassie Mitkin was plump, and soft, and huggable, and she was short too. Mitchell waited for his mother to answer but she just stared up at him, glassy-eyed. Doctor Wagner stirred the thick mood of the room.

"Well, it looks like this, Martin." He turned and faced everyone. "The cancer's there, and it's spreading. The liver function test was elevated, and I think the biopsy will show the same thing. That's what I want to do next, now." The scuffling of an elderly patient could be heard outside the door, while a faraway nurse dropped a bedpan. Mitchell Mitkin reached to take Doctor Wagner's clipboard, and Martin Mitkin did not move much except to rearrange himself under the lightweight blanket which covered him up to his midsection.

"And then?" said Mitkin.

"We'll have to see, Mitch, but I've seen this before, and you too, probably, if there is a micrometastasis outside the lung we must go with chemo. Just have to."

Cassie Mitkin began to sob. Her head bobbed up and down slightly. Mitkin tried, but could not muster sympathy for her. He disliked her ignorance about chemotherapy and was disgusted by her lack of faith. Hadn't her husband worked his whole life in pursuit of better medicine? Didn't that count for anything or was it just a waste? It seemed to Mitchell that this illness was an opportunity. Sure it was sad, but it wasn't over. Mitkin had what his mother did not: faith. He believed in the religion of reason, rationalism, concrete thinking and the principles of science. At the age of nineteen there were answers to all the questions of death and suffering, and though we hadn't discovered them all, we would if only we cared enough to, and worked hard enough to, and employed the right minds. Mitkin believed he was one of those hard working minds, and he was; he was a little genius. But he was also a young man of little tact. His mother continued to sob, even as Doctor Wagner walked her out of the room for tissues, looking over his shoulder with a kind expression. Martin Mitkin nodded back knowingly, while Mitchell took his mother's seat and put his chin in his hand. He hunched his back and took on the posture of Rodin's Thinker. He looked at his father whose face was staid and whose eyes were clear. A quiet glinted there. Learned lines rumpled his face. His lips, thin and red, formed a sorrowful smile. "She's afraid Mitchell, let her be afraid." Mitkin nodded slightly.

"You don't want chemo, do you Father?"

"Yes, I'd love it. Could I box some leftovers for you?" He grinned sheepishly. "No, Mitchell, I don't want chemo. Nobody wants chemo. The question is, do I need chemotherapy? If Jim is telling me I need it, then I do."

"No you don't," said Mitkin.

"Oh really? Let me quote what Jim said before you got here, when it was just the two of us in the room. He said, 'Martin, without chemo you're toast.' If Jim Wagner says I need it, I need it."

"But he's wrong, you don't." The younger Mitkin stared directly into his father's eyes. "There are other ways of dealing with this Dad. Have you heard of antibody therapy? They extract a tumor cell, monoclone it in a surrogate and then reinject it, and it fights for you, it fights the cancer. There are new ways like this, ways that change the whole paradigm of cancer treatment." Mitkin was serious. "I've been studying them, because I knew that one day you'd be sitting right here,

I knew that chemo would come up and that Mom would cry. Seriously, I'm not some half-wit." He was getting stirred up. "Dad, I want to talk to Doctor Wagner."

"Why?"

"He should change his therapy."

His father breathed a laugh. "Well, for now you will speak with me. Mitchell, you are a smart boy who is bound to be great. But I am a sick man, and soon I will be a dead man. In the meantime, I expect you to rule out rushed judgments and schemes that come from your heart and not your head. Don't be afraid for me Son. Don't fear death so much. The body, like all things, just gets old, changes, fights and ultimately dies. Mitchell look at me." He looked at his son forcefully, gesturing with his index finger. "When you are afraid, you must face your fears, not succumb to them by shouting everyone down and trampling on an entire room full of opinions." He finished, still looking directly at Mitkin.

"But Father, I am not trampling. I just believe—"

"What, that you know more than old Jim Wagner? Is that what you believe?" asked his father.

"No. But I believe that what I know is more important in this situation than what he knows. I don't know more, I just know more about this."

Martin looked at Mitkin wearily. He shook his head silently and that chaffed his son. Mitkin did not move but inside his mind worked overtime: "My father," he thought, "has lost respect for me." He felt his throat tighten. "He doesn't need chemotherapy, I know he doesn't need it. It will just kill him slowly, and he'll be in pain." He spoke aloud to his father, but through a quivering voice.

"Dad, I've got a feeling on this." Mitkin removed his hand from his father's hand and balled it into a fist. "Think about it, Dad, please, just think about it. I don't want to challenge Doctor Wagner, but there are other ways and he knows it."

"Well if he knows it, then why doesn't he recommend these ways? Does he want to see me suffer, Son?"

Mitkin wagged his head no. "Why do some old men choose to live when their life is nothing but pain and suffering? I mean why don't they just ask their doctors to assist them, reduce their pain forever? You know what I'm saying Dad. Why don't their doctors do it themselves, finish it for them, or at least encourage it?"

His father began to respond.

Mitkin interrupted, "Dad, it's because they are set in their ways and still slaves to ridiculous claims about 'dignity' or 'nobility,' or whatever. Doctor Wagner is a good man but he's like those old men and their doctors; he knows what he knows he knows, and that's all. In our case he knows chemo. That's it." He stood up and looked down kindly on his father, a regnant, willful prince still in love with his dying king. "Dad, he's one of those dinosaur doctors down deep. He is."

"Don't pull this crap, Son, you know how I feel about that. We agree. But I don't think those doctors are anything like Jim Wagner. Mitchell, he just doesn't believe the other therapies will work." He struggled and sat up even further in his bed. "Isn't that clear?"

"No, it's not."

Martin Mitkin's eyes narrowed to an exasperated squint, his lips straightened and his forehead wrinkled. Slowly, he leaned back and ensconced himself in the bed. He never took his blue eyes off of his son, however. He sighed and drew in a deep breath, letting it out as he pointed profoundly to a little white paper cup. Mitkin handed it over and he sipped some water, and then, as if taking back the conversation, he pointed at the chair and spoke softly. "Have a seat, Son." Mitkin obeyed. After some time spent in silence, Martin Mitkin spoke again. "Is it possible that you are scared, Mitchell? Are you acting this way because you are afraid for my life?"

Mitkin shifted in his chair.

"No Father, it's not that."

"I don't believe you," replied Mitkin's father.

"But—"

"Son," Martin Mitkin broke in again, "what do you think death is?"

The look on Mitkin's face changed from a flat and fixed confidence to a corrugated confusion. "Death?"

"Yes, what is its significance? What happens when we die, when I die?"

"Why do you ask?" said Mitkin evasively.

In a baritone, Martin repeated forcefully, "What is death, Son?"

"Well," he glanced straight up at the ceiling, nervously. "I guess what happens is what you've always told me happens. Our body loses its resiliency due to one trauma or another. Next its inability to repair itself leads to secondary and tertiary malfunctions and eventually to a massive breakdown in all systems, including the heart. Without fuel, the body collapses. If it remains in this collapsed state for too long it will remain in it forever, or at least until it is no longer what we recognize as a body. Then it is nothing but material fodder for other organisms. Essentially we become nothing."

"Good," said his father. "And does this nothingness scare you?"

"It's natural."

"But does it scare you? Does it make you want to believe in something more?" His father spoke with solemnity.

"Dad, I don't get all of this. First of all, you're not dying and won't die. If you would just take a look at some options and not just accept Doctor Wagner's chemo diagnosis, well, you might just live another fifty years. I mean, what is all this morbid talk for?"

"For posterity, for your future son. I want you to realize that an enlightened mind faces a grim reality. Our lives as we know them are no more than a series of titillations where the body reacts to stimuli. When we no longer register any titillation, we are dead, Son. There are no fantasies to look forward too, no afterworlds full of magical immortality. This is the way it is Son, and believing this, as I know you do, I do, is courageous. See, we choose the tougher road, the cold but true road, and we must understand this. Don't cop out, Son. Copping out is what brings delusion; it's like a drug that makes life easier. We're more heroic, like warriors, because we choose empirical truth, grim or not." Mitchell Mitkin looked at his father. His bottom lip hung low on his open mouth. His father continued. "Death is the end of an organism, don't make it more than it is. And if you have to, realize you do so to succor your weakness."

The sun slid behind a rogue cloud. The room went a shade darker and Mitchell Mitkin was dumbfounded. How could his father think he was going to die? Worse, how could he think that his son would be scared if he did? *Scared?* He at his father. "That's not it at all, sir," he said aloud, eyes narrowing. "I just know I'm right on this. I know."

His father watched him, then looked away and nodded. "Fine, Son. Fine." A long silence followed, and then the sun again moved back into place, out from behind the clouds, bright and glaring outside the window. Cassie Mitkin and Doctor Wagner returned. Cassie was smiling again.

Mitkin would tell me how for two years this moment hardened him. His father's challenge to remain committed to scientific materialism in the face of death had hidden him from the subtleties of the soul and things unseen. This repression, he would go on to say, led to his looming miasma. But for the time being, the battle in which the enemy was his father's physical pain would serve as a means for survival.

CHAPTER IV

Family Matters

About the time Mitkin was hitting a comfortable stride and rounding Grant's tomb with its beautiful ivory pillars and classic Roman dome, Raphaella and I were in a confused conversation about a visit to her mother's house. Simon, her oldest brother, was having a birthday party and I wanted to go. But, somehow my words got twisted. We always had these cursed conversations in the sober light of day, and in the midst of it, I longed for the night.

"Whatever, Davey. You can go or not, do what feels good for you baby."

She called me Davey for one of two reasons. One, she was absolutely enamored with me, or two, she was about to tell me to *hit the road* because she was starting to tire of me.

"But, I don't mind going at all," I said. I looked for an answer, but she had gone to the back of the apartment, to a closet, where she whisked a summer scarf off the shelf, around her neck and over her head. It was pink and white and stylish. Next she grabbed her cat-eye sunglasses, her purse and keys, and spoke to me as she went.

"Then go, Davey. It's just that you're doing that thing again, that high eyebrow thing where you want me to feel your answer instead of you just saying it, straight. You know, like a man."

I frowned. "Do you want me to go, Raphaella?"

"My brother does."

Her brother. I liked him, I liked all of her brothers and her mother too, but I didn't care that her brother wanted me there. What about her? My puerile heart wanted a slobbering show of devotion, but she just didn't get it. I hated her for not getting it. Not getting me. I thought of leaving her that very moment, but I stayed. I always stayed, always waiting for things to change, for her to do all the tender things I saw lovers do on sitcoms, or on the benches of Central Park. I was such a fool. I took the frames of people's lives for the entire reel and then tried to live the fairy tale. And on this hot August day, I would do just that, live a fairy tale that seemed always *about* to deliver something other than the drab, damp shades of confused, misguided love.

"So that's it," I said. "That's it?"

"Yeah, that's it," she sighed. "Yeah Davey, I think it's time for us, or me, or you, or whoever the hell is headin' out to this party, to hit the road." She snatched her sunglasses from her face and eyed them. "What's this?" she said using her shirt to wipe a smudge clean. Then as if doing the same with the conversation, she said, "You hittin' it with me or not?"

I swallowed hard and tried not to show my anger. "Let's go."

We'd almost reached her mother's house when traffic backed up and I realized it would remain this way until the invading suburban Yankee fans slipped safely back to New Jersey with their car windows rolled up real tight. This was how I'd come to think about the South Bronx since getting to know Raphaella and her family. I'd made their town my own, though I'd neither lived nor worked there. And I didn't share the same skin color as most of its residents. I was a liberal white kid who wanted desperately to relate to a world I had only read about. Dating Raphaella, a mixed girl from the boogie-down Bronx, well, that just about made me authentic. I liked feeling authentic. Waiting in traffic, I was free to grumble at the stupid "outsiders" who hypocritically came to the jungle for some entertainment. I could smugly honk my horn and holler for them to "go back to the burbs." In short, I could be what I always wanted to be, a New Yorker.

Of course, I wanted to be a happy New Yorker, not one under the enslaving spell of an enigmatic girlfriend with magnificent cheekbones. I shifted the car like a third world taxi-man and looked over at Raphaella. Would she at least say something civil before reaching the party? She didn't look back. I shifted and looked at her again, this time purposefully in an attempt to start conversation. The silence she loved killed me.

"Come on, Raphie, lighten up. I don't want your mom to see us fighting, besides, why are we fighting? What is it, huh? What's wrong?"

"Well, one thing that's really wrong is Michael Jackson. His skin is getting lighter every year. Don't you find that odd?" She turned to me. "And what about famine in Mozambique?" She said Mozambique incorrectly, making it come out *Mozambeekee*.

"Mozambique," I said.

"Exactly."

I shifted again, and stared.

"David, do you have trouble dealing with silence?"

"No."

"Then why all the angst?" Her beautiful scarf slipped back on her head, settling around her neck as if it were meant to be there all the while. Contrary to every rational thought, I wanted to kiss her.

"I don't have angst," I said.

"Ahh, yes you do."

"Alright so I do, dammit," I said just cracking a smile. "But not enough to make you torture me. You like torturing me, don't you?"

"No, but you like the thought of me liking the thought of torturing you, because if I'm torturing you I'm caring for you in a sick kind of way, and then at least you feel wanted." She laughed like she'd just seen a man slip on a banana peel and fall on his face. So smug.

Ouch.

"It's a damn good thing you are a fine looking young man," she added. "Sometimes, well, I could just kick your ass, and then kiss your ass."

We were now only a block from 172nd Street, the street where her mother and brothers lived.

"Yeah, well," I said. "Don't think I couldn't do the same."

"Sshhhhhh…" she said. "Silence." After a pause she yipped, "Yes! Get that spot." She shimmied. "I love getting a good parking spot. Isn't it just the greatest thing to get a good parking spot, Davey?" She pointed.

"I can't get in there."

"You can do it, Davey." She lifted a fist. "You can do anything, I believe in you."

I slowed and she clicked her door open. Peering out the door and over her shoulder, she directed me. She always did this, a sort of instinctual act of distrust. I bumped the car behind me and Raphaella clapped and hollered with her thumbs up, "Yeah baby." A few more bumps and I was in. We both got out and made our way into the big brown building.

The place where Raphaella had spent the last two years of her high school life was unremarkable. There were six floors. The outside of the building was old brick but without character. A big, wide-open black gate lackadaisically guarded the entrance to the building. Just inside was a little cement courtyard. A parched and defunct fountain sat in the middle, its rust-red water scars running vertical where water had leaked. A handful of teenage kids sat on the fountain's retaining wall. They looked bored. When we walked in, they followed me with their eyes. One kid I recognized from the few times I had come on my own to visit Raphaella's mother. I hoped he would give me a familiar nod. Nope. We rang the battered directory board where it said HURSTON, and waited to be buzzed in.

Since moving to New York three years earlier, I had spent much of my time waiting to be buzzed up and into diverse buildings where friends and acquaintances kept watch over the solitary part of their selves. This was the ironic thing about New York. Without much effort, a man could become a recluse above the teeming streets. The rooms inside the pre-war apartment buildings were modern man's phylactery, a place to store and mull over sacred memories before heading back out into the breaking waves of the city. Some folks, I imagined while staring up at the windows, never come out from these places. They live solitary lives with their televisions. There they remain detached from real people and real relationships, from eyes with horrible stories to tell, outstretched hands in search of lunch, or lips that hammer away in conversation all around them. Entering any building in New York was, in many ways, like entering someone's soul. Holy holes in the wall, I thought as I stared. Some holes were open, others had lids.

"I love you, Raphie, let's not fight upstairs, okay?"

"Alright Dave, don't worry." She moved toward the elevator. "No fighting." She smiled.

All three boys would be at Simon's nineteenth birthday party. Anthony was the youngest. At thirteen, he should have spent most of his time at school, but in fact, he managed to spend most of his time in his uncle's "music shack," a basement with recording gear. Anthony was going to be a rapper, and he never left the house without his new-style baggy pants made popular in the jail cells of Rikers Island. Julius was the middle brother. He was seventeen and close to Simon. They did everything together, though Julius read more books than Simon. Actually, everyone read more than Simon as it wasn't clear that he could read at all. Julius was also a better athlete than Simon, and often schooled him on the basketball court. Simon, the birthday boy, was the oldest of the boys and at nineteen, three years younger than Raphaella. His baggy face and heavy jowls made him look more like thirty-nine, not nineteen. But his eyes were young, and they danced with enthusiasm for life. He was big and burly and much darker than Raphaella.

All three of her brothers were darker because they had a different father. Their daddy was Carl. He had been the "steady man" to Arlene for nearly ten years. Then Carl left, just two weeks before Simon's eleventh birthday, because he sensed himself getting sewn in and too "tied down to it all." Arlene learned later he left because he had a major gambling debt that would soon be knocking on the family door. As far as Arlene was concerned, he left to protect her and was to be commended for his courage. Everyone, however, knew there was more to it, and that Carl was an addict of gambling, or at least one of those skinny guys who hangs out in OTB's and eventually loses lots of money and pretty much all dignity. The family didn't talk much of this, everyone that is but Simon. He'd come right out with clipped phrases like "rat cheat," and "punk ass fool," and diatribes about how Carl couldn't support his woman. Simon never mentioned his own pain directly, but rather wrapped it up in a withering defense of his beloved mother. Simon never spoke as if he were owed something; he was too proud.

And then there was Raphaella's father, the white phantom. He had come and gone long before, leaving only his business card and a baby, my girlfriend. He was the mystery man of the Hurston family, a white man who was the punch line in more than a few Hurston family jokes. The boys called him The Roman, thinking this was what you called people from Romania. They'd put on a nasal white-man accent and Groucho Marx nose glasses. They'd tease Raphaella about her "white girl butt" and then wonder aloud if Raphaella's father may have been the first man ever to have no ass, whatsoever. "A modern medical phenomenon," Simon would say. "The man with no ass. Excuse me, sir," he'd say, "but you have no ass." He'd laugh. "You know he had to kneel on the toilet!" In general, Simon and Julius were merciless. They'd take her stockings and wear them over their head, parading around and "combing" their "white" hair. They'd put her frilliest panties on over their jeans and saunter around the house, just because. Simon called her Starsky because her hair positively bounced in the morning, just like Starsky's did when he'd rush out of the striped Dodge Charger with Hutch, in pursuit of the bad guys. He swore that Raphaella had inherited the ultimate phantom gene, officially known as *White Man's Vinegar Smell*. "Yep, you got the vinegar curse, Raphie, no doubt." Then he'd put his nose in the air and say, "You smell just like the subway stop at Wall Street, straight up. They say the only way to get rid of it is to shave it off. Too bad for you."

They teased her because they loved her and because she was different, good different. She was exotic and interesting and quirky, and she was their sister, entirely, wonderfully. When they crossed the line, Raphaella would let them know with medieval reprisals like duct tape and rat-tailed towels. She remained their elder. Still, for all the jokes and all the love, Raphaella's center, her core, remained inviolable. Even to Simon, her closest brother, serious conversation was too ticklish, too uncomfortable, too filled with silent moments and perilous pauses. Besides, she was different, and not just older. She was restless and combustible. As Raphaella grew up, she eschewed the common causes of the ghetto. The righteous gripes of black rappers, black buppies, black Jacksons and black Muslims, all of them eluded Raphaella, even as her irreverent iconoclasm made her attractive for many a cause. "I'll be a nigger for nobody," she'd say. And that's how she got her nickname, the only one that would ever really stick. "You just don't fit nowhere sister," said Simon one day after Raphaella turned down tickets to the Beacon Theatre to see a rap act called Doug E. Fresh. "You're like one of those birds that's a bird, but don't fly."

"An Ostrich?" she said.

"No, the other one."

"A Kiwi?"

"That's the one. You're a damn Kiwi Raphaella. A regular Kiwi."

It stuck, and I guess it makes sense, really. She was a different kind of bird, different from the very people that raised her and nurtured her, if you can call it that. The gambling addict, the Indian black named Freck, the music shack, the pigeons on the roof, and the loop-the-loop hairdos, all of it was unique. But most of all there was the Roman, the baker out there somewhere, selling little creamy delights to hungry Transylvanians without thinking much about the dark and mysterious Bronx, the place a daughter named Raphaella called home. For me, a rather simple product of two happily married people, the story was real scary and painful and reeking of disintegration, massive irresponsibility and urban decay. I rarely brought it up. It was too much like a caricature of slum living, the absentee father paradigm, the image that so many white, suburban Americans fear and disdain. It wasn't *really* this of course, but I was too sentimental, too idealistic to see it otherwise. Besides, being so close to black family ruin allowed me to show I was more flexible than the next guy, the next white guy anyway. I could deal with a little big city dysfunction, no problem, piece of cake. I'm a liberal person,

I thought. Go for it. Show how humane and tolerant you are. Rubbing shoulders with the dispossessed, now that was cool.

But for the Hurstons, their past was less loaded and nothing to be ashamed of; surely nothing massive or particularly inglorious. When they brought it up it was to make fun of Raphaella's honky nose. Why not? The family was boisterous and raucous. They were classically fun, fun like white people in the suburbs think of law abiding black people in the city, if they think of them at all. They barbecued, went to family reunions (Raphaella always missed these since becoming an adult), had unruly "dancing" parties, played basketball in the park, went to the local roller rink, and had loud conversations about semi-personal stuff on entirely public transport. I wanted to love it all, and after I had dated their beloved Raphaella for two years, they loved me, though in a sad, kind of sympathetic way. It was as if they looked at me and said, "God bless your hopelessly overmatched soul, son." I wondered if they knew something I didn't, or worse, would not know, ever.

The elevator door opened, and the brothers pounced. Simon and Julius threw their arms around us, Anthony sort of stood off, posing almost.

"It's a roof gig today, people," said Simon before pushing us back on the elevator. "You'll like it David, you can get some sun. You could use some sun." He smacked me on the back and looked at Raphaella. "You too, Kiwi. You don't get out?"

"No Simon. I've been sick. Hemorrhagic meningitis." She stared plainly. "In the hospital. Why haven't you come to visit me?"

"You lying."

"Yes, *I* lying."

Simon snickered and looked at me. "She crazy, right?" I looked at her and nodded. We all nodded.

"Nice belly, Kiwi," said Julius, reaching over and rubbing her smooth stomach. "I'm gonna be an uncle."

"Yes you are Julius."

"Do you know yet if it's a boy or girl?" asked Anthony, standing in the corner of the elevator.

"We don't know yet, but what do you think Anthony? What are you hoping for?"

"Boy," he said.

"Me too," said Simon, and then the elevator stopped. The doors opened with a jerk. Simon led us around a corner, down a long hall and around to a cramped staircase. Rickety stairs had been pulled down like stairs to an old attic. These stairs were precarious. Climbing these things has to be illegal, I thought. Light from above streamed down and formed a square on the floor where we stood, the heat of the summer simmering inside it. Bass beats boomed above, and I could hear giggles. A pretty girl poked her head through the opening to the roof, spilled her drink in gulps, and said, "Oh, look, men."

The boys climbed those illegal stairs real fast, with bright smiles on their faces. So did I. I was happy to be near the good food, pretty girls and the party music. The sky above was so blue and on the roof like this I could look down on that suffocating canopy of steel and brick which otherwise hovered over me as I moved about New York. Walking to the building's southern edge I could see the colossal bend of Yankee stadium, its bright white awnings contrasting against the sea-blue, upper deck seats, some of which were spotted with spectators. I strained to hear the roar of the crowd but could not.

Turning around, I surveyed the rooftop and its green artificial turf. It had been converted into a social hall of sorts, and now nearly thirty people stood in little groups all about the roof. Someone, I guessed Simon, had hauled a fat and tall portable stereo up the stairs and at least four couples were swaying to its sweet, sugary rhythm. I saw a table full of food. There was more food than guests to eat it, and though Arlene's dancing parties were usually like this, it still reminded me of Thanksgiving with all the leftovers and lovehandles. The baked macaroni and cheese was the only dish anywhere near empty, but it wasn't because people weren't eating. It had more to do with the industrial-size tins all the food came in. A pile of greens, dug out in the middle, poured out the smell of simple, country living. Getting closer, I could see a big bowl filled with chunky mashed potatoes, dotted in the middle with a soapy heap of daisy-yellow butter. I caught a wisp of honey-basted ham and then a hint of chili beans, specks of green and red peppers and chunks of white onions flecked throughout. The bouquet moved easily through the fresh open air. A garbage can full of beers got drenched from melting ice. I dug around in the icy can, fished one out and grabbed a chair. I was ready to eat.

Someone yelled, "Hey, good-looking." With a fork full of greens poised at my mouth, I turned to see a large black woman, sprawled in a lounge chair, yelling at me with her hand out. "Hey there now, don't try to ack like you don't see me son." Son? Shit. Of course, Arlene. Here I was, laid out with a beer, a fork full of food, and a flashing hunger-grin, and there she was, the mother of my girl, the grandmother of my unborn baby, and the hostess with a most fanatical jones for party decorum. This was Arlene Hurston, the dame of the uptown. And she was a dame, in the most classic sense. She loved drama. Big earrings, big long fingernails, big loud he-said-she-said fights, big dramatic pauses, and big hair. Today she had the hoop hair, that's what I called the kiddy racer set on her head. It was like one of those loop-the-loop race car courses, the kind a father sets up late on Christmas Eve. She had three loops, they were shiny and hard and they rattled ever so slightly in the wind. She could press it like this because, as she often said, "I was blessed with some good hair, child." Good hair equaled straight hair, simply. And she had good hair, dammit, even if Raphie and I had seen her at the Unisex just three days before getting a perm. "That wasn't no perm," she said, "that was a touch-up." She was a big woman, hardy, curvy, sexy if not a little scary. Today she was wearing a long dress that looked like a bathrobe to me, or maybe a housecoat. It was dark blue and satin. It glimmered. She looked good, somehow. She always looked good somehow. I think it was her face. Like her daughter's, it was chiseled. High cheekbones drew in full lips that sat puckered above a strong jawbone. "I have full-on Cherokee blood in me. Anyone can see that," she'd say. "You gotta be a fool to miss the Indian in me, my grand's married into a whole teepee full of red-blooded Cherokees." She could have been Cherokee from what I could see, but Raphie used to laugh at that.

"She's Cherokee like I'm Roman," she'd say.

Yes, Arlene Hurston was a real piece of work. She was a mother of four, lover to many, and wife to none. Sitting there grinning and grinding on a tough piece of beef I wondered how bad I'd get skewered up there on that roof.

"Hey, Momma Hurston," I said, saying *momma* just like she'd taught me. "The mac-cheese looks great."

"Had any yet?"

"No, I was—"

"Where's crazy Kiwi?" She took a quick look around and then used her pinky nail to pick at a beef tendril caught in her teeth. "She puttin' on a lot of weight?"

"Well, the usual," I said, having no idea what that meant.

"Keep an eye on her. When I had Simon I must a put on four, five hundred pounds. It was like that child had six heads inside of me. Turns out he barely got his self half-a-head. Go figure."

I nodded and said, "Go figure."

Simon walked up and put his big hand on my back. "I like this fool Mom. I like the way he treats Raphaella, like he actually likes her. She pretended to like you yet, boy?"

Arlene chimed in, "My Kiwi don't pretend about nothing son, don't listen to Simon, David. Last time I ever seen Raphaella do anything but speak her mind is when I caught her runnin' round in my bedroom with the super's son. She did a little pretending that day all right. But you don't have to worry David, if she's with you, that's enough to let you know she likes you just fine, even if she ack evil all the time." She scooped up some potato salad and ate. "Simon's just jealous. I mean, look at him."

"What's that supposed to mean, Ma?"

"Where the girls at in this party Simon? Everyone I see round here is related to you. Don't girls like you no more?"

"Tina's here," he said, pointing across the roof to the same girl who had spilled her beer moments ago.

"She's a whore, she don't count."

"Relax Ma. Damn. Tina's all right, plus, she'll fight you."

"She'll lose. I got my Vaseline and some knuckles right here in this pocketbook." And like it was a Derringer, she patted it.

"You crazy, Mom. You crazier than Kiwi." He left us with a dismissive wave. As he walked away I leaned a bit closer to Arlene and recalled something she had just said.

"You really think Raphaella is happy with me, you know, loves me?"

"Sure son, why not. She lucky to have you. You a steady young white boy."

"Yeah, well," I paused, "I wish Raphie knew that." And the next moment a very saucy grin stretched out across her face.

"Okay then, here she comes, we'll fix it up." She raised her hand and sort of motioned me aside, "Raphaella, come on over here a minute." Then looking back at me she snapped her fingers. "I'll fix it up just like that." She looked Raphaella up and down as she approached. "Kiwi, David and I were just talking…"

Oh God, I thought. Jump. Cover your head, run screaming and just throw yourself over the edge. Do it, I thought. Do it. I didn't do it, instead I smiled like a man trying to disguise the onset of very bad gas.

"Hi Raphie," I said, barely.

"Hey, David." She spoke clearly, kindly.

"Raphie," said Arlene, breaking in loudly, still splayed in her lawn chair, "why you so evil with this boy here. He's telling me he's not even sure you love him, and with the baby coming and all, why you being so evil?"

"He what?" She was wearing her cat-eye shades and I couldn't read her eyes. "He's wondering if I love him?"

"I know! I told him that the whole idea is just ridiculous, but he had to hear it from you I guess. So tell him honey, tell him it's all just fine."

I broke in, "Well it wasn't exactly that I needed to know if—" but I didn't have a chance to finish.

"Go on, Raphie, tell him how much this baby means and how much you love him, and how having *his* baby is so special, and how he'll always be the father of your child and all that, and yeah, why don't y'allf get married? I never got married ya know, never found the right guy. But hey, David here, he's a good steady white boy."

"A good steady white boy, huh?" said Raphaella.

Her mother nodded. "I mean I don't know how he does in the rollin' round hours, but he seems like a steady boy to me."

"Sure Mom, he's steady all day and all night, too. He's a real champ." She looked at me and took my hand. "I'm gonna steal him from you for a minute, Ma, you mind?"

"Not one bit. I just wanted you to know, air some things out now with the baby coming and all, you know, do some mothering at this motherly time. Air some things out for y'all." Raphaella nodded and so did I. "You look so good together."

Still holding my hand, she walked ahead of me so I looked like I was being led to the yellow-bus stop, or maybe the gallows. Oh boy, I thought, this isn't going well. Idiot. Maybe next time I could just wear a sign, something that read:

IGNORE ME BECAUSE CHANCES ARE I WILL SAY SOMETHING VERY STUPID VERY SOON, AND I'M NOT SURE WHY, OTHER THAN A DEEP

SEATED DESIRE TO HAVE OTHERS LISTEN TO ME, AND COMMENT ON HOW GREAT I AM, OR WILL BE, OR COULD BE, IF ONLY I WAS LOVED LIKE I NEEDED TO BE.

But that wouldn't fit on one sign, I thought. And still she led me, closer and closer to the edge of the rooftop. I heard echoes wafting up from the alley far below.

She leaned against the edge and said, "When you were a kid, were you left alone a lot, maybe locked in a closet, because you're freakin' me out David. I mean, telling my mom? You really think that she's gonna help you?"

"Yeah, well, I sort of messed that up."

"Yeah, you sort of did." She gazed out onto the horizon. There was silence. "She's not like your mom, David. She's not always trying to make things better. She's not like that."

I wiped my brow. "I guess I was just nervous, wondering about us and the future. My folks, you know, think this whole thing is a bad idea. They keep telling me we blew it when we had sex, and how we kept the baby, and how we won't get married. And I just can't shake the idea that maybe they are right."

"All right Davey, what the hell is this all about? Let's go. Get it out."

"I want to get married. Look Raphaella, I know I don't make much money and I can't write for crap, not yet anyway, but still, I want to do something right. Something right, just once."

A breeze blew a black, chocolate strand of hair across her face. I wanted dearly to remove it but didn't dare, not now. She lifted her long brown hands and removed it with the back of her thumb. "David, look over there at those people." Her nostrils flared slightly. "Look at them. Do you see one person standing over there who knows the first thing about doing something right?" I turned and did as she said, and the simple faces I'd become accustomed to slowed and waned and each became insipid somehow, each became trite, fleeting. "Now picture the faces of your friends, your parents even, your sister and her husband in their little suburban home with their pretty white boat. Do they know anything about doing something right, really right?" I did as she asked and all the faces I pictured came and went without a hint of sagacity, this even though I loved most of them dearly. It was the way she was saying *right* that made it hard to picture. "Well?" she said.

"Yeah," I replied.

"Picture me then. Look at me." She took a step back, and with flair widened her feet and stiffened up, standing like a superhero. "Do I look like I have the first clue about what it means to do something right, something really, really right? Perfect? Do I?" I stared and thought, she is beautiful. But this was getting too intense, more than just a pretty moment. She stepped up to me, took my face in her hand, squeezed it puppy-style, and shook it. "Do I?"

"I don't know, Raphie."

"And neither do I," she stopped and let go. "Neither do I."

A pigeon coasted to a stop only a few feet away, sailing in like a fat, speckled snowflake. We stood still. I tried to say something like, "Yes, you do," but she interrupted.

"So. There you have your answer, David. We can't get married because you know nothing, and I know nothing. All together, we know nothing about doing something right. But you want to marry me anyway."

Then through a sassy chortle she repeated it. "You want to marry me." She laughed loudly. "Just looking at you right now tells me you can't handle marriage, and especially not a marriage where you and I are involved. But that's okay," she turned aside, "why would you want to anyway?" She was talking to herself now, looking out again. "Wake up, stop trying so hard."

"But, what is going on with you, Raphie, what's wrong? I love you. I'll help you."

"Oh shit," she laughed. "Why do you keep trying to love me?"

Almost in a whisper I said, "You used to know love, Raphie."

Her eyes flashed. "I've never known it, David. I know something else, something fake. I know that sounds harsh but it's true. It's the closest thing to truth I know." I looked at her profile and wondered what had crept so profoundly into her soul.

"Raphie," I leaned nearer, "what's wrong with you?" She didn't move. "What the hell is it? Is it Mitkin? Are you in love with him or something?" I turned and looked out too. "Could it be Mitkin?"

"Maybe," she said. "No," she started, "not maybe. It's not him I'm in love with, it's his love that I love. Yeah," she sighed, "watch him sometime. Look at the way he believes in everything he does, every minute—like it's all fail-safe and true. He doubts nothing, even when he's an idiot, even when he's aware everyone is calling him an idiot. He just goes on. I love that about him, I love his faith in his world. I love *it*."

"But you don't even know it, this thing, with Mitkin." I paused. "Or do you? Have you, Raphie? Have you been seeing him?" A primal pang fizzed in my stomach, I was afraid of her answer. "This is about more than just one or two random meetings isn't it, isn't it?"

"No, David, I don't lie. We talked twice before today. But truth be told, that's enough, isn't it? When you see something that gives you a rush you don't question it, do you? Haven't you ever seen a photo and bam, just like that, you know the man in it, immediately. You're a writer, David, doesn't this make sense to you?" She faced me squarely with entreaty in her eyes.

"Of course it does," I said. "But to be so into a kid, one you hardly know, uh, that's not really sensible, Raphie. Can't you see that?"

"Yeah, if I was saying all that. But you're not listening. I am not attracted to him, it's his thing, his gig." She turned and leaned on the wall and looked down into the street and shrugged. A few little boys played stickball there and she watched them. "The boys are playing in the street," she said.

I looked down and saw what I'd seen many times before. But this time I felt an original sadness, a sense of loss deeper than I'd ever known. My brow wrinkled. "What do you want, Raphaella?"

"I want what he has." She turned and walked away.

***

I went home. Not conspicuously. I didn't make a scene and ruin the party for Simon, though his mother and his cousins seemed well on their way. I went home, to my place downtown, far away from the Bronx and the little Harlem apartment on 103rd Street. Raphie told me she would get a ride with Simon in her mother's car, or take the train, and that I wasn't to worry. But I did.

It seemed to me that Mitchell Mitkin was stealing my girl and that he was doing it without wanting to, in fact, without even knowing it. Alone in my bedroom the feelings of rejection which began on the roof continued. I slammed the door and ransacked my little room. Fatigued, I stood ankle-deep in debris, ankle-deep in a flood of ruin. Then I entered that pit of childhood despair where a tender heart is soothed by pathetic, milk-warm tears for one's own self. I cried these tears curled up on the couch. That she wasn't really falling in love with someone else did not matter. It was inconsequential that she loved a hope and not a man. I told myself what I wanted to hear because doing that made the tears warmer and more medicinal and the whole thing more romantic and cinematic, easier to cry over.

The other part, the part about loving what he loves and his idealism made no sense, at least not then and there, on my ragged futon in the poorly lit room. Mitkin wasn't in any way ideal. His crude boorishness wasn't ideal, and neither was his bitter wit. It was true that I'd seen glimpses of a compelling character, but these weren't the things of romance. Besides, her beauty would kill him. The whole thing was ridiculous. If it really was a crisis of meaning she was having then why didn't she come to me for help, come to me lovingly with her head on my shoulder, asking about the finer questions of life? After all as a writer, that's what I did. Insight. Sure, I wasn't published, or even writing on a regular basis, but that didn't matter. One doesn't need fame to enlighten others. What a terrible nightmare it all was.

I envisioned my parents with entirely justified scowls. I saw my mother waving her index finger; their warnings of doom were stupid and alarmist two years ago but now they were, well, right on the frickin' money. They were right, and compared to the unruly Hurston family my folks became sages, insightful, prudent. I started to brood about my predicament. I began to hate everything uptown and everything New York. My little desktop light struggled against the blackness of the stodgy room and I felt that the night wanted to suffocate me, it being my current life and the bane of my existence. I bemoaned having ever run into Raphaella at the club. I worked backwards in my mind until I reached the stainless days before our relationship and I waned over them until they became like a mighty golden cruise ship whose journey knew no rain and whose nights knew no displeasure. Everything about singledom came back to me as idyllic, and everything after, disastrous. I kept seeing myself watching other women, enjoying the innocence in it, and reveling in the vision of myself before her. Back then I was free, accountable to no one, a slave to no soul.

I wanted to be without her. I would be without her, I thought. Then I thought again, and remembered I was already a father. A *father*. It was the thought of the baby that ended my freewheeling run through faux history. There was a new history swimming in her womb, a history that I could not change, and one I was responsible for. That sobered me. I returned to the one thought needful. I was a father and I had to work it out with my wife. Wife. How funny is that? I was so far from being a husband that the word *wife* made me laugh.

I rolled over onto my back and began in earnest to formulate a plan to win Raphaella back. The plan was simple. Do exactly what she says, all the time, exactly. No more, no less. Be her little slave. Yes, don't ask for favors and don't even volunteer them. Sleep over when she asks, and only make love when *she* says so (though I think this had always been the case). I would win her with my obedience; that would do it, utter and dispassionate vassalage. That was it. I wiped my drying eyes. Be a father to your child, this was my mantra.

I sat up straight in my bed, ready to kill the dissonance that infested our relationship. I would leave Mitchell Mitkin alone. I told myself this was the mature decision; he, after all, was not the active ingredient in all of this, it was us, and on this night I decided I would act to put the *us*, the ugly, broken us, back together. I got out of my crying bed energized and began an entry in my journal. I was writing again, and by the time I crawled back into bed, my head swam with hope, and the balled-up sweatshirt I used for a pillow felt no harder than the night before. I was in love again. Again.

CHAPTER V

Dinner

I sat on my plan for two days, refusing to call Raphaella until I felt ready. I went to work and wrote continuously. I even reworked a short story I had set aside three months earlier. Being alone was tremendously efficient but the thought of my life out there, up there, at 103rd Street, always hit back in my most self-assured moments. On the third day, I called Raphaella and told her I wanted to see her. She sounded like she always did, blithe and satirical, but I would not be deterred. I went to work that afternoon with my bags packed for a night uptown.

The workday was sluggish. Rain covered Manhattan like a balmy blanket. It fell through thick, humid August air. I was a counselor for a non-profit support group called The Plateau. The Plateau set up offices in troubled high schools around the city and provided services to young people mired in life's difficulties. My title was *Employment Specialist*. There were four other counselors in the office with me. Summertime, especially late summer, was the easiest, most lackadaisical time of the year. Few kids remained involved with outside agencies such as ours, and of the thirty kids I had on my summer caseload, twenty-five were strong characters in need of little direction. The other five kept me just busy enough to avoid an overwhelming feeling of guilt.

I got the job a year earlier because I begged the founder of the program to help me out. He had been my professor at NYU where my studies and my New York odyssey had begun. I started at NYU as an education student but dropped out after two years. Ostensibly it was a cash problem. I told my folks I didn't think taking loans to teach was a good idea. I remember my father mumbling relieved approval on the phone while my mother immediately moved to confront me, a son who was "jeopardizing his future." She was kind about the whole thing, but in the end my father's approval and my insistence got me out of NYU full-time. I re-enrolled part-time, this time as a student of literature.

Studying the great wordsmiths made me more comfortable, and it allowed me to swill the New York nightlife and peruse the chic, clandestine East Village, writing clichés without a hint of remorse. At the time it was an exciting idea, and it would have remained exciting if I had continued to pursue the obvious: writing. But writing simply lost out to the one million other options available to a twenty-two-year-old in New York, and most of these options had long legs. I was always on the lookout for love. If I found myself bleary-eyed and broke, it was always with a beautiful companion. All of this was like a compost pile for writing, I told myself. I had to experience life before I could write about it. Of course, this was a dismissal of the rather simple assertion that perhaps, maybe, I could do both at the same time. Eventually one of the distractions became the only distraction, and that, of course, was Raphaella.

At work, with the rain and humidity, I became lost in the undulations of love and self-enrapture, which meant I didn't do crap all day. On the verge of reprimand from another counselor who was slouching through a list of summer students in need of re-adjusted paychecks, I waxed on, oblivious. (This was far too banal a chore for someone like myself. I was in need of deep, romantic, philosophical thought, clearly.) He looked at what must have been a rather glassy-eyed dolt. I looked back and smiled.

"Hey Mel, how's that list coming? It's quite a list, huh?"

Mel continued to finger the fat pile of paper. It was printed on unwieldy green computer paper, the kind with holes all along the edges and folded back to back. Leafing through it all was like swimming through seaweed. One of the pages had folded unevenly and Mel was having a hard time getting it unfolded. He tried to coax the wrinkled paper back into shape but could not. Finally he took an oversized dictionary and slammed it down on the pesky paper, grinning menacingly at me.

"Yep, David, quite a list all right." He leered. "Maybe you'd like to take a look at it, maybe retrieve some of these names from it. I don't know," he paused, "maybe earn a dollar or two, what'ya say?"

I took the list because I was afraid if I didn't, he'd report me. Then on top of losing my girl, I'd lose my job. Mel slipped on his leather jacket with aplomb, like a biker guy. The jacket jingled. It had many long, dangling tassels and beads and gilded decals. His hair was long too, nearly greasy, and he had a bushy goatee. He looked more like a murderer than a man dedicated to inner city kids. He didn't fit here the same way I didn't fit there, with Raphaella and her family. But didn't I have to fit? I mean, I was going to be a father. I had to be right for Raphaella, I had no choice. Of course, this wasn't really true. I could leave and avoid this future.

I could tread back to my family home, a failure in the city, a father without his child, just another man who couldn't hack the repercussions of a night's passions. I could do this. It wasn't impossible. My mother would frown a bit but my father would ultimately open his doors and give me a bed.

The thought of such a scenario was enticing; it tugged at me as I put my raincoat on. I could do it now, immediately, without having to face Raphaella's discerning eyes, and her bewildering ways. I could, I thought as I locked up. The clank of the door reverberated up and down the cavernous corridors of the big school. Because it was summer, everything that had been waxed and polished was still waxed and polished, clean and antiseptic. The walls were free of posters and announcements put up by aspiring school leaders. One I remember from the school year read, *Don't Be Wack, Vote for Mack.* It was gone now. Only the clip-clop of my shoes escorted me through the gaunt hall. I left the building and wove my way to the subway where I stood and looked at a sign reading *Downtown-Uptown.* I thought, *Comfort-Pain.* I fiddled in my pocket for a subway token. *Downtown-Uptown, Comfort-Pain…*

I chose pain, and sure enough, got it. The lock had been changed. Mitkin had done as he said he'd do and now I stood in front of her place a stranger. I rang the bell and looked through the front door into the apartment just as Mitkin had done before. I looked frantically for anyone who could let me in. I even banged on the window to the first floor apartment, a bay window just within reach to my left. No one had lived there as long as I'd known Raphaella, but I banged anyway. I buzzed again and started the process of killing myself with my imagination. He must be up there right now, I thought. Right at this very moment, Mitkin is probably kissing her neck. Right now. I looked in again. No one came. Surely they were locked in some scientific love embrace meant to maximize the orgasmic potential of a woman. That was it, I thought. I banged again. It was 6:15 p.m.; I was right on time. I peeked in the window yet again and came to the conclusion that in three short days Raphaella had given up a life of would-be marital bliss with the father of her child for the cold, reptilian love of an intellect she'd known for less than a week (no matter what she said about knowing him from before). My resolve to serve her was ebbing away. The heat melted it like it was melting me. I began to sweat. I was a mess. Mitchell Mitkin confirmed this for me when he appeared on the sidewalk behind, carrying a bucket of something, a hammer, and a painter's dropcloth over his shoulder.

"Wow, David." He looked me up and down. "I sure hope it's the heat or you're about to go into cardiac arrest." He dipped his shoulder and off fell the tarp. "I don't sweat," he said, "I try to avoid it by keeping my system clean of pollutants."

I started to answer but didn't know if this was a greeting or a command or an attempt to humor me, or what. I just looked at him, confused. A bead of sweat darted off my scalp and into my eye.

"Raphaella's not answering because she's on her way back from the hardware store. She's helping me paint my apartment. It's a kind of payback for running some telephone wire in hers." He smiled amiably and without inference. I smiled back trying to keep my teary-eyed promise of just three nights before, the one that would make me a willing slave. "She's right around the corner, or at least she should be. She's picking up Chinese food." He smiled. "There's enough for you if you'd like some." He was on the stoop now and standing next to me, smelling tart, his ruddy face wrought with activity, indicative of a mind in motion. He was wearing a T-shirt with sleeves cut off, and his sinewy arms and defined triceps nearly rubbed against mine. I did not look at him, afraid I would become very angry.

"Do you think she'll be here soon?" I asked. "I'd like to speak with her, if I could." But of course I could talk to her, I thought. Why was I asking him, the new neighbor, if I could talk to her, my old girlfriend? I wanted to reclaim my dainty petition, but of course, it was too late. Mitkin spoke up and over the rattling door, which he now opened.

"Why couldn't you speak to her? I mean, I think she'll speak to you. She doesn't have laryngitis or anything if that's what you mean."

I nodded and hid a leer, and was inside by the time I realized Raphaella was right behind me. I stood in the front door while Mitkin held the inside foyer door open with his foot. Raphaella waited for us to enter, holding in her hand a plastic bag stuffed with Chinese food, the customary red and white Styrofoam cartons peeking through. Her face betrayed no anxiety. I stared until I got a smile from her, and then I looked at the food. It looked good, until I realized it wasn't for me.

"Don't worry," she said, "I got General Tso for you. It's still your favorite even in exile, right?" I shot her a look and grabbed the bag. The three of us made our way up the stairs to the third floor. We went single file, Mitkin first and Raphaella last. I was in the middle.

Thankfully, Mitkin broke the silence by talking. A lot. He rambled on and on about things I'd never considered. Most of what he said concerned epistemology, a dry subject he made fascinating. He was pretty good with words, not that they were poetic or majestic, to the contrary. His words were cunningly conserved, streamlined and without excess. He spoke adroitly about everything he chose to speak about. Where he did not know, there he did not speak. This precise silence made him appear wise. I must admit, I liked to watch him talk. How could this kid be nineteen? I listened to him and Raphaella all night. In the course of our dinner conversation, Raphaella sought to question most of what he said, and that surprised me. It was not what I expected, given her outburst about "wanting what he's got," and "loving his gig." At one point, as we all sat on couches around her low glass table, she asked him why he thought religion was a waste of time. He started in with a mouth full of chicken lo mein.

"Because, it takes no discipline. It," he paused to swallow, "is inspiration, not dedication. That is what has always angered me about these real didactic types who spend their lives trying to find a proof for God. I mean God has to elude proofs or he's not God. That is the first and only logical premise of theology. But in history it has not been this way at all. Instead, little balding men spend wasted lifetimes researching the un-researchable, if I may use that word. I guess another way to say it is, if you're going to be a scientist, be a scientist. Accept what science says, and what it doesn't say."

"And what doesn't it say?" asked Raphaella.

"It doesn't say anything about God. It says we have no empirical proof that God exists."

"And that's the end of it?" Raphaella reached for her drink.

"That, Raphie, is the end of it."

"How do you know what exists then?" I asked, trying to get into the thick.

He sort of lurched. "You know the answer already. What exists is what your senses tell you exist. Like I told you about the philosopher David Hume, your namesake, we are what our bodies and brains tell us we are, and no more." A smug calm could be seen on Mitkin's face. He liked this conversation.

"Miracles?" said Raphaella, chewing.

"What about them?"

"Aren't they proof of something else?"

"It's all excess. Someone has some psychological baggage, maybe a fear from childhood or the belief in demons, and in turn they create an occurrence which relieves them of their baggage, frees them from the freedom of life." He held up both his hands, palms down. "Think of a see-saw, Raphaella. Miracles are the unstable person's *see*; a response to their exaggerated *saw*."

She looked at me with her hands positioned just like Mitchell's, palms down, seeing and sawing. She smiled. "See and saw, right." And just slightly, she rolled her eyes. I liked that she rolled her eyes.

"You crazy, Mitchell." She kept smiling. "See and saw. Who says that? Crazy." He smiled too, but a bit awkwardly. Raphaella leaned back into the couch, and rubbing her belly, struck an earnest expression.

"But something's not right. What about the gut, gut feelings? Huh?"

Mitchell Mitkin reached across the table and speared a potsticker with his chopsticks. He dripped soy sauce across the table and dragged the damp, cooling aroma of lukewarm vegetable with it. "Gut feelings are, well, something, but not something worth a whole lot of attention." He pointed at Raphaella with his chopsticks and potsticker. "Even they are a product of the empirical."

"A product of the empirical, wow," she said, grinning. "Something I can trust?"

"Right, but it's still worthless."

"My own gut feelings are worthless? Who can believe that, Mitchell?"

"I can. See, the objective realities arrived at by man's collective and constant scientific inquiry, that's what's important." He took a breath. "This is what gives us everything we know today. Microwaves, and microchips, and cars, and catalytic converters, this is the mind of a race which chooses to move forward, always improving." He motioned out and up with his arm, as if climbing a ladder. "Free to be anything he wants to be. Perfection exists for us, ultimately." He looked at Raphaella with resolute eyes. "Your gut feeling is just a hunch until you get out and prove it." Mitchell stood straight up, "Test it!" He sauntered down the hallway where Raphaella and I could hear the refrigerator open. Bits of ice plinked. "You gotta doubt everything!" He returned with a bottle of brandy and three stout glasses of ice. "Now for the ultimate empirical reality." He poured. "You're about to partake of my father's favorite. Thank the distilleries for such perfection." He beamed a *cheers* and we drank. Raphaella took a tiny, polite sip and put it aside. Mitkin nodded in approval.

All three of us liked learned conversation. I liked it because I was taught to. Raphie liked it because she was naturally curious and simply smart as hell. But neither of us were like Mitkin. He liked it because it was his destiny. He was an intellectual. He knew he was an intellectual, and by his gestures and haughty speech, so did everyone he spoke with. He just knew that one day he would write a great book or coin a tumultuous phrase, basically change the lives of millions. It unnerved me a bit that he could so easily command our attention and talk to us as children, and it made me helpless too. With him in the room, I could never impress Raphaella. But strangely, I was not urged to with Mitkin around; it was only after he'd gone that I'd feel nervous. It was his absence and the impending silence which I feared most. I watched Mitkin go on and on.

"Take for example, this uproar over fetal tissue. Why not use it for experimentation? Do you know they have been trying to learn about fetal tissue since 1922! 1922 and all we get are roadblocks, roadblocks and more roadblocks. Why are people scared? What is there to be afraid of? Change is the answer. Most are just afraid that some fictitious past will be forgotten in favor of the evil future. What a waste. I say heave-ho, chuck it and go forward. It's not like a man is more than what he makes of himself, and I don't mean that like my mother means it. When she says it, it has this pseudo-mythic sentimentality." He imitated a female soprano and spoke, "Be all you can be Son, don't let anyone say you can't. Say *oh yes I can*. You know, this little engine that could crap. I mean, man used to be weak and susceptible to any multitude of viruses: bubonic, influenza, consumption, polio and the lists go on. Today, man is more than these diseases. We have fought back." He looked at Raphaella. "Haven't we?"

"Cancer?"

"Soon there'll be no cancer either, Raphie. I am not saying that man's scientific mind is flawless, it requires data. I'm just saying that we make ourselves great when we apply our minds collectively in pursuit of empirical truth. The end of cancer is coming too, you'll see."

Raphaella wagged her head and smirked a little. "If you say so, but it sounds like you're just spouting your father's stuff. Come on, most of this comes from him, right?"

Mitkin looked perplexed, hurt almost. He took another sip from his brandy. "I didn't get this from anybody," he said swallowing. "Knowing the world is a vocation, it's a higher calling. It's religious really. Who do you think the priests of the future will be? Shrinks, Raphie, shrinks. Get sick, feeling a little depressed? Visit the shrink. Priests will run to them, too. Heck they already do. *I'm an alky, I like boys, fix me up, Doc. Thanks, Amen.* It's all science, Raphie. All of it is calling, it's all out there for us. I just hear the call louder, maybe. But everybody should be investigating something."

"Like jobs?" I said. "I already do that. My latest investigation tells me there ain't enough of them." I wanted to laugh at my self-sissification, but Mitkin just kept on.

"Yes, like jobs. If economics was done more accurately and without such reverence for intangible indicators it would make for better policy." He spoke coldly. "The same goes for sociology and psychology. Everything we do should be systematic and ordered."

"I think we're already too ordered," I said.

"Who? You? Are you telling me that you, David, the guy who wants to be a writer, are too ordered? There's nothing you'd like more reasonably ordered in your life?" He sipped his brandy again, pointing with the glass as he put it down. "Nothing?"

"I meant we, as a society."

"But you're pretty representative of society, aren't you? Would you say there are more *you's* in the world or more *me's*? Honestly now, David?"

"You know, Mitchell," said Raphaella, "you talk a lot. If you talked less, you'd make more friends." Like crawling into a warm bed, I felt comforted by Raphaella's rescue.

"What, am I boring you?" asked Mitkin lightly.

Raphaella glinted. He wasn't. Mitkin smiled and nodded.

"But wait," Raphaella started. "There's something missing here. People mess up all the time, we regret things. It just doesn't seem like we are naturally the way you say we are. I mean, humans really aren't very rational at all."

"Yes we are." He was unrelenting. "We are just ignorant, unaware of all the data we need for each important decision in our lives. I don't debate our ignorance. If we had more data, we'd make better decisions." He leaned forward in his seat. "Let's say you knew more about your future financial status. Knowing you'd be dirt poor or disabled or both, you'd probably make a reasonable decision to have an abortion right now."

"You sure?" said a thin-eyed Raphaella.

"I'm not sure that you'd choose an abortion, but I am sure that such information would give you the opportunity to make a more informed and rational decision. A decision closer to correct."

"Well, big deal," Raphaella retorted. "I agree. I make decisions based on what I know. But what I know doesn't change what is right. If I *know* giving up my child's hiding spot to killers will save my life, I still can't give her up. I mean, we can know a whole lot a shit and still do the wrong thing, can't we?"

"Not if you choose rationally. A truly rational man gathers as much knowledge as possible, assesses his desires and makes a decision that contributes greatest to his assembly of wants. Then, with a smile on his face, he calls his decision the right thing. Why do you think people live together before getting married? Knowledge. They want more empirical data on their mate. Eating habits, cleanliness, bed sheet preferences and bathroom hours. The more you know, the better your decision. Right and wrong change; change of data, change of values."

"But Mitchell, there must be more to right and wrong than just getting a good deal for yourself?"

He held up his hand. "Look. The more you know, the closer to good, if you want to call it that, your decision will be. But the decision is only good because it is informed. You guys keep thinking that empirical truth is like an emotion. It's not. It's revealed."

I was on the verge of confusion. And restlessness.

But what did Mitchell care? He hid his brandy behind his back and then slowly wound it around and into the open without spilling a drop.

Okay? I thought. What's with the hidden brandy trick? And why the heck is this creepy kid drinking brandy in the first place?

"See, truth is just hidden behind ignorance. Brandy is good, but as we learn more about drunkenness and what it does to the body, well, it's not so good. It's like fetal tissue." He smiled. "Fetal tissue has always been advantageous, it's just we've only now in this century pulled back the curtain to reveal this. These facts exist whether we like them or not."

I decided to weigh in. "So it's just like that scene from Wizard of Oz where Oz gets exposed by Toto. That curtain was green, emerald really, and Toto yanked it back and there he was: Oz. Even though it was clear that Oz was also the guard and the servant, Dorothy was sort of stupid on that one."

Mitkin looked at me deadpan. Raphaella shook, holding back a belly laugh.

"You're messing with me, David," he said flatly. "Go ahead, but it doesn't change what I'm saying."

I started to lighten him up with an apology of sorts, but Raphaella just waved it off. "Relax, Mitch, we are having a conversation between friends, that's all."

Friends, I thought. Yeah, I guess so.

I noticed that dusk had fallen. The room was smeared in it. Raphaella lit a candle, as she loved to do, and its glow mingled with the new night creating a gentle mysterium. A simple painting grew louder on the wall. In it, a yellow man looked up and out and into the yonder of space, where, in a deep and distant corner, a little yellow dot of a man looked back. It was the yellow I remember best. It glowed under the light of Raphaella's candle, while at the same time Mitkin's discerning voice grew more incongruous, scraping shrill against the gloaming of the setting sun. I looked at him. He was sipping another brandy and smacking his slender lips as if preparing to speak.

"Once a friend of mine told me I'm the way I am because I was afraid of what I'd find beyond the data of my existence."

He was foundering a bit and I interrupted. "He said it like that?"

Mitkin smirked. "Next he made reference to my father. Said he had no heart, said he wasn't human." He drank and scowled. "He's no longer my friend."

"But I thought... I mean, technically, your friend is right. According to you, your father doesn't have a heart, in that way. You see?"

"He was a sap! Don't you get it, David? He was dishonoring my father by appealing to emotions. Waa, waa, waa, childish emotions, sentimental crap. The truth of the matter is he was just revealing his own insecurities. His father abandoned him when he was two, there's the information of importance. *Now* do you see? There's the key."

There was a sliver of silence.

"So did mine," said Raphaella.

Remarkably, Mitkin became like a child. He sat up and cocked his head slightly and squinted; he was disbelieving. "Your father, too? He left you? Why?" It was the first non-rhetorical question Mitkin had asked all night.

Raphaella leaned all the way back into the thickest and most comfortable part of her couch. "Issues, I guess."

"But you haven't told me anything," said Mitkin.

"Because I don't know anything," said Raphaella. "My father was a Romanian. He had a two-week affair with a black woman from New York City. He had urges, macho stuff. You tell me, Mitchell, can we explain that rationally? Does it make any sense? A man makes a baby and then abandons that baby? I mean, what led him to make that decision? It sure feels like he was missing some crucial information to me, like how his daughter would feel." She smirked. "Yeah, in fact, that's a good question for you. His best interest was not mine, does that mean you can't call him wrong for abandoning me?" The coupling of the personal and theoretical charged the room. Raphaella was irritated, though I did not see the great depths of resentment I'd become accustomed to between us. She was not bitter or dismissive; a bit of her was reserved in homage to Mitkin and his stalwart love of an idea. I wanted to see the resentment, I wanted to see her hurt him. I poured another drink.

"That depends," replied Mitkin, unencumbered and clearly intoxicated. "He may have done himself more damage by hanging around here. He may have done more damage to you, but that's not even the point really. The point is this: If he weighed his options sensibly and if he chose soundly, without emotion and sentimentality, then he chose rightly. Pain, I'm afraid," he averted his eyes, "is not part of the equation."

Raphaella stoically found his averted gaze, and looking directly at him said, "Well for some, anyway."

They were locked in some sort of soul-defying eye battle and I felt a little left out. With my face warm from drink, I added, "And when her father dies? Won't he regret all of this on his deathbed?"

"If he's on a bed when he dies, he might," shot Mitkin. "Who's to say he won't be incinerated in a terrorist attack or spontaneously combust? Who's to say he'll have time for the cartoon deathbed scene?" I felt the root of anger waggle inside me, but it did not move me to act. Raphaella spoke up.

"So, okay then, he might feel pain, good enough for me. How about a new topic, something, well, further from home?" She smiled resolvedly.

Mitkin was not finished, however. His voice ran on, higher now, a voice filled with the sing-song of appeasement. "Don't get me wrong, Raphie. While the goal is to minimize regret by making good decisions, I don't consider your father's decision a good one. A father should stay with his children." He smiled, oddly. "A father should serve his daughter." Mitkin was gushing and it was not befitting.

And then that feeling hit me again, it rushed into my head and exploded. *It's for love.*

My innards turned flush red. He loves her. He loves her, dammit. Just like I felt on the roof the other night, the same thing! I brooded on this. I felt like my head was swelling to absurd and grotesque dimensions, my pride was bloating and breaking the skin in which I was trapped. Don't let her notice, I thought, it will only piss her off. I was shaking. Can she tell? Don't let her see. Go to the kitchen. Why though? I'm her man, not this guy, this boring twig. I sucked down my brandy. She'd think I was an idiot if she could see my jealousy, *but I know he loves her.*

I was a wreck. I looked at him. Now, eighteen years later, I don't imagine he was doing anything particularly crass or spiteful, but sitting there, I was convinced he was mocking me. Arrogant bastard. Look at the way he's holding his mouth, he's ugly. What is he doing with his mouth anyway? And then, on cue, Raphaella spoke as if to pop my bloated self.

"How about your love life, Mr. Mitchell Mitkin?" I groaned inside.

"There's nothing to discuss," he said, getting up and going to the kitchen again. Where had Mitkin gone? Was he going for more tasty toxicants, more seduce juice? I surveyed the room. Little rice crumbs dotted the rug where I sat, and the couch was strewn with chopsticks and chicken carrion in Styrofoam cartons. But no, Mitkin's area was less chaotic. He had not spilled his food, bastard. He lingered in the kitchen, browsing through Raphaella's refrigerator. A legion of jealous minions marched in my breast; refrigerators, I thought, are personal items. I looked at Raphaella. She didn't seem to care at all, she was stretched all the way out on her couch. That's my couch, I thought. I bought it on one optimistic Saturday at the local resale store on the corner. The recliner Mitkin had just vacated retained the imprint of his butt. Ugly butt, I thought. I searched the hall for his return, but heard only more rumbling. I turned to Raphaella and broke down, quietly, with my eyes. I felt myself giving in to that warm, pitying emotion men know so well when faced with the specter of a woman's rejection. If she recognized my pain, she showed no signs.

I let go into the silence. "I brought my bag, you know. I've been thinking, I want things to change between us. Can we have some time together later?"

She didn't respond immediately; she didn't want to have this conversation. I could tell by the way she ignored me. Cold neglect. What I wanted to talk about paled next to the buoyant, heady conversation of Mitchell Mitkin. She sighed. I should have realized right then that my decision to start this conversation was not in my best interest. Everything that I had suppressed for three days came back. Confused love, envy, desire, security and sex all welled up and I wanted Mitkin to leave. I searched again for him. He was there, this time carrying three bowls of ice cream. Cold.

A relieved smile curled on Raphaella's thick, kissable lips, and the whole scene was murderous. I thought about screaming at the top of my lungs, flipping a chair or two, running top speed out the door. Anything I do, I thought, will just be met with an invitation to leave or a Mitkin discourse on the merits of dispassion. I was without recourse, pinned down by enemy fire so strong I felt I would forever crawl on my belly. Mitkin gave me the bowl of ice cream. I wondered where he'd gotten it. Was it a last-minute pickup or a scoop from his very own carton, stored in her freezer, like a lover stores underwear in his partner's dresser? I was ornery and sexual and I had forgotten about my pledge of submission. I remember thinking, I'm a mess and I don't give a damn. And Mitkin? He just sat back down on his ugly buttocks indentation, reminding me of his permanence. This frickin' guy lives downstairs, I thought, how would I ever catch him cavorting? My mind, a minute ago comfortable and enjoying the undulating waters of our conversation was now loosed from its moors. I stood up abruptly. Mitkin eyed me, surprised.

"Raphie, is it over between us?"

Raphaella rolled her eyes. "David, sit down."

I stared dumbly.

"Sit down, David."

"I want to know. What's the deal? I've made many promises to myself. I promised that I would make this relationship work and that I'd be the father that your father was not. I've promised to always be there for you, to listen to you, obey you. I'll do whatever it takes, Kiwi, whatever."

"It takes sitting down," she said. I sat down. It grew very silent. I looked around the room and found Mitkin staring at me while pulling a loaded spoonful of ice cream through his lips, flattening the top of the frothy, rounded scoop. His blue eyes did not commiserate with mine, but neither were they opportunistic like he'd been waiting for us to blow up, waiting to take her from me when the time was right. He was just studying me to see why I was acting the way I was. I wished he'd find out, because at that point I didn't know myself. I had abandoned the plan, and seemingly against my will. I looked starvingly at Raphaella. In her eyes, I saw a congealed mix of pity, irritation and anger. And then, for a moment only, I saw profound sorrow. She looked at Mitkin.

"As you can see, we've been having our problems. David doesn't think that I know he'll be a great father." I entered a half-catharsis. It wasn't like she said I love you, but still, I thought, it's a start. I wanted to give her a kiss, but she was still looking at Mitkin. She wanted a response so she could get on with less anxious conversation, but of course, the little word-general did not oblige. He just scooped up another spoonful of ice cream and slowly slid it between his lips. The room remained loaded. Raphaella scooped and ate too, and I sat still. The little candle in the corner burnt itself out, and the conversation was over. In the yellowish dark of the room, Mitkin got up and the three of us exchanged niceties.

"I'll have to ask you about that love life some other time," said Raphaella. I glanced at her. She ushered Mitkin out the door, but to add to my drunken angst, he left all the items he'd brought. Raphaella said something else about seeing him later and shut the door. She turned around and stood looking at me. I stared back and smiled.

"That went well," I said. I gave her a hug, but she did not hug back. I gave her another, this one was more repentant. "I think I'll clean up a bit and meet you in bed." She remained in her silence. It was another of her many forms of torture, and she shoved off to the back of the apartment. I wandered into the front room and stared at the mess. Reason, rational thought, it's all bullshit. Mitkin is wrong about life, our impulsive life together was testimony to this. Alone in the dark, I wondered if I'd ever find happiness with the woman who carried my child.

By the time I got into bed, Raphaella was nearly asleep. She was on her side, facing the wall. I crawled in and felt my head spin. I gently laid my hand on her hip and then fit it snugly over her maternal belly. She was crying. "Baby, what is it?"

"It's nothing, David. Go to sleep."

"Should I worry?" I said.

"Yeah, you should worry. Worry a lot. You're out of control, David."

"But what am I supposed to do? I love you."

"You don't even know what that means. I don't even…" and she began to cry again. Her sobs were deep and she shook. She cried uncontrollably. I had never seen her cry this way, I had never seen her cry at all.

"What is it, Raphie? Tell me."

"Something is happening to me, something I can't explain." I held her tighter but she did not respond. I was there, but she was alone. I hung on for a long time, long enough to see the dark shades of night grow lighter and whiter. And then I let go and fell asleep.

CHAPTER VI

Descent

I left town. The next morning, I silently gathered my things, took a train downtown and packed up my apartment. I was afraid of the sorrow I saw in Raphaella's eyes, it was something I did not know but oddly felt a part of. I imagined that it was me, my foibles, there in her eyes. I imagined myself as the thing that was happening to her, and I could no longer bear being that. I did something, something I vowed I would never do: I left before my child was born.

I went home to California where I began work as a legal assistant in my father's law firm. I sent money to Raphaella regularly and routinely requested pictures of my daughter. She was beautiful, my Dana. I went out to visit once each year and enjoyed the visits, but I could see that in Raphaella the unseen still moved, inchoate. I felt like she was pregnant again, but not with a baby. We always parted amiably, but her sorrowful eyes always made me worry. Her mother called me when she heard I'd left. She chewed me out, and then told me I wasn't to blame, given Raphaella's confusing and independent ways. She added something about how "Raphie got too much of me in her. Chasing men away and all. Like I did her own daddy..." Simon wrote me a letter. He misspelled every other word but I could see he missed me and the thought of his sister with her *husband*.

I heard little of Mitchell Mitkin. In one of Raphaella's letters, I got the feeling he was still quite involved. And then he actually wrote to me. I was suspicious. Maybe Raphaella had urged him on as a way to reconcile, as preparation for the big announcement, the one of their impending marriage. His letter was actually an addendum to hers, a little note saying he was one year from graduation and planning to teach high school for one or two years. He said it would be "a service to the city and to education as an institution." Same old Mitkin. It was timely, because I too was working on my teaching certificate. I had not decided where I'd teach, but the thought of returning to New York lingered. My father was adamantly against it. He warned me to avoid the den of deceit and destruction, the place that ruined me and got me into real, life-altering trouble.

That I was home and working in my father's law office made my mother happy, but she wasn't convinced that I'd done the right thing. As much as she loved me she knew that I had a child out there, and that made her very sad. Besides, she knew I was no teacher and surely I didn't belong in a law office. She nagged me about writing, asked me if I needed more creative outlets, if she could buy me a new word processor, or even one of those newfangled home computers. I always assured her I was fine and that the writing would take care of itself, but that wasn't happening. I hadn't written anything since arriving in California, and that included journal entries.

I did read every chance I could. I read a great deal of history and some philosophy. I did not, however, become passionate about anything while in California. I kept saying to myself, one day I'll discover passion for something and then, there, among flashes of desire I'll become great, a true light in the darkness. It never happened. Instead I went to many Mexican-style happy hours and reminisced with old high school friends. I often drank too much, and they did too. Most of them, like me, hadn't graduated from college and together we had little to talk about, except the past. And it was an ignominious past.

I didn't tell anyone about Raphaella and Dana, and I took special care to keep all my dates in the dark. It wasn't that I was trying to conceal some detrimental piece of information; I just never felt close enough to any of them. In my bosom, or someplace akin to a bosom, a heart or a gut maybe, I knew I would eventually end up with Raphaella, and telling simple, dull women who wanted to sleep with me about the woman I loved reeked of betrayal. And sleep I did. But each time I regretted it, sometimes just a little, sometimes just for a day, other times for a week. But my regret was always more than a moment.

By July of my third year away, I knew that it was time to go back. I wrote a letter to Raphaella telling her my plans. I would take a huge course load and finish my undergraduate degree locally. Then I'd leave California and teach in New York, and I would start in the fall. That's all I said. I did not ask for a place to stay or even a suggestion. I just wrote, "See you in the fall."

I left on my twenty-sixth birthday, taking a bus cross-country. I had always wanted to take such a trip; such a trip just had to be good for a writer, it just had to be. So it was that I mounted a shiny Greyhound bus, captained by an overweight Native American with very long black hair. I sat in the front so I could chat with the big man whenever I wanted. I loved talking to drivers: truck drivers, bus drivers, taxi drivers. They know so much about the passage of time and the meaning of returning home. I wanted to hear some wise words from this modern day Odysseus.

"People? Most are just assholes," he said.

And that was about all he said until Denver. Okay, I thought, I'll watch America pass by in this window. It was the sunsets that I liked best. They uncoiled flat against the dry earth, pressing down and out in all colors, following me, romantically. And then nightfall, it was then that I'd look at my reflection in the window, staring dumbly while listening to my heart. It would at once tell me I'd made the right decision to return and then it would bang a beat of doubt and reverse itself. I'd picture Dana's face as I swaggered home and into the room. She was always glowing and a perfect image of love, and I knew she would take me in. Then I'd picture Raphaella—she was different. She smiled sympathetically, as if forcing the love her daughter felt, as if partaking in it, but not as her own. The effort was tormenting. I'd always stop daydreaming at this point and instead tune in a baseball game played far away. I caught a Yankee game played in Chicago and listened intently, living vicariously through the players whose names had changed, but who still were spoken of with respect, as if more important for their pinstripes. They were the New York Yankees, the team of the past, the team of kids' dreams.

After three full days, I reached my destination. I hopped a cab and headed downtown where I met a friend. I remember well my first full day back in New York. It was late August, the same time of year I'd left three years before. It was hot and extremely humid, and empty. It sounds odd but a Manhattan August is barren. Echoes bounce louder between the great steel canyons and the streets run fast like raging rivulets, yellow beads of sweat galloping from light to light in search of fares. In August, Manhattan becomes a red-hot steel village. I walked down 8th Avenue pulling my luggage behind me, looking forward to dumping it at my friend's apartment as planned. We were supposed to meet at our favorite restaurant, an African joint, where I looked forward to getting something cool to drink. My friend's name was Jamel, and he lived in a flat above the restaurant, coming and going, making that restaurant his second home. While working at The Plateau, I found him a summer job at a law office and he had done well there, impressing the thin-lipped and very Caucasian woman he worked for. Her name was Ms. Polk, and her firm had never worked with The Plateau. I could tell that

Ms. Polk, whom Jamel called "The Brown Shirt," was quite nervous about this placement. But Jamel was the best. He excelled and impressed everyone. They offered him an extension on his summer job, and when I left he was still working there and getting ready to graduate from high school. A letter from him told me he had now graduated and that he was attending Pace University as a political science major. He would become a lawyer, he wrote.

It was lunchtime and the little, easygoing Malian restaurant was just opening—late according to the sign on the front door. I stowed my bags in a corner and scanned for Jamel. I found him sitting with a tall African girl in the back near the kitchen. They were laughing. He looked bigger and older, more mature. A little tuft of hair sat on his chin. He no longer had a flat-top. Now he sported a ragged half-dreadlock thing, *nappy* some might say, but uniquely stylish. His clothes were deftly coordinated. Everything on him hung loosely and intimated a cool chic. I hollered. He turned and squinted.

"Is it Big D?"

"'Tis," I said, extending a hand and a hug. He pulled up a chair, backwards, and laid his arms atop the rest. I leaned back in mine and smiled.

"So where's old Brown Shirt?" I asked.

"She's back on the grill, she's no good with the public." He grinned.

"You didn't burn bridges did you?"

"Hell, no Dave, I blew them up." He laughed and then slapped my hand again. "Everything's cool D, all is under control. Besides, you're the one who's got questions to answer." He stared at me.

"I'm back. What can I say? I figured I'd had enough of California. Too many blondes for me."

"You always were the uptown type, D. I figured you'd be back sooner. You left in a rush, you know. I know some people 'round here are still a bit upset, if you know what I mean."

I did. I'm sure he was talking about my boss at The Plateau. It had to be. I knew he couldn't be referring to Raphaella. Or maybe he was?

"Have you spoken to Raphaella?" I asked sheepishly.

"Haven't seen her one bit, at least not lately. Right after you left, she and I had a little sit down. I went up to see her figuring she was broken up."

I looked at him, wanting him to continue. Was she broken up? He caught on. "She seemed sad, real sad, Dave. But I got the feeling she thought it was for the better. You know how she is."

"Well that was a long time ago." I took a sip of my ice water, eyes down. "How about you?"

"You mean with Cheryl?"

Jamel and I had grown close because we had similar stories to tell. Both of us loved women who didn't love us back, or at least this is what we told one another. He, like me, had a baby with his woman. He, like me, made a calculated decision to stay out of their collective lives. He, like me, blamed most of his tribulations on her, calling her hardheaded and selfish and whatever else came to mind. Together we girded the other's insecurities and helped each other through difficult situations. After three years, I was very interested in his story. Could it be as bad as mine?

"She's still crazy," he said. "Last time I checked she was with some dude, some older business type. She can do her little love thing as long as she remembers whose child she's raising. I'm still that baby's father." He nodded, affirming his own words. I nodded too but only because it seemed like the right thing to do. The impulse to raise my child had subsided slightly. I was more cautious and less obsessive about my relationship now. At least that was the way I felt sitting there with Jamel.

"You're here to get back together, aren't you Dave? You're taking the big chance huh?"

On the long bus ride east I had answered this question solidly. *Yes* was the answer, but now, back in town and faced with a real human being and not just my distorted image in a Greyhound bus window, it sure felt shaky. Jamel stared at me as I wondered how the two of us had gotten to this point in our lives. We were absent fathers and confounded lovers. "Tell me something Jamel, why are we still like this? Why are we still bitching and moaning about our women? What is it? Is it us?" The whole question came out more earnestly than the situation called for. It sent him thinking. He cocked his head and studied his shoes, an unlikely place for an answer. I interrupted. "I took a bus here and had time to think. I thought about my three years in California and how I'd done nothing, really. I thought about how I'd always known I'd come back and how I couldn't abandon my family. But now, sitting here, about to go uptown and see Raphaella, I'm getting these big-question blues, Jamel. I don't mean to make this too sappy, but why is life between men and women so difficult?"

"Because life is difficult, bro. Women are like everything else in life, sort of messed up, ya know?"

"So our troubles are normal then?"

"Well, look around. Every other man I know has a baby and a woman somewhere, someone he loves but can't stand to be around. It's a shame, but not a damn shame."

"I don't know," I said shaking my head. "There's more to it than that. Gotta be."

"Well, in your case maybe, but us black folks are just dealing with what you white folks cooked up for us. I mean two hundred years of broken families just doesn't fix itself because a man thinks he's in love. That's a whole 'nother story though, ain't it, D?" He grinned.

"Yes it is. It's just that when I think of Raphaella and of our baby, I think maybe there is more to it than just love or whatever."

He nodded. "So, you are back to get with her then."

"Okay Jamel, yeah, I'm here to put things back together with Raphaella."

He nodded knowingly. "Well when you do, give me a ring and help me out. In the meantime, call me when she makes you want to crack a head or cry some tears. And she will."

We went on talking for a while. He told me about Pace and his studies. Watching him speak I felt good about my work at The Plateau. Jamel was a success story, a standard of excellence. The Plateau and I had engineered a soul for the world and I thought how that was good. Leaving, I gave him another embrace and my new address. He gave me his number. I left the little restaurant and strolled north on 8th Avenue planning to catch the D-train after a browse through Times Square. The August air felt like wet curtains and as I approached Times Square, the cluttered, neon epicenter of the world, it was true; there was no turning back. An incautious hope emoted in me and I took in the giddy, celebratory excess of this very American square. I beamed. A preacher barked at me from the corner of 42nd Street while a flood of lunch-timers waded into and around me, jostling me ahead and to the corner of 43rd Street. I left it all and slipped underground, into the subway. A bead of sweat broke over my ear as I stood waiting for the train that would take me to see Raphaella.

***

I found her on the stoop. She was cleaning up, scrubbing some crag or other, bent over, her marvelous back bending against a cotton blouse. I watched her as I walked slowly up the street. It had been three years since I'd really conversed with Raphaella. I had seen her several times since leaving for California—baby daddy visits. From these meetings, I surmised she was still racked by that intangible desire to know more about love and truth and beauty and whatever. It was that look in her eye. It hadn't changed since the last night, the night before the day I left, and if anything, it had become more intense. Coming down the street, I experienced a pang of anxiety and then, laying eyes on her, a long, broad stroke of nostalgia. It warmed me and I did what I believe most men do, I practiced. Under my breath, standing across the street from Raphaella, unnoticed, I ran through a litany of opening lines. They were valiant, valiant lines, oh yeah:

"Time won't separate us again, I won't let it…"

"I'm ready to be a man now, please give me the opportunity…"

"Can I tell you about how much I need you…?"

"I want to love you for who you are… please!"

And finally the one I almost rested on, "Three years have taught me what I needed to know. I love you…"

I said this one again, out loud, clearly, as if meaning it. It sounded as bad as it does now. I cringed to a stop. All of my phrases were gross, I thought. Rehearsal was dangerous with such a woman; she was simply too earnest. I stopped practicing and propped myself against the wall of an apartment building, directly across the street from Raphaella. The unique three-story brownstone she lived in preened itself while below Raphaella continued her cleaning. Like an old friend, the little building reveled in her touch. It had a new paint job; its bricks were more brown than I remember, richer. I looked at the top floor and its bay window. That was the floor I knew best, or at least thought I knew best. I looked at the middle floor. Mitkin's face came to mind—the brash student. Looking at the window, it was clear he still lived there. Various items, coffee mugs, books, a fishbowl, all sat disheveled on the big sill. I wanted to see Mitkin there too, perched in the window, feet dangling out and onto the fire escape. But I didn't. He was probably at school, I thought. And then I thought how surprising it was that I could feel such a strong curiosity towards this odd man. I followed the tracery down to the first floor. There the big window sat as it did before, bare and apparently unoccupied.

Could it be that after so many years, no one had moved in? How could Martin Mitkin go so long without the rent income? Was Mitkin's father dead? I also noted that nothing had gone up beside the old brownstone. On one side, the left side as you stood in front, the lot was the same as three years before. Fat shards of rusty red bricks pocked the lot. Two discarded car tires lay waiting for burial, defying the elements. They were there three years ago too, and just as defiant. The stout fence that encircled the lot had been taken down, and on the other side, the right side, a vital patch of green had burgeoned where formerly bricks had lain. It was a community garden now, a fresh tract of hope, I thought. All the way in the back, beyond all the color of the garden, sat a pack of women. They were having fun cheating each other in a good game of cards. The entire scene was very meaningful at this moment. It had that cinematic quality to it, a foreshadowing effect, as if the great director of life had chosen this moment to elucidate all those to come. Even the few clouds overhead did their job by standing still, hovering for a moment, like a spirit, floating and intimating something profound, pointing out redemption with a wistful wink. And there at the base, still bent over and scrubbing, was Raphaella. She wiped her brow, stood straight up, and turned around, just as I moved to cross the street. She stared at me but then returned to her work. Had she seen me? I doubted everything in the time it took me to step off the curb. Everything. But I kept going, pulled along by the imperative of having come at all.

"What are you scrubbing?" was my first line. That was it. "What are you scrubbing?"

She smiled a broad, rich smile, wide and supple across her face. I felt welcome. On the stoop I hugged her, we released, and she held me at arm's length and smiled again. I felt the needles of anxiety retreat, and in their place came the sweet calm of acceptance.

"I've come to teach. I thought I could make the biggest difference here. And I wanted to see you."

"It's good to see you," she replied.

"You look good, Raphaella. You seem happy. Where's Dana?"

"At her cousin's."

In the silence I heard the laughter of the women next door. "You seem happy," I said again.

She looked down and toed a pebble with her sandaled foot. "Yeah, well, it's a work in progress," she said. I looked at her quizzically. "Let's just say..." She took me by the forearm. "Forget that. Come on, let's get something to eat."

I paused.

"I'm sorry," she said. "Do you have a few minutes?"

"Sure," I said. "Sure, let's go."

We walked down the street toward her favorite diner where we took a table in the corner. She made sure I was snugly in before she went to the counter and spoke momentarily with the big burly restaurateur who seemed to be in charge. Watching her go, I noticed she was still beautiful, still thin and shapely.

"Simon had a baby," she said as she sat down.

"Simon? Your brother Simon?"

"Yep, baby girl. Don't ask who the baby's mother is." I asked, of course, and she told me it was Tina, the same one her mother had called a whore three years before.

"He's happy," she said, "but he doesn't know the first thing about babying. He has no idea what he's into... does he?"

The question was our history. I nodded with absolute certainty and felt like an old and wily boxer. I sipped my beer hoping to come up with an appropriate topic for conversation. I didn't want this to be a sappy "remember when" session. I really just wanted to see Raphaella and begin the long process, the one that would bring me back to her and our daughter. A little period of silence broke out and I mostly stared at my beer.

"How's Dana?" I finally asked. It seemed like the right question, even if I'd asked it already.

"Quite a bit has changed since you left."

"Uh-huh," I muttered.

"We're getting along David, without men. I hope that doesn't offend you."

Confuse me, is more like it. "Without men? Like without boyfriends or without me?" Her long smile and good mood had turned to a familiar earnestness.

"Both, I guess."

"So, no dating at all?" I asked.

"No. None. All the men I meet are so... I don't know, content."

"How awful, content men."

"Not that it's bad to be content, I'm talking about the shallow thing. They aren't really searching, I guess. That's what I meant to say." The big smarmy waiter appeared with two heaping bowls of salad, one for each of us. "These aren't on the menu, I had him make them for us, eat that." She pointed to what looked like a splayed mushroom. Spread over the whole leafy thing was feta cheese. "Eat it."

"Have you figured it out yet?" I said after a few bites.

"What?"

"What you're looking for?"

"Wow, the big questions so soon. A man on a mission all right. You get the feeling I'm looking, David?"

"Always," I said flatly. "Mmmhuh. At least I did when I left. I felt like what you searched for ruined what you had."

"And what I had was you," she said kindly, affectionately and without malice.

"What you had was the beginning of something. Something good. If you'd like, you can have it again." Achh, I thought, this is too quick, too heavy, but I couldn't stop.

Raphaella was calm. She picked an olive from her plate and held it between her fingers. She popped it in her mouth as she replied. "Have you ever seen a baptism, David?"

"When I was a kid at church."

"What was it like? Did you like it?"

I furrowed my brow. "I was fidgety."

"Well, I went to one about three months ago. Yeah, I did." She leaned forward. "Would you like to hear what happened while I was there?"

She changed the subject and was now talking about a baby's baptism. I wanted to find out more about *us*, but at the same time I knew I should slow down with the *us* conversations, they always got me in trouble. The tug and pull between what I wanted to talk about and what was good to talk about paralyzed me. Raphaella spoke over my paralysis.

"It was nice, real nice. For three months that place, and that music has stayed with me." This was a change. Though Raphaella had always had a quirky desire for "more," religion was never the answer. It was the enemy in many ways. I remember her saying just that, long ago, shortly after I'd met her. "Religion makes people slaves," she told me. "Death scares people, and religion gets them to follow

these powerful dudes, men mostly, who tell them how to beat death. It's a scam."
That's what she said four years earlier, but now she spoke curiously about God.
She put her fork down and clasped her hands, elbows on the table. Her eyes danced.

"First of all, the church was pretty dark. They didn't have the lights on, just
bunches of candles. An old woman told me you should never have the lights on in
the church."

How about that, I thought. Un-enlightenment.

"It was a small church, not much bigger than this diner really, with high
ceilings. Right in the middle of the ceiling, way up on top, was a painting of Jesus
with outstretched arms. He was dressed with robes, not dying all bloody, but like
a king. Strong, I liked that. Icons were all over the place, and most of them had an
oil lamp dangling in front, and this made them glow nicely. It was beautiful. All
the people had lit candles and placed them around the church in these prayer box
things. Also there were candle stands just around, you could walk around easily
because there were no long benches or chairs. Well, there were a few, but out of
the way, along the walls. And everyone made the cross sign in front of them, it
seemed like all the time." She demonstrated. It did not suit her.

"Where were you?"

"I stood in the back with Dana. Dana was good. I think the music made her
calm. It was chant, all chant, nothing was spoken during the entire service.
Everything was chanted. And incense was everywhere. It smelled like 125th Street
in the summer. I think it was jasmine or myrrh or something."

"How did you find this place?" I interrupted.

"Wait. I'm not to the good part yet." Her innocent adoration was out of
character. "You should have seen the priest. Actually there were two, one had a
long beard, I'm talking real long, like those ZZ Top biker guys. The other was
bearded too, but slightly, like he was just getting started. And they had great
clothes, man. Their robes were white with gold lace and tiny, handcrafted patterns.
They were so beautiful that I just wanted to wrap myself up in them, like I used to
wrap my Barbies in my mom's best cotton napkins. Can you see how ancient and
beautiful it was?" I nodded, just slightly. "I was just loving it, but it was tiring, too.
Standing up is hard if you aren't used to it, but now I'm getting better."

"Better?" I said.

"Yeah, at standing."

"In church, you're better at standing now? You've been back?"

"Just wait," she said. "Everything about the service was primitive, right. It made me feel like I was a part of some great sacrifice, like an ancient ritual was happening right in front of me. My mind couldn't grasp everything that was happening, but you know David, I don't think I was supposed to. I liked that. I liked the primal thing. Anyway, the part I want to tell you about was when the three people were baptized. Two of them were babies, darling little babies, his baby," she nodded to the guy behind the counter again. "Anyway, the other one getting baptized was a big burly man, he looked foreign, you know, hair on his back. The priest had set up this big pool, almost like a summer yard-pool, but dignified and lined with beautiful lace. I kept staring, thinking that this big man was about to get into that little pool, in church! I was loving it. Grown people acting like they'd lost their minds. But he did. David, he went all the way under the water—the priest dunked him. Part of me was saying, this is just weird shit. A half-naked man and a little tub, I mean what's all that about?"

"Yeah," I said. "What is all that about?"

"But I loved it. It had this absurd feel to it, but not the kind of absurd feel I get when I swipe my subway card like a lemming and stand with thousands of people crammed together, none of us talking, nobody really caring about the other person except if they get in their space, and then caring a lot. That's absurd too, but not like this was absurd. This was innocent, simple."

"Simply absurd. Okay," I said.

"Yeah well, you're the writer, write it for me one day, huh." She paused and cracked a smile, but she wasn't finished. "So, the big guy, they held him under, three times. The kids got dunked too, but in a smaller font. They cried as they were wrapped up real neatly and given to their parents, or godparents or whoever it was. And then the babies and the big man got blown on by the priests."

It was getting creepy. "Blown on?"

"Yeah, the priests said prayers about devils and stuff and blew on them, the breath of the Holy Spirit or something. And then they brushed oil on them using a paintbrush thingy. I know I am just going on but all of the ritual was familiar somehow. I don't know, it wasn't that the people were real friendly, they weren't, they sort of wondered who we were. And the priests weren't real fiery or great talkers. It was about something else. Something familiar."

"Interesting," I said. But this church talk made me fidgety, just like being in church made me feel as a child. I bleated, "So you liked it?"

"I don't know, David. It's not like I'm born again or anything, it's just that Dana and I felt... felt... I don't know, David. It goes back to what I've been feeling for two or three years now."

"How's that?"

"It's the death of one world and the birth of another. That is what the priest said in his short talk."

"Like starting over," I said.

"No, like going back."

"Back?"

"Back to what's really, really right. Perfection David, back to perfection." Her words were eerily similar and eerily ominous. I waved to the big guy and ordered another beer.

"So where was this place?" I asked.

"You see the guy you just waved to, his family goes there, it's a church in Queens." I looked at the smarmy fellow again. I imagined him in Greece dancing to some real bouncy music and swilling Ouzo. Not the pious type, I thought.

"*That* guy's church," I said. "He goes to church?"

She cocked her head, "Yes, I went to that guy's church, with that guy and his family. So what?"

The anxious fog of our history settled over me and fidgety became really fidgety.

"I wonder why you went," I said, trying to sound innocent and less suspicious. I truly wanted to be less suspicious and more innocent, I really did.

"You really want to know?" She searched my eyes and I believe she found the part of me that really wanted to know. "It's exhaustion. I'm tired as hell, David. For three years I have been raising a child, running from job to job in search of the best day care, living to work, eating to stay alive, searching for more and coming nowhere close to finding it. You know I've doubted my decision, to you know, go through with Dana's pregnancy. I have. Isn't that terrible?" She poked at her salad. "My life is just like that. Everything about it confuses everything about it. One thing to the next, one plan to the next, and all I end up with is nothing, nothing worth having. And I wonder what the hell is worth having and why bother, anyway? If I die with two houses, two boats, college educated kids and lots and lots of money, what's the point? What does it all mean?" She laughed painfully, "But I'm probably just saying all of this because I'm poor and ain't got shit really. You think?"

"I don't think that's it, Raphie."

"Well, I hope not, damn I hope not." She ate a bit and relaxed a bit, her jaw slackened. "This city, it's tough. Seems like the only way you get measured is by what you do, you know, put out there. It's not about who you are, I mean your, your…"

"Soul," I said.

"Yeah, that's it, exactly. But life can't be that way, can it?" Her sincerity was inspiring.

"No, it can't," I said.

"You agree, don't you?"

Now, here was a connection, an honest connection. Really, I thought, life could not be about how much you make or how valuable you are to a company. She was right, and I was right, and we, incredibly, were together. Together. Amazing.

"Do you remember how it was when we first met? Can you remember how much I loved life? Do you remember the Hamptons weekend we had, Ellis and his girl and that other couple you invited from work? Remember how we drank and danced and how wild we got afterwards? Remember that house we stayed in with its perfect deck on the ocean and the big bedrooms? And the food? You were good to me David, taking me to get my favorite seafood at all hours, waiting on me hand and foot, loving me. Remember how peaceful everything was between us, how good the romance was, how we were just lost in the living? Well, for two years I held on to that weekend as the perfect weekend, the thing to live for. I really thought that was it. I used it as a marker. When we started to fight I thought about that weekend. When Dana came and life changed, when I felt sad, and no longer free, I thought about that weekend. The weekend became a sort of goal, a sort of way of coping. And this weekend way of thinking, I did it with other things too. Maybe I would plan a big get-together with my girlfriends, or I'd think about saving money to buy a car, the right car, the one that would take me in style to places like the Hamptons or the Jersey Shore, good places, I thought. I planned to buy a house and worked long hours to make the money I needed. Do you remember how hard I worked that first summer when we met? I had a plan. I wanted to line everything up just right, but every time I thought I was there, ready to cash in, something came up. Maybe I got married like an idiot, got pregnant, got an abortion, got into a fight with you, maybe I borrowed too much, bailed out Simon too often. It was always something. I never got the things I wanted, I never got the weekend back. Look around Dave, nothing. And now I've lost you, too."

"But it seemed like you wanted to lose me," I said.

"I did."

"Well I don't get it then."

"I don't either. I just know that there is no plan if it's all about this stuff, this, this," she looked up and around, "this world. And so, you got to hear about this baptism, man. It wasn't like all of this. Don't ask me what it was, I only know it wasn't this," she waved her hand in the air.

"Yeah, I hear you, Raphie," I said. "But, it's not all bad. Living isn't just all a horror show."

"Look, I hope I'm not sounding too burned out, but isn't there something kind of horrific about a whole country working like plow horses so they can afford the upgrade and get car seats lined with animal skin?" With her fork still prodding the salad her voice trailed off, frustrated.

"So are you going to convert or something?" I asked flashing a hint of bitterness. After all, I had just clanged out of a Greyhound bus that could have used some leather interior, if you ask me.

"I don't know, maybe. Who knows? I like that place though. It's peaceful."

"You've been going back?"

"Yeah, now and then. And to another place too, a monastery uptown. Go slow, I say. It's just that one day I want to find..." Silence, and then a little more. "Whatever it is I'm looking for, whatever it is, Dana and I need it."

I started to tell her I was back to give her just that, but she interrupted with a quick, exaggerated turn of her head, like in the old black and white movies.

"Don't mind me, David. I'm sorry for all of this, this outburst." She shrunk into herself after having been uncharacteristically exposed and excited. "Another beer?" she said.

"Naw," I said, and we sat in silence for more than a few moments.

"How's Mitkin?" I finally asked.

Dragging his name through her mouth she said, slowly, "Mitchell Mitkin. Mitch is still plugging along, confident, conceited, and as unlovable as ever."

"You like that about him, don't you?"

"I guess so. He's just so ridiculously sure in a world where nothing seems sure. He acts like a really smart two-year-old sometimes, but it's what I like about him."

"And his father?" I asked.

"His father is almost dead."

"I'm sorry," I said.

"I'm worried. You should go visit him." She paused and leaned back wiping her mouth with a clean, crisp napkin. "You know since you left, Mitchell and I have become good friends. He just graduated this summer. He graduated a year early."

"I heard he'd do that, in fact he told me in one of *your* letters." I let the letter info slip and looked for a reaction. She didn't even flinch, telling me that their joint letter was probably just that, and nothing more, and that maybe I should just relax a little. I continued, "He told me he was planning on teaching. He doesn't seem like a teacher to me. Could it be true?"

"As far as I know. He has certain principles you know, he feels some debt must be paid. He said, 'I must contribute something to the backbone of western society, public education.'"

"But he went to prep school and then to Columbia."

"I know. That's really why he's doing it. Guilt."

The conversation was running low. I didn't want to talk about Mitkin anymore; everything seemed the same with him. But with us, I had seen something that moved me. California and the emptiness I had experienced there made an impression on me. I had lived with a touch of that angst that Raphaella had been trying to describe. There was hope for us because of this, and I was buoyant. I could have gone on, queried her more concerning the religion thing but that was a conversation I wasn't really equipped to have, or at least willing to have. I wanted to leave things where they were, afraid to over-water and suffocate the burgeoning soul flowers popping up all around. I'd returned to live the stoic, moral, comfortable, responsible, American dream. My only fear was she wouldn't see it that way, or wouldn't want it that way. Maybe that's why I let the church conversation go, let it dangle. I just wanted her to say to me, "Let's be good people, together." That was it. I didn't need the complications of anything mystical. Forget the magic stuff and just accept what your heart tells you, I thought. I have needs, she has needs, together we assess what those needs are and pledge ourselves to one another in an attempt to fill each other's needs. That was the key to happiness.

My mind catalogued these thoughts in split second screen shots, rolling through, looking for a safe topic, but like I said, the conversation had run dry. We finished with some talk of Dana and visitation schedules, and this made things clean and happy, fresh and a perfect way to end the conversation. I'd be seeing her again, and soon. We hugged outside the doors of the diner.

"Very good then, David," she said to me straightforwardly.

"Very good then, Kiwi," I said in return. "See you soon."

I took a subway back downtown, contemplating my new apartment and my new life. When I finally picked up my bags from Jamel's and located the superintendent of my new building, I was very tired. The super was a little man, a friendly Puerto Rican with leathery skin. He watched as I waded about the empty space acting happy and excited. I had to. The place was already paid for, at least for three months. My mother and I had signed the lease blind. Soon, through various glances (like the one he gave me when I checked under the sink and found rat droppings that looked like neatly curled chocolate frosting), we established that this place was a hellhole, a very cheap hellhole. I thought about our (Raphaella's) apartment with its long hall, capacious bedrooms, inviting living room and decorative window wells, and I laughed impulsively. I laughed to avoid despair, I think.

The little man, his name was Rico, helped me retrieve my stuff and even prepared a little dinner for me in his basement apartment. Speaking to me through a thick accent and a thick mustache, I didn't understand much of what he said. I just kept smiling and nodding.

In bed, the rhythmic rumble of motorized New York kept me awake and thinking. I thought about my job and the first day of teaching, and whether I'd run into Mitkin. I thought about Dana and about how her mother might ruin her, or make her the perfect human being. I fell asleep and dreamt of her baptism, but this time I was there. I was praying or at least trying to. Everyone around me was doing the same. I saw Raphaella in the dream, waiting in a white robe, stolid-faced and stern, preparing for change. As she stepped forward to be dunked, she looked at me and nodded me forward, urging me to join her. The monotone chant welled and enclosed around us. The dream ended just as Raphaella began her descent toward submersion. Everything but her head was under water when I woke to a humid and bleary Manhattan morn. In my new place, I was lost for a few seconds. The walls were bare and the floor dull and scratched, its old, cheap tiles exposed. My big suitcases were unzipped and their contents spilled about. I rummaged through a bag and pulled out a wrinkled shirt that would get me through the day.

***

Mitchell Mitkin is sipping from a bottle of water. He is about to reflect on the day I returned to New York City.

"Three years, huh," he says. "I remember, because it was the same day I went to the Board of Education in search of my placement papers."

He had gone for his last dose of bureaucratic medicine. "I got it all right; they assigned me to the South Bronx High School of Science." He rolls his eyes and smiles an affectionate smile. "I was very happy at the time. I was starting a new, tidy career, one that would pay back a little to the great institution called public education. My father thought I should teach for a while before becoming a research scientist. He loved public education you know. He was committed to it. It was his life. It would be mine, too. That is what I believed then. I mean, I really believed it. I wasn't all bad, I guess." This was also the day Mitchell Mitkin's father died.

CHAPTER VII

Revelation

Mitchell went from Brooklyn and the Board of Education directly to Presbyterian Hospital and his father's room. He ran the last two blocks with his teaching assignment in hand, excited and proud. He would be like his father, a teacher. He had other reasons to be happy. He was brilliant, healthy, good-looking in his own way and a recent graduate of Columbia University, and as expected, he was number one in his class. He was heir to his father's foundation and he was in love. For Mitchell Mitkin it was the future he courted, and all of it, stretched out in front of him, was beautiful. He believed in the perfection of man, in mankind's ability to overcome nature. He was sober and yet able to wander into the spectacle of creation and its majesty, and there feel something like love.

Now in front of the colossal hospital, its twin towers showering cool shade upon his sweating brow, he met his father. His father was a part of this building, a dedicated member of the whole, a granite rock in the foundation of the cathedral of science. This is why the hospital never scared Mitkin. Thoughts of it as a place of death never mingled with thoughts of his father. He had grown adept at separating the two. The hospital *was* good. Besides, Jim Wagner was sure to try another treatment now. For three years, Jim Wagner never wavered from his decision to use chemotherapy, but now the radiation was no longer effective. Because of this, Doctor Wagner had begun to explore Mitchell's ideas on antibody therapy. Mitchell was ecstatic, but he was also bitter that so much time had been wasted. Waving amicably at the nurses in their stations, Mitkin ducked into the finest room in the building, his father's room.

He was met by the lone sound of a sucking valve. It sucked its way up and down, and Mitkin slowed. His mother was there, just as she always was, though, uncharacteristically, she was silent. Mitchell moved closer.

"Mitchell?" She sighed. "You've made it. Martin's just fallen asleep."

Mitchell nodded. His mother invited him to sit down and he took the little chair at the foot of his father's bed. She began flatly, "He's tired. He's trying so hard now, he's real tired." She did not look at her son.

"Yes, Mother," he said, expressionless. "How long has he been sleeping?"

"Not long."

"How long, Mother? Exactly."

Startled, she said, "A half hour I think."

His father was not sleeping. Mitkin could see he was not present, and that thought was disturbing when applied to a man so thoroughly present all his life. He studied his father's face, the skin barely hanging on, his neck withered, feet pale and sticking out just beyond a thin blue blanket. "So bony," thought Mitkin. The absence of his father's mind made Mitchell look hard at his father's body. Everywhere it was emaciated and Mitkin thought how ridiculous the body looks apart from the mind, and then a sickening feeling overcame him, a feeling that his father had never been alive; like everything he had been was a mirage, an illusion that was now whisked away and made to disappear like a sweet dove in a magic show. He heard his father's words: "Death is the end of an organism, don't make it more than it is, Son." He stared at his mother's hand so close to her husband's, one pink and alive, the other ashen and dead.

"Ring for the nurse Mother. He's dead."

Cassie Mitkin looked at her son. She was spent and very sad; she would not be strong. "No Son," she said. "He's sleeping."

Mitkin pointed to the chest. "Watch it. It hasn't heaved since I arrived. Father is dead."

She studied her husband and then quickly looked back at her son. "What about the alarm? Why hasn't anyone come?" She stared at the inert body, the pallid aura of death loose in the room. "Oh my God." She covered her mouth. "Go! Go Mitchell, get Jim." She screamed, "Doctor Wagner!"

Mitkin didn't go, and no one came.

"Go now, my God!" And seeing that Mitchell wasn't moving, Cassie Mitkin ran out of the room. A great deal of commotion could be heard outside, but still Mitchell did not move.

"Don't be a coward. Don't cop out." He used his father's words again. "The death of an organism, that's what this is. The death of an organism, nature's course, that is all." He reached out and touched the graying toe. "The body's inability to repair itself leads to secondary and tertiary malfunctions and eventually to a massive breakdown. The heart's malfunction leaves the body bereft of fuel and absolute breakdown ensues. We all are destined for the same thing. Nature's course—it is natural. Don't be a coward, don't be a hypocrite." And then gripping the toe, he spoke aloud.

"Be strong."

A single nurse ran into the room. Immediately, she ran back out. Next came a horde of others, a team. There was pounding and prodding and poking, tubes wiggling here and there. One went into the gaping mouth. Doctor Jim Wagner came running, too. He had a look of anxious aggression, but there was fear there, too. Mitkin remained in his chair at the foot of the bed, moving only slightly and just enough to give the pounding nurses room to work. He laced his fingers together and placed his hands on his lap. More medical personnel entered. Mitkin's mother wailed. She screamed orders and cried between ugly, phlegmy coughs. Nurses and doctors hustled in and out, back and forth. They stepped on Mitkin's feet and bumped his knees, but Mitkin sat, ambivalent. "So, this is it?" A gray pall settled over him. He stared mechanically. A bewildering sense of separation bled between him and everything manic in the room, and in this space quiet grew. It all became mute, like a silent movie, as he stared at his father's face. It rattled from the pumping, shaking like a doll. But it was the eyes that got him, the left eye, to be more specific. He couldn't shake it, couldn't take his eyes off of it. It mesmerized him, sucked him in. It was open but empty, void, and nil. Whatever was there was gone now, gone somewhere else, not far off, not very far off at all. *And it had been there.* He looked at the ceiling and at the window and then again at the eye. Empty eye.

The power of the past gripped him, and he reeled from images of his father in a tuxedo on New Year's Eve, in his pajamas on Sunday morning, at a ballgame in Yankee Stadium. He recalled an idyllic lakeside cottage in winter, one that would fill up in the summer with voices and life, and he thought how his father, too, would fill up, one day, with that thing which had just now left the room. It would come back—it was loose and this was a terrifyingly wonderful thing. It made Mitkin sweat. He began to feel lightheaded, just as the distant, lonely cry ascended from the depths of his soul. It fought through his mind and burst in his heart. "My father lied to me. There is more, there was more!" He fought back tears and struggled to his feet. "Nature's course is a curse, nature's course." He repeated with clenched teeth and watery eyes. "Nature's course…"

He walked out unnoticed.

***

"A liar?" I say, confused.

"That's what came to mind, dominated my mind, really. It's what was revealed to me." I mentally note this, that Mitkin thought his father was duplicitous, but these notes don't make sense when compared with my mental notes. How could Martin Mitkin have been a liar just like that, alive an icon, dead a liar? Besides, what did that mean for Mitkin? How could he deal with this thing, this new truth? I ask him.

"I didn't deal with it. Look around. Prison, Dave, we are sitting in a prison and I'm the prisoner."

"Okay," I say, "but what about the harsh judgment? One minute one thing, the next, he's out, over, a liar. What's up with that?"

He is getting agitated, squirrelly. "See," he says with his hands up and out, like he is about to measure something, or maybe begin instructions, but in an agitated way, like a foreman on the job. "How can I tell it?" Now his hands go to his head and he is out of character for a moment. He seems confused. He gets out of his chair. "My father died, and I think there were two things right in that room with me. Fear. Fear was one. The other thing was guilt. I felt afraid because death was so final, so inexplicably final and I was afraid that everything I knew about it, death, was a lie. And everything I learned about death, and life, and living, was learned at the feet of my father, and so, I thought, no, the thoughts just came, that he had lied to me, misled me. His corpse, lying there so empty, made me rethink his life, and by extension my own. I was afraid of this." He is still standing, but with an embarrassed air about him now. He fixes one arm across his chest and stands. He is, well, lovable, somehow.

"What can I tell you, David? It was a revelation. That kind of fear was something I'd never experienced, not even close. And the guilt, I couldn't believe I was so afraid, so unable to continue with his ideas, his philosophies, his truth. It ran out of me the minute, the second he was gone. I was like a soldier who turns and vomits and cries the minute death starts to pop off all around him. I was soft. It was a bad day."

I stare at him. He is so earnest, still.

"Do you remember how much of a mess I was, David?"

"I do," I say. "Raphaella told me you disappeared after the funeral. What happened?"

He says through a laugh, "A whole lot happened." And then he smiles and says it again. "A whole heck of a lot happened, and all of it right up here."

"Up here," he says pointing to his head, and I know that this is where the answers are, the answers to my questions, to the one question that has led me into his life and this prison. I lean over to see the recorder still churning away, and I shift in my seat as if the previews have just ended and the feature film is ready to begin. He continues, undeterred.

CHAPTER VIII

Faith

"It's Sam, Raphaella, Sam Mitkin." Two big thronging bangs rattled the door. "Sam Mitkin! Raphaella, hello, are you there?"

It was Saturday, and I was alone in the apartment with Dana. We were playing in the living room under the big bay window, Dana seemingly content with me, and I just beginning to feel like her father, her once-a-week father. The big bangs startled us. Dana even blurted out a little *hoo* as if she'd just fallen off her chair. I went to the door just as Sam Mitkin began to whack the door again with the fat underside of his fist.

Opening the door, I was greeted with, "Excuse me please, but," Sam Mitkin stuck his head in the door, "have you seen Mitchell?" He was a tall and wiry man, dressed entirely in black. His suit was functional, comfortable, sturdy but not stylish. He wore thick black glasses. His eyes darted back and forth, and he was very agitated. "I'm sorry, but we are looking for Mitchell. I'm his uncle. Have you seen him?"

I thought how I'd been here before, me on the third floor, in Raphie's apartment, a Mitkin down below, banging, manic in that very Mitkinesque way. Part of me wanted to be curt and impolite, but in the end I just said, "Haven't seen him."

Looking past me, Sam Mitkin said, "Has Raphaella seen him?"

"Aren't they at the funeral?"

"They were," he said. "But Mitchell ran away, and then Raphaella chased after him, just as they put him in the ground. Now we can't find either of them."

"I can see that," I said, noticing that Dana had crept her way into the doorway, underfoot. Then, like a sweet little lamb, she offered the skinny oddball sleuth a drink from her very own Kool-Aid cup. She just stuck her hand up over her head and said, "Want some?" Sam Mitkin's face bunched up and a clear case of emotional gridlock overcame him.

"Princess," he said while nodding at her, and then he was gone.

I turned to my daughter, and comforted her with, "It will all be fine, sweetheart. She'll show up soon." I tried to conceal serious consternation. "They'll show up, don't worry."

And they did, just before midnight, wet and weary like cats caught in the rain. My stomach was in knots, and I felt at any moment I might punch an inanimate object, Mitkin maybe. Looking at him, however, that thought quickly gave way to something more like sympathy. He was muddy from head to toe. On one cheek dried foliage of some sort clung disturbingly, and the other seemed to have been finger painted with mud. His hair was heavy and matted like a shaggy doormat. Raphaella was a tangled mess of dirt and rain and hair. I heard them rumbling around downstairs and poked my head out. Below, on the stairway, I could see Mitkin fumbling with his keys, while Raphaella held him under the arm. I hurried down.

"Don't ask," she said.

"Why not?"

"Because she said so," Mitkin suddenly growled. He tottered.

"Can you help me with him?" asked Raphaella. I took him under the other arm, and together we held him steady.

"David, she's stronger than you," said Mitkin, again sourly. I gripped him a little harder and twisted slightly. How's that, I thought.

"Could you stay the night, David?"

"With him?"

"Well, one of us here, the other upstairs, could you?" She opened the door into his very ugly apartment. What used to be an immaculate abode had become a disaster. A plate of half-eaten spaghetti sat on the floor in the living room, an overturned beer bottle nearby. His music collection, and who would think he even had one of these, seemed to have exploded right there in the room, and his dirty clothes bin with it, apparently. I saw at least ten ties sprawled across the apartment, and, unfortunately, more than a few pairs of dirty underwear. His kitchen sink was piled with dishes, and there was a terrible smell in or behind the refrigerator. Helping Mitkin to his room, we passed the bathroom and I noticed flecks of facial hair ringing the white porcelain basin. Passing through this battlefield, it was easy to avoid Raphaella's question, and it was quite a question, him sleeping with her or me sleeping with him? Great. *How about, I just leave.*

"How's Dana?" she asked as we put Mitkin on his bed.

"Fine, sleeping."

"The goddamned boat had holes, Raphie, it had big bullet holes, like it was in a war... Crimean..." said Mitkin, succumbing to the succor of his pillow. "Damned Crimean Russian bastards..."

I looked sideways and thought, Crimean War?

We moved out into the living room and she said, "I tried to call three times but the pay phone was messed up, and the one time I got through nobody answered. Were you home?"

"We went to get something to eat, but that's it," I said, and she nodded.

"Look, I'm sorry. I am. Forgive me. I just couldn't leave him. He was gonna do something terrible, hurt himself or someone else, I could see it. He wanted to drink and I thought the bar, in public you know, would be good, calm him down. We went to the Ostrich. Then, he just went blazing like a crackhead into Central Park, black suit, tie, little black loafers, right into the pond."

"A very muddy pond, apparently," I said.

"He dug out an old boat and tried to launch it, what a disaster. It sunk and I went in after him. I just wanted to help him somehow." She was tired. "He was wild, out of control. Wow. He's coming apart, he needed help."

"Is that why you got drunk together?"

"I'm not drunk."

Then, from the bedroom came a burst of words, "We're all drunk you idiots. Drunk, blind, confused, intoxi—" There was a pause, and then, "Cabby! Take me to him, did you know my father's dead? Would you like a word with him?"

From somewhere came a whispered plea, "Mommy?" We both turned and saw the silhouette of Dana in the doorway, her nightgown wrinkled like her sleep-filled face. "Mommy you're back, Mommy you came home."

They hugged and then Dana hugged me too, both of us, together and at the same time. Raphaella was shaken. "I am so sorry, honey. I had an emergency and now everything is okay, don't worry baby. Let's go to sleep now, okay honey?"

Dana nodded, relieved, and that sealed the deal. I'd be sleeping with the drunk. I crawled onto Mitkin's couch, turned over on my back and was immediately met with the sound of tepid air wheezing in and out of his drunken orifices. These were horrid snores—cranky, sputtering sounds, like a machine on the fritz. I don't know how I managed to fall asleep, but I know how I managed to wake up the first time that night. It was 2:20 a.m. and he was yelling, "Daddy, Daddy!" and then, "Father, Father, hey!"

Then later, seemingly in my ear, "What the hell is this?" Defying all laws of near-death intoxication, Mitkin had gotten up very early, slipped on a natty, beige terrycloth bathrobe, and even brewed a pot of coffee. Oh, and he also managed to get really close to my face, so close that I wished he'd taken a minute or two to brush his teeth.

"What are you doing here David?"

"Huh? What?"

"You, what are you doing here?"

I rolled onto my side and covered my face with my arm. "I'm the cavalry. I'm here to protect you."

He scratched his head and sipped his coffee, and waited for me to say something else. Still on my side I managed to say, "I'm doing Raphaella a favor." He took another sip from his coffee and cocked his eyebrow. He was back in his bedroom and back to his melancholic, dirty life before I finally pulled myself off the couch. Getting myself together I yelled, "She didn't want to sleep here and she didn't want to leave you alone, so there you go."

A cough from his room was followed by a scratchy, "What do you want, a Nobel Peace Prize or something?"

The new Mitkin, I thought. "I'm leaving."

"Bye-bye," he squawked. "Bye-bye."

I trudged upstairs and stood in front of Raphaella's door. It had a rainbow pinned proudly on a message board, the name Dana scribbled in the center. Each little letter of her name had been innocently and earnestly squeezed through her little left hand, delicately and with abundant hope. I imagined Raphaella holding that little hand as it went. The cool air reminded me it was still very early and that they were surely still asleep, so I dropped my fist and did not knock. Instead, I descended the stairs very quietly so that Mitchell Mitkin would not hear and gain the satisfaction of knowing I'd never gotten to say goodbye.

***

On the subway ride home and subsequent walk to my apartment, I was plague-ridden with runaway ruminations.

"I bet they got naked in that pond, oh, no doubt, and then they probably rolled around all nudie, sandwich style, flip-flop like a wrestling thing. He just bolted his dad's funeral, it's too bizarre, no one would believe it. He's ugly, anyway. She loves him like a brother, of course, like a crazy, creepy, brother who moved away and lost track of you and never calls, yeah, brother all right. Too bad about his pop, he's just not transitioning well, but what the hell, he should transition with someone else's would-be-wife, and that could be just about anyone including Raphaella I guess, so I guess he can be with her then, wait, strike that thought… Will I be a puddle like that when my father dies? I was pretty cool last night, I obeyed, it worked out well, I'm the man… She probably doesn't even want to sleep with him anyway, who would? I could take him in a fight unless he turned psycho on me, but he's already a little psycho so be careful about fighting him, thumb outside, never inside, broken thumb otherwise. Broken hand bad. Pain."

With my head down and my mind racing, I marched down the street and up my stoop where my knee cracked a kid's jaw. The kid's name was Elvis, the handsome, lazy, sixteen-year-old son of Rico, the super. Elvis was probably the most introverted person I'd ever known, but now that would all end, my knee had become acquainted with his face as he sat calmly there on the stoop.

"Damn, yo. What the F—"

"Oh no, my fault," I said. "Sorry about that kid." Elvis stood up real fast and puffed his chest. His fists curled and he cock-walked to within an inch of me. "I wasn't paying attention, I was thinking about some stuff, you know, sorry. I didn't see—"

Then, that kid punched me. Real square, right on the chin. I stumbled back against the stone banister and held my face. He waited for my reaction, but I was in a daze. "Five dollars," he said, and pointed.

"What?"

"Five dollars punk, you kicked my drink over."

I looked down and saw a sideways beer bottle. It oozed foamy beer. "What? You want money for that? You shouldn't even be drinking that, and in the morning? Forget that. Forget you."

He stepped up to me again and this time I cracked him, a glancing blow to the chin and neck. We got tangled up and, well, I was in a fight with Elvis. I punched him in the back once or twice and then he bit me and ran. He bit me. I hadn't even showered yet, and already I had a black eye and bite marks on my arm. All I needed now was a gasoline tire ignited around my neck, or maybe a good quartering. Better yet, how about sheer and utter bureaucratic bafflement at Martin Luther High School, my new place of employment and home to thousands of kids, just like lovely Elvis.

I had to get ready for school, and as I preened in the bathroom mirror I noticed how nicely my new khaki slacks went with my black eye and bite marks. I looked like an idiot. But what could I do? It was my first day of work and three thousand students from all around the city waited for me at Martin Luther High School. MLHS was a magnet school for kids from all five boroughs, but mostly it was a thug school. Luther High attracted very mediocre students every year, a cycle the Board of Education found difficult to break. I was going to be a history teacher— a green, white, rookie. But was I worried? Not really. I was a nice guy, I thought, everyone will love me. I imagined the days ahead; students clapping and cheering as I finished my lecture, girls and boys lingering after class, asking questions about history and life, kids getting a compass reading on their future. I imagined myself tousling the head of a young whipper-snapper, encouraging him with a heartfelt, "It's all within your grasp, you can do it, Jerome," or maybe something like this: "The lessons of degradation we see in Eastern Europe after the war can be applied to our very own history right here in urban America, right here in our own neighborhood." What a teacher I'd be. I'd reach the Elvises of the world all right.

Then I met the chairman of my department. This man was a well-oiled curriculum machine, a computer really, and he loved handouts. He walked me through files and files of old handouts, the kind made by Rexograph machines about the time James Dean died. "Follow the handouts," he'd say. "They'll take you where you need to go." And he wanted me to log all of my lessons, my witty, instinctive, spontaneous lessons; he wanted them *logged*. At one point during that first day he actually gave me a sticky:

> *Rexo #'s 1-25 can be picked up*
> *in my office today. Don't forget to*
> *LOG YOUR LESSONS.*
> *—Krugs*

That was his name, Mr. Krugs. Later, during the second week when he had more time, he actually took me into an empty classroom and went through a series of, what he called, abstracts.

"And if he curses, here," he pointed to a row of empty chairs, "do you immediately send him out?" He waited but this was rhetorical. "And here again, two more students taking the lead of the first troublemaker, what then?" Then, I'm screwed, I thought. "And do you ever physically restrain the combatants?"

"No?" I peeped.

"Precisely, Mr. Higgins." I waited for him to salute, but he just hunched his shoulders and said, "Now, it's only in the doing son. Good luck."

Why had Mr. Krugs ever chosen to be a teacher? Had he wanted to heal a failed relationship in a faraway city, be a writer, do something good and give something back? Did he just love kids? Did he imagine himself getting standing ovations too? Looking at him I thought, wouldn't he be better off operating an abacus somewhere? But what did I know, really? Twenty-six years of handouts lie decaying, and I, this new guy named Higgins wasn't about to stem the great Rexo tide, no chance.

My first day had gone well, at least that's what Hill said. Hill was short for Hillray, Hillray M. Johnson, but this Hill was anything but short. He was about six-foot-six, 255 pounds. He shaved his head bald, and when he shook hands you were very afraid. He had been at Luther High for seventeen years and knew what I needed to know.

"But they didn't really listen to me," I said.

"Think about that for a minute. What you teaching on the first day that they need to be listening to ya? Yep, exactly. It's if they ain't listening next month that we need to keep an eye on. You just go ahead and make it mean something to 'em, they'll listen."

Good advice, I thought. He shook my hand, I tried to shake back, but mostly he just moved my arm up and down. Then he just up and walked out the front door of the high school. I looked at my watch—it was only 1:30 p.m., a little early to be leaving, I thought. Looking around I realized that just about everyone was gone on this first day, an administrative day. I decided to use the time to go and see how Dana was doing after her first day of school.

I ran into Mitchell Mitkin struggling with his keys at the front door of the brownstone. He turned around quickly, suspiciously.

"Oh, David."

"Mitch, how are you?"

Turning back around and trying another key he said, "I don't know, how do I look?"

"You look okay," I lied. He was a mismatched, disheveled mess, and he seemed to have spilled coffee on his shirt, down his pants even. "I am sorry about your father. Really, it is, well…" I didn't know what to say.

He chimed in, "One of life's tragedies? Whatever." He opened the door and went inside, letting the door slam with me still on the other side looking in. He mounted the steps, two of them, and stopped. I followed him in and saw him there, waiting. He looked down at me and choked out a throat-clearing cough. I waited for him to speak but he didn't, he seemed seized by something. I spoke up.

"I'm teaching you know, Mitch. Both of us. If you ever want to talk about teaching and, well, whatever…" There was lugubrious silence. "I got your letter, you know, about how you were going to teach this fall. Looks like you've just finished your first day, huh?"

"Yeah, mmmhuh," he said, oddly. He continued his ascent, disappearing into his second-story room. He had left a loathsome wake.

Upstairs, Raphaella wanted to know if Mitchell had returned. "Yep, he's back from work, just came in," I whispered while pointing down the stairwell.

"Did he talk to you?" she asked.

"Not really."

"I haven't seen him since the funeral." She motioned me inside and shut the door. "The kid's losing it."

Inside, I saw that everything had changed. Raphaella had taken her vacation time to repaint and refurbish her apartment, a project paid for by Sam Mitkin, the building's proprietor now. This was the kind of relationship she had with the Mitkin family. She had lived there eight years and not once had she paid a late rent. The family had come to trust her with building matters, and after her "rescue" at the funeral, they had begun to trust her on a personal level. With a thin white smock wrapped lazily around her and a wet paintbrush about to drip a resplendent rose onto her hardwood floor, she stood before me.

"Hold it up," I said.

"Hold it up?"

"The brush, it's about to drip." I grabbed her gently, and turned the brush. I felt the sinew of her supple wrist.

"Wow, to the rescue," she said. "Thanks."

"For Dana's room?" I said.

"Yep. It's nice right?" I nodded. "Dana's in the back, sleeping. She doesn't feel well."

"Did she go to school?"

"No. She's sick. Sore throat." It was her first day and I was disappointed she hadn't gone. Part of me wanted to scold Raphaella slightly, tell her that the first day is important and maybe reflect a bit on my first day, on my insider's perspective now that I was a full-blown educator. But I didn't say anything. I actually fought the urge. Instead, I went with my thoughts on Mitchell.

"He's always looking a little dirty these days, have you noticed?"

"The man's father just died," she said. "I mean, come on. He loved his father."

"Yeah, but why isn't he taking care of himself? What's that all about?"

"Look, the guy loved his father, he believed in every word his father said. He was devoted. Life's totally empty without his father."

"What about his mother?" I asked. Raphaella shrugged. "Don't they get along?"

"Let's just say he doesn't get along." I could tell she knew more but didn't want to talk about it. I got the feeling she wanted to protect Mitkin. "They just aren't that close," she repeated.

"Anyway, I hope he feels better. I'm still waiting for someone I love to die. I've been lucky so far."

She nodded and said, "Maybe it's not luck, David."

"Maybe…" I trailed off. "But that's not what I'm here to talk about. Actually, I'm not here to talk about anything, I came to see Dana. But she's sick, so, how about you and I watch a movie? I'll run out and rent one."

She laughed and said, "I'm working."

"Well, quit working and come over here and sit down with me." I cleared a space on the couch and patted it, inviting her.

"What movie, David?"

"Whatever you want, *Wall Street* just came out on video."

"*Wall Street*? Okay." She gave me the rental card for P.J.'s Video. I ran very, very fast and grabbed the movie and was back before she had taken her painter's smock off. She smiled and we sat down. The movie clipped by and I sat close enough to feel her warmth, but I didn't touch her intimately. No slick arm sling followed by a cough, no lazy prostration where her lap became my pillow. I sat, and she sat, but we sat together.

It was a good movie, but I sensed she didn't think so.

"Sort of sad, isn't it?" she said at the end.

"How's that?"

"How doing one thing, like selling stocks, makes it almost impossible to do another, like being good."

"But selling stocks is good, at least as far as Gekko saw it. It's the same thing. Selling *is* being good, it's the point of being American."

"Yeah, I heard. Greed is good. The only problem is, it's not true. It ain't good. Greed is bad."

"But that depends, doesn't it?"

"I don't think so." Then, as if collecting all of her courage, she said, "God is good. God, not greed."

There it is, I thought, everything keeps coming back to the same idea. I sensed that this notion of hers was always on the verge of escape, seeping out against her will as if she were possessed by it, as if it were too big for her body. It was unnerving in those days after my return from California.

"You know, Raphie, my mother always taught me to avoid two topics in polite conversation—"

"Yeah, I know David, you've told me before. God and politics."

"Well," I said, trying to be funny, "given my very recent return to New York, this still qualifies as, well, polite conversation. And so, technically, you're breaking my mother's rule, aren't you?"

"Yeah, but you know what, David? We've always had nothing but polite-ass conversation. Sorry, I'm not angry as much as, well, clear, you know? I mean, when did we, lovers I remind you, ever talk in depth about anything? When did we ever really have great, deep, hopeful conversation? I mean shouldn't lovers, of all people, be talking about good things, about love, about things not of this world?"

That was an odd phrase I thought. Not hers.

"Shouldn't we?" she pleaded.

"Of course, that's why I came back."

"Are you sure about that? Are you sure?"

"Yeah, I'm sure mostly." I was near a laugh when she sucked her teeth.

"You're a loser, David," she said, also on the verge of laughter.

"See, relax," I said, smiling. "It's just a movie and we're just talking. Relax." I patted her knee. "See there, nice and easy. Relax."

"I'm relaxed already. Shut up. Seriously, David, you have to wonder about what I am saying. You and I just don't go very deep."

Straightening my face, I endeavored to hear her. "Okay then, tell me about this not-of-this-world idea. You think love is not from this world?" I was trying.

"It's from God. It's not biological, you know, like a result of our brain activity, or brain maturity or whatever."

"Some people would disagree with you, you know."

"You mean some person like Mitchell. Yeah, he would. But he's wrong too. I think."

"Mitkin's wrong? Wow, that's different."

"Look, David, you need to know a few things about Mitchell and me. Mitchell came into my life when I was on the verge of a real crisis. Having your child was one of the toughest decisions I've ever made and I am not trying to hurt you by saying that. I think you know, now anyway, that what we had wasn't real good. Having a baby together wasn't exactly smart, but I had the baby anyway. Do you know why?" I shook my head though I thought for sure I knew why. "Because I couldn't have another abortion. I couldn't stand another cold instrument inside me, another stranger poking around down there. And there was another reason. I wanted to marry you. Really. I wanted you to sweep me off my feet with a proposal the minute I told you I was pregnant." She looked at me, directly. "But it didn't work that way, and the rest is history. So that's what went on in my mind."

"But why didn't you tell me? I could never have known all that, especially given the way you treated me."

"I should have told you, but don't you see? You didn't know this stuff for the same reason you don't know my feelings about God. We, David, were simply incapable of deep conversation. Everything was about something else, everything was just a distraction, a game. I mean shit, David, I was having your baby. Don't you remember?" I did, clearly. She suddenly got up and peeked into the living room. Dana was fast asleep. She sat back down, focused on finishing this conversation. She was not upset or irritated. She was closer to inspired. "This is not an indictment, but it wasn't love we had."

"Sometimes we had it. Don't you think? Early on maybe?"

She turned a circumspect eye my way. "Oh yeah, like the time I had you crying at the nightclub because you thought I had gone home with the big, leathery guy. Or was it the other time, early on, when you got so mad you dumped me on the side of the freeway upstate? I stood on that damn freeway for almost an hour you know." It was longer than that, I thought, I couldn't find a place to turn around. "Or how about the time you took that trip to Minnesota, that guys' weekend thing? You called me every hour, do you remember that? Every hour, like a freaked-out puppy dog." She spoke with a bemused twinkle in her eye.

"Yeah, but you were there, right there, sitting with some other guy, doing, well, doing a whole lot."

"That's right. You're making my argument now, dumbass. We never had love."

"So what was it then? What were we missing?"

Soberly she looked right at me. "I went to see the priest, the one I told you about."

"Yeah, so?"

"He had an answer to that question."

I oozed an "Aaaand…" while picturing her on a couch talking about neurosis and her fatherless childhood. I imagined my name being thrown around while both priest and patient connived to make me the bad guy. "What did he say?"

"He said without suffering, there is no joy, and that without sacrifice there is no meaning."

Sitting there numb I wanted to add an *ooooh* or an *aaaahhh*, anything to make his weighty words more palatable and less embarrassing for the both of us. Instead I leapt to defend myself, whining, "So I didn't sacrifice? Love?" I paused and looked around the room. "We lacked suffering? I don't get it."

"Yeah David, maybe." She pointed at herself. "When did I ever give up what I wanted so you could have what you wanted?" She scoffed, and waited for me to answer, but honestly, I was afraid to answer that crafty question. "For a long time I've been thinking that I could have done more," she went on. "But the problem is, when I get right down to it, I don't know what that means. It's like the whole idea of love and suffering is just theory for me. When it comes to actually making the change, the hard part, the whole thing falls to pieces. Do you know what I mean?" I nodded, but I think she knew I was thinking about something else. And what was I thinking about? Reality. Reality starkly protruded through the thin veil of hope I had created for us. The reality was simple; she could no longer entertain any idea of us without entertaining the higher notions of Him. It was like a freshwater lake overrun by a saltwater river.

"So you buy this guy's premise, about sacrifice?" I said.

"I think so."

I curled my lip, "Come on, Raphie. You're telling me that if you hit the jackpot you'd sacrifice the money, give it to someone else."

"Geez, David, you don't listen too well, do you? I said I don't know what I'd do. In fact, my history with you tells me I'd keep it all for myself. But that doesn't change the idea of, of, doing it right. Of the one thing that *is*." She was speaking slowly, confusedly. "It's the idea, the great idea..." She shook her head and her hands as if to dismiss her words. "Look, don't miss the whole point, David."

"But when did you start believing in God, Raphaella?"

She moved down the couch slightly, looking at me as if to get a clearer perspective. "I don't know if I do believe in God, David. I'm just wondering."

"Then what's with the priest already?"

"He seems so sincere, I guess. I felt at home with him."

"Look, I know a little bit about priests, okay. My father's side of the family includes a Catholic priest and one of those reader guys. I've been churched you know, and a priest is just a man. Don't get too caught up by the robes and all that." She was listening. "I could tell you some stories, Raphie."

"About?"

"Priests."

"Yeah, duh, David. But what about priests?"

"Well, one my uncle knows kept a diary of all his confessions. He was going to write a book and use the stories, but when the guy in charge found out, the bishop I guess, he just gave him a slap on the wrist, didn't even stop him from hearing confessions. It's the same when they're caught molesting little boys. Sweep it under the rug, that's what they do all the time. You may be talking to some crazy molester priest, who knows?"

She shook her head vehemently. "It's not like that! This isn't about the actual guy, it's about something else, about the idea. It's the idea, David, don't you get it?" She was squeezing the couch pads with her hands. "It's the idea. Some ideas are just closer to true than others, don't you think?"

"I think so, I guess."

"Then aren't some *men* truer than others?"

"You mean do some people have the truth? No."

"That's it? Just, no?"

"That's it. Nobody can just be the truth, or know it completely. That's what I think." I was growing tired.

"But you're irrational. If some people can come closer to truth than others, can't some reach the truth?" She pleaded with upturned palms.

I was struck by the word she used to describe me. Irrational? I was the irrational one, yet she was the one going to see a priest? But that was just it. Who could understand what was going on at this point? It wasn't the same Raphaella I knew, but, in some ways, this was a good thing. She had lost her acidic tongue, the one that burned me unmercifully when we fought. I sensed a new deliberateness, a stillness that made her less prone to sarcastic attacks. And she was less sure of herself, more inclined to say "I don't know." I could envision this conversation coming to a happy end, and that was definitely something new. That's not to say I still wasn't convinced she or I could really know truth, but I didn't care about that, even as I continued. "Truth is sort of like a gas, or a cloud, I'd rather deal with things that I can get my hands around," I said. With that, I wanted to give her a big grin and a knowing glance, but restrained myself.

Then, as if detached from the conversation, she said, "The more you want to know things, the more pain you get." Her words were soft between her lips.

"Who said that?"

"The same priest you think is collecting notes on my confession, the double molester guy." She paused and grimaced. "Ouch, imagine that. My confession as screenplay, written by a pedophile. "

It was funny, but I didn't laugh. "You had confession with him?"

She just rolled her emerald eyes and shook her head, deeming my question unworthy of an answer. Her corkscrew hair settled over her sculpted face and I was just about to lean and pet it when Dana let out a tired groan. Raphaella went out of the room and I was alone for a moment, in front of the television, a blue screen marking the end of our movie and my visit to 103rd Street. I waited for Raphie to emerge and then gently said goodbye. As I walked the sidewalk to the subway, the setting sun made an impression on me—I had to hurry. Raphaella was moving in a direction that confounded me, and yet, I loved her more than I'd ever loved her before.

CHAPTER IX

Ed Taughtauer

Meanwhile, Mitchell Mitkin tried to live. He was the youngest science teacher in his school but this was the least of his problems. Internally he was at war. For most of his senior year at Columbia, he had looked forward to teaching in a tough, inner city high school, romanticizing the impact he would make and the kids he would meet. He looked forward to the curriculum, to teaching science and the tangible world of empirical data. His father had looked forward with him; before his death he shared all his fondest memories of youth. "Teaching," his father told him, "taught me about myself." It was cliché but true. Mitchell Mitkin was learning a great deal about himself, none of it particularly pretty. He was wrought with abysmal emotion, a cocktail of polarities; one day he was lethargic, the next frantic. And he was skeptical. Trite lessons about cells and gravity, about "life's little building blocks," were suddenly impossible. Inertia became familiar while gravity became so tediously heavy that he imagined he might scream out in class one day. In short, he mourned his father by bemoaning his work. He became cagy.

"Today I want to talk to you about compounds," he said, one day shortly after his father's death. "Before we break into groups, be sure to recognize the aim of today's experiment please. From the reading, who can tell me what you are trying to accomplish today?" He was standing straight up like a stork. His head bobbed from side to side looking for an answer. "Anyone?"

No one. "Nobody out there can tell me why you're suited up and ready to mix compounds?" A black and brown pond of faces rippled with confusion. "So you're basically wearing these stupid little masks and yellow gloves because somebody you barely know told you to, is that it?" More than a few students nodded. One shook his head, and with an amateur's flair, Mitkin called on the "no."

"I am doing it 'cause if I don't my mother will beat the hell out of me. I don't do something because you tell me to, you can believe dat." The child's cool clarity washed over Mitkin and momentarily cleansed him of his brackishness. This young man became Mitkin's favorite.

"Honesty," he pointed at the brash student. "This kid is honest. You all should be so honest. I mean what else is there? Huh? Huh?" Mitkin's approach confused the students and made them edgy, in need of direction. Mitkin too was in need of direction, standing there with a room full of kids, some good, some bad, some just wanting to get a grade, but all wanting direction. Mitkin was no leader. He turned to his new favorite student and said, "Is your father alive?" The kid rumpled his face.

"My father's in South Carolina."

"But he's alive?" Mitkin asked. The boy was getting suspicious. No teacher had spoken to him like this.

"Yeah he's alive, what you trying to say?"

The question went directly to the root of Mitkin's soul. He couldn't answer. He stared out over the class where a smallish girl shuffled her feet. Someone fiddled with a candy wrapper. "I'm..." He mumbled incoherently. All activity stopped now.

"I'm trying to say something about, about organisms I guess, and death and chaos and anarchy and reality." He was rolling now, carefree. "Something about lies, something about courage, about confusion. I, uh, I, don't know what I am trying to say. Do you?"

Another student spoke up. "Hey Mr. Mitkin, you shoulda called in sick, yo. Hey y'all, maybe he mixed one of these beakers all wrong last period. He looks sick, yo." A contagious laughter splintered about and the students began to murmur one to the other. A girl snappily dressed and wearing a great deal of lipstick chimed in.

"Yeah, Mister, and if you go home make sure you dress yourself in the mirror this time." Everyone burst out; hunting season was wide open. A wad of paper sailed toward the garbage can and a spindly boy followed the miss with a mock slam-dunk.

"Why is this happening?" thought Mitkin. "Why am I here?" He stretched himself tall but this had no effect on the jailbreak around him. "I don't care about these kids. I don't care about compounds, this job. This is all bullshit." He looked out over a tempestuous pond, a flood really. No one wanted direction anymore and Mitkin was inconsequential. It grew very loud. Two kids in the back, two small, very quiet South American immigrants began a shoving match. In rushed the provocateurs. The words *fight* and *kick his ass* could be heard even beyond the closed classroom doors. Mitkin ran to the back and jumped onto a long black lab table. He kicked a glass test tube and it shattered, releasing an acerbic stench. Kids covered their faces, one girl cried.

"Order!" yelled Mitkin. "Order!"

He was high above them all, standing on the table, shouting. "Look at me!" One by one, they did and Mitkin quietly shuddered inside.

"There must be order!" He trembled. "Sit down, people. Sit down now!" He pointed at the well-dressed girl. "You, back to your seat." With his forefinger trained like a laser, he guided her back to her chair. He did the same with another student. Methodically, he moved each student back with his finger, seizing each in his sights and steering them with a profound intensity.

The students muttered as they moved.

"What's up with this guy yo?"

"What's wrong with the schizo?"

"This white boy is trippin'."

The honest student spoke directly to Mitkin. "What's wrong with you, Mitkin?"

Mitkin paused. "My father died two weeks ago." He slumped pathetically. "That's as much as I can tell you."

"Is that why you come to school looking all busted?" said the well-dressed girl. Mitkin nodded while glaring at her. She whispered something to her friend, and there was an uneasy silence. Mitkin regretted mentioning his father.

Then a peep from the back. "My father left us two weeks ago. I can't understand why." The little girl who spoke had a dark and chiseled face that reminded Mitkin of Raphaella. This girl would suffer and her face seemed to say as much. Many of the others, too, had that look. Suddenly Mitkin felt embarrassed. The sum of one's suffering is an unsightly thing when offered before the pain of a child, he thought. He felt like a coward, like the coward his father warned him about. His stomach turned. He felt queasy. Mitkin was not well. He was so far from the unwavering Mitchell Mitkin, the confident son, the valedictorian of Columbia University. Confusion crept back into the room. It crept into Mitkin's eyes, standing there so absurdly, high up on that table.

The bell saved him—the bell saved all of them really—the discomfort in the room was murderous. Mitkin dismounted. He still had the bulky, protective goggles stretched over his forehead, sticking up like a miner on lunch break. At the back of the room, a tall, plastic, scrawny human skeleton stood grinning at Mitkin, its bones numbered and its eye sockets filled with bulging, anatomically correct eyeballs. Mitkin pondered death, but his genius was obsolete. He turned and fingered the drawer to his desk and grabbed a brown bag filled with food. He started for the door and walked steadfastly to the little room reserved for teachers and their lunches.

"Mr. Mitchell," cried a voice from the corner. "The young superstar of South Bronx Science, yep, yep. What's that you've got in the old brown bag, Mitch?" Mitkin's lunch bag wasn't even visible. "I bet you've got bananas," sang the voice. "Yep, yep."

This was Ed Taughtauer, a most disproportionate and unattractive man. His neck was long, his face was long, his nose was long and so were his spindly legs. But in the middle was his belly, a rotund thing full of junk food and sweet drinks. He had a distinctly British face, and that means no chin. He was balding, but that didn't stop him from wearing what little hair he had long, back, and nearly to his shoulders, almost like a tail. He was a jocular fellow who always greeted Mitkin, be it in the hallways, in the teacher's elevator, or here, in the teachers' lounge.

"Two bananas and a ham sandwich," Mitkin said with hesitation. Taughtauer crossed the room, side stepping a teacher eating lunch. He slipped past two others with their brown-bag lunches strewn across undersized desktops, the same desks used by students in the classroom. Mitkin thought how Taughtauer looked like a drunk. He waited on him, perturbed. Taughtauer sat down with his mouth still filled with food, and Mitkin could smell corned beef.

"You look rundown, teaching these kids," he paused to swallow, "It's hell you know." Mitkin cheesed a smile and nodded. "Don't get me wrong, it's not the kids who make it hell, it's the administration. They kindle it, hot like the nether regions." He pointed to his crotch and took another bite. "You and I oughta get together for lunch sometime, talk about some things. Talk about things that matter. Really. I'll buy." He got closer and quieter. "Most of these teachers don't know jack shit. I mean look around this place. Ain't a brain in the bunch."

Again Mitkin nodded, pretending to agree. He peeled a banana and was about to bite in when Taughtauer drew closer still. His desk scratched against the hard Formica floor as he slip-jerked it closer. He whispered, "If I thought I could get away with it I'd take the whole goddamned history curriculum and bury it in the Chancellor's ass. I'd teach these kids a few things they'll never learn in, and I quote, *respectable society*." He nodded. "Mmmhuh. That's what I'd do. We should get some guts and do it together." Then in a voice not a whisper, he said, "Oh, but you don't have tenure, do you?"

"No," said Mitkin derisively, "I've been here a week. I thought you'd know that. You seem to notice things like that."

"Oh you mean I seem to be watching you?" He picked at his teeth nonchalantly.

"Yeah, you seem to be watching me." Mitkin was half-revived by the combative blood rushing through his veins.

"Here's the deal. I have been watching you. I saw you at the first all-staff meeting, when you got up and questioned the assistant principal about homework, about, what was it, systematic evaluations?" He smiled. "Yeah, I liked that you stood up. You seem like the real deal, Mitch. Most new teachers, you know, got no guts, no courage, most are just looking for a paycheck."

"Yeah, and why are you here?"

Taughtauer leaned back slightly and grinned. "Oh Mitch, so much anger. I started teaching because I imagined year-long investigations into what matters in this world, you know, unearthing powerful, courageous creatures ready to change the world. That's why I came here, I wanted to teach some supermen, Mitchy. But the system sees to it that supermen die, oh yeah. Die." His sudden intensity was contradictory—he didn't look like any of this. He continued with a sideways look at Mitkin. "Do you know why I'm staying though?" Mitkin shook his head. "Rebellion." He repeated *rebellion* in a whisper, his eyes darting back and forth cartoonishly. Mitkin looked at Taughtauer and wondered if he wasn't maybe a fool, a patient in a ward somewhere. Taughtauer just stared back, grinning. "And you, Mitch?"

"Me, Mitch?" said Mitkin.

"Yeah, you Mitchy. Why are you here? Still. I've seen some leave after an hour in this shithole."

Mitkin remembered his pledge to public education but that was a pre-death pledge, one that seemed empty now. Besides, Taughtauer didn't really care, or did he? "I just wanted to teach."

"Thou wraith telleth a lie, good Mr. Mitchell. Have not you come to spy a damsel's eye?" He grinned a giant grin and warmly patted Mitkin on the back. "No?"

"No what?"

"You're telling me you wouldn't like a little teaching assistance from that one, come on Mr. Mitchell." Both eyed a young, semi-attractive woman. With Taughtauer so close to him and so intent on talking sex, Mitchell felt slimy, like a rotted onion cut too thin.

"You're too much," said Mitkin.

"Now, Mr. Mitchell, that's positively meaningless. You're educated. You can come up with something a little more... yep, yep, illustrative. Can't you? Come on, describe me better than that."

Mitkin sucked twice on his upper lip. Then he cocked his head, regaining a confidence he had lost of late. "I read this once: 'Where a man does not know, there that man must not speak.' Here's the point. You are a weak man who has no friends and in order to deal with this very debilitating reality, you have assumed certain things about me that are untrue. The first being that I am interested in talking to you." It was the old Mitkin, just for a moment.

"Ludwig Wittgenstein."

"What?"

"Ludwig Wittgenstein is the architect of your little quote, Mitchy. He was referring to his inability to understand things metaphysical. He copped out basically." Taughtauer reached into his own brown bag and started on some chips. "He was a fraud."

"He was no fraud, he was one of this world's great thinkers. Anyone who knows anything about mathematics knows that."

"Well, then I guess I'll settle for knowing a lot about something else, something like the real world, something Wittgenstein had no clue about." Gnawed bits of chips flew from his mouth when he said *Wittgenstein*. Mitkin brushed them off and leered at Taughtauer. "Oh, come on Mitch, relax. I know something about you that you don't know I know. Smile and I'll tell you."

"What makes you think I care?"

"You care because what I know about you tells me you care." He sighed as if bothered. "It's the whole point."

"What's the whole point, what the hell are you talking about?"

"Whoa there, Mitchy. The whole point is this. I've read your stuff. I read the article you published in the *Columbia Reader*. Yep. Loved it. You're a real man of the mind. Really, good, good stuff." He chomped on another chip. The little window in the door to the teachers' lounge filled with a pretty face, and the girl waved at Taughtauer. Taughtauer invited her in. She was a strong girl who possessed poise, and Mitkin thought how could a sharp student like this be enamored with a boor like Taughtauer? Mitkin looked at Taughtauer who smiled back. "She's a beauty, huh, and smart, and, best of all, she's got moxie. A good kid." He looked Mitkin up and down. "You've got moxie too, right Mitch?"

"You really read my article in a college newspaper? Are you kidding me?"

"Nope, not kidding. Yep, did read it. Do you know how I found out about it? I read 'em all. I'm a graduate—philosophy, class of seventy. Never miss an issue. Hell, I'm still paying for the damn thing, aren't I? Anyway, I loved your stuff. *A Call to Reason*, yep, yep, good stuff."

"I didn't write the headline," said Mitkin.

"Yeah, but you did write the part about Columbia's abandonment of rational thinking, the part about sentimental policy decisions and unnecessary pandering to special interest groups. You wrote that, right? But the best, seriously, the best was when you brought the whole thing home, the whole thing right into the laps of the dogs who run the joint. And I quote you sir: 'One day reason will bring us to conclude that those who educate us are no longer serving our best interest, and at that point we will have no choice but to tear down what they have built, tear it all down to the ground.'" Taughtauer leaned back in his chair as if blown by a big wind. "Right down to the ground! My sentiments exactly! Bravo, old boy."

Mitkin looked hard at Taughtauer. This was no joke. This freakish individual *had* read his article. In Taughtauer's birdie eyes there was real satisfaction, a genuine admiration, an admiration so profound that Mitkin shuddered. Flatly and fearfully he said, "What do you want?"

"Me?" Taughtauer raised an eyebrow. "What do I want?" He pointed at his own chest. "Why, what makes you ask such large questions, Mr. Mitchell? I mean I want lots of things in this world."

"What do you want from me?"

Taughtauer got up and stood looking down on Mitkin. He finished a cheek-full of chips and then threw the bag into a wastebasket some feet away. "It's not time yet. I just wanted to see if you were as brilliant as your father said you were, and I have my answer." Taughtauer walked out of the room without looking back. Mitkin was bewildered. Confusion flooded in again, and on this fifth day of teaching, he could honestly say he disliked it all—the classroom, the administration, the students, himself, Taughtauer—he hated it all. But the thought of Taughtauer is what lingered. He could not dismiss this zealot, this odd man. He left the teachers' lounge with its messy bookshelves and full garbage cans and returned to teach about simple compounds.

CHAPTER X

Someone New Moves In

Raphaella heard a knock at her door.

"Raphaella, it's me," came a voice. "Are you there, please?"

It was Mitkin. He had not come to visit in nearly a month, longer than he'd gone between visits for nearly three years. She opened the door and let him in. "Where have you been, Mitchell? Are you okay?"

"I've been thinking."

"Downstairs, the whole time, in your room? Why didn't you visit, or at least answer the door?" He didn't respond. "David said he saw you, but he said you just growled at him." He looked at her with forlorn eyes. "What is it?" She opened the door wide. "Come, have dinner with us. You must."

He took up her invitation because he was hungry and lonely, and because she said that he must. Still wearing his teacher clothes, the outfit the students called mismatched, he followed Raphaella down the thin hallway into the kitchen.

"Raphaella, do you know how much I admire you?"

Raphaella stole a peek at Mitkin. He was staring down at his shoes like a broken man. "Admire?" she said.

"It's true. Before my father died, I could not have told you this, but I think, well, I think I've always loved you."

Raphaella shrunk. Loved? How loved? She loved him too, but this was different. This was a conversation grounded in fear and crisis, and the worst kind of desperation. Raphaella walked over and sat down across from Mitkin. She held his hand and looked at him sincerely. "Mitchell, tell me about your father and his death. What is happening to you, inside?" Mitkin slumped in his chair as the boiling water bubbled behind him. "Tell me," she said again.

"I hate what is happening to me. I am no longer sure about anything. Nothing makes sense. The dream I had, the dream about teaching science and paying back for a few years, well, that's gone. It went with my father. All of it is dead, everything from the past is gone." Irritated, he got up and meandered for a moment.

He stopped and pointed. "The water." Raphaella reached and turned the heat down on the stove.

"But that's not true," she replied. "What about science and everything you've ever told me? Your father's death doesn't change all that."

"He lied, Raphaella. He told me death was one thing, and it turns out it's something clsc. And he taught me that I was a coward if I was swayed by my emotions, but I can't help it. There was more to his death than he thought. It was not the end."

"But—"

"Have you ever seen someone die, Raphaella?"

"Yeah, I have."

"Tell me what you felt."

"What I felt?"

"Yes, felt, not thought."

Raphaella was carried back to her teenage years. On the corner of 175th and Creston she had seen a young man, a boy who had always had a crush on her, shot in the head. She was the first on the scene and now, because Mitkin had asked, she tried to remember. "I felt helpless."

He nodded. "Did you feel betrayed?"

"By J.J.? Not really."

"Did you feel very, very insignificant?"

"I think that was part of it, yeah."

"When I saw my father die, the first thing I felt was betrayal. Do you know why?" He spoke in typical Mitkin style, chin out and hands demanding attention. "Because when he died, when his system broke down, there was something in my body that corresponded with no physical or material constituent part. It wasn't my pituitary gland or some highly evolved electrical system that moved me. Raphie, in one solitary second, one damn second, I was moved to question everything my father had taught me. That's not normal. You see, something's wrong with that. How could I hate him, or hate what he stood for so quickly? It's not normal. How could his lie become so, so blatant, so fast? He was a fucking liar."

She recoiled, and there was silence. "Mitch, maybe you need to find out more about the science of emotion or something. Psychology maybe." Raphaella wanted to give him hope, something that he, the logician, could identify with, even if for her the answer lay elsewhere.

But he knew she was pandering. "You don't believe in that shit." *Mitkin cursing?* "Raphie, you are the most spiritual person I know. Since I've known you, I've known you to be different and now I know why. Help me, Raphaella." Ill at ease, Raphaella got up and poured some rice into the boiled water. She brought the heat back up and went to the cupboard for a chopping board. His eyes followed her, their friendship seeming to hang in the balance. Raphaella did not want to lose him despite his rude ways and this new, manic adoration. She wanted to shake herself clean like a muddy puppy might, start over again, maybe return to the door and re-open it and invite in some other spirits, not the ones that came in just a few minutes ago, the spirits of anguish and agony and absolute timidity. She sat down again and smiled a broad, comforting smile.

"We're all like you, Mitchell. We all learn something from death. There was more to your father than he said, but ignorance isn't a crime, is it?"

"But what am I then? I'm not rational, I'm not clear. I don't have the answers anymore. Raphaella, I can't even get through a lesson on compounds, simple compounds." He shrugged and looked around the room and then up toward the ceiling. "What is happening to me?"

"What's happening is the same thing that happens to every earnest person when they think about life and death. Brain smoke."

"Brain smoke, that's good, but it's more than my brain, isn't it? Isn't it, Raphie?" he repeated like a hopeful schoolboy.

"Maybe," she said. "Maybe."

"And you?" he asked with piercing blue eyes. "Has it ever happened to you?"

"It's happening right now." She took his hand and held it. "It happens to me every day." Right there, in the kitchen with their hands together, Mitkin found a resting place. For the first time since his father's death, he had found peace. She was his friend and he loved her. He wanted to hug her and thank her and stay the night, on the couch, protected by fellowship, but he could not bring himself to ask such things. His eyes darted from side to side as he waited for her to ask him. But she didn't, she got up and went to finish preparing dinner.

***

Then that week, for the first time, someone settled into the first floor apartment, the one just below Mitkin. His name was Andrew Seever. He was a big, hardy guy from Wisconsin. He spoke as if in no hurry, his vowels long and lazy, his accent nearly Norwegian, his predilections purely American. I met him like I'd met Mitkin, moving in.

"Hey there, don't let me get in your way now. I'm gonna prop these doors so nobody'll have to worry about 'em. Alrighty then?" He smiled and bounced a little. "Do you live here?"

"No, not really," I said.

"Well I'm Andy Seever. I'm brand new to the city, just graduated from college, Wisconsin in Madison. The Badgers, ever hear of 'em?" He welled with pride.

"Sure have."

"I played baseball there. You like sports?"

"Sure," I fibbed. I hadn't followed any sport for a couple of years and lost interest about the time I graduated from high school. I was never coordinated enough to play, or patient enough to watch.

"Do you know of any softball leagues around here? It's about all I can do now. Besides, I won't have time with my new job." Seever had a real endearing way, the type of guy who thought simple things aloud.

"New job, huh?" I felt obliged to ask.

"I'm going to be an underwriter for an insurance company downtown. Good bucks, good bennies, solid retirement plan. I'm real psyched. My mom's sister, my aunt, she got me the job, said I'd make more money in New York than Milwaukee or Madison. My parents were a little nervous about the whole deal, you know, going away and all. But what the heck, I figure, why not?" He paused and then flexed like a muscle man, "I'm young. Besides, I hear most big guys don't have problems, even in Harlem, hey. A black guy told me that, on the train coming out here."

"A black guy, huh?"

"Yeah, he was a real nice black guy. Gave me his number, told me he'd show me around. I thought, no way, New Yorkers are supposed to be jerk-offs." He smiled and then quickly put a conciliatory hand on my shoulder. "No offense." I nodded a smile. "So, how's this place? How's the landlord? They seemed real unorganized when I went to sign the lease, like they were just trying to figure everything out."

"Where did you go?"

"To a place in the burbs. It was someone's house."

"Well, the landlord just died and I guess things are a bit confused. Anyway, my," I stumbled, "girlfriend hasn't had any problems and she's lived here almost eight years now."

"Is that her that I saw? The girl with the green eyes, upstairs?"

"Is she my girlfriend?"

"Yeah, that's your... wow." He whistled. "She's really something. She's like from another world or something. Boy, you're lucky all right. New York girls are so exotical."

I waited and then thought, why bother, *exotical*, *exotic*, whatever. Plus, I thought, let him think she's my girlfriend, she is, basically, sort of my girlfriend.

"Anyway, now all I need to worry about is getting a car. I want something solid but cool, like a Firebird maybe. Do you like cars?"

I was no longer interested in the conversation, and by pretending I was, I was only prolonging the pain. I should have told him he didn't need a car in Manhattan, and then said something like, "See you around," but instead I said, "Cars? Love 'em, just don't own 'em."

"Yeah lots of people told me not to buy a car in the city but I thought, hey that's crazy, I'm gonna need to escape, you know? Plus, I've had a car ever since I was fifteen, that's when I fixed up an old Dodge—"

I jumped in, "Sorry Andy, I'm a little late, I'll see you around." He yelled to me before I'd reached the second flight.

"What's your name, buddy?"

"David," I said.

"David, do you know of a good gym around here, a Gold's maybe, or one with a tanning booth?"

I quickly answered, "Ninety-second and Third. Go down ten blocks or so. See ya." A tanning booth? This would be interesting, I thought, Mitchell Mitkin and the tanning booth guy in the same building.

I told Raphaella about her new neighbor while I waited for Dana to get dressed. She thought having a third tenant was a good thing and that maybe he would befriend Mitkin when Mitkin needed it most. But in the back of my mind, this didn't seem possible. The exceptionally pensive Mitkin had lived a long time with an exceptionally inquisitive Raphaella, and now the two were being asked to reside with an exceptionally simple all-American, a good guy, a suburban stud. For me, it wouldn't work, but it really didn't have to "work." There was no reason any of them had to talk to one another, ever. This was a false expectation fostered by the close relationship Raphaella and Mitkin had developed, a relationship that had included Mitkin's father.

As I opened the front door to leave, Dana in tow, I said, "Why don't you join us? We're going to the aquarium. You'll love it."

Dana cheered, "Come on Mom, you will. The whales!"

To my amazement, she said yes. We waited for a moment as she threw on some clothes, great clothes, clothes that she didn't give a second thought to, but clothes that worked well. Brown leather boots, perfect jeans, a familiar white cotton shirt and a well-worn leather jacket with embroidery on the cuffs. She quickly put her hair into two ponytails and we left. We watched the whales as a trio, Dana between us, our hands in hers, her cries of "Mommy this," and "Daddy that," lending a profound sense of normality to everything we did. On the way home, I rushed them off the subway at Times Square and we caught a concert in Bryant Park. It was classical music by the New York Philharmonic, and it was perfect. The fall air was crisp but not cold, Dana fell asleep in my arms as the final piece came to an end, and I bought Raphaella a bouquet of yellow flowers. The entire day was medicinal, curative, and I wouldn't forget it. Perhaps, most importantly, I truly believed that she wouldn't either, that she too was enamored, hopeful. She held my arm as I carried our daughter out of the subway and up to the front door of the apartment. She curled her long fingers tight around my bicep like she was my date.

"She's heavy when she sleeps," I said.

"Very. Let me take her up." She scooped Dana out of my arms and paused. "I'm glad we went together. Thanks, David."

"Me too," I said, and we kissed, lightly, on the cheek. I waited for her to get safely inside, and then telling myself to go ahead, go on, I stood still. The streetlight behind beamed rosy and bright, and I didn't want to move.

CHAPTER XI

Les Misérables

Meanwhile, Mitchell Mitkin was in search of a new paradigm. Like me, he was re-examining his relationship with Raphaella, and like me, he just knew he was the one for her. He began to visit her regularly. Every time I visited, he was there. I often found his books stacked against the wall beside the couch, a couch on which, I surmised, he must have slept. They had apparently started a reading club of some sort, though later I found out it was not so much a club as a spontaneous clique; the two of them read poetry and discussed novels and essays. I saw Rousseau's *Emile* on the floor behind the couch, a book that looked more like work than pleasure. Mitkin chose Thoreau and Wordsworth, Blake and Goethe. Exuberance and the "love of living" were the common denominator and Mitkin's new definition for beauty. He loved that he could call himself an "uncontrollable animal" whose "great joy was joy" and whose "character was love." He delved deep into the idea of intuition and inspiration; he began to make himself over again, and all at the feet of Raphaella. He imagined that she was all of these things. He believed that in her he had found the archetype of beauty, the *vernal wood*. Like a child he ran to her so that she might listen.

"Sometimes, Raphie, when I look at you, you're like a light sitting there, a beacon, a sort of saving force for me. Do you know that, Raphie? I can talk to you."

"Relax a little, Mitch. We've always talked together, haven't we?"

"But not about this stuff." He held up *Songs of Experience* by William Blake. "This is a drug almost, and we are doing it together." Raphaella nodded. "I'm torn you know," he went on but almost as if he didn't know how to, "I want to tell you something, but..." He waited for her.

"Go ahead, Mitch," she said, ever so slightly irritated. "It's okay."

"These last few weeks, ever since I started coming here, since school started and everything else, you've made me, well, I feel free here. I feel like the past is falling away, and I'm liberated." He was beaming. He stared and smiled at Raphaella, and in his eyes she saw a manic happiness, the look of an unconvinced man. "I don't know how to thank you for taking me under your wing like you have. I know that sometimes I'm maybe a little too talkative, but I don't mean to be. I'm just, well, recovering I guess. You're making it easier for me."

Raphaella nodded awkwardly.

Together they read on and lived on, closer and closer each day, or so it appeared to me. Raphaella read his book choices obediently, and would often let him choose for her. Together they read Victor Hugo and then, very predictably, crowned their little reading club with a trip to Broadway and *Les Misérables*. At the box office, the salesman called them a nice-looking couple as Mitkin smiled and put his arm around Raphaella.

"I bought the best, Raphaella, we should be way down there," and he pointed to the orchestra. "Only the best." They took their seats and waited as the mid-size crowd meandered up and down the aisles behind them. Mitkin moved excitedly in his seat, turning and looking directly at Raphaella.

"I would never have gone to a Broadway show before. This is so artsy, but so perfect too. Are you having fun?"

Raphaella laughed nervously under her breath. "Yes, Mitch, I'm having fun."

Mitkin had one thought. It conquered him and held him captive the whole night. When will I take her hand and hold it? Each minute that passed marked a missed opportunity. "Now?" he'd muse. "What about this moment? Do it." He wondered if she was thinking the same, and in a fit of anxiety turned to her. The orchestra had not yet started to play the overture, but she was counting. One by one, she pointed and enumerated the marble gargoyles that stared down from the domed ceiling. Like a child unaware she counted, "...eleven, twelve, thirteen..." And then she began to count the figures on the walls, above the stage, and around the orchestra. "Counting?" thought Mitkin, "Should I take her hand while she is counting?" She turned around and began to count the carvings behind her. She counted to forty-one before Mitchell stopped her, riven with confusion.

"What are you doing?" he cried.

She was startled. "I'm counting."

"What?"

"The details. If you look closely at the walls you can see that each section has sets of little sculptures, and each one of those has something religious in it, which, if you look closely, has its own little story to tell. Together they tell some big story."

She squinted, "The whole theater is like a giant narrative. Somebody really cared about this joint."

"Or they cared about money," he said from the side of his mouth.

"Money?" She grimaced. "All this for money?"

"No. All right," he moved in his seat. "No, I don't think so. You're right, probably not." He mumbled, "Not for money." He turned away from her slightly and then back again, resuming his stare. Raphaella was heedless. Without looking, she tapped him on the thigh with her rolled up program and pointed.

"The show's over there." The lights went down and the show indeed began.

When it was over, he wanted to talk. He hurried her up the long row of seats and across the aisle out of the theater. He grabbed her hand (yes, he'd deferred for almost three hours) and pulled her through the thick crowd. They popped out on 42nd Street. Bright neon lights swamped the street and chased the night. A surreal setting ensued. Everything seemed bigger and better, brighter. Still holding her hand, Mitkin pulled Raphaella through the street and into a pizza shop where she politely wriggled free. He helped her with her chair, and then went to the counter to order. Standing there, with his back to her, Mitkin considered her thoughts. Maybe she had begun to love him, too? Maybe she saw their compatibility, their natural affection for one another? Maybe she saw his devotion for her, his desire to build a beautiful theater together? She had gone out of her way to help him, she had shown how much she cared by letting him into her life, and he liked what was happening to her, too. That she had questions about her own life made him trust her more. That, he told himself, was the center of their love. That they both asked questions and searched for meaning in the world would get them through it all, the whole of life, together.

Mitkin became very sentimental. He imagined the pizza as an offering, a primal gift, given from one heart to another, a ready-made offering. He pictured a simple life with her. He wanted to experience the vernal woods with this woman and do it now, right there, transported on the chariot of man's good nature, into the heavens reserved for him and her from before all time. His heart was a fluttering feather. The show, with its eternal themes, themes he romanticized, repeated itself in him and he grew confident. He was convinced that she was ready to ride away with him, and that he need only ask. (Clearly she was too polite to ask him, even as she fought the urge to). He whisked the pizza sacrifice off the high counter and slid three one-dollar bills toward an unassuming prep cook. He placed the offering in front of her and gallantly sat down.

"Hey, Mitch, you tipped the counter guy three bucks. Do you always do that?"

He shrugged. "Why not?"

She shrugged too. "Yeah, why not?" She hissed and hooed as the hot pizza rolled around in her mouth. "Oh, hot," she managed, chewing delicately. "Did you like it?"

"The show? I loved it."

"What was your favorite part?"

"You tell me yours first," said Mitkin. He waited wide-eyed while she finished a bite.

"The part when the bishop gives him all the silver even though Valjean stole from him. There's no story without that." She smiled. "That's what gives Valjean courage and everything else that matters for the rest of the show."

Mitkin nodded, but did not agree. "That was a good scene."

"Was it your favorite?"

"Sure," said Mitkin.

"Come on, seriously. I can see you're just saying that."

"Well, all right. I liked the barricade. The fight. That was the center of the story for me."

"Why?" she asked.

"They loved life, a great robust life. It was simple, too. I'm right, you're wrong, the end, kill the ones who disagree. It's refreshing."

"But it's the center of the story?" she asked again.

"Well, no. It doesn't matter."

She waited.

He saw that she was pressing him, and he liked the attention. "It's the center for me these days, anyway. I've learned a lot. I think the key is the emotions, the wild belief, like the fighters of the barricade had. They loved freedom."

"But Valjean didn't. He… This whole thing is stupid. We're idiots. This isn't real life." She rolled her eyes. "I just thought the center of it all was repentance, you know. Love."

"I agree!" He was pleading nearly. "Love of life, of breath, of freedom. That's what the whole story is about."

Raphaella sat uneasily. "Yeah, but not like you're saying it exactly." She finished her pizza, wiped her mouth and put down two dollars. Mitkin pulled back suddenly.

"No way, keep it, please, Raphie," he said pushing the money away.

"Mitchell," she said, "take the money." And then, trying to lighten the mood, added, "How about some ice cream? I'll buy." He sort of stared and nodded slightly. "Ice cream and then we've got to go," she continued, "Dana's sitter is expecting me by 11:30."

Mitkin put his jacket on. He did not finish his pizza. He had not even touched it.

CHAPTER XII

Ripe

The bell rang and science class was over. It had gone much better this week, as a steady rain seemed to calm the students. Raphaella had told Mitkin that this would be the case. She was often right, and good and beautiful, he thought. She was exactly what he needed to survive his new life. As students filed out, one girl, a little girl in short-shorts, filed in.

"Sol, where have you been?" said Mitkin.

Snapping her gum the girl said, "I got a pass, Mister, here, it's from Ed."

"Ed?"

"Mister Taughtauer, dang. He said I could stay with him and then he gave me this note. It's my pass."

Mitkin was exasperated. "Could you be here on time from now on please," he said as he shook his head.

"Dang, whatever, Ed just said you'd understand and that you weren't such a little bitch, but I guess not."

"Leave, Sol," said Mitkin. She rolled her eyes and huffed off. Seeing her go, he rested his body against a table and began to read.

M. Mitkin:

The short version.

An organism is dying and must be put out of its misery. It is no longer able to continue the life it was designed for, and so, a few elite members of that organism do the noble thing and end the life of that organism. Its death is good for everyone involved. Its death is very good for the people the organism was designed to serve. In fact, death is so good that in the place of that dead organism truth blossoms, truth and tranquility and the root of goodness, a root long since withered. All of this is natural, it is all meant to be. One could say the organism needed to die in order for its seed to survive. One could say that, don't you think?

I will be in my room after school waiting for you. I hope you will not be afraid to come. Please don't be afraid, you are the man for the job. Your father told me so.

—ED

Mitkin dropped his hands and scanned the room. He read the last line again: *Your father told me so.*

"Taughtauer," he thought, "has nerve." He shook his head. "My father didn't tell him anything, when would they have met?" He looked one more time at the letter and folded it into his back pocket. He meandered about the room. It was the letter that now occupied him and not the art of instruction. In fact, the letter blotted out the haunting image of his father's dead body and, incredibly, resurrected his father. Mitkin pictured the two of them talking at Columbia over coffee, during some lecture series, or, he thought aloud, "At the conference Columbia had for teachers of science. Yes, that's it! But Taughtauer teaches history doesn't he?" He rushed all of this through his mind, but could not place Taughtauer with his father.

The next set of students barged their way into the classroom, but everything that Mitkin set out to teach was overwhelmed by thoughts of Taughtauer. He had traded one obsession for another, death for derangement, but he was not entirely unhappy with this trade. It was the mysterious tone that attracted him. It promised something, a forecast of hope. He decided that he would go see Taughtauer, and besides, he thought, he could always yell at Taughtauer for keeping Sol out of class. Yes, he could always do that. He turned the corner of the long corridor that led to Room 409 and Ed Taughtauer.

The paunchy man was at his desk, hunched over some papers and surrounded by a canopy of color that exploded from the walls, the floor, and from every corner and cranny. Taughtauer's walls were the canvas for a giant collage. Anything a student accomplished Taughtauer put there. Portraits, posters, test papers and pictorials combined with maps, mosaics, murals and magazine covers. They were everywhere. A blanket-size relief map of Australia stared down from the ceiling. A giant timeline encircled the entire classroom running from 440 BC to NOW. A slide pointer rested at 1890. Mitkin was impressed. Still standing in the doorway, he saw Taughtauer's red pen flying over white lined paper, scribbling even as Mitkin made his way in. He got as close as an arm's length before Taughtauer spoke without looking up.

"I thought you'd come, I really did. It's simply too good, too you, and I knew you'd know it. Yep, just too good."

"Cut the crap. Don't take my students out of class for your experiments or whatever it is you do in here. Do you understand?"

Still looking down, Taughtauer said, "Not why you came."

"What?"

Gleefully, Taughtauer looked up. "That's not why you came, Mitch."

Mitkin huffed. "I want to know in clear and coherent terms what you want." Mitkin stood nearly at attention, very taut and about to break. "And how did you know my father?"

"Well, geez Mitch, that's all you had to say," said Taughtauer, swiveling his chair and reclining with his hands behind his head, like an arrogant policeman. "Well, it's like this basically. Actually why don't you sit down." He pointed toward a desk. Mitkin did not move. "Come on, Mr. Mitchell, just have a seat." Mitkin acquiesced. Taughtauer smiled.

"He's greasy," thought Mitkin.

"I met your father about eight years ago. He ran a seminar for science teachers, something about how to get funds for science projects. He was in charge of a great deal of money. The chairman as you know, the chairman of *Science Now*."

Mitkin shook his head. "He was the founder of *Science Now*, his way of paying back."

"I know what it was. I talked to him that day for about an hour. We even went out afterwards, had a drink, talked shop. I was impressed with your father. He had many good ideas about this country, this very confused country. His best idea was science."

"What is that supposed to mean exactly?"

Taughtauer grinned. "It means he loved, no, worshipped science." Then he grinned and stuck his index finger in the air. "He was scienterrific!"

"You're an idiot," said Mitkin.

"No, not an idiot, just a guy who disagreed with your father about what he called a 'reverential dedication to the natural sciences,' or the 'hard science's salvation of public education.'" He pinched his nose between his thumb and forefinger, itching it, grubbing at it. "I didn't agree that a foundation dedicated to pumping private funds into public school science departments could save public education. No. But I did agree with him that public schools could be saved, I did agree with him, with his eyes really." He paused and leaned over, and whispered ever so slightly. "He was a zealot, Mitch. I agreed with his love for the human mind. I liked him. I liked him a lot. But I never told him."

"Why would he care?"

"I never told him about my plans, dummy, not that I liked him." Taughtauer leaned forward, his nose seeming to grow as he got closer. "I never told him about the revolution." He stayed fixed on Mitkin. "The revolution, Mitch. It's why you're here."

Mitkin looked around the room. Taughtauer's wispy voice made him very aware of himself and he suddenly felt subversive, and though this feeling was entirely alien to him, he liked it. He had spent his whole life outside, in the sun, spewing natural truths and holding his chin up high. But, with death had come visceral doubt and danger. Since his father's death, the call to purpose had vanished, but in Taughtauer's room, a novice to the veteran, Mitkin felt let in, accepted and welcome. He felt called again, even if by such an underground eccentric as Taughtauer, especially perhaps. He looked at Taughtauer, hoping to see a less greasy character and to hear more about the revolution. "It's why I'm here?" he asked.

"It is why you are here." Taughtauer said each word slowly as if to separate one from the other, and he pointed at Mitkin as he did so. "You are here to help me help these poor sons of bitches who society has left to a slow, intellectual rot. Look at the kids in your classroom, they are abandoned, every one of them, by this system. They've got no one who loves them in this system, Mitch. Oh don't get me wrong, a few teachers here and there love them, a few give out their phone numbers and feel like martyrs when students call for extra help. Sure, there are some sweet apples in a sour lot, but let's face some sound and safe facts ole Mr. Mitchell. These kids are screwed because the people charged with looking out for them don't. They don't care, try, love, teach, administer, budget, you name it, they don't do it. I'm talking about the people at the top, Mitch, the gray-suited elite who move from office to office and school chancellery to school chancellery and those who call themselves principals, superintendents and board members—especially board members. They are the God-awful worst. The whole lot doesn't give two shits about these kids, and so, to borrow from a rarely wise Founding Father, now that the school government has become unable to secure a student's right to education it is the right of my students to abolish this government and institute a new one, one that secures a student's right to knowledge and lays the foundation for the pursuit of individual happiness!" He grinned a self-satisfied grin. "Basically Mitch, I propose a mass rebellion of the governed against the governors—in this case, masters is more appropriate. And I propose that you help me in this endeavor. I want you to write for me, Mitch. I want you to be our mouthpiecc."

A portentous pause filled the room, and into it spilled the pounding a cappella of *Carmina Burana*. It had been playing the whole time, but now the music had grown to a crescendo and Mitkin was filled with what Taughtauer hoped he would be: purpose. Sheepishly, Mitkin spoke up. "You want me to work for the overthrow of the New York City Board of Education?" The words hung in the air. "It sounds like you're planning to overthrow the Board of Ed, is that what you are planning? I mean, come on."

Taughtauer smiled comically. "The Board of Ed, The Board of Me, The Bored Ed... Ha. I like that. I like that a lot." And then dripping with bravado and much sarcasm, he continued, "You're not doubting, not you Mitchell? The brilliant son, and I did hear of your brilliance from independent sources, sounding like every other partially dedicated functionaire who lives to work and loves his weekends as his life? Not you too, Mitch? You're not like every teacher that's ever decided he'd teach because he had nothing else to do, are you? You're not like the everyday suit more interested in tie sales than students? You aren't just *every man*, are you, Mitch?"

"I'm just asking."

"I'm just answering. When a system no longer serves the people it is created to serve, it must be torn down. What is so difficult to understand about that? Your father understood it. He spent his whole life, his whole philanthropic life anyway, trying to tear down this system in order to replace it with something better. Didn't he?"

"Sure, but he was missing the edge. You sound like you want to take something over, kill someone. I can see it in your eyes."

"No, what you see in my eyes is courage to do what is right. What is right, what is true, and what is good. That's what you see." He was very earnest now. "And seeing it disturbs you, doesn't it? Yeah, I can see it's gone—truth is missing in your life, courage too. You look tired and worn down. Yep, looking at you I get

the feeling you don't believe in anything. Maybe I was wrong about you actually."
Taughtauer returned to his grading.

"But you haven't told me anything. What, in concrete terms, are you proposing?"

Taughtauer's head was down again. "Fire."

"Fire?" peeped Mitkin.

"Fire."

"You mean like lighting a fire?"

"Yeah, Mitchy, like lighting a fucking fire. But, first we'd take the building for a few days, maybe ten hostages, maybe more, and then the fire." Taughtauer reached over and purposefully turned up *Burana*. A slow, trembling wail joined the two teachers in the room.

"Hostages?"

"Hostages. And fires, and destruction and jail, hey and maybe death. So what? Hello! When's the last time an elected politician gave into the demands of underage niggers—and I use that phrase familiarly."

"Nobody is going to listen to them anyway, fire or no fire." Mitkin looked around the room into a sea of dedication. "Why give all of this up? You are making a difference here, Ed."

Taughtauer mocked Mitkin with a whiny voice, wagging his head. "You're making a difference here, Ed." His eyes flashed. "Come on, Mitchy! Get some backbone." Then, in a soft and disturbing voice he added, "You called me Ed. I like that, Mitch. Who knows? Maybe we can be friends." He looked out. "You like my room?"

Mitkin nodded.

"It can be better. Look, I could sit here right now and tell you about the kids I've come to know in eighteen years on the job. I could tell you about drug dealers and valedictorians and the rest. You would get squeamish about some things, like incest and rape and addiction and concerning some other things you'd just nod. And then you'd nod a little bit more, and if I hadn't brought up the fire and hostages you'd leave. By tomorrow my sad stories would become cheap anecdotes you'd use to impress girls at parties, and in two weeks my sad stories would be forgotten. But I guarantee you that in two years you'll still remember the wacko who talked about burning down Livingston Street, and this, even though we didn't do it! If we actually pulled it off, you'd be talking about it for decades, centuries, and in fact, and you know I am telling the truth, one day kids would read about it in their goddamned history books. That's the truth, the truth, unadulterated, no bullshit. Incontrovertible." Taughtauer stopped, turned his head and invited Mitkin to disagree. "Big words, big ideas, big truth. Am I wrong?"

"No, but—"

"But... Here comes the crap. Don't *but*, just *do*. The only real question for you Mitch is, are you courageous enough to do what is right, to start over?" Taughtauer got up and walked to the back of the classroom where he stopped in front of a maudlin painting. It depicted rows and rows of sepia brick buildings, identical in design and stretching for miles into a sinking sun. Tawny yellows and rusty reds dominated the sky and a gloomy film covered it all. Taughtauer motioned Mitkin over with his chin. Mitkin walked over and stood square in front of the painting, trading glances between the painting and the grave, gray eyes of Taughtauer.

"Can you feel it?" asked Taughtauer.

"What?"

"The despair, Mr. Mitchell, the despair?"

Mitkin felt it. "Who did it?"

"James Clay."

"Clay? I've got a student Willie Clay. Are they related?"

"Were."

"Were what?"

"Related. Your Willie had a brother named James. James is dead. Died on the street a year ago. Couldn't add, couldn't subtract, couldn't find a job, couldn't do much. But he sure could paint. Of course, it didn't help that not one school in this district offered art, real art where kids are classically trained. Have you seen our art room? A joke."

Mitkin looked at the painting and admired the long straight lines and the dark mood. He felt the name James Clay in the painting, and he imagined what the boy was like. His own melancholia mixed with the despair of the painting and he asked, "Was he your student?"

"He was our student, Mitch, he was my student and yours, he was our responsibility and we let him down. Look at the talent wasted by the system. Look at it." Mitkin, of course, already had. He turned and began to walk out of the room.

"He's the reason you came to teach Mitchell, don't cop out now." Taughtauer raised his voice. "Don't be a coward, Mitchell."

Mitkin reached the doorway and hung his head. "I don't know why I'm here anymore." He moved to leave but couldn't. Curiosity held him there, it swelled against the stark realization that outside there was nothing anymore. He thought about amoeba worksheets and gravity quizzes and his putrid apartment and his intolerable mother with her pathetic tears. He thought about all his father's causes, the foundations, the hundreds of thousands of dollars going round and round and never seeming to pacify the pain of the world. He thought about his father's life again and then, as he always did when the memory of his father surfaced, he thought about his dead body and the lie. The urge to destroy something scurried out of his head and into his arms and to his hands and he balled a fist, raised it and smashed it on an empty desk. Taughtauer watched it all calmly.

"Why are you doing this to me?" cried Mitkin through clenched teeth. Taughtauer continued to stare. "What do you want from me?"

"I've told you."

"But it's all too crazy."

"Then leave." He pointed to the door. "Just leave and see how fast it all seems perfectly sane. Besides you've got nothing else now, I can see it. Your god is dead, yep. It's time for a new paradigm, Mr. Mitchell."

"But when you burn down Livingston Street, what comes next?"

"Chicago's Livingston Street."

"Come on Taughtauer, Chicago? And then L.A., right?"

"If that's what the students want. And they do. We're already there, too."

"They'll be dead on the streets before they burn anything down."

"They're already dead, Mitchy, at least as far as America is concerned. Besides, you're missing the point. When a kid commits, you should see what happens. I've got one kid who has been in on the planning for six months now. Guess what Mitch? He's an A student, a perfect honor roll kid, but guess what else? He doesn't give a crap. What he cares about is the revolution, he cares about change and equality and justice and the big bombs of life. His grades are only a reflection of his awakened mind, don't you get it? I don't know what will be built on the ash pile, but I don't care. Whatever it is, it will be built by renewed hands, renewed minds."

"Are there others?" asked Mitkin.

"There are, many, but I am not at liberty to tell you who they are." *Burana* clicked off in the background.

"How many students, Taughtauer?"

"Not at liberty," Taughtauer said in a whisper and through a wry grin.

"What will I write?"

"Not at liberty."

"So what do I do?"

"Come tonight. I'll leave an address in your box downstairs. Don't tell anyone. Be on time and bring a notebook." His eyes narrowed. "Look for the note." Taughtauer went to the door and opened it wide, inviting Mitkin to leave. As Mitkin turned and left, a loud, high-pitched bell howled in the hall.

***

"Did you go to Taughtauer that night?" I ask.

"No, David. Not that night. I still loved Raphaella."

I think about how I loved her too, at that time, really loved her as I hadn't loved her before. And so both of us had loved the same woman, we really had, in very much the same way. We had been in competition for her, just like I thought we were, just like I kept telling myself I was. I had been right. "So Raphaella kept you from going? How's that though?"

"My hope for one life stopped me from joining another. Isn't it always like this?" He eyes me.

"What happened then? Why'd you end up with him?"

He is light and airy. "The Cloisters happened, David. The Cloisters had to happen, didn't it?"

CHAPTER XIII

The Cloisters

The Cloisters is an old, Catholic monastery sitting at the highest point of Washington Heights, a neighborhood in northern Manhattan famous for its hilltop brownstones and eclectic mix of elderly Jews, Columbia University med students, and vibrant, tough Latino immigrants, most from the Dominican Republic. It is an odd place for a monastery, and within its walls, removed from the gridlocked streets and swarming sidewalks, one feels something of what the monks of the 18th and 19th centuries must have felt. Of course, The Cloisters is no longer a monastery but a museum. Various works by religious and irreligious artists alike hang on the walls amid a tepid quiet the curators have parlayed into a churchly calm.

It was early winter when they visited. Mitkin had suggested the date a week before, and for the entire week fought a sinking feeling, one that had him saying all the wrong things and doing all the wrong things, and generally ruining everything that he imagined he and Raphaella had.

"You never would have joined me here two years ago," Raphaella said as they ascended a steep path winding through a rocky outcropping in the incongruous Manhattan woodland. Looking up, they could see an old bell tower affixed against the crisp, pewter-blue winter sky. A jet rumbled above on its way out of the city while the afternoon sun jabbed slightly through the scanty canopy, throwing little diamonds of white light on the ground. "Of course, two years ago I never would have come here. I'm happy we're here."

They reached the monastery and went in. There were not many people inside. The few that were, coupled up. One pair held hands as they perused the finely carved votives and exquisite tracery cut into the stone cornices. Another couple walked arm in arm, each enveloping the other as if trying to stay warm. Raphaella and Mitkin walked apart. When Raphaella stopped, Mitkin would stop. Where she saw something interesting, so did he. She spied a cross.

"That is Byzantine."

"I like it," he said, and they continued. A hardy breeze with an icy sting slapped their faces as they turned to head outside where a garden filled with graves awaited. It was part of the museum. Various friends of the monastery had been buried there, buried in simple, well-kept plots all surrounded by a retaining wall of knee-high planters. Only one of the planters contained anything living; an early morning glory sprouted against the cold odds of winter.

"Do you remember when I told you I loved you?" asked Mitkin. She nodded. "Did you know what I meant?"

"I think so," she responded as they weaved through the grave markers in silence, Mitkin's palms moistening, his heart growing wild. At the back of the little ossuary, they found the same path that had brought them up the hill to the monastery. Mitkin watched as Raphaella entered it for the descent. He stirred in agitation. The bell tower now stood tall beside them, but soon, if they continued down, it would sink into the hillside, out of sight. Raphaella smelled something burning and slowed. "Can you smell that?"

He nodded but did not respond. "What did I mean?" he intoned, sternly.

"About love? You meant you love me. We understand one another. You're searching, like me."

"That is not what I meant." He stopped and waited for her to do the same. "Raphaella, I didn't mean that when I used the word love."

She stopped. "What did you mean?"

"I meant love, sensual love. I meant the most basic desire known, the one I've denied for so long." He took a step but then stopped again, turning to her quickly. "If you give a man long enough, he will believe in anything. I believed my own thing for a long time, but I was wrong about that. My father was wrong, too. I've rethought everything now. I've rethought absolutely everything. Do you remember when I first met you, how I measured your fetus, your baby, with my hand? Do you remember my hand on your belly, on your skin? I think I said that he would be big-boned and early. Well, that was a joke. The whole encounter was not what I made it seem. I was acting like that because I had been trained to take all of my insides, my deep passions, and turn them into cold calculations. I was like a pervert, because I wanted to touch you differently and wouldn't admit it. I was a pervert, see, I buried what I wanted in a sick way. I always wanted you Raphaella, even when you were pregnant. Does that bother you?" He took a step closer. "David thought I was courting you when I put my ear to your belly, and he was right. I was courting you, I was falling in love with you, I was wanting you, and so what? I fell in love with you in my own way, it was scientific and stupid, but now it's different, now I've gotten rid of all that baggage and found a new way. I love you, Raphaella."

They were on a steep set of stairs that traversed the craggy hills on top of which sat the monastery itself. They were standing together about halfway down. She stood one step above him and looked down on him, he looking up, close enough to touch. When a cold breeze blew a thick bushel of hair into Raphaella's face, he took her hand and held it forcefully. With his other hand he combed her hair back slowly. "I will never stop loving you, Raphaella."

"You can't love me, Mitchell."

"Don't say that, Raphaella. You're strong, you're silent and thoughtful and you have what you need in this life."

"Doubt is what I have," she said beneath her breath.

"How odd," he said, then louder, and aggressively. "How odd it is you say that, because I was about to say how confident you are." He paused, "I was going to say how much your confidence attracts me. It's the thing that I need now, the thing I need the most." His hands moved slightly to take her but she stopped him.

"See, we are no good, Mitchell. I am not what I seem. Please Mitchell, don't talk about love anymore. Please. There is nothing between us." He stared coldly at her. "Nothing, Mitchell. Do you hear me? Nothing."

Mitchell Mitkin stopped staring at her, took a slight step back, and looked up through the tall trees. The sun found his eyes and he squinted. A ridge built of piled rock stood crooked at the bottom of the hill, the only sign of the city below. He buttoned the top of his jacket and tugged on his knit hat, pulling it nearly over his eyes. Then, heaving, he took a step up and took Raphaella by the shoulders with force, and as he did his hands slid up slowly until they were snug around her throat.

"You must love me, Raphie. I need you, you're not like the others down there." He held her too tightly for a moment and she recoiled, throwing herself to the ground, afraid. His chest grew tight and he pitied himself. There in the little wood under the monastery he swore his life meant nothing. Every attempt to make sense of it ended the same. She had betrayed him and his pride would not have it.

"Get up," he cried as she crab-crawled away from him, her back ramming the step behind her. "Get up!"

"Please, Mitchell, what is it?"

He tried to grab her, but she refused, her face filled with fear. He raised his hand to strike her, but stopped. "Fine, whatever then, I'll leave," he said, pointing down the path. "I'm finished with all of this. You're right. You don't know what love is. Not you, not anybody. You are just like the rest." He dismissed her with a wave and curled his lip. "Love is shit." Still sitting on the ground, Raphaella watched him descend the steps, down and out of view he went, his image growing darker and darker in the shadows, until finally it disappeared into the street below.

CHAPTER XIV

The Monk Seraphim

Meanwhile, as Christmas drew near, I grew closer to my daughter. I had great plans for this Christmas, our first real Christmas together. It was a weekend I believe, and I was sharing lunch with Dana. We picked up a bucket of chicken and were enjoying a little picnic on an exceptionally warm winter day. We were in Central Park near Walden's Pond. Crisp, cool air freshened our faces while above, the towering, gilded cornices of Central Park South soared. It was a place I loved to go.

"Daddy, can I have your potatoes?" asked Dana.

"Sure honey, but first eat your chicken."

She picked up a leg and then quickly put it back down. "Oops, I can't eat that, Daddy."

I admonished her, "Sure you can, aren't you hungry?"

"Mommy says that if I remember, and if I want to, I should not eat meat right now, not until Christmas."

Dana's face was wrought with angst. Her brow was stiff as she dug through the bag for a spoon. The chicken lay untouched on her paper plate.

"Go ahead, Dana," I pointed. "Eat the chicken. I'll tell Mommy it's okay."

"I don't think so, Daddy. I'm more hungry for potatoes." She scooped a pale white glob into her mouth. I looked at her chicken and then at our daughter and thought, *this* is weird. Denial at age four?

"Eat the chicken, Dana," I said.

"But—"

"I said eat the chicken." Startled, she quickly picked up her plate, rolling her chicken leg like a log from one side to the other. She squealed as the leg rolled again, back and forth across her plate until it crashed onto the sandiest patch of Manhattan real estate known to man.

"Oops," she moaned.

I fumed and said, "Pick it up." She did. I snatched it out of her hands and tried to brush off the sandy skin before handing it back. She gave me a furtive glance and clenched her teeth. "Dana," I said loudly. She stared at me and then, obediently, began to bite in. I snatched the chicken away before she got to it.

"I'm sorry, Dana, it's just that you should be eating Kentucky Fried Chicken like everybody else. Here, eat this one, it's not so sandy." She took it and we sat quietly, chewing. Finally, it was time to go home.

"Ready?" I said.

She nodded. I drove home, hurriedly.

"It's called fasting," said Raphaella, pointing Dana to her room while at the same time dealing with me. "It's no big deal, people all around the world do it. Relax."

"Why relax? Flogging at four? Don't you think that's a little much, a little ridiculous?" I was more irritated than I'd hoped to be.

"It's not flogging, David. And no, fasting is not ridiculous."

"I think it is. Whose idea is this anyway?"

"It's my idea."

"I don't believe you. I think it's the priest's idea. How often do you go to that church now? Huh?"

"As often as we can, so what?"

"Well, I think he's got you brainwashed. That's what I think."

"Well I am sorry you think so little of me, but I'm not brainwashed. I made a conscious decision to fast. I explained my decision to my daughter and she has decided to fast with me. Big deal."

"It is a big deal. Now I'm dating someone who starves herself, some guru of the gods, while my baby daughter learns the great lessons of self-deprivation. What's next, the frickin' iron maiden?"

"First of all, you're not dating anybody. Secondly, it's easy to say what you're saying David. Try to look a little deeper."

"Oh, I have Raphaella. I spent three years in California looking deeper." She rolled her eyes. "Okay, I couldn't love you correctly, I hated that. I came back in to do the right thing. I've done everything you've asked of me since returning. I haven't pushed you into anything sexual, into dating, into being a couple. I'm just trying to do what's right." And now, I guess I blew a gasket. "I mean Dana's my daughter too, right?"

"Not the point," she said.

"So how about a little consultation before turning her into Mother Teresa?"

"And that would be so bad?"

"You know what I mean."

"You know what? I don't. I really, really don't, David."

"I mean stop subjecting her to somebody else's ideas of what is right. Do what your heart tells you, everything you need to know is in your heart, just follow it, gosh." I was running out of words and I kept wanting to say, "You know what I mean." More than anything though, I wanted to start this whole conversation over. We had been doing so well together.

"That's why I fast, David, to get to my heart, to uncover it and know it." She had been nearly yelling, and suddenly she lowered her voice, looking for Dana. Near to a whisper she said, "David, don't think it's all just black and white for me. I'm struggling to understand all of it, too. I'm searching, so what?"

"Whatever," I said. "I just want to know one thing. Will we ever be together? Am I just fooling myself? Am I an idiot?" But of course, I was an idiot. All of the peace treaties and good-boy credits had just gone out of the window because I just had to drop the big one. The together question.

"I don't know if we'll be together," she said. "I really don't know."

There was no way to stay in that room now. How badly I wanted to take my daughter and leave, to get out of the wooliness of it all, to move into the outside where buildings were buildings and streets were streets and right was right and wrong was wrong. It was so uncomfortable inside. Just say goddamned yes, I wanted to blurt out. Just say, *hell yes, I will be with you starting now, this moment, now and forever*, quickly say *yes, yes, yes, yes... yes!* Instead, a mercurial mood overcame me, and I blurted out.

"I want to meet the priest. Tomorrow."

She looked at me.

"I said I want to meet this guy. I'm free at five, I'll meet you here at six."

"If that's what you want. But that's not really it, is it?" she said.

"Yeah, that's really it. Yeah."

I left. I don't remember anything about the day after that. I was consumed with her and her priest and her new creepy life. The next day, at 5:59 p.m. I knocked on her door. We walked in the first snow of the winter season. Large feathery flakes swept back and forth before us, dancing on the icy winds of late

December. It had been coming down for more than an hour and was beginning to stick. Buses and cars, black on the bottom from oily precipitation, chewed their way up and down 5th Avenue. We crossed over to Madison Avenue where few cars and fewer people made the city disappear behind abandoned buildings and sparse gravel lots. I covered my head with the hood of my jacket, covering also the color of my skin. Walking with Raphaella this far uptown, this deep into Harlem, with the snow and the desolation of abandonment all around, I was moved to hide who I was. We did not hold hands, though at this point in our relationship that was rare regardless of where we walked. A pinch of sulfur hung in the air, a product of salt trucks dumping their wares up and down the main avenues. We passed a hospital. Its windows gleamed with warmth, and I thought of white-hot stars blazing through the thick haze of a snowy cosmos. At 124th Street, we again saw signs of life. Little hooded men on each corner, their hands in their pockets, swayed slightly to sounds of rhythmic rap. One raggedy bodega challenged the rap with merengue beats. Two men moved their hips slightly, dancing with invisible partners, swigging on large bottles of bagged beer.

We continued uptown and reached 125th, the epicenter of Harlem. Yellow light from skinny streetlamps illuminated a lively world. Heavy pedestrian traffic and big black gypsy cabs cock sparred for space in the crowded crosswalks. They crept along on either side of the street, honking occasionally, trawling for cold and tired mothers on their way home from a full day's work. Sidewalk vendors hawked jackets and caps. A young man displayed a card table full of cassettes, a failing boom box blared Bob Marley. African merchants displayed leather belts and wood carvings. Sweet incense hung in the frosty air, and no one seemed to notice the snow. We headed east again, down 127th Street and the world left us. With each passing block, a hint of darkness returned. Streetlamps failed again. One blinked on and off, its broken rays splintering in every direction. An abandoned building with gaping, paneless windows stood frail before us. Like lightning, the streetlamp broke above and I imagined the face of a child peeking out at us. I saw a mother too, and together they held tight to each other, shivering in their decrepit home and searching the night for rest from the cold. Another burst of light and they were gone.

We crossed the street and arrived at the foot of a tall stoop. Raphaella pointed up at a thick black door with a gilded cross looming above. Next to the door was mounted a box of some kind. It held in its open face an oil lamp and a picture. A mother and a child kissed gently, he looking up and she, tenderly down. Raphaella began up the stoop, and for a moment I changed my mind. I wanted to leave and forget all of it—the fasting, the praying, the all-controlling change of direction. I wanted to let her go. I waffled and watched as she climbed, steadfast. Up she went, gingerly getting a foothold on the damp, snow-covered steps. She stopped at the top of the stoop and looked down to see if I was coming. Her bright eyes shone through the melee of winter, inviting me up. I cowered imperceptibly beneath the weight of my petulance, while all the while she kept her stare. Finally, I followed.

"Does he live alone here, Raphie?"

"Oh no, there are three other monks here with him."

We heard footsteps inside and I again felt the pang of regret trickle through me, pricking hard in my stomach and reminding me that this was all very, very odd, and too foreign. The door opened. A tall man, dressed entirely in black and wearing a long, thin beard greeted us.

"Is Father here?" asked Raphaella.

The man nodded and motioned us inside. Raphaella went first. Inside, we immediately mounted more steps and on the second floor we turned again to climb yet another flight. We trudged upward. I kept looking for other monks and nooks and crannies where I'd find little robed men bent over and bobbing up and down to some icy chant. We passed a candlelit room with many more of the paintings I had seen mounted outside. After another flight of stairs we reached a landing that opened into a big room filled with couches and chairs. I looked behind me for the man who let us in, but he was gone. We stood in the fourth floor foyer alone, waiting for something. Raphaella rang a little bell that hung over the door. Another man in black robes appeared. He too had a long beard and like the other, greeted us with a nod.

"Good evening, Raphaella. Father will be right out."

We sat down. The monk took our jackets and dissolved into a back room.

"What's next?" I asked.

"Father Seraphim," replied Raphaella.

I sat stiff, trying to remember why I had come. It was not easy as my mind kept focusing on little things, a tiny painting of a skinny man holding his own decapitated head, another of a malnourished woman and her companions, a skull and a lion. A skull and a lion, I thought. The Wizard of Oz? There was a dog's head carved into the back of a rugged dining chair, a pair of large black slippers, an 18th century candle lamp, complete with a large reflecting mirror for reading, and there was a black cane. I turned slowly, half-expecting to spy an iron maiden. On the other side of the room there was a television. Okay, good, I thought. Raphaella seemed more at ease than I was. She sat humbly, reverently even. She looked at me and made a face somewhere between a smile and a sneer.

It was the paintings that stuck with me. There were many of them. All were done without a three-dimensional perspective, and all of them seemed so simple. The bodies of the saints seemed misshapen; a head too big for a body here, hands too small to hold a cross there, or children painted as adults. An oil lamp dangled in front of many of them. If I had come here under different circumstances, alone or on a field trip for school, let's say, I would not have had such disquiet. It was Raphaella that unnerved me, really. She wasn't watching all of this as I was; she was beginning to belong to it. For this reason, all of it, the ancient paintings, the oil lamps, the big tattered books, the black robes and thick beards, the dim candlelight, the chant I did not hear, all of it became animated and filled with life, alive and working to capture her, the woman who was part of me, the woman whose flesh I'd had and in whose womb I had placed a life. She was slipping away, and I was, too. I needed a handle, something to hold. I tried to return to more tangible concepts, the ones that brought me here, the thought of her and me splitting apart, the thought of me hoping and trying, and of her drifting, and in which direction, and to whom? To him, of course, the priest, to this place and these ideas, all of this was stealing my woman from me and I would not let it happen. This thought, this new direction, was simple and in thinking it, I became calm. I had purpose.

A door opened, Raphaella stood up, and then so did I. A big man with a cane approached.

"Hello, Raphaella." He nodded and then looked at me, square. "And you're David, right?" He gestured with an open hand. "Sit down, please. Would you like something to drink? A cookie?"

I didn't think about the cookie while nodding. I was thinking about this guy's get-up. He was wearing a long black robe cinched at the waist by a thick black leather belt. The robe didn't have a hood like I'd seen other monks wear, but it was full-length and old-fashioned. He wore big black boots as if he were about to go out into the snow, and he wore a round black hat pulled down quite low on his head, almost covering his eyebrows. His hands were very large, I thought, and they were very strong and thick, while his eyes were kind and soft. And blue, bright blue, so blue. He didn't seem to be Slavic or Greek or smarmy in that Old World way, mostly because his eyes were like the sky. I wondered about this for a moment, but more than anything, sitting there, I thought about how long this guy's beard was, and how gray. Let's just say his beard could easily have gotten stuck in his thick black belt, maybe as he got dressed in the morning, bent over and cinched up. I'm sure he could have made a real mess of his morning, yanking on his beard, pulling his head and face almost off. That's what I thought of, I couldn't help it. What a beard!

The same monk who had earlier disappeared, now reappeared, this time with Oreo cookies. "Fasting food," the priest said, nodding to the cookies. We ate the cookies in silence.

"Oh, forgive me, David," said Raphaella. "This is Father Seraphim, the priest I told you about."

I nodded, and so did the priest.

"What a night last night," he said. "Two men from El Salvador just showed up at about two in the morning, dirty and tired. I still don't know how they found us. Father Silhouan thinks old Albert down the block told them we had a Spanish-speaking monk here, and that they thought we were Roman Catholics. Wait until they wake up and find out we're not Catholics, ha!" He said Catholics like *cat-liks*, laughing. And then within just a few seconds, he composed himself and spoke to me in a deep, clear, clipped baritone voice. "So why are you here, David?"

"Well," I said, "I wanted to know about fasting and why my little girl has to fast?"

"Dana?" he said.

"Yes, my daughter. Why does she have to skip meat, when she is growing?"

"Well, she doesn't. Nobody does." I shot a look at Raphaella. "Nobody has to fast, David. Nobody has to do anything, unless they want to. I mean, you didn't have to come here, but here you are."

"Sure, but she isn't eating meat because she thinks eating meat is bad. Her mother here thinks so too. I mean come on, how bad can it be?"

Father Seraphim had been sitting like my mother sits when she drinks coffee, legs crossed and to the side, back resting against the armrest of her big, comfortable favorite chair. Now he unfolded himself and leaned forward, his elbows on his knees, boots squared up in front of me. He was suddenly very masculine. I shot another look at Raphaella.

"It can be very bad, David. Sin is very bad, missing the mark is very bad because when we miss the mark we distance ourselves from God, and God is love, and so, we distance ourselves from love. From the thing that makes us like God."

Wow, I thought, and then I blurted out, "Come on, eating meat does that?"

There was a pause, and then he pointed at me. "Let's say that you played basketball for a living. You know, you were good at it. Let's say you had the season coming up and you needed to get ready for the year by getting in shape, and so you started your workout regime and cut back on certain foods and hit the weights. Then one day a buddy tells you about this great party with beer and girls and cake and pork rinds and I don't know, you imagine." He gesticulated with his big hands. "First of all, would you go to that party? Maybe. If you went would you hang around the pork rind table, the chocolate float table? Maybe, you might even eat at those tables, and it might taste really good, and you might be happy. But you wouldn't be a world-class basketball player, would you? You would be something else, especially if you didn't understand why you weren't supposed to eat from those tables. Some tables are just off limits. And so what? Everyone would understand because they'd know you are trying to be the best you can. Good, they'd say. They might even help you by giving you some other food, tasty food, but the kind that makes training easier for you, not harder. They might even help you."

The priest pointed at David again. "They might even help you to make the mark, to reach your goal, to be a star ball player. They might even do that, if they believed you had it in you."

He leaned back and crossed his legs. I just tried to process the whole thing, tried to relate it to my daughter. I mean, sure, the basic concept was clear, but why my daughter? She just wants to go to school, just wants to play with dolls already. Like a hawk, he watched me think.

Then he said, "If you believe that we are spirit first and flesh second, then the goals of the spirit must come first. Love, joy, sacrifice, but mostly love for God and others, these are the things of the spirit. But the flesh, well, you know your body. You know how it works. We like stuff, we like warm baths and ice cream every day, and sex. But these things must happen in conjunction with, no," he shook his head slightly, "in concert with, the spirit. If not, well, it's just all so frustrating and short-lived. You know?"

Yeah, I thought, I guess so. But I wasn't sure enough to nod my head or even acknowledge his words. Instead, I just sat there, inexplicably waiting for more.

"Dana doesn't have to fast. Eating meat is not a sin. Ever. But if you desire that she find truth and love, it may be that foregoing meat is a means to a very beautiful end. But she is not Orthodox, and she is not seven. At seven, the Church instructs its children to fast so that they may begin to train their body to obey their soul. Of course, if you don't sin, you don't have to fast. So don't sin, and there you go."

"But I don't even believe there is such a thing as sin," I said.

"Yeah, I figured that."

"You figured that?"

"Sure, it was the look on your face. You have a real dilemma on your hands, don't you? Here is this woman, this crazy woman that believes in sin and is also the mother of your child, and there you are, a father and a guy who doesn't believe in sin, and between the two of you nothing is working. Not even close."

I thought to myself that this guy was mean. He thinks he knows a lot about me, about us. I mean here he is just laying his opinions on me like he is right, and that is that. I looked around and all the old paintings, as quaint as they were only moments ago, became irritations and reminders of the irrational, the pre-enlightenment mumbo-jumbo about souls and spirits and voodoo and witches and iron maidens. There just had to be an iron maiden in this joint somewhere. I looked at the old priest and decided to dive in.

"But, this is just some belief that you have about spirits and souls. It's just a hope, isn't it?"

"No. It is the truth."

"But only as you know it."

"Well, how else would the truth be known?"

"Well, like scientifically. Provable." I looked at Raphaella and sensed that she was uneasy with the turn in the conversation.

"David. Why? Why did you come here?"

"I told you," I said.

"Fasting?"

"Yeah, and Dana and just the whole thing. I want to know what the heck happened to Raphaella."

The priest sat with his legs crossed and a big hand stroking his long beard. "Do you have a minute?" he asked.

Almost against my will I said, "Well, I have to go..." And then I stopped and sort of got stuck on what I wanted to say, and where I had to go. He just kept stroking his beard. "I have to go in a little while."

"So do I," he responded, leaning over and sipping his coffee. Swallowing, he started with, "How old are you?" I told him I was twenty-six. He nodded. "Were you in New York three years ago?"

"I, well, I was in California."

"Do you remember the story of the little boy from the Bronx? Ty Ty they called him." I shook my head and he looked at Raphaella. "What is with this Ty Ty by the way? Was it for Tyrone or something?"

"I think so," she said.

"Whatever it was, his name was Ty Ty, and Ty Ty was a crack baby, and his mother ran a crack house. Actually his mother ran a whole drug dealing operation, pretty much as big as it gets for a while there. She was good at what she did, but she had been a user during her pregnancy with the boy. So he had all kinds of neurological complications and all kinds of kidney issues. You could say he was sick, but some might say he was kind of crazy, a little bit wacko. He would wander all the time, and talk to himself, and bob, you know, like an autistic boy. But he was like a dove, too. Just as gentle as can be. I met him many times, used to see him when I'd walk up to visit an old Catholic friend of mine who ran a soup kitchen at St. Ann's. I'd see the boy walking and bobbing and holding a pack of baseball cards, always with his cards, flipping through them at top speed, saying each player's name as he went. He had a little clumpy Afro, matted half the time and he had this stare, this real simple, innocent stare that just went out of his little beaten body, and you weren't sure if he was looking at you or at something behind you or at something entirely not of this world. He'd take the same exact route each time he'd go wandering. Looking at people and buildings, birds, trash, just always staring and walking." The priest sipped his coffee.

"Anyway, he grew up in his mother's crack den basically, but he hated that place. His mother would beat him when he came back from his day trips, but that didn't stop him. He started wandering at night, too. He wasn't in school, and nobody paid any attention to what school he should attend. The closest thing he had to a parent was his grandmother on his mother's side. She would walk with him some days, give him new clothes when she could borrow a few dollars, and even read to him. She wasn't always around but she was very kind and tried to do what she could. She loved him. One day, I guess this would have been about two summers ago, maybe three, she took him to see the Yankees. Ty Ty bobbed all the way to the park and sat there bobbing in his seat and his Grandma didn't think he was understanding much of what was going on, but she didn't leave. She stayed to the end and he bobbed away, talking to himself with his baseball cards flying through his hands, and well, the Yankees won. Do you remember Don Mattingly?" he looked at me.

"First baseman?" I said.

"He hit the game winning home run that day. Apparently the Yankees weren't very good and that was a rare win for them. Is that right?" I nodded. "Well, Ty Ty came back after that game and kept up his wandering and everything seemed just the same as before, except that from time to time the little boy didn't come home at all, for the whole night, and even his mother began to worry. This continued for a while. Entire nights and days would pass and that little boy would not come home. I guess he was about seven now. When he'd get a beating, he would just cry silently, mend his wounds and continue with his wandering. Apparently his mother continued selling her drugs, though it appears she wasn't doing them so much now. She was getting rich, actually."

I nodded, but the story was long. "Then, in the fall, and I remember this as clear as day, I saw little Ty doing his thing on the sidewalk, and I stopped him and put my hand on his head and said 'Hello, son,' like I had done many times before. He looked at me, well around me, in his way, so sad and deep, and then he slipped out from under my hand and onto the stoop of an abandoned building. He scooted inside and I thought, this little crazy kid is living in this building! I followed him inside and what'ya know, I found an immaculate room, swept neat as new. It was a huge, empty room. On the floor was this perfect, I mean perfect, re-creation of Yankee stadium. It covered the floor. It *was* the room. An infield had been taped to the tiles, hundreds of long strips of masking tape lined up over and over again, in the shape of an infield. There was a pitcher's mound too, a home plate and a backstop, all just like Yankee Stadium. There was the light blue outfield wall made out of cereal boxes and constructed to the exact proportions of the real field. There were thousands of tiny little seats, thousands of them, placed in tiers just like the stadium, all of them fashioned individually out of thousands of gum wrappers, each glued down. There was the little museum out in left field, everything immaculately drawn or painted to scale. Even the scoreboard looked exactly as it is, or at least as I've seen it on television. I've never been, have you?" he asked, looking at me.

"Yeah," I said. "The wall is blue."

"Well, yes it is. I was just dumbfounded. There was all of this and then thousands of baseball cards, organized nicely in shoeboxes, team by team. He must have had all the players from all the teams. It's up there with the most manic things I've ever seen. And I've known some real manic people, trust me. I stood there astounded."

Raphaella, who I had nearly forgotten about, wondered aloud, "What did the boy do when he saw you there?"

"He just started playing."

"Playing what?" I asked.

"The game. Flick 'em. He started playing Flick 'em. That's what all the neighborhood boys called it."

"Flick 'em?"

"Yes, of course. He motioned me to my knees, him on one side of the field, the first base side, and me on the other." The priest got out of his chair and pulling up his cassock, got down on all fours. "Like this," he said, "he handed me a card, a pitcher I guess, and showed me how to flick this little tin ball that he had. You flicked it with the card of your player, and in my case I was supposed to flick the ball at his card, the batter, standing at home plate. So I did and guess what, he cracked that little ball, and it flew out and over his perfect model of Yankee Stadium." Still on his knees he pointed out across the room, like Babe Ruth before his famous home run call. "That little tin ball flew over the wall and landed in the seats of center field. It was brilliant. He was a genius. And best of all, after some more of this, I noticed that he was keeping score, or something like that, in a book. I paged through his book and he had hundreds of scorecards, like old men keep when they watch or listen to the games on the radio. Hundreds!"

The priest got off of his knees and hardily made his way back into his seat. "He was the commissioner basically, I mean he had a league of Flick 'em, and he played with all of the neighborhood kids, every one of them knew about this spot.

It was Ty Ty's spot. He had been coming here for so long, creating this game, this world. And his favorite card was Don Mattingly. He kept it in his pocket at all times. He was a crazy kid, but not so crazy really. Not so crazy at all. I left him when some other boys came over and wondered why a man in a black gown was hanging around ruining their Flick 'em games."

"How did you know it was called Flick 'em?" I said.

"That is what the *Daily News* writer called it when he did a story on the little boy. They called him the Yankee Dandy and he became quite a little celebrity in this town. He met with Mayor Koch and got himself into a good school and he even had someone buy the rights to his Flick 'em game. But then the darndest thing happened. Ty Ty got beat up one day real bad. Some thugs thought he had money after all the fuss in the papers. They beat him pretty bad with some rebar. He got tetanus from that rebar, but his mother didn't know because she never managed to leave the crack den and he, well, he died. He died all alone. Sure the city came out for him, and he was back in the papers as a little hero and a sad case of how the system fails kids and all of that. His mother was demonized. She was run out of town and sent to prison, but what people didn't know is that after his death and before her trial, she had already begun to change. Something took hold of her after this little boy's death, something that made her want him back. Grief, sure. Guilt, sorrow. But I think she also saw something else. I think she saw the love that so many of these very normal neighbor boys had for her son. They loved him, went to his funeral, even cheered at his funeral when Don Mattingly showed up and gave a wonderful speech. These were little lives and they were touched by her son, and I think she saw in them the thing she had missed while her son was alive." He sat forward on the edge of his big chair. "She wanted that. She wanted that thing that he had, that he had given."

He got up and walked into the kitchen. I wondered where he had gone. From out of sight, he yelled, "Cookies?"

"No, thank you," said Raphaella.

"I'm fine," I said. He came back into the room with a tin of cookies.

"Russian," he said. "Great cookies, but don't eat too many, the Russians don't know how to moderate their food, or their passions for that matter." He popped one in his mouth. "So sweet."

Was the story over? I thought. I watched as Raphaella gave in and plucked a cookie out of the tin. It looked good, light and crunchy, but I held back. "So, what about the story. Is that it?" I asked.

"Well, not really. She gave all of the money she had, and she had a bunch from his sale of the Flick 'em game, to build baseball lots in the neighborhood where Ty Ty had become a fixture. And they were all mini Yankee Stadiums."

"That's what those are?" I said, knowingly.

"Yep. You've seen them then?"

"Yeah, when I go up to see Raphie. Sure. Those are because of this kid? They're nice."

"Yes, they are nice," he said.

He got up and slipped on a black wool coat, long and simple, and heavy. "So, now *I've* got to go." He buttoned his coat carefully and fetched one last cookie. As he prepared to leave, Raphaella got up and went to him with her hands together, palms up. Crouching ever so slightly, she extended her hands as if begging. The priest made a crossing motion and placed his hand in hers. She kissed it.

He turned and looked at me. "Nice meeting you, David. Please come back and see us again, maybe go out with the monks to feed the homeless, or come to a vespers if you'd like." He looked down at me, and I realized I was still sitting. "You can stay if you'd like. No problem."

I hopped up and retrieved my jacket, sort of shaking off the fog of his story, and his crossing, and her kissing. "No, that's fine, thanks anyway," I said. I looked at Raphaella and she smiled, sheepishly. He buttoned the top buttons of his coat as he descended the three flights of stairs. We stood above, in silence, half-listening to the tap-pop of his boots on the stairs below.

When all was quiet, I turned to Raphaella and said, "Flick 'em?"

She nodded.

"But don't you think he sort of, I don't know, skipped a few things. Maybe sort of swerved a bit, off the track." I straightened my arm and pointed with a flourish. "Like frickin' Stanley and Livingstone off the track?"

She was staid. "Maybe," she said. "Maybe."

On the way back, neither Raphie nor I spoke much. The only thing I could get myself to say was, "Nice place." Whenever I went to question the whole story and its relevance I was met with resistance, a sort of gust of dread. Outside, the snow had stopped and the night had grown clear and cold. The moon was so bright, and

Harlem gleamed beneath it. A man with a long, shabby beard sat all alone next to a heap of cans. His swollen hands gripped a cup of hot coffee and his eyes glared out at us. There was something fearful in his look. Raphaella nodded to him and we walked on until reaching the stoop of her apartment. I forlornly looked up at the door, doing what I'd done so many times since my return from California, begging inaudibly to come up, and in, for the night. But this time, in the midst of my performance, I stopped. I couldn't keep my stare, I couldn't keep the syrupy, shallow strokes of my lashes in tow. I turned my head.

"Good night, Raphaella. I'll call you about Dana's next visit. Tell her I love her." She extended her hand. I shook it and left.

CHAPTER XV

The Garage Sale

Raphaella began to lose her sense of humor, at least that's the way I saw it. She no longer was able to command a room and instead sank back into the corners, content to watch and listen and rarely talk. She was not a brooding figure; one never felt threatened by her silence, unless, like me, you knew her before her baptism. If not, you'd think she was just a quiet, kind woman. But I knew more of course. I knew her when she used to make love to me in the car as we drove, curse at cabbies, drink and gossip. I remembered Raphaella Hurston, but this was someone else. This woman prayed daily, three times daily, and always before meals. She told me that she had started praying many years before but always fell out of habit and that now, finally, she had maintained the habit. I asked her how she prayed, but she politely refused to show me, saying it would be odd.

One night, however, I found her praying in her room. She crossed herself and bowed, and I realized she didn't know I was watching. She went prostrate from her knees, reciting words that had something to do with attaining a clean heart. She did this three times and then she began to chant, aloud. The chanting was monotone, and she repeated the same words again and again, something about Jesus Christ and having mercy. With each little prayer, she moved her thumb over a knot on a long rope, a wool rope that I'd seen before. She did this for what seemed like more than ten minutes, interspersing her repeated prayer with prayers for people. She faced a corner, the eastern corner of her room, where on the wall a myriad of at least twenty paintings hung side by side, creating a colorful collage of icons. These old paintings, some of them prints, had sort of multiplied as I'd never seen them there in such numbers. Standing there like a voyeur, I remember thinking how she had plenty of room for more, because, well, she'd given away just about everything she owned.

Her things went with the winter. She had a rummage sale the first day of spring, downstairs in the little lot where the neighborhood green thumbs kept their gardens. They were happy to accommodate her and even felt honor-bound after she hoed their hardened garden plots one winter day. So, with their help, Raphaella undid in one day what it took me two years to do. She unfurnished like a banshee. She sold her television, two couches, one bookshelf, two stout end-tables, her bed, her portable stereo, three boxes of books, a recliner (the one she had so often called her *love chair*), a giant box of record albums, a beautiful burnt-brown ottoman, a baby stool, a perfectly puffy red bean bag chair, a giant pile of perfectly good clothes, a box of beautiful jewelry, the sketch of the Brooklyn Bridge (one of my favorites because we watched the guy do it, and plus the frame was very nice), and finally the painting of the pear.

She did all of this in one spring day, a day that just about killed me. See, I could not deal with the immoderacy of it all. I couldn't stand to see my gifts piled along the street with her garbage. But not all of it was garbage, not at all. Most of it was great stuff, gobbled up as though it was the buy of the damn century. And it was. Raphie's prices were ridiculous. Nothing, not even the bed, was priced higher than fifteen dollars. People were laughing that sucker-laugh all day, and I spent most of the day assuring neighbors and acquaintances that the price was not mismarked. "No, that's right," I'd say. "The stereo is really eight dollars." And, "Yes, it does work, really." All day was like this, and more than once I asked myself the question, why was I there? Why had I said I'd help, in fact, volunteered to help?

At the time, I think I did it as part of my contract to Dana and to show I was committed to Raphaella and the new life she had chosen. I helped, even as I argued that this whole event would hurt our daughter. I said that her asceticism demonstrated a lack of care, and an irresponsible attitude toward possessions. I argued that she would make Dana bitter, especially when Dana started to see the relative wealth of her friends. I was sure Dana would become even more materialistic because she lacked material wealth. My arguments made good logical sense, oh yeah, but she sold on. I handled her craziness, at least until she wheeled out my four-month-old Christmas present, a microwave oven. Apparently someone had asked if there was one for sale.

"Sir," I said as he reached into his pocket for a few, paltry dollars, "that's not for sale."

"Really?" he gesticulated. "But the young woman say she got a microwave for me. What's a matter, is it broke?"

"No," I spoke in a monotone shout, "it is not broken, it's just not for sale."

"He's right, James," said Raphaella, "I brought it down so you could have it. I'm not asking anything for it. I'd like you to take it. We don't have the space for it anymore, so here you are."

Space? I thought. Space? That's all you've got up there is space. No. I don't think so! Not this time, not the microwave, no way. And so right there, in front of the neighbors and the vaunted microwave, I made my stand. "Sir, please put the microwave down. I can't allow you to take the microwave." He looked at me and then at her. "Please sir, put the microwave down."

"David—"

"No, Raphaella," I interrupted, "don't even try it. This microwave is not going anywhere. Sir, put the microwave down and back away. Do it now. Please. Pick something else, I'm sure the prices will agree with you. In fact, forget prices, take something else, anything, just not the microwave." He put it down. "Thank you," I said.

When he left, I was alone with Raphaella, and I expected recriminations, a yelling spell complete with a good slap. She had never allowed me to thwart her in public, especially not in front of a neighbor. She looked at me, and I saw a flash of the old soul and then a tidal wave of the new. It swept over her and into her and out of her eyes. Those emerald orbs closed in a slow blink and she sighed.

"I'm sorry. It was the wrong time for that, forgive me." She took the microwave in her arms and nearly tripped on the curb. "David, could you help me?" I did. Together we walked the microwave up the stairs and put it back in the empty apartment. It sat cockeyed in the tidiness of the kitchen's far corner. The day ended with more giveaways and more angst, but there was no angst for Raphaella. She and Dana merrily returned to their empty apartment and counted their money. Three-hundred dollars and twenty-one cents, more than Raphaella had hoped. I watched as Dana put on a pair of sweatpants and a sweatshirt, and then put her hand in mine.

"Daddy, now we have lots of money for McDonald's. I'm hungry, let's go."

"Okay, sweetheart." I turned to her mother. "What will you do with the money?"

"Do you need some?" she asked.

"No."

"If you do, let me know. Otherwise there's a man I know from the monastery who needs two hundred seventy bucks to buy a plane ticket. He wants to go see his father. They've never met."

"You'll give it to him?"

"Should I?" she asked. All I could manage was to watch my feet and they did not move. Big... mute... feet, I thought. "Are you sure you don't need any money, David?"

I grabbed Dana's hand. "Come on Dana, let's go get that burger. We'll be back soon." We left her and the microwave and went down the stairs. "I'm getting a double something honey, maybe a double Big Mac," I said.

"They don't make that do they?" Dana asked.

"Today they will, for us both." I smiled and squeezed her hand. Looking down, however, I was submarined by the feeling that she would have to order some nasty meatless meal, maybe just dine on the fries and skip the shake. Was it a fast day? Oh, brother.

"Dana," I said, gently. "Can you eat a burger today?"

"A burger? Sure, why not?"

"Are you fasting?"

"Oh no, Daddy, not this week. This is a bright week, Mommy says we don't fast at all this week. It's bright like a feasty table."

Bright like a feasty table.

"We can eat burgers today, Daddy. You, too."

"Good," I said. "Let's celebrate."

***

"Did you see how she was changing?" I ask. "Did you notice how odd she was becoming?"

"I did," responds Mitkin. He scratches the tip of his long, straight nose. "I liked it."

"But you said you wanted to hurt her when she rejected you."

"But that was me, not her. It was me who had the problem because all I could see was myself. If I really loved her, I would have loved even her rejection of me, because—" He drops his chin. "Because she wanted to know something deeper than conjugal love for man."

I knew that, I say to myself. I recognized that. I could see then that she didn't want sex, that was clear, but I also knew she was searching for something, and I even told her I'd like to search with her. Didn't I? Didn't I tell her that? "Did she ever tell you about us?"

"No, not really," he replies. "Well, actually, that's not true. Early on she used to tell me about you. She griped usually. Most of her gripes were typical: 'We don't get along,' or 'He's too pushy,' but she loved you." I start to ask more and he interrupts. "But that was not how things ended. By the time I went to work with Taughtauer, she had stopped telling me about you. All she ever spoke about was me, all she ever asked about was my wellbeing, or she'd just be very quiet, watchful."

"She was in love with you after all?" I say, leaning closer.

"No, not like that. She was in me, she minded me more than herself. It is hard to explain. She was meticulous about me. She was always aware that words made a difference, and she minded her words. They were tender, the same way she dealt with me."

"You mean about school?"

"Yes, about school and Taughtauer and the movement." And then he starts a long narrative. As he speaks he winds a black beaded rope through his fingers, back and forth. He keeps vigil with his eyes too, rarely do they wander, rarely does he look away from his hand and the beads. When he does, it is to look at me, and there I see diffidence, a look that I associate with a broken, contrite heart.

CHAPTER XVI

A Believer

In May, Taughtauer was fired. He was asked to leave when it was alleged he'd had an inappropriate relationship with one of his students. He had. He was proud of it. Mitkin learned of the firing from one of Taughtauer's revolutionaries. They were alone in the hall and it was late in the day, the end of the last period of the day, when most kids at the large, vacuous school had already gone home. Teachers often requested ninth period because they appreciated the smaller numbers. Taughtauer was one of these teachers, though he had more profound reasons for staying; he used the end of the day to indoctrinate. Ninth period was when he kneaded his students and baked them, quietly, systematically fashioning each one. He looked for kids with courage, savvy, intelligence, vision, resolve and the ability to hate. Edwin Elrod passed every one of Taughtauer's tests, a confident kid whose large frame made him intimidating. He was angry like his teacher, and best of all, Edwin Elrod was disinvested, a kid who never bought the dream of capitalism because he'd simply been too poor. He was a perfect disciple and now his hulking frame was standing in front of Mitchell Mitkin.

"Edwin, I thought you loved Taughtauer's class, why are you cutting?" Mitkin looked up into Edwin's eyes.

"He's gone," he said, before resuming his stride down the long empty hall.

"He's absent today?" asked Mitkin, pausing and then walking briskly to catch up. "Out sick?"

Edwin stopped. "He's fired, cut loose, slashed, as in not coming back. Don't act like you didn't know yo, every old-body in this place knows because everybody wanted him out."

"I didn't—"

Edwin interrupted, "You didn't do shit to keep him here. You just went about your business like every other teacher, just earning a paycheck. That's why he's gone. He cared." On the big youth's face was a mix of wrath and confusion.

"I didn't know," muttered Mitkin.

"No shit, that's just it." Edwin turned a corner and was gone. He cut the corner deftly, his body taut with rage. Mitkin followed but did not keep up. He retraced his steps and went into Taughtauer's classroom, clumsily.

A meeting of about thirty kids, nearly twenty more than usual, crowded the middle of the room. One boy, a thin light-skinned Latino seemed to lead. Near the front of the room, far away from the students sat an elderly woman hunched behind *The New York Times*. It was Ms. Schneider. She was always around, filling various posts vacated by absent teachers, an expert substitute because she knew exactly what it took to get through a harrowing day of disrespect. Besides using her newspaper as a shield, she'd memorized the security codes and knew exactly how long it took the guards to respond to "011" or assault in progress. "Six minutes in the morning," she'd coach, "and nine minutes in the afternoon. Six and nine," she'd tell anyone who'd listen, "six and nine." The security officers were big, young men renowned for their afternoon siestas. Mitkin always thought how the guards were just uniformed versions of his most rowdy students, dropouts with a job. But they loved old Ms. Schneider.

Ms. Schneider was not thinking about calling security at this point, no, she seemed content to read her paper and count the minutes which for her moved interminably slow. But not for them. For the students in the heart of the classroom, the minutes moved by like a blitzkrieg. This urgency, of course, resulted from the removal of their mentor and chief. These kids were Taughtauer's core, the elite soldiers of the movement. They were the ones who gave more than their time. They believed everything Taughtauer said and, more importantly, were able to imbibe Taughtauer's moods, his rancor, and his slicing cynicism. They were exceptionally bright and willing to give up what they considered largely pilfered lives.

Taughtauer had created in them a reason to come to school and a reason to leave school, and they had become obsessed. Now that Taughtauer was gone, they were reeling, and in an imperceptible, primeval way, Mitkin saw their faces as his own, because they, like him, were alone. They had embarked and then suddenly found themselves in a rudderless ship. He identified with these lost souls, and next to the foundering image of his despotic boss, the evil administrator, Mitkin's love for these victims grew. He wanted to help, truly help, for the first time since taking the job as a teacher. Empathy washed over him and in the melee of his mind the specter of Taughtauer and the "Taughtauer Rebellion" softened. The man appeared less sinister, and his cause seemed lofty beside the gallant faces of young, devoted souls. Their search for meaning in a meaningless world translated well in the battered spirit of Mitchell Mitkin, and it took seeing the pain of others to know his own, and so, in what he would later call his "most mystical moment," an idea settled in Mitkin's mind. That idea made it possible to see Taughtauer as more than a mischievous malcontent. He was a hero more than anything else. He was the real educator. Mitkin began to understand that everything he and his famous father strove for was meaningless unless accompanied by the real forceful devotion of a rebel. "Rebels," thought Mitkin. "We need them."

He was wrong to dismiss Taughtauer so easily, and Taughtauer was right to come on so forcefully. Strength, a will to accomplish and to achieve in the world, these were appealing themes. They were also concrete. They were not the quiet musings of Raphaella who seemed to mulch the plain and simple into an indigestible existentialism. "This is why she rejects me," thought Mitkin. "She can't stand the particular. This is the whole crux. I have been brought to a place, have been privy to a death, have been given a mind for a purpose, on this earth, here, in the flesh. I am called to be somebody now, not there, in an ivory tower, but here and now." Thoughts whipped through his mind. "In fact, that is ridiculous. Heaven is here, where you make it. Raphaella's entire pursuit is something less." Rousseau welled up in him. "If we made it bad then we, as the authors of our own destiny, can make it good. These children need us to make it good, to help them."

While looking at the students, something peculiar happened to Mitkin. On the far fringes of the room, Mitkin saw and felt a chill. He saw frost on the walls in the form of art and graphs and charts and the intellectual accomplishments of Taughtauer's students. He felt a cold witchy wind in the heart of the old woman who seemed incapable of relation, the unoccupied desks scattered about the room grew icy and inert, and the tall cabinets near the back, the ones with big, clumsy, silver handles struck him as upright coffins, repositories for the dead. Everything outside the circle of humanity grew cold and hollow next to the warm, rushing, living waters of love and life. Within the students was the hallowed good of which the great writers, the ones Mitkin now loved, Rousseau, Thoreau, and James, spoke. Rapture materialized right there. Goodness became flesh in front of him and he was overwhelmed.

Mitkin could not contain his tears as he watched the stoic leader pass around a piece of paper that each and every child solemnly signed. Then each student took notes diligently, more diligently than Mitkin had ever seen them work. From one pair of hands to another, the paper made its way around and as it did, the little leader, thrust into his role, made rounds. He talked with smaller groups of students, five by five, systematically pointing and nodding and descriptively moving his hands back and forth, pushing gently on a shoulder, pounding a hand coolly. Mitkin overheard him talking to one group. "You can't bullshit yourself, if you signed then you believe. Think about the future. You ain't got nothing if you ain't got your pride. Be proud. Get your groove on." His voice trailed off as he again gave a fist pound to a fellow comrade. Then he saw Mitkin. Through his tears and in his mind, Mitkin had forged an alliance with the students. Suddenly he loved them. He wanted them to know about all the things that had shifted and shaken in his heart over the last six months, in the last six seconds! He felt an intense desire to tell them all of his faults and let them know that he was just a simple fool who had believed the world a simple place. He wanted to join them and their innocence and live renewed, even if it meant corporeal danger and incarceration. But now, with the leader staring him down, the reality of relationship and human misperception stung hard. "Yo, what you looking at?" Mitkin wiped a tear.

"He's Mitkin," said a young girl. "He's a science teacher."

"I came to see Taughtauer," said Mitkin.

The elderly substitute put her paper down. Naked and unprotected, she glanced at Mitkin and then at the students. "That man's been released. Is there a problem, sir?"

"No, no, everything's fine." Mitkin looked at the students, who had not stopped staring. "Everything is just fine." He nodded resolutely to the leader, but the young man did not nod back. He just continued his stare. Mitkin nodded again, very deliberately and painfully, trying to build a bond. Nothing. He smiled and then left. On a mission, Mitkin went immediately to the assistant principal's office and took a seat.

Richard Borly was the assistant principal. He was a portly man who wore a mustache in the style of the old Tammany bosses. His fat mustache and haughty speech earned him the nickname "Lip." He was all monologue, no dialogue, ever. He was the kind of person everyone knows but no one ever knows himself to be. On more than one occasion, Mitkin had been forced to stand and listen to Lip, lots of loose and flailing lip about the state of education in America. He was the caricature of a bad administrator, a man who knew students as numbers and teachers as salaries. He loved to twist and turn figures, grope them, make loveless love to them until all of his vaunted programs were paid for. Most of the programs in Borly's budgets were pork barrel favors given to loyal teachers and "valued" stewards. His programs were like him—detached and most of the time just vehicles for teacher overtime. He ran the school's scheduling, he hired teachers, he supervised department chairs and he was the one who fired Taughtauer. Outside of his office, Mitkin tapped a toe determined to wait as long as it took to see Borly.

The long, shrill wail of the day's final bell sent whatever students were left into the hallways, and a din of chatter went up all about, some of it seeping into Borly's little waiting room where Mitkiń sat. Peering into the hallway Mitkin saw two of Taughtauer's faithful students waiting outside. Mitkin checked Borly's door, then peeked into the hall, and then back at Borly's door. Outside, more of Taughtauer's loyal foot soldiers gathered. Had they come to confront Borly? Had they come after him? Surely they didn't plan to raise hell about Taughtauer, not if they wanted to remain underground about the movement. More students, nearly twenty now, gathered in front of the office and Mitkin felt a fine trickle of sweat crawl through the hairs under his arm. It made its way down and out of the pit, creeping slowly by his flank where it ran into his already soiled shirt.

Mitkin looked down at himself. Gradually, over the previous six months, his personal appearance had changed. He no longer anticipated the day by laying out a clean outfit, and no longer attempted to match colors or press his shirts. He stopped wearing a tie and never considered wearing a dress jacket. Jeans and T-shirts and white socks and old sneakers were his choice now. And Mitkin's hair had grown, too. Before his father's death he wore it short, closely trimmed and brushed to the side. Into it, he would hand-comb some mousse. Now it grew long and wiry, and on most days, it was greasy. He grew a beard as well, though the cheek hairs could not keep up with the chin hairs. In fact, he grew a goatee, a sad, shaggy goatee. But this was good, all good, he thought, as he associated his rhapsodic empathy for the students with his new, simple, natural, even ignorant look. "I like myself this way," he thought. Slowly his consciousness hoisted itself out and above his body. There he saw himself slouched timidly in the chair, waiting with fear for the small-minded Borly. He didn't like it. He straightened his back and pulled his shoulders even. His ego was renewed sitting there. Right there he became a born-again rebel.

Mr. Borly's door opened and out scurried a little mousy woman who exchanged comments with herself. "Gotta write the first by ten, and then the second by… oh, and also the trip forms." She looked up at Mitkin. "What, no, Mr. Borly's busy. You must make an appointment." Mitkin watched her walk safely out of the room. The door remained open just a crack. He looked into the hall and then took two big steps toward Borly's door. He entered without knocking.

Borly's office was a mess. From floor to ceiling he had piled various binders and files which overflowed and stuck out in every direction. Every windowsill was packed crooked with papers and coffee cups and paperweights. In the far corner of the room, a wooden Indian held cigars in an outstretched palm. The old mannequin had become a makeshift coat rack, a storage bin for golfing hats, fishing hats and winter coats. A spring slicker dangled from his wooden feathers. Then there was Borly himself, stuffed behind his desk, rattling on over the phone but staring askance at Mitkin. He did not point for Mitkin to sit down or nod a chin to acknowledge his presence. He just stared out of the corner of his eye. Mitkin tried to stare back but the large sea lion mustache distracted him. It bumped up and down as Borly spoke, and in it was caught bits of a cream cheesed-bagel. It was too much to look at. Mitkin stole a glance out the door and saw the slight kid, the leader from the movement, standing in the half-opened doorway watching Mitkin, not unlike Mitkin had done upstairs only minutes before. His arms were crossed, legs spread slightly. His lips were drawn across his face but he wasn't smiling. He was studying Mitkin and Mitkin knew why; the boy was afraid. He believed Mitkin had come to destroy the movement. That was it. It had to be. Why would he have followed him here? Mitkin's mind rushed while the two sets of eyes gripped him from either side of the door. Borly talked on, and the little leader stared on.

"Mr. Borly, I've come to talk to you about Mr. Taughtauer, please hang up the phone." He was loud and direct. The frail secretary could be heard fumbling at her desk. The next moment, she was in the doorway.

"Mr. Borly can't talk to you right now sir, please step outside and wait."

"He will talk with me now. Mr. Borly, hang up the phone." Mitkin wagged a look at the leader. "Borly, hang up the phone," he cried loudly.

Borly covered the receiver and growled, "What is it, Mr. Mitkin? Can't you see I'm busy? Helen, get him out of here please." She mumbled a bit about being too frail and how she might fall, then Mitkin heard her call for the guards.

"You should have never fired Taughtauer, Borly. These kids trusted him. It was wrong and I will not abide it."

"You won't abide it? Are you nuts? You're a first-year teacher who, frankly, is a joke. You're a mess, Mitkin. Now please, see yourself out."

"I won't let it happen, Borly," Mitkin said. He stood still, speaking without hand gestures, a paragon of confidence. "You work for these kids." Then with a jerk, he pointed out the door, toward the leader. "They are your job. Put the phone down, Mr. Borly."

Borly slammed the phone down and fumbled to get up, his face turning red. "You're babbling like an idiot, Mitkin." Mitkin did not move. "I'm calling security myself."

Mitkin had crossed over now, gone to a place where nothing Borly said or did mattered. He could have bullwhipped Mitkin, clapped him in the stocks, burned him at the stake. Mitkin would have suffered it all. "Call security," he said calmly. "Go ahead, Mr. Borly, do what you need to do."

Borly spoke under his breath as he dialed, "And your father was such a good man."

"What did you say about my father, Borly?"

"I said he was such a good man."

Mitkin moved to within an arm's length of Borly and then, grabbing his tie, pulled himself to within an inch of Borly's nose, unbelievably. Borly tried to slap Mitkin's hand away but failed. He ended up off balance and wide-eyed as Mitkin spoke.

"My father was like you, Mr. Borly, a good liar. The only difference is that he believed his lies." He let go of Borly's tie only to condescendingly cup his face, like a father grabs the face of his little boy. "Good bye and good luck to you Mr. Borly." Then from over his shoulder he screamed as he left, "You're gonna need it!"

There was a crush of bodies in the hallway as Mitkin was escorted out of the school by three security guards. At least fifteen of Taughtauer's students followed Mitkin, watching. They had all gathered outside of Borly's office and had seen it all. Walkie-talkies buzzed on and off as school guards called for other school guards, and as the crowd grew, Mitkin soaked it up. He watched kids growing excited as an exceptional mix of chaos and hope charged the room. The word *riot* was on everyone's lips. Two students applauded him loudly, "You are the man,

Mitkin! Don't let them mess with you, Mitkin! You did right, stay strong, yo!" The young chief of Taughtauer's movement followed at a distance, watching surreptitiously.

Mitkin had changed. He was gaining courage and confidence because for the first time since his father's death, he had stood up and been counted as a believer. Their love gave him courage. They were alive, buoyant, fervent, and strong. They looked at him as they had looked at Taughtauer their mentor, and Mitkin was swept up in the romance. He smiled broadly and even shouted out, uncontrollably. "You count for something, you are good, good, good, good!" He yelled over his shoulder toward the leader, "I'm with you!"

One security guard hollered at Mitkin, "Cut the drama already, asshole. Get off campus now."

Mitkin lurched back. "Life is all drama, don't let the dead fool you!" The guard just shoved Mitkin forward, squeezing him and his crowd through the front door before leaving them curtly on the curb. The students mobbed him in an unforgettable show of elation.

"Are you fired, Mitkin?"

"Did you smack Borly down?"

"Is Taughtauer back, yo?"

Through the din he heard the silky voice of the young chief. "Do you believe what you said in there, Mitkin?"

Mitkin seized the young man and held him by the shoulders. "Yes."

"Will you fight?"

Mitkin looked around. Most of the hangers-on had begun to leave, already bored by the inrushing reality that nobody had thrown a punch. Only a small group remained, a group of Taughtauer's toughest disciples. They listened closely. Mitkin looked at them all and said, "Don't you get it? I was trying to tell you before, before Borly, upstairs, in the classroom. Yes, I will fight. Just tell me what to do."

The young man did not flinch, and a moment passed between the two. Then, as if satisfied he said, "Taughtauer will call you." He turned and left and most everyone left with him. Only a young girl remained. Her name was Jasmine, one of Mitkin's students, the one who had confessed about her father. "I like you, Mr. Mitkin. More kids than you think like you, too, they do. Keep fighting, kids you don't even see are listening. They are out there."

Jasmine left and Mitkin was alone in front of the school. An old fallen billboard faced him. The billboard had once trumpeted the opening of South Bronx High School of Science. It was hand painted. On one half of the mural a green-pocked globe stood surrounded by smiling teens of all colors. They held hands and seemed to skip in a circle around the world. Their clothes were multicolored, a beautiful kaleidoscope of the dissimilar in harmony. Above the dancing teens a caption read: WHEN WE DO. On the other half of the mural a gray hue served as background for nefarious behavior. There were three scenes. In the first a boy with a gun stood over a bleeding man. The second featured a deathly thin woman huddled into a corner and smoking a crack pipe. The third was of a thinly surfaced hillside cemetery replete with wiry, winter, windblown trees and icy gravestones. Over these portraits was the caption: WHEN WE DON'T. The whole rectangular billboard sat precariously on its end-corner, a decrepit reminder of an optimistic past. Mitkin studied it. For the first time in his life he had taken bold action, and he was drunk with it. He had never felt such bodily courage. Everything had always been hypothetical, but now theory meant nothing. He was an unemployed teacher, but in truth, he wasn't that at all. He was now a man of intent, a wondrous, powerful animation, a creature pledged to support fierce students who wanted to violently overthrow their school system. Just like that he had recovered himself and he thought of Raphaella. "Where she prays, I take action, and in our actions is her salvation." The irony was powerful and he loved the deep swath of emotion the whole scene had carved in his soul. The word *soul* now became a possibility for him, it entered his vocabulary and it became a description of what he was. He was a soulful scientist now, a spirit using different tools with which to measure the world. This time it was his passion that measured the movements, demonstrated the depths, and it was through his soul that he saw. Raphaella was right. There was more. There was action and the will to do what was right, and right was right there, simplified for all to see, painted by children but indelible on the hearts of men. He headed for home.

***

"And so now you were unemployed?" I ask.

"I didn't care that I was unemployed. There was something I wanted at that point. It was like a sudden addiction. I wanted to do things, to take action all over the place. I was insatiably active." Mitkin rolls to the other side of his seat. He crosses his legs. "I had a sort of rebirth, but it was incomplete."

"Why incomplete?" I ask.

"Because, it... it was all for me." He trails off with his answer and doesn't convince me that he is convinced. "I mean the whole thing, every move, every flier, every speech, the whole thing, it wasn't for them. It was for me." He finishes with his head down. I wait.

"And that was bad?" I ask.

"I think it was now." He looks up. "Now, yes, I think it was."

"Did anyone notice your new self?" I press him.

"I don't know. What about you, David, did you notice?"

I think about it, and I wonder why he asks me. "I can't say I did. I think I just wrote you off. I always thought you were a little, well, you know, odd. If you became more eccentric, I guess it just made sense to me." My pen nibbles at my notepad, I doodle a fountain of lines coming from a box, or going in perhaps. Mitkin waits for a more direct answer. There is silence. He stares at me waiting. "I guess I didn't notice, really. I missed it, Mitkin."

"Taughtauer didn't. He saw everything. He knew I was confused. He knew I was of use to him if I felt important. And I did, David, I really did."

"Did you ever think for a moment that it was a bad idea, back then, while it was happening?"

"No. I was utterly convinced of my mission. I was all sentiment, and I saw that as good. Have you ever read Rousseau, David?" He folds his arms on his chest like a farmer.

"No. Not Rousseau."

"Well, read his words sometime. You'll understand better. He had me convinced that I could engineer the world from the outside in, you know change who I was by changing how I live, how society is. See, we've all got a little Jean-Jacques in us now; we all believe we are the authors of our own lives. I believed it."

I look at him for a moment, his sandy blond hair neat on his head, his muscular arms bulging a bit, folded on his chest. I can see he is not finished with this thought, and neither am I. I wonder how anyone could believe we are anything but the author of our own lives. "I think I believed it too," I say. "Still do maybe."

"Well, don't." He squeezes an irritated grin through pursed lips. "We believe first, and create accordingly. But I am full of it really, I can't explain it, don't listen to me." He turns away. I see his profile clearly. He is a handsome man, clean shaven and nothing like the man I remember, at least not that maniacal man who came into my life and changed it forever.

CHAPTER XVII

World of Darkness

The phone rang. Mitkin, alone in his apartment, picked it up. The line went dead. It rang again immediately. Mitkin let it ring this time. Again and again, it rang echoing through Mitkin's apartment. He picked it up one more time.

"Hello."

Silence.

"Hello, who is this?" said Mitkin.

"You did it."

"Who is this?"

Again silence, and then Mitkin heard lips part on the other end of the phone. "Yep, yep, you did it."

"Taughtauer?"

"The kids told me you acted like a real rebel, a real piece of work. They told me they believed in you. But what I want to know is, do you believe in you?"

Mitkin screwed up his eyes and looked around the room. "I just did what was right. I was overcome with, Taughtauer, this *is* you right?" Mitkin was hesitant because this voice was sweeter and more melodious than Taughtauer's.

"Go to the zoo," said the voice. "I'll meet you there in two hours. Meet by the bats. Don't be late. Noon. No later."

"I won't go unless you tell me who you are."

"You know who I am." The phone clicked dead.

Mitkin looked into the receiver and mused. "You know who I am?" He searched his memory, "Yep, yep..." It has to be Taughtauer. He looked around the room and found the clock. The second hand moved sluggishly over the hour hand while outside the sun shone bright and the quiet of a mid-morning workday infused Mitkin with a sense of purpose. He should be at work. He said aloud, "They said he would call, it was him. Had to be." He moved through his apartment looking for a shirt. "But why the zoo?" A wrinkled pullover peeked out at him from the shelving in his closet. "I'll go, why not? I haven't been to the zoo for a while anyway. Had to be him besides. Had to be." He laced on a pair of sneakers and stuffed two subway tokens in his front pocket. "Why not?" He crept out the front door, patting his pockets and checking twice to make sure he had his keys. He shut the door behind him and the words *lock it* came to mind.

It wasn't until he got to the street that he remembered his book. He stood still debating a return. The sun peeked out from behind the clouds and a kind breeze blew through the building-framed block, and a pleasant, life-affirming sensation moved through his body. He remembered the words of Thoreau, "Follow the impulse of the vernal woods, all that comes from her will be true." He beamed and stepped into the street and crossed against traffic quickly, skipping toward the subway stop and his train north to the Bronx.

Mitkin had broken new ground. In four years of living in the city, he had never taken the subway without a book to read. He cherished the reading he did on the subway and pitied the people who sat stone-faced and weather-beaten, and without a book. "They," he would say to himself, "are wasting their lives away." But now, absent a book, he was one of those he once pitied. For the first time in his life he sat looking up, looking *out*, and it was upon the faces of passengers on the subway that he looked. So many faces. He journeyed from one to another—a tall Slavic woman with tired jowls and a heavy frown bouncing slightly in her seat as the train rolled. She stared out the window and Mitkin imagined her with her grandchildren, laughing. "Her face was beautiful when it laughed," he thought. A slight, brown-skinned man in his fifties sat across from Mitkin. Deliberately, unabashedly, he dug in his nose. Then he pulled a handkerchief from his pocket and blew unembarrassed. Mitkin smirked. "Even he must love, even he," thought Mitkin. And he imagined him smiling, too.

Up and down the train, Mitkin wandered with his eyes. A diverse mosaic sat in that car and each one was like him, alive, breathing, sucking up the gift of air and life and living, and each, like him, deserved more than what this train and this life was offering. He remembered again the vernal woods, and in his soul he measured the tremors of emotion he identified as love. "This is love!" He chastised himself, "I've been so stupid for so long, but now, now I know. This is love!" A great irrational, untamed joy swelled in Mitkin, just as it had the day before. These people were like his students, they were the culmination of creation, the noble beasts of nature and heirs to the world and no matter what had come before each of them, and him too, all were now magical, special, tender, beloved creatures and

Mitkin loved them. "I am free to love them," he thought, "I am free to love all of it now!"

He continued in his elation until the train stopped for the final time. Mitkin had missed his stop but he did not care. Together with his new brothers and sisters, Mitkin disembarked dreamily, no rush in his step, no care for what would come next. He wandered along the platform and casually made his way out. By the time he reached the exit, he was the last one in the station. He peered into the dark tunnel down the tracks and shouted "Hello!" in a long melodious greeting to anyone who might care. He made one last pirouette, a little bunny hop of joy, and headed up the stairs toward the street. A transit worker, selling tokens from behind three-inch bulletproof glass, frowned when Mitkin greeted her, wide-eyed and smiling. The clock behind her read 11:48.

The zoo was big. The land on which the zoo was built was still forest, some of the oldest forested land in North America. Much of it had been preserved and worked into the landscape of the zoo itself. Thick, rich, green oaks lined the path that led Mitkin to the entrance. The sting of the sun disappeared behind the fat trunks of the aging trees. The path beneath his feet was that welcoming pin-gravel that kids love to kick and slide on, those little rocks adults associate with parks and places of natural refuge. These sentiments mixed easily with Mitkin's already magical mood and carried him airily between the two large stone gates that guarded the entrance to the Bronx Zoo. He paid quickly and noticed there were no lines.

"What time is it, sir?" Mitkin asked the teller.

"Ten after twelve."

Mitkin nodded and went inside. The path diverged and became many paths. He stopped and read various wooden placards, each carved to an arrow-point like kitsch road markers from some imperial playground, and searched for the one that would lead him to the bats, to the World of Darkness. He spun once around in vain, and then, there it was, the bat house marker. He passed a giant pool of water crowned with boulders of artificial granite on which lolled three giant bull seals. Mitkin stopped and watched as one crept toward the water. It pulled itself with its flippers, and in the flippers Mitkin saw malformed hands and imagined the seal as a handicapped human. "Amazing," thought Mitkin. Then the seal slipped into the water and was transformed into an entirely new creature. He was fast and sleek, a greasy flash of black lightning. He sailed in circles underwater, swam on his side and occasionally surfaced with a whinny and a spray. Like this, the seal was anything but handicapped and Mitkin reveled in nature's perfection.

Down the path he encountered other animal environs. He crossed a bridge under which sat the grassland habitat of big cats. A pack of four female lions huddled together under a tree. The biggest one, its coat a shiny and golden brown, yawned mightily, displaying an insouciance that Mitkin associated with profound contentment. He went further down the path and deeper into the park, leaving all the sounds of the city behind. A giant ostrich poked its head in and out of a healthy mulberry bush. Nothing moved hurriedly here. He passed a grizzly bear sleeping on a rock. An impala and some of its smaller gazelle cousins strolled easily between two small ponds, their hinds powerfully propelling their spindly legs lightly along the ground. The slow, rich wail of a crane sounded in the distance. Mitkin came to a fork in the path and to his left, rising from a slight knoll, stood the World of Darkness, and outside, perched comfortably on a railing was Taughtauer. He was smoking a cigarette. Mitkin started to wave, but a green pickup truck filled with zoo workmen came barreling along, honking him off the path. He jumped to safety with a start while Taughtauer watched it all with cool reserve, dragging on a cigarette and then flicking it to the ground. He smashed the butt with the ball of his foot and without a glance, ducked into the cave building.

"Did he see me?" thought Mitkin. Not moving, he waited for the man to poke his head out and wave him in. "It was Taughtauer, wasn't it?" After another moment, he moved forward up the path, toward the World of Darkness, propelled by curiosity.

In the dark he called out, "Taughtauer, where are you?" Slowly Mitkin's eyes adjusted to the artificial darkness and he began to see large glass encasements of mini-forests holding various nocturnal species. He skulked past one that housed a giant fruit bat. "Taughtauer?" He continued on what seemed like the main corridor, stopping in front of a case filled with four-legged rat-like creatures for which he did not know the name. The fattest of them slid along the bottom and into a hole near the back. Mitkin looked behind himself and saw the thick image of a man. He turned and started toward it. "Taughtauer, it's Mitchell. Are you hiding from me?"

"Excuse me?" replied a voice, not Taughtauer's.

"Sorry."

Mitkin continued down the dark alleyway and began to doubt his mission. "Was it really him?" And then he felt a hand on his arm. "Taughtauer?"

"Do you like the bats?" came a voice.

"Is that you?"

"Of course it is, Mitch. Didn't you see me out in front, I mean that is why you came in, right?"

"Sure, but what's with the hide and seek?"

"I've been here the whole time, Mitch. I've been waiting right here the whole time." There was a pause. "It's hard to see in here you know."

"Yes, but it's not hard to hear. I yelled your name twice. What's with the games? And what's with the smoking? That's banned in the zoo." Mitkin pulled his arm away.

"Banned in the zoo?" Taughtauer laughed. "Yeah, sorry. Whatever. And I wasn't playing games, Mitch. No more games, Mitch. The games are over now."

Mitkin stood still and looked hard into the darkness trying to get a clear view of the man with whom he spoke. "Did you call me this morning?"

"Yep."

"You sounded funny on the phone. Are you sure that you called me this morning?"

"Mitch, you're acting skittish. Of course I called you this morning. I set this whole thing up. Everything is going just as we planned. Now, do you like the bats or not?" Taughtauer moved closer to the bat box, and in the glow of the case Mitkin could see the sharp lines of a face he knew. "Do you like the way they hang, upside down, inverted like that?"

"I like the seals better," said Mitkin sharply.

"To each his own I guess."

Mitkin looked around for the man he mistakenly took for Taughtauer but he could see nothing. It seemed that they were alone. Taughtauer continued his silent stare, a damp heat hanging in the air. "I like it here," he said. "I like how things scurry around."

"Is that why we're meeting here?"

"Well, sure why not. I figure two men, both unemployed, both single, both with a lot on their minds might find a little solace among the mighty creatures of this world. The only problem is, Mitch, when you get right down to it, these animals aren't so mighty in these cages. In fact, they're really pretty pathetic." He rapped on the glass enclosure. "They aren't mighty at all are they, Mitch?" Taughtauer turned to Mitkin. "It's kind of like the kids at school, isn't it?"

Mitkin remembered the sign outside the school sitting crooked and halfway off its moorings. *WHEN WE DO. WHEN WE DON'T.* He stretched out his hand and felt the glass that imprisoned Taughtauer's fruit bat.

"Wouldn't you like to let him out, Mitch?"

With his fingers still going over the glass, Mitkin did not respond. Taughtauer waited patiently. After another few moments, Mitkin nodded.

"Good, then let's do it." Taughtauer took Mitkin by the shoulder and together they walked toward the exit, and as they did the light from outside blinded Mitkin. With his eyes adjusted, they sat down on a bench and Taughtauer pulled off his backpack, producing a finely bound black book. He opened it and inside Mitkin saw pages and pages of handwritten notes. Taughtauer flipped through it and found the page he wanted. He tapped it with his forefinger and slid closer, exposing the book for Mitkin to see.

"We have three months. In that time we have to consolidate our support in these schools. If we don't get these schools then I'm afraid we won't get the turnover we need in the smaller schools. I need you to work in these schools, Mitch." He ran his finger over the list.

"Get them?" asked Mitkin. "To do what?"

"Maybe I should start from the beginning, yep. See Mitch, it's like this." Taughtauer closed the book and leaned back on the bench resting his head against the brick wall. "We believe that every student consigned to half-ass education inherently understands his consignment. My kids all confirm this, but not every kid can really articulate it. See, they can't all verbalize the implications of their consignment. Am I losing you?"

This was not difficult to understand, and expression on Mitkin's face betrayed his annoyance.

Taughtauer continued, "I forget, Mitch, you're a smart guy, sure. So the most articulate ones become the most angry and make the best martyrs. Basically, my kids are the ones who will kick some ass. Look at Elrod. Elrod hates the school system, but before he came to us, he thought his hate was for others, for individuals. But, of course, it wasn't. Individuals are good and pure like you told me. No, what Elrod hates is the system that the slave masters create: parents, policemen, teachers and administrators. We weave an ugly web Mitch, and Elrod is pissed. He's pissed because he lacks freedom and yet he knows he's meant to be free. Tom Jefferson and his cronies knew this, just look at all their rhetoric. The problem is they didn't go far enough, Mitch. Sometimes, when I feel generous, I think of Tom and the boys as the Founding Fathers of the true revolution, the earliest voices for absolute individuality and the underground architects of a movement to destroy all authority, the king being only the first to fall, see. I think that maybe they saw it all, they saw perfect individual freedom, anarchy, Mitch, and they desired it, and to achieve it they created a manifesto—the United States Constitution. Wouldn't that be brilliant?" He clapped his hands together like an excited child. "Brilliant! But I don't think they were up to all that, not quite courageous enough, really." Taughtauer sat up. "Look, Elrod understands that authority thwarts who he is. He has been shown the truth and our job is to show others the same thing."

"Sounds like you want me to brainwash them."

Taughtauer slumped on the bench. "Aw, Mitch. Do you, or don't you think that mankind has the right to life, liberty and the pursuit of happiness?" Taughtauer put his hands out quizzically.

"I think we do," chirped Mitkin.

"Then how can restoring liberty be brainwashing? It seems to me they've already been brainwashed the other way, to believe in slavery." Taughtauer turned to Mitkin. "This isn't rocket-fucking-science, Mitch. But let me put it to you another way. You believed your father when he told you about the world, right? You never doubted that man was a great machine destined for the dunghill, right? Then your daddy died, and by dying he taught you the truth. And now you say, 'Darn, we are more than just machines. My father was wrong.' And you're right. Man is more! He *is* freedom. You, Mr. Mitchell, were living a lie. Elrod, Mr. Mitchell, was living a lie. Students who submit to authority are living a lie. Leaving people ignorant is cruel, Mitch. As educators, we must try to make people free, and aware. Am I making myself clear?"

Mitkin heard these words and they did make sense to him. He had been deluded, but now it seemed the only real thing was death. Wasn't death all there was in the end? He put the question to Taughtauer.

"Death is real," said Taughtauer lightly. "But the legacy of one's life is what lives on, it's what counts. We should live for liberty and create heaven right here on earth. You can achieve heaven right here, Mitch, by being who you are. I mean, watch these kids! They have it together. You'll see them and then you'll know. Forget the fairy tale heaven, it isn't somewhere else, out there, waiting. It's right now, right here, inside. Hell too, right now. And what's hell, Mitch? Hell is the life of those people who accept a bogus version of who they are. They are never fulfilled because they don't even know what that means. Slaves to authority live in hell. Masters of its destruction live in heaven."

Since his youth, Mitkin had always loved to hear his father string words together. It enthralled him. Like a guard dog, he would sit and bark for his father whenever he argued a point with a friend or gave a lecture to his mother. The silky sounds of a great orator were like chocolate for Mitkin, and he would have made a good wunderkind in earlier times.

"How do you know so much about me?" Mitkin asked.

"I do my homework."

"Yeah, but why me?"

"Your father's genes and especially your father's balls. I admired him." Taughtauer began to go through his book.

Mitkin stammered, "I did too, I mean, I don't believe the things he taught me as a child."

"I know you don't, Mitch, but I also know you loved him very much and he loved you. Mitch, do you know how long all of our plans have been in the works?"

"How long?"

"Your father knew about our plans when he still worked full-time for *Science Now*."

Mitkin said slowly, "*Science Now*? That was—"

"Twelve years ago, yep. He knew about what we wanted to do."

Ashen, Mitkin turned to Taughtauer. "My father knew you planned to burn down the Board of Education?"

"Yep, yep, old Mitch. He knew. And I've got one more for you. He recommended that I use you to do it, how do you think I know so much about you, Mitch? Why do you think you wound up teaching at South Bronx? Put it together now, come on." Mitkin felt nauseous. He blinked his eyes very hard and turned his head away from Taughtauer, trying to avoid his gray eyes. He could not respond. "He knew," continued Taughtauer. "He was as sick and tired of all the bureaucratic bullshit as I was. After all, it was the school board that spent, or should I say, stole his money year after year. Yep, Mitch, your father knew. He'd be proud of you right now."

It didn't make sense. His father wasn't a subversive, he wasn't like Taughtauer. Taughtauer appeared devious and edgy, a charlatan. Mitkin's father respected authority, he wasn't some half-baked anarchist.

"I think you are lying," said Mitkin.

"Mitch, why would I tell you something like this? I have nothing to gain from it. You're already here, you've already decided to join the movement. Telling you this would just jeopardize my plans, right?"

A rivulet of tepid, rusty water ran out a drainpipe that jutted from the World of Darkness. It trickled over the cemented ground and against Mitkin's heel and then around his shoes and toward a patch of grass a few feet beyond them both. "Bat bowels," thought Mitkin, as he raised his foot and let out a mild curse. On a little patch of green grass, he wiped his shoe clean. Taughtauer stayed on the bench. "Mitch, it's like this. Do you, or do you not, believe in changing the school system?"

"It's not like *that*! It's just not so easy," Mitkin yelled from just off the path. "You're talking about killing people and now you're telling me that my dad was talking about it too?" He looked around and lowered his voice again, almost to a whisper. "I mean, what the hell is going on here?"

But he knew he could answer his own question.

Mitkin neared Taughtauer on the bench. "What makes me want to believe you?"

"Because you're a genius," said Taughtauer. "Stop questioning yourself. You're here because you recognize what millions of Americans don't. We are all living in delusion. There is no salvation in things, only action. You realize this. You're here! Shit, Mitchy, you're here because you realize the truth! Stop feeling for the brakes, let go man. Your father served you well."

It was a hard thing to understand, but Mitkin was weak and tired, too tired to fight and too weak to believe otherwise. He had been a depressed wreck for six months and now he was that same wreck, but without a job. The only sanguine moments in his life had come during deeds of insurrection. Meeting here was one such act and quitting in Borly's face was another. He still believed that his father was wrong about human life and truth, but he saw now that he still loved his father and still cared about his legacy.

"Come on, Mitch, walk with me," said Taughtauer finally. Mitkin thought about these things as they meandered through the zoo. They walked slowly and for a long time, quietly. It was unlike Taughtauer to be so still, almost stone-like, but his effort was working as Mitkin began to trust him. Mitkin glanced at Taughtauer several times and saw a forsaken man, a man rejected by society. He was not loved by the school board, he was not loved by school administrators, he was not loved by any women, at least not the women with whom he worked at school, and as far as Mitkin could tell he lacked the love of a family. He was alone in the world except for his kids, his students, and walking on that path, thinking many thoughts Mitkin, managed to imagine an ebullient Taughtauer just as he had imagined the joy-filled subway car. Every conjured vision of joy placed Taughtauer among his students. Mitkin settled inside.

"Why aren't you married?" he asked.

"Oh Mitch, not women, come on."

"Seriously. Why not?"

"Look at me, Mitch." Taughtauer stopped and waved his hand like a wand over his body.

"And?" said Mitkin.

"If you were a woman? This package?" He waved his hand again, "You gotta be pretty hungry to want some of this. Am I lying?"

"Are you gay?" Mitchell asked stone-faced. Taughtauer laughed and resumed a stroll.

"No, not gay, not gay, Mitch. Just ugly."

"So that's it. Ugly. That explains everything?"

"Mitch, you're alright. I figured we'd get along one day. Is this the day, Mitch?" Taughtauer gently slapped him on the back. They walked a few more feet and Taughtauer stopped again. "I love ideas, that's all. I love the idea of my students being one-hundred percent happy. Happiness, that's what I love. Like on the Fourth of July when their faces light up under the fireworks. That's an idea I love with all my heart." He was filling with energy. "Okay, so it's a little cliché, but to me it's the only idea in this world worth living for. So that's what I do; I try to love." He took a breath as if to continue, but he stopped. "You understand, don't you?"

Mitkin nodded. "You're in love."

Taughtauer nodded and flashed a winsome smile. "Yep, yep. I'm in love. So are my friends."

"You've got friends?" Mitkin asked.

"Yep, Mitch I've got friends. Boy, do I have friends." Taughtauer opened his black book. Over their shoulders and behind a high chain link fence, a pair of monkeys chased each other. The little one screamed and excited the others. "These are the lists," said Taughtauer, hunched over his book. "I've got pledges from over nine hundred teachers—nearly eight per high school."

"Pledges to do what?"

"Support student centered administrations." Taughtauer turned the page.

"But not to burn down Livingston Street?"

"That's this list." Taughtauer said as he showed him a much shorter list. "Here are the teacher martyrs, here are the most dedicated, and here," he turned to yet another page, "I've got the student martyrs." This list was short too. "Each of them has pledged, and I mean been baptized, to support the rebellion to the last. These are my bishops." Information was detailed and included addresses, schools and a third entry entitled *Dependability*. Mitkin asked what this meant.

"Later," said Taughtauer, briskly opening to another page. "This is what I have in mind for you. We need more priests by September. I'm confident that for every priest we recruit, we can get three deacons, and for every deacon at least four laypeople. We need more laity and that's why you're here."

"Okay, what's with the church names? It's a little creepy, Ed."

"I learned a long time ago to admire the Catholics, Mitch. They do what we all should, they shoot for the moon. People have it wrong about the Pope—they think he forces you to do something you don't want to. Wrong. The Pope is just providing a way, a path to the idea, and then, if people believe in the idea, they follow the path. See, people are free to follow or not. People just don't like to follow the rules because they don't like the path—the path to the idea is a real thorny bitch. The idea itself, well that's real nice. I mean, Jesus is real nice."

"So why not be a Catholic?"

"Because I don't believe in the Pope's ideal. There's no Jesus, no god-man. Nope. There is only the individual and his freedom. Freedom's my ideal. When you put an outside god into it, you just stick authority in there, and authority, remember, is a tool for the rich and powerful."

"Over the poor and powerless. Yeah, I know," said Mitkin sardonically.

"Watch it, Mitch. Sarcasm is a faith-killer."

Mitkin began but went silent.

"Good. Now. We need more laity, the ones that will be there when the revolution is in the balance. We need numbers, Mitch."

It was easy, once there and listening, to get excited. Taughtauer had already arranged a substitute job for Mitkin in one of the key rebellion schools; money would be no problem. He had no treasured friendships, no girlfriends that might interfere with his subversive deeds; Raphaella had seen to this. His mother had moved, and she would not investigate. And of course, his father was dead. Death was at the center of the momentum pushing Mitkin toward Taughtauer. He knew it was coming, he knew death as giant locusts on the outskirts of town, leaping and seething and flattening, undaunted and indomitable and forever ready to devour everything, everywhere. And unlike most everyone else in the world, Mitkin could not put down or subvert the idea of death. It was always with him now, and perhaps it had always been, even in those moments he recalled as his childhood. Perhaps it was always death that moved him to act, become, think, create. Perhaps it was the specter of death that moved everything.

"So, Mitch," said Taughtauer, "I want you to be a martyr. Will you be a martyr?"

"This is kind of crazy."

"You said that already. Yes or no?"

Mitkin smiled lazily. He shook his head and then looked down at his feet as they passed indifferently along the pebble-strewn path. He turned and stared at Taughtauer and nodded. "Yeah. Yes, I'll do it. Yeah."

"Then," Taughtauer clapped, "let's go get you baptized."

CHAPTER XVIII

Going Under

It was two weeks later, after more walks in the park and Chinese lunch specials, that Taughtauer arranged the baptism. They met at the corner of Reservoir Avenue and 205th Street in the Bedford Park section of the Bronx. Taughtauer was wearing crisp gray pants and a high-collared short-sleeved dress shirt, hair combed back. Mitkin was more casual, if not just less ironed.

"This way," said Taughtauer. "To my house. Good to see you."

The sidewalks were alive with children, their unbounded energy spilling into the streets. A little tune came to Mitchell and he sang it in his head:

School's out, school's out, teacher's let the monkeys out, one went east, one went west, one went up the teacher's dress.

He grinned. A tiny child ducked against his legs while a playmate pursued with a water balloon. Mitkin pretended fisticuffs while Taughtauer chased the bigger kid. Everyone laughed. A car horn bellowed in front of a game of street tag, bicycles and jump ropes zipped and twirled. On the quaint block, children ran in and out of their row houses while local bodegas, bloated with candy-buying kids, blared rapid Latin rhythms. Cries of *mira* and *papi* could be heard.

"This is what school should be like, Mitch," said Taughtauer. "It should be like this all the time."

They crossed a large thoroughfare and turned up a tiny street. Taughtauer pointed at a church at the end of the street. "That's where Ricky goes, do you know Ricky Cuevas?" asked Taughtauer.

"The quiet kid from South Bronx Science?"

"That's the one." Taughtauer then pointed at a thick brown building. "Ricky lives in that house there. He'll be by later, everyone will be. All the martyrs are coming for your baptism."

Mitkin pictured himself dunked in water.

Cool. Bubbles from the mouth run to the surface. A big hand with knobby calluses and long, rangy fingers is pushing. There is muffled talk and distorted faces peer in through a clear glass font. There is water pressure on the pupils, the water settles, and the crumpled chatter ceases. The leathery hand holds on. Quiet. For a long time there is a midnight silence and it is agreeable. There is no struggle and there are no dilemmas, no intellectual calculations, no right and no wrong. There is only silence. The eyes close, and against the silence darkness blots out everything. Coolness. Blackness. An embryo. Stay, stay, let go! No breathing. No nothing. Be baptized. No breathing. Darkness. Be baptized. A squeeze and then a tug and then heavy soggy hair covers the face. Noises again. People are cheering and thumping on tables and hooting. With a skinny thumb wet hair and water are moved aside and there is a man in front of him, unhanding him and hugging him. That is like love, and that is odd for this man. But it isn't, suddenly, it seems normal. Everything is new. There is hope between them, a familial longing, and between the others too. Love. There is something in it all that must be love.

"Mitch?"

Mitkin turned with a start.

"Mitch, are you listening to me?"

"Yeah, sure. Is there going to be water at the baptism?"

"Of course there's going to be water. There's no real baptism without water. It's elemental."

Mitkin moved his head approvingly as a harried man in a tight-fitting business suit loped in full stride toward him, his head and eyes down checking his watch. His briefcase nearly gutted Mitkin.

"Wow, how about that guy?" said Taughtauer turning like a matador. "See what happens to us, Mitch?" He shook his head. "Slaves." Suddenly he stopped, ebullient and untroubled but pensive as always. He stuck his hand in the air, forefinger first, and shouted through a grin, "Damn, I'd like to burn it down today. Right now. I mean what else is there? Suits and bank accounts. Ridiculous." He moved his head to and fro in disapproval. A little boy stopped and stared. Taughtauer let out a growl and playfully chased the boy up the block and waited for Mitkin to catch up.

"That's my house," said Taughtauer pointing to the church. "Nice, huh?"

Mitkin laughed.

"Of course, you know it really is my house. Me and those guys, we're brothers. We both want the same thing, peace. What is it? Peace on earth, good will toward mice?"

"Yeah, mice," replied Mitkin, wistfully. He was thinking of Raphaella. *She's really not very peaceful, most of what she does divides people actually.* He shook his head and spoke out loud, "I bet you've never even been inside that church."

Taughtauer straightened his neck. "In there? I don't need to, they've been coming to me four times a year for twenty-five years. I know just about all of them in some form or another."

"You mean teacher-parent nights?"

"More. Most of the earliest ideas for the movement are a reaction to these Christian people who bitch and moan about the system they trust their kids to. The problem is most of them don't realize that they are as much to blame as the system. They, after all, believe in the lie of authority, I mean they *are* authority. The system relates to their kids the same way they do—as a behemoth overseer, as one above the other, all this 'in charge' crap. Yet they hate it; they hate the heavy hand when it comes to their kids. They want," he sugar-coated his voice, "caring teachers who'll take an interest in my child." Yeah, right. They're all confused and deluded."

"But there are exceptions," said Mitkin.

"Yeah, the exceptions all put their kids in home school or private school if they can afford it. The almost-rebels move to some tundra commune somewhere in California and regret it deep down."

They walked one more block. "Here's my house, really."

In front of them stood a tall, two-story house with an attic. It was painted navy blue. All of its borders were done in canary yellow giving the house a foreign feel, almost like a Swiss chalet. The front yard was tiny and newly laid with luscious green sod. Neat little beds of fetching flowers rimmed the yard. Red orchids and yellow daisies sat side by side with hardy roses.

"You did all of this?" asked Mitkin.

Taughtauer nodded. A short banister led to an open porch on which sat a rocking chair. The porch reminded Mitkin of something from the South. It was inviting, like a bed and breakfast. Taughtauer opened the door and led Mitkin inside. The first things he noticed were two televisions, one giant and the other smaller, just to the side. Both were tuned to news channels. In the far corner sat three army-style cots lined up in a neat row. Below each lay bundled bedding and other personal belongings including the latest black and red striped Air Jordans. Mitkin waited in the foyer while Taughtauer went up and down the stairs, prowling about the house searching for something. He rifled through the cots and their belongings and then went to the phone and turned it upside down. He then went out the back door where Mitkin lost sight of him.

The back door slammed and Taughtauer's voice could be heard, "Okay, Mitch, you can come in now. Nobody's been here."

"What about the TVs?" Mitkin hollered.

"They're always on."

"Okey-dokey, then," Mitkin said under his breath.

Mitkin met Taughtauer in the kitchen where he was stirring some iced tea. He poured a glass and gave it to Mitkin.

"This is our headquarters, yep. Everything that goes on here is absolutely top secret. As you know, there are many forces out there with an interest in seeing the movement fail."

"Top secret, huh?"

"Yep, yep. Top secret."

"Have you ever been arrested, Ed?"

"No. Harassed yeah, arrested no. They've got nothing to arrest me for. Now, as for the kids, we've got a few societal degenerates, if you know what I mean."

Mitkin sipped his tea. "Like who?"

"You tell me when they get here. You've met most of them before. But if you pay attention, you'll notice that the kids with the longest rap sheets are also our best martyrs. That's how I persuade so many teachers to join us. The whole movement is transformational." The doorbell rang.

Two teens appeared in the kitchen. Mitkin recognized one of them immediately. His name was José Hernández, a student at South Bronx School of Science, a popular student whose dyed hair, this day yellow, was his trademark. His face was uneven—big teeth, oafish lips and a meager mustache gave him a doltish appearance—but his eyes were kind. He was staring at Mitkin now, hard, he and his friend giving the once-over. Mitkin's stomach turned and his heart raced. It was like a coming-out party.

"So, it is true!" José Hernández stiffened his hand and stuck it out. "You're really with us, you really are *the man*."

Mitkin nodded.

"I was there at Borly's, I saw it all."

Still nodding Mitkin said, "Nice hair." José patted it down coolly and pointed at Mitkin's head.

"Yours too, papi."

The other student stepped forward. "James Hunt," he said. He wore cornrows and an oversized black leather jacket. His skin was very dark, the color of a rich stout, and his eyes were piercing. Even in the jacket, it was easy to see his athletic build. Together all three went into the living room, Mitkin trailing the two boys. Taughtauer sat in a recliner with a bowl of chips. "I've already told Mitch about his recruiting mission. He says he's the man for the job, right, Mitch?"

"You liked the idea?" asked José. "It's mine, you know. I'm working on it with you, me and Richie. Do you know Richie?"

"No."

"He's a trip, yo. You'll like him though, smart as hell, right, James?" James nodded. "I brought you this stuff," he pointed to a black bag, "it's a notebook and some drawing paper. And here's some art pencils, chalk, a what-cha-call it. Oh and here is my favorite." He pulled a floppy disk from the bag. "A program so we can upgrade our MacArt. This bad boy will let us do anything we want, and fast." He handed the glossy box to Mitkin. "You work on computers?"

"Yes," said Mitkin.

"Good, Richie will love you."

There was a quick knock and the front door opened again. A skinny teen slipped his way in and with a grin on his face searched the room ravenously for something or someone.

"It's gotta be you, you the only white boy in here," he said, looking at Mitkin. "A new teacher martyr and the son of Martin Mitkin. Damn, skippy!" Mitkin raised an eyebrow. They slapped hands. "Richie Rovers," said the thin boy. "I hope you know some shit about computers, yo."

Another teen was soon inside too. Mitkin knew this one. They exchanged glances, but unlike the lightsome Richie Rovers, this lean kid was aloof. He made his way into the kitchen without greeting anyone but Taughtauer. Richie squawked on, "How much you know?"

Mitkin shook his head confused.

"About the movement, motherfucker? Did Taughtauer show you the lists yet?" Mitkin went to answer but Richie kept talking, "Did he take you to the World of Darkness, yo?"

"He did."

"So you really in, man. This white boy is really down, huh? This shit is real." He fisted both hands like he'd just scored the winning basket. "I love saying that. This shit *is* real!"

The room was filling up, and as it did the boy with whom Mitkin had exchanged glances returned. He meandered over and sat on the rug opposite Mitkin, sipped from his drink, nodded, and then held his glass to the sky, slightly, reverently.

"Cheers, Mitkin. I told you we'd call." His voice was silky.

"Yes. Yes you did." Mitkin raised his glass. "Cheers. Your name is?"

"Enrico Cuevas. Ricky 'round here."

"Ricky Cuevas. The one in charge." Mitkin recognized him as the leader from the classroom.

The boy put his drink down and leaned backward, onto his palms. Almost imperceptibly he began to rock to a gentle rhythm and did not answer Mitkin. He was very cool, calm, as if he were there for something else, not banter. And of course he was; he was there for Mitkin's initiation.

Mitkin's mood began to change. He thought how his father had planned for this moment, and how much his father had loved him. He thought how this movement had begun to change his life, and a great vitality rose within him. In his mind, he managed the words *holy warrior* as a description of himself. Indeed, he was about to embark on a holy war.

Taughtauer set a large table. Some clanking in the kitchen and a sweet aroma reminded Mitkin of Thanksgiving dinners past when his mother would feed his father's aging but agile friends, each of them tanner than normal. He heard a dry coil creak as someone opened the oven door, he heard the chopping of food on a butcher's block, an electric can opener grinding, the cork popping out of a bottle. Curiously, these holiday sounds brought with them thoughts of Raphaella and an ironic melancholy seized him. "Were we this close that I can't shake her now, thoughts of her?" He imagined her prostrate before her sacred trinkets on a cold Christmas Eve. "If only she'd dump all of that," he thought. He wanted her to join him. "She would be a star here." He thought about going wantonly after her, rushing through the streets and finding her with a hug and a kiss and then brusquely carrying her back, to the hideout, where she, too, would be cleansed in the baptismal waters. Eager agitation shot through Mitkin's soul and he stood up, walked over to Taughtauer, and with a heedless hand took him by the elbow. Taughtauer, taken by surprise, followed.

"Whoa, Mitch, take it easy, my elbow. Relax." Mitkin, still holding tight, directed Taughtauer to the back porch.

"I'm ready to be baptized."

"I know, Mitch, you already told me. Take a seat. We're all going to eat and then a little meeting and then the water. Take a little break and get something to eat."

"But you're not getting it, Ed. I really *want* to be baptized. It's not like at the zoo before, I want it like food or water. Do you understand?" Taughtauer flashed a broad grin. "Don't look at me like that," said Mitkin. "I'm not some experiment. This has been coming ever since my father's death and now it's hitting me. It feels like gravity."

"It feels like gravity?" Taughtauer put his hands on his hips and smirked, "Let's call that God for lack of, well, a definitive term. That's God calling you, Mitch."

"Yeah, well, maybe. I don't know what it is here," he said pointing to his head. "But there's more. I can feel it and I don't want it to go away. Did you know that for the first time since his death I feel at home? I think I must feel like they do." He nodded toward the kids. "Were they like this before they came to you?"

"Mitch, we are all like that, we just don't all wake up and realize it. These kids are closer to who they are."

"Freedom," Mitkin said knowingly.

"Freedom, you got it, Mitch." It would be Taughtauer's mantra for the next three months. Over and over he would drive it in, and he would not waver. Other ideas revolved around the ideal: justice, goodness, equality, something he called the "intolerable shackles of authority" (he usually said this in a state of near ecstasy), and of course his battle cry of "constructive destruction." But it was young hearts and freedom that made Taughtauer tick, and in turn, the movement itself. Mitkin loved the ideal too, but it was not freedom that made him so ecstatic. It was the physicality of it all. He had left the books and created real relationships. Being there he felt at home, and seeing the unquestioned allegiance of these students, day in and day out changed him. He came to know how they silently lent money to one another, fed and washed each other's babies, shared bus rides late at night, and volunteered to risk their lives collecting guns and money. For Mitkin, as lonely as he was, it didn't matter so much that these kids worked to change the system, it just mattered that they worked together, united, lovingly, patiently, side by side. Out on the porch that evening all of this came as a blur, an intimation of something good.

"Funnel your idealism," said Taughtauer. "Be reckless, but just wreck the right stuff."

Taughtauer had set nine places. A bench had been dragged from the back porch and on it sat Richie Rovers and James Hunt. Mitkin sat to Taughtauer's right, as Taughtauer sat at the head of the table. On the other end, at the head, Ricky Cuevas sat tall in a grandly carved wooden chair. He commanded the circular passing of dishes and calmly, keenly, directed traffic on everything from potato salad to the wine and beer bottles. Imperceptibly, like a ripe married couple, Cuevas and Taughtauer communicated their authority (though Taughtauer would have denied such authority; that was against the mantra).

"That ain't eatin'," said a young woman to Mitkin's right. "I could eat that for a snack, come on now."

"Just getting started," said Mitkin.

"Ain't that the truth," she laughed the words through her teeth. "Ain't that the truth..." This was Nicole and her baby girl, Tiana. She was James Hunt's girl and one of the sharpest martyrs at the table. With a high voice and a strong hand, she took Tiana by the wrist and waved at James who sat far away at the other end of the table. "Hey Daddy, hey old man." James Hunt waved back meekly, embarrassed. "Tiana's planned," Nicole told Mitkin.

"Oh, you're married?" asked Mitkin.

"No. Not the way you thinking anyway. We together though, he needs me 'cause without me he wouldn't talk to nobody never. Probably end up mute from not using words, like the kid in *Jungle Book*. We love each other though." Mitkin chewed slowly and looked at James. James never raised his eyes from his plate.

"How long have you been together?" asked Mitkin.

Taughtauer pushed his way into the conversation. "Just as long as they've known of the movement. It was freshman year that you met, my first full year recruiting martyrs. I waited on your class for fifteen years." He smiled and looked at them all. "Fifteen years!"

"I remember, too," said Nicole. "I just got off suspension when James told me to take your class. You taught crazy stuff in that class. That's when I first learned the word anarchy."

Mitkin turned to Taughtauer. "What class was that?"

"Study hall."

"Oh," peeped Mitkin, winsomely. "Of course."

"Every one of these kids took that course. Yep. Every one." Taughtauer raised his glass and gave Mitkin a wicked wink. "Aah-tahn-cion people. I would like to make a toast." A few forks could be heard tapping against cheap crystal. Taughtauer waited like a thespian, his back straight and pinky finger extended. "This is a toast to family. Every one of us is ordained to live in a family—" He was interrupted.

"Ed, you better explain what means for these fools, especially José over there," said Richie Rovers.

Taughtauer smiled and continued. "Living in a family is a needful thing. Thanks to this movement, every one of us has a family now. And I know every one of us is grateful for that." He looked surreptitiously at Richie. "But we must continue to grow and share our wealth. Today we do just that. I'd like to present for baptism a new martyr, the son of an old ally, and, I might add, a young teacher with ample intellect and a mighty mettle." Taughtauer looked at Mitkin and resumed, his vocabulary just as pompous and ridiculous as ever. "Yep, good folks, I give you Mitchell Mitkin." Everyone toasted. Mitkin nodded while the martyrs sipped. He watched each of them, afraid he'd find some evidence of unbelief, a boyish giggle or a ridiculous belly laugh. But he didn't. They believed and so he marched forward, his progress measured instantaneously in little soul-seconds, deeper and darker into the night of his soul he went, groping to believe and stumbling forward, standing taller with each doubtful breath overcome. They were done clapping and he was done doubting. He drank the toast to himself, finishing it and filling it again, blissfully swilling. "Thank you," he finally said aloud. "Thank you."

The wine and beer flowed. A huge carafe of red wine glimmered as if dappled on the table. All around were tall cans of malt liquor. Conversation broke out in all corners. Nicole, sitting next to Mitkin, served as a sort of interpreter. In hushed tones, she retold the tales that were being passed around, tales of old friends and high school adventures. Taughtauer needed no translation as he laughed along with all of his followers, baying at their jokes.

"Richie hadn't even learned to read yet," said José, snorting. "You remember, Rich? You used to come to me and ask me to read for you."

"It was Spanish, fool."

"Richie, the United States Constitution was not written in Spanish, man." Everyone rolled.

Taughtauer turned to Mitkin and then to Richie. "Rich, tell Mitchell about how far you've come. Tell him about junior high."

Richie curled his lip and shrugged his shoulders. "Come on, Ed, that's old news."

"Go ahead, Rich," said Alysha, a tall good-looking girl of eighteen. "Tell him about Woodson and woodworking class. That's all, just woodworking."

The whole table stopped chatting. Richie slowly warmed to his audience, convincing Mitkin that he had wanted to perform his story all along. He stood up.

"This is how the story ends." He pulled up his loose fitting shirt and exposed a giant scar that ran up his flank. He did so plainly. "Now for the beginning. See, I had this woodworking teacher named Woodson. We called him Woodie. He was always trippin' in class. He used to make these crazy-ass motherfucking wood blocks. He made a woodblock look like a dick once, I mean it had all the right parts, balls, the whole thing." Mitkin looked around the room and waited for embarrassed laughter but none came. "One time he made this death scene out of wood. It had a guy on the ground with a knife going through him. He was real good with the wood yo, seriously, but he was always trippin'. Woodie loved to make jokes. He would put on plays in class and use what he carved as props. One-man plays, man, like he'd talk to himself and use these characters and then use their voices to teach with. Like still use them even after the play was over."

Richie put on a voice. It was a deep Russian voice complete with the obligatory *da* and *nyet*. "Vee vill kroosh Amerika," he mocked, "like an ahnt beneath my shooo…" Richie feigned stepping on an ant. "I remember my favorite voice was his English accent. It was that real, real uppity voice like of royalty. Every time he did it he talked about having sex, though, like he'd say," Richie twisted his hand into the air and stuck out his jaw, "James, could you fetch the wench, please." There was laughter. "The one with the big bootay." Then, still in character, Richie pranced off in pursuit of the wench. He returned laughing and loose, his skinny body rubbery and ecstatic. "And that little bitch used to put on wigs too. Some kids liked him a lot, yo, they said his class was the only fun one. Me too, I liked his class, but I never really liked him 'cause he reminded me too much of my pervert uncle. So that shit was always going through my mind, every time I saw old Woody."

Alysha urged him on, "So get to Chucky and the saw."

"Damn, Alysha, you act like you bought a ticket or some shit. I got this, don't worry." He nodded as someone laughed. "So after a couple of months I got into a beef with this little Spanish kid they called Chucky. He was real light-skinned and I guess I picked on him for that, but it was no big deal, at least not until I caught Chucky and Woody doing the nasty after school one day." Mitkin looked at Taughtauer who was chewing with his head down, slowly, deliberately. "I ran out that mother fast as I could and figured I'd tell somebody the next day but the next day came and I got scared. The whole past with my uncle and all scared me, and so I just went to class and tried to forget about it. But I couldn't. I saw Chucky and he was real embarrassed and he started crying. I felt real bad and then I got this rush of anger. It came out and I couldn't really control myself. It was like waking up, yo. I took Chucky by the arm and walked him into Woody's carving class and picked up a chisel, you know those sharp things, and jumped Woody. All the while I was whacking him, I could hear Chucky crying and that made me whack him even harder until I could feel his blood on me, dripping down my cheek. I stopped then but he wasn't hurt as bad as I thought 'cause before I knew it I was pulling a screwdriver out of my side." He pulled up his shirt again. "That screwdriver." Nicole winced ceremoniously. "I just wished he hadn't got hold of that."

Mitkin's mouth was open.

"That was in seventh grade, right, Richie?" said Taughtauer still with his head down.

"Seventh grade."

"Seventh grade?" repeated Mitkin.

"Yep," said Richie. "Seventh grade. I didn't go there in eighth."

"No shit?" said José sarcastically. "They had enough *Texas Chainsaw* for one day, huh?"

"Where did you go?" asked Mitkin.

"Spofford Correctional Facility. Great place if you like being caged like a fucking ferret all day."

"What about Woody?"

"Woody? He retired. He's probably chilling somewhere in the Keys right now. That's where he always said he'd like to live, the Florida Keys." Richie sighed and sat down. "That's the end of my funny story. Eat up."

"Mmmmm, thanks, Richie," said Nicole.

"Tell it again, no really," said José.

And then, under the din of general conversation, Nicole gave Mitkin the translation. Chucky wasn't the only one who Woody had molested. Richie had been a victim, too. "But we still love him anyway and he's still the funniest of all these niggas and the cutest, except," she smiled, "for his stupid tail-braid coming down the back a his neck." She laughed. "We love him. A real rude boy."

The baby cried and Nicole took her for a change of diapers. The doorbell rang. Taughtauer motioned James to the door and he went quietly. Two older people walked in. They were both a little overweight and both a little ruddy. One, the man, wore his hair combed to one side and neat, like a mannequin might. His black hair was thick and jet. The woman wore her hair up and in a bun under a broad-brimmed summer hat. She warmly opened her arms, and with a smoky voice greeted the people.

"Ed, you've got a damn good-looking bunch of revolutionaries here, a damn fine lot." She looked at him. "And you're not such a bad old white man either. Of course, I excuse myself."

"Yes, you do Judy. Yes, indeed you do," lolled Taughtauer.

The man with the deep black hair removed his windbreaker and searched the table for a place to sit. "Is that free?" he asked Mitkin, eyes up and bright. "Hey, wait, are you Mitch? What am I saying—you must be Mitch." He picked up his foot and like a horse to a gallop, he charged for the seat. "I'm gonna sit right here." He plopped down. "You don't mind, do you?"

Taughtauer spoke, "Roger meet Mitchell Mitkin. Mitch, this is Roger Nin, coordinator of teacher affairs. He's also been on board longer than anyone but the old hag over there. These are two of my five teacher martyrs. Get to know them, it's in your best interest." Mitkin shook Roger Nin's hand. "Good Rog, now go find yourself another chair, that's Nicole's." Taughtauer pointed and then returned to his plate. "Some food, too," he finished with his mouth full.

Judy Strand approached. She shook every kid's hand all the way around the table, bowing to each and reverencing the males with a curtsy. She got to Mitkin and fell, wryly to one knee. She was very spry for her age, her legs looking strong in her sheer pantyhose. "Bless me, son of Martin. A pat upon the head is all I want, oh young master. Mitkin tentatively obliged, his palm resting lightly against her big-haired head. Strand looked enchantingly at Taughtauer. "And he has a sense of humor too. Ed, what a perfect child you've brought us."

Taughtauer shooed her out of the way as well. "There's a seat in there, go find Rog. Go ahead, git." Strand grabbed Taughtauer's hand and kissed it all over. "Forgive dear, sire, forgive… Boy, I'm getting old."

"Like wine," shouted Richie from the other end of the table.

"Or Old English," followed Ricky. The young leader then turned to Taughtauer. "Is that everyone for tonight then?"

"Yep, yep."

As if on cue, the martyrs all looked at Mitkin. Whispering wings fluttered in his stomach and he got up.

"Not yet, Mitch," said Taughtauer. "Let's finish our meal first, okay?"

Mitkin sat back down.

"But make a toast, Mitchell, that's what we need, a good toast. Give us one would ya Mitch?"

Slightly dizzy, Mitkin got to his feet and held up his drink. The others did the same. The acceptance he felt rose within him, warmed by the camaraderie and cheap wine. A faint image of what he wanted to say belched up from below and he reeled as he began. "I guess I want to toast to you. I feel saved by you really. There is something about you all, together, that is good. Over the past months, something intangible and spiritual but more real than rock, has started happening to me, and has led me here to this room tonight. It's freedom I think. Freedom is the only prerequisite for happiness, and so fighting for it and teaching others to do the same, well, it's changing my life. It makes me happy.

"Since my father's death, I have been a mess, you know. I have been unable to find my way in the world and at times have considered leaving it. It seems like a cruel joke sometimes, but meeting you guys has rejuvenated me. You have allowed me to see the beauty of life. You people have embraced love and life and a spirit that I've spent my short and naive life denying, and being here has enlightened me. I can see that no matter what happens to us and this movement, we will have lived struggling for freedom, the only thing worth living for. It's maybe not a good comparison, but I feel like I accepted Jesus. Like I've thrown myself on the ground and it feels good. Here's to the ground."

No one moved. Some gaped. Mitkin, too, stood still. He stared and then, suddenly, remembered to drink. They all followed and the dignified mood broke. Chatter resumed. A bit sheepish, Mitkin sat down.

"Nicole, was I an idiot?"

"Hell, no. You just kept it real."

Mitkin looked at Taughtauer. "Was it too much?"

"Absolutely not." Taughtauer leaned back and patted his belly. "Yep, Mitch, you definitely are the man for the job. Yep, yep, you are a great, great man, the *only* one for the job. They love you, too." He plunged a food-filled fork into his mouth and washed it all down with a glass of wine. Mitkin breathed deeply.

Dinner wound down and one by one the martyrs got up and cleared their places. They began to do the dishes and clean the dining room. No one handed out orders and no one slacked off. Only Taughtauer could be called lazy. He stayed in the living room in a leather chair, finishing his wine and smoking a cigar. Mitkin watched as the spindly man called his followers to him, one by one, talking quietly, earnestly. Judy Strand and Roger Nin sat on either side of their chief, like sentries. After a few minutes, Taughtauer called to Mitkin and then motioned for the others to leave. Mitkin walked through the smoky mist and sat where Nin had just been. He noticed that both Strand and Nin watched him intently as he got closer to Taughtauer.

"It's just about time now," said Taughtauer. "I will be your sponsor. All you need to do is listen to me, in fact that is all you will do. Right now, I want you to go on your own into the basement and look around. Just stroll around and get a feel for the place. So go ahead down there now. You'll see a font, but don't touch it, or anything, just go down and look. And relax. These rituals are all for a reason. You'll know the reason." Mitkin got up and followed Taughtauer's outstretched forefinger until he found the hallway and the little door that led to the basement. "Yep, yep, right there. Go on down."

There was no light in the stairwell, only an oily-black abyss looming against the puny hallway light in which Mitkin now stood. The stairs stretched interminably into the dark, as if falling forever, down and down into oblivion. He reached around the corner and fumbled for a switch. His hand ran smoothly over a poorly papered wall and made a slick sliding sound as it went. He felt unsteady but found nothing and reached further into the stairwell, leaning a bit, over the stairs and into the black. His fingers were taut and spread wide, the tendrils on the back of his hand raised and rigid. He found nothing. Behind him, he heard the chitchat of his compatriots. Two steps down he went. Again he rushed his hand over the wall and still he found nothing. The sound of his sliding hand was all there was.

Step by step, he made his way down. The wall fell away on either side and he experienced a sudden space, wobbling a little. He imagined he was close to the floor and began to point his toes with each step. He waved his arms above his head looking for a dangling chain switch, the kind he had in his childhood basement. There was nothing there. His gulps for air grew louder in his own ear. The dim light from above petered out now, and he was enveloped by the pitch darkness. His own hand was invisible in front of his face. He toed the next step. It came to him and beneath his foot he recognized a new surface, cement, the floor. All the way down now, he recognized the air of the basement. It was tepid and heavy, just like his own basement had been, and he remembered playing there, in a fantasy land designed by his father, one replete with jungle gyms and a giant sandbox city. Slowly treading along, his shin knocked hard against a post and he wanted to go back up. Finally he found a cast-plastic switch. Light flooded the room and he squinted. A well-kept room came slowly into focus and he saw that it was filled with chairs and what he immediately thought of as a giant birdbath. "The font," he thought.

It was filled with glistening water. He looked and saw his reflection, and then that face, his face, in so many places from the past. He was with his father on a fishing trip, he was with his mother as a little boy, naked and happy and being bathed by her florid hands, he was with Raphaella as they walked in Central Park, and at his father's bedside. He was at Columbia taking an exam and he was at school teaching. He saw himself upstairs, only moments before, giving his toast, smiling ferociously, talking eloquently again in front of his new friends. And he was here, in the basement, staring back at himself, his eyes blue and bold, his strong nose centered perfectly on his angular face, lips laying thin and still. Boldly he raised his hand and plunged it into the water. It was cool like a spring from the ground, like juice from the forbidden fruit. It comforted him. With two hands, he cupped it and washed with care. Slowly and gently he scrubbed his face, massaging it into his skin. He traced his nose and eyes and ears and felt the bones behind them. He felt every bone in his face, one by one, like a caring lover might. He rubbed each gently and envisioned his skull below. He ground his palms against his face and pulled his skin tight. Again and again he washed, and water began to splash out and onto his feet, death and life changed places in his soul until finally he was finished. A thick strand of wet hair dangled in his eye and water ran nimbly down his back.

And then he heard footsteps above, many moving feet. One by one they all came down and gathered around him. They were quiet and somber, though none of them had changed clothes or put on anything shiny or new. Taughtauer was the last to join them. He approached Mitkin and patted him on the head slightly. "Seems like you got an early start."

"I was just washing."

But Taughtauer put a finger to his lips to stop him. Everyone put their heads down as he spoke.

"Many people think that ritual is a waste of time. Modern people are embarrassed by it; they think that it is superstitious and foolish. So why are you here, about to be dunked in this water, and why water, and why rituals at all? The reason is simple, Mitch. You believe, as we do, that the world can change and that making a commitment to change makes you a better man. With this water, we will separate you from the old man, the one who did not believe, or who did not care, or who simply did not know that freedom is possible and that children can live freely in this world. When you go under this water, Mitchell, you will be released from this old, pessimistic man, and become the new man, the one you know is good. So the time is now. Repeat after me."

The words flowed. There were invocations of hope and truth and commitment. There were incantations about brotherhood and success and keeping secrets. The crowd of martyrs spoke up too, acting as witnesses for Mitkin's transformation and promising to assist him in times of fear and turmoil. There was talk about the crimes to come, how each martyr must be willing to die for the movement. All the while Mitkin stood only half-listening; he was focused on the thick fingers of Taughtauer who now gripped him behind the neck like a child. Taughtauer was gently massaging Mitkin, not in a sensual way, but as if to calm and prepare him properly. The words faded until finally the room fell quiet.

Taughtauer edged Mitkin closer to the font and then pushed him slightly, bending him at the waist so his face looked directly into the water. Then, starting with Ricky Cuevas, each martyr stepped up and pushed his head deep into the water, one by one they initiated him, and little by little he felt unable to catch his breath, just as in his daydream. He groped about and lurched for air and by the time Taughtauer took him by the neck again, he believed he would die. In his ear he heard Taughtauer say, "Welcome, Mitchell. You've done it. We have done it together."

With a towel around his soaking wet neck, Mitkin walked slowly up the stairs and back to the big table where dinner had been served. Eventually he would put on a dry T-shirt, one of Taughtauer's, and curl up on one of the army style cots he'd noticed upon his arrival. He slept there that night, a new man and a martyr.

CHAPTER XIX
Bums and Dads

It was May when Mitkin left school and was baptized, and it was that same month that Raphaella, too, began something new. After selling nearly everything she owned, Raphaella set out to shelter the homeless, literally. She had gotten involved by sitting with them, those folks that we pass in the street, the ones we hope won't ask us for something, or worse, follow us for companionship. She'd sit with them before and after work, getting to know them right in the street, introducing them to Dana and learning their names. She and Dana would make extra food on Sunday afternoons and then spend long hours delivering it on foot, cul-de-sac by cul-de-sac. In essence, they ran their own little soup kitchen, the mother and child.

I went with them once, a Monday in May. We took the subway to the center of Manhattan, a place called Columbus Circle where on any given day, scores of homeless gathered. We pushed a shopping cart filled with food and drink until we found a cache of needy people. We found them huddled in the corners of the Columbus Circle subway stop, meandering in the crosswalks surrounding the tourist bureau, in boxes beneath storefront awnings, and along the benches in nearby Central Park. Many more could be found at Port Authority bus terminal and Grand Central Station; they were everywhere and so was Raphaella. She would pack food in neatly folded little lunch bags, the same ones she'd use for Dana's school lunches.

They found time for all this salvation because Raphaella's boss was like her, a badly bleeding heart. His name was Vinnie Ferrare, a doctor and specialist in social medicine, and a man who adored Raphaella who worked for him as an office manager; her razor-sharp organization skills were an asset to his practice. He and his wife, a generous woman who wrote books on child welfare and public policy, insisted on leniency for single mothers like Raphaella. They showered her with time off for college classes and child care, and of course, the homeless. Raphaella graciously accepted their gifts, and often spoke of how much she respected the Ferrares.

Dana loved the homeless, and the homeless loved her. They appreciated her innocence and childish benevolence, and her simple honesty. Most of all, they loved her willingness to have a conversation not about their past, their future or their misfortune. She just wanted to talk, and they too, together.

All of this was nice and good, at least until Raphaella told our daughter to imagine each of them, each vagrant, as her brother or sister, father or mother. This was a nice little teaching mechanism to be sure, but one that I didn't really appreciate.

"If you have to tell her something, tell her they're like brothers, not fathers, okay?"

We were in the park at 96th Street and Lexington, and I was nearly shouting. I mention the park because it was not a place for yelling. No, this park was middle class with middle class families who considered it their backyard.

"I've told her that, David."

"Then why did she tell me, and I quote, 'The homeless people are like daddies'?" I raised an eyebrow. "What is that all about for Christ's sake?" I was standing over her in a way that might have made nearby strangers nervous. She kept checking to make sure Dana was out of earshot, motioning to me to sit down.

"David, here," she said patting the park bench gently. "Come."

"I don't think so." I knew not sitting would irritate her, or at least would have irritated the woman I fell in love with so many years before. She smiled a helpless smile and patted again. "Raphaella, you are going too fast with all of this. These bums are not her daddy, I am. Do you think that associating them with me is going to help rebuild our relationship? I mean I'm not even the husband of her mother."

"What?" said Raphaella, trying to follow.

"I don't even see her as much as the bums do. Could you just stop with the homeless stuff already?"

"Why?"

"What'ya mean, why? Don't try to be some peace-loving nun or whatever. It's dangerous. Just go like every other bleeding heart and serve soup at some Catholic mission. Why can't you just go and do that?" I was nearly whining.

"I could, but this just seems right." Her eyes blinked like a doe.

"These people have problems food won't fix, Raphie, mental problems."

"But so?" In an impulsive moment she summoned a heap of words that poured rapidly from a cauldron of thought. "Isn't all of it dangerous? Life, generally? What is safety? What about greed? What about my ego, those dangers? What about people who care only about themselves. Hmm?" I tried to interrupt, but she wouldn't stop. "The world is a dangerous place, David, and I'd rather die doing something good then something selfish, wouldn't you?"

"Raphie, don't even try to make the comparison. Please. I mean, how is all of that the same as getting killed by a crazy person under some godforsaken bridge." I paused and became loud again. "How?"

"How? Because death is death. It's all the same. I'm sinful, David. I've got all kinds of crap piled up in my heart, piles of garbage, hundreds of thousands of ugly images, messed-up impulses. Dying isn't much when, if you think about it, you're already dead." She paused and shrugged her shoulders. She smiled like a penitent. "You wanted to know."

"No, really though, Raphie. What are you talking about? Seriously, you sound, I don't know, just off."

"Look. I see a fat guy on the street wearing tight clothes ten years out of style, and what's the first thing I think of? How stupid he looks. Why do I do that?"

"Because he looks stupid."

"Compared to what, David? Compared to what? What's my standard?"

"Yourself. You have a high standard. You're beautiful."

"So my standard should be based on bone structure that I'm not even responsible for? That's it then? I can think nasty thoughts about him because I have good bones? Could it be just bones?"

"Okay, it's not bones, it's a look, advertising, the capitalist machine, and like that, you've got the look. You look good."

"David," she shook her head and moaned slightly, "you are so far off, man, you're not even on the same planet. I mean you're standing right here and I can see you, but, you're an, an..." I know she wanted to say idiot but she didn't. "God is beauty." A group of kids ran by, screaming curse words at one another. "And you can't see God if you don't have a pure heart." That was a change of direction, I thought.

"So, is the fat guy beautiful, Raphie?" I said.

"He would be if we had the eyes to see. The world is groaning and moaning and waiting for me David—waiting for me to wake up and know who I am. We're all sacred, and always have been, but we keep falling, refusing to recognize that we are divine. We've done this to ourselves and that's why the angels cry."

The mood was changing. I had started in anger and now there surfaced in her that incorporeal pain. It was a profound sadness about the state of being, a deep-seated vision of what she called mankind's fall. She was sad in the truest sense of the word and I could not be angry next to her. Part of me wanted to console her but knew from experience that I did not possess the words. Instead, I just sat with my elbows on my knees. She turned to me and with a look of utter sorrow, confessed.

"Um, David, well I have to tell you something else. I've allowed a homeless couple to sleep in my apartment. They stay in the front room. I bought them sleeping bags." She looked down as if embarrassed. She reminded me of an addict out of control.

"They sleep overnight, every night?"

"Some nights yes, other nights no."

"You gave them keys?"

"No, they come and go. I believe their story. They say they are reunited lovers who both have drug problems. They say they are attending a rehab program on the Lower East Side, but it's not an overnight program." There were more children playing and then Dana appeared, worn out. The May sun was beginning to inch down toward the horizon, fantastic auburn rays bursting against the windows of the surrounding buildings. A window high up seemed filled with the sun itself and Dana looked up.

"The sun lives there," she said. "Doesn't it look like the sun lives in that house, Mommy?" Her mother nodded.

"Dana, can you go swing one more time for Daddy, just once more and then we'll go. Okay?" She went.

"So," I huffed, "they do, or do not, have keys?" I said.

"Do not," replied Raphaella.

"Will they be there tonight?"

"They might."

I could not believe this was happening. First, my daughter was confusing homeless people with me, and now, incredibly, those same homeless people were invited to sleep where I, the real daddy, could not. I had handled the fasting, and then the fire sale of everything she owned, but now she expected me to handle the outright endangerment of my flesh and blood. I wanted to snatch Dana and leave the freak alone in the park with her "fellow beautiful souls," the ones whom she loved more than me, and even more than her own daughter it seemed. I got up and then sat back down again. I pointed at her and then turned away.

Turning back around I asked, "Have you told your mother about this?"

"She wouldn't understand."

"Yeah, I bet," I said. "Have you told your friends?"

"They think I'm stupid. They've been thinking that for some time now." Raphaella flatly smiled.

"What about your priest? Have you told him?" I was afraid of her answer.

"Mmmhuh. He wishes I would bring them to the monastery. But he hasn't forbid me from helping them. They are my friends, really. If you could see, you would know."

"So your priest is at the bottom of all this. It's always that guy. Always. But this time I'm not taking it, Raphie. You cannot bring strangers into your house and jeopardize my daughter. It's a legal thing, I'm sorry. I won't allow it. I'll be by tonight to move them out."

"They've got nothing to move, David."

"Well then, I'll push their bodies out." Then loudly, like a drunk, I yelled, "They are leaving!" Alarmed, she gathered her things and stood straight up. "Out of the house!" I screamed. She beckoned Dana and the two of them left quickly, moving lithely without me, trying to shield themselves from me with their resolute strides. I trailed just behind yelling questions at Raphaella.

"Who do you think you are? You're not alone in this world you know. Why don't you wake up from your little selfish search? Hello!"

Haranguing her like this, I followed them for nearly two blocks. Finally, just before reaching 3rd Avenue she stopped, turned like a fierce animal, and protectively put Dana behind her. Stepping close enough to whisper she shot words down my spine.

"You punk ass motherfucker, you're not worried about Dana, you're jealous." She spoke with her teeth clenched. "If you were worried about her, you would have never left. That was danger. This," she raised a pointy finger within an inch of my nose, "is us trying to live a life worth living. Check yourself, David." She wheeled and turned away, but as she did she began to cry. I put out a hand, but they moved on. The old Raphaella had stopped me dead in my tracks, while the new one, the crying one, confounded me. Standing there, all I could do was watch them go.

I did not go by that night, and I procrastinated in telling the authorities, settling instead with a phone message to Sam Mitkin. He never returned my call, so I assumed that he was working on the "problem." I found out from her later, however, that she continued to house her new friends, and there were many of them. She went so far as to rearrange her front room. It now slept eight, and on most nights she filled it. She did not make keys but made sure to be home at the same time every day so each needy person could get in. All of this put an end to her portable relief efforts, as this new project was all she could handle. The lodgers were asking for money and pleading for food and they stole from her, but since the garage sale, she hadn't anything worth taking.

A tired devotion filled her emerald eyes as she acquired the look of a simple servant. Everyone she met immediately saw the change in her. But of course, that look, that simplicity, it just about broke my heart.

When I saw that look, I saw the sins of my past, though I never called them sins, of course. I described them as the *trouble we had* or *the tough times*, something innocuous that spread the blame. On other days I was less generous; I believed she was the great evil one, the unloving, unforgiving taskmaster whose new humane life was simply an effective payback, the means of my torture. She just wants to hurt me, I'd think to myself. Thinking this way comforted me and took me far away from the real questions, the truest and most difficult of all being: What was happening to Raphaella?

By June, a group of seven women lived quietly with Raphaella. The men who needed help went to Father Seraphim's monastery uptown, where they received hot meals and a cot. She had decided to preclude men when two made lewd comments and threatened her. Good, I thought, at least she's not a total nut. The women, hardened women, had suggested kicking the men out and whispered under their breath that it should have been done long ago.

The ones who stayed were an eclectic group. Of the seven, five were black and from Harlem. They had kids, but rarely brought the kids around the apartment. They used the apartment as a place to dry out. Kitty was the youngest of all the Harlem women. She was sixteen and sick with a sexually transmitted disease, one for which she refused to go and see a doctor. It just wasn't important to her. She had very little desire to be well and she'd say, "Because life's a little short thing, when it's too long it gets real boring, and you get ugly, too." She had seen nearly everyone in her family die early, and many of her friends too. Her appearance was unforgettable. She was short with thick, difficult hair, the kind of hair other black girls called bad hair, and the kind that took poorly to sheen and straighteners. She had let it become ragged and usually wore a baseball cap in the summer, a knit cap in the winter. She was shapely at sixteen and knew it, sometimes supporting herself with her body if she needed the money. She was called Kitty because she, rather unoriginally, likened herself to a cat. "Living's like being a cat in a dog pound," she said. "We da smart, tricky cats, they da dumb, dirty dogs."

But it wasn't the words that told the story, it was Kitty's sullen eyes. They were portholes to pain and that she spoke in worn out clichés made these portholes even darker, deeper, more rutted in a sadly predictable way. She rarely smiled and rarely thanked anyone for anything. When she first met Raphaella, she dismissed her as arrogant. Kitty considered most people of mixed ancestry arrogant. It was quite uncomplicated really; white blood equaled money, money equaled snobbery. Everyone she met was either friend or foe, and at first, the strange mixed lady with the green eyes, well, she was foe. "I thought you was a bitch," she told Raphaella more than once. "I thought you were trying to feel better by helping me out, like you was guilty a something." She decided to stay with Raphaella after another wanderer named Diamond Lee convinced her to.

"She not a bitch, little Kitty," said Diamond Lee, "she's just really crazy. She thinks wanting shit makes life shitty so she likes giving shit away."

Diamond Lee was harder than Kitty and the first to come as a full-time lodger. She had been an "associate" of the young thieving couple Raphaella told me about. "They," said Diamond Lee, "ain't no kinda married people, they just trash, period. And they ain't going on no bus trip, Raphaella, they smoking that ticket right now, believe you me."

It was Diamond Lee who moved in first after their departure. She was exceptionally skinny and very nosy. She never stopped talking and loved to tell Dana stories about the streets. Apparently her mother had given her to welfare authorities when she was two, and Diamond Lee had spent the rest of her life in foster care in a South Brooklyn neighborhood called Red Hook. She had come to Harlem to live with a boyfriend named Jimmy. He lived in a corner apartment above a bodega where, in cahoots with the bodega owner, sold cocaine, lots of it. The owner got shot one day and Diamond Lee was left alone. She started selling cocaine herself but smoked the profits and soon fell into debt. To fix that problem, she started to sell her body and the rest of the story can be found on the streets. At the house she was still a mess, but in Raphaella she had found a friend, though she would never admit it. She'd rather be called a deputy, Raphaella's deputy. Diamond Lee enforced the rules around the house that summer, and it was a good thing, too, because her deliberate and forthright style compensated for Raphaella who was growing extraordinarily quiet. This is not to say she grew self-indulgent or sentimental. She was simply reflective, a reflective woman in constant motion around the house, a woman who served. She was always picking up after the women or washing clothes or fixing dinners. She was assiduous and rarely went to bed before midnight. Few of the lodgers ever spoke directly with her for any extended period. Diamond Lee did the talking for her. Raphaella became an angel in that house, and Diamond Lee her guardian.

I remember watching Raphaella one Saturday as she sat and listened to the women discuss men. It was morning, and I had come to get Dana for the weekend. A great stream of light ran through the large bay window and into the packed apartment where it fell hotly on the half-sleeping women. They tossed on their little foam mattresses and moaned for someone to shut the curtains but no one did. "Get up welfare moms," said Diamond Lee, sipping coffee and laughing. "We have ourselves a little visitor boy." She looked at me. "Hi, Davey." I knew Diamond Lee from the week before when she assaulted me with questions about who I thought I was, and why I had caused Raphaella so much grief. "You're the little California beach guy, the little surfer punk, right?" Now, on this morning, I was apparently welcome. She even ogled me suggestively, causing me to gulp involuntarily. I saw neat little piles of clean clothes, each pile, I guessed, belonging to one of the lounging women. I got the impression that Raphaella had prepared the coffee and washed the clothes, and it occurred to me that Raphaella had been up for hours doing chores and serving these women as they slept. This irritated me. It was like free hotel accommodations for lazy people. I waited near the door, a stilted smile on my face, uncomfortable but curious. Diamond Lee used my presence as a starting point.

"So you gonna marry this boy, Raphie?" she said looking me up and down. "He seems a little antsy, like he got the crabs or something." She looked at me directly while shouting toward the back bedroom, "Is he any good in bed?" A woman, buried under her covers, giggled a girl's giggle and shuddered uncontrollably, like a third grader who'd just passed gas.

"I'll take him if you ain't gonna," she said through a laugh, still faceless under the sheets. "I'll take anybody who'll help pay the rent."

Diamond Lee shot back. "That's your problem, girl. You settle. Try shootin' a little higher, damn." She shook her head sarcastically. "Like me," she added sucking her teeth. "Shoot high like me. I mean look 'round, I'm the queen of this here place, the goddamned queen a Harlem." She nodded to herself and Raphaella appeared, nonplussed. "Oh, come on now, Raphaella. You love me, honey, you know it." Raphaella smiled.

An older woman named Annie lay on her side listening to the conversation. Her head was up and her eyes perky as she listened. She was rotund and wore tight clothes exposing her belly and the large, bulbous "half-belly" obese people often have just above the crotch. She had been discharged from a mental institution and into her brother's care eight years before, but her brother turned out to be crazier than she was. She'd been on the street for years. She wore thick black glasses and a wig that inevitably swiveled on her head. When she adjusted her wig, she handled it as if it were a hat.

"I never had no man," she said. Her voice was high and childish. "No man never wanted me." She put her head back down, her wig crooked again.

"Well, as far as I'm concerned you better off for it," chimed Diamond Lee. "Ain't nothing but dogs, just like Kitty here is always saying, ain't nothing but ass-licking dogs. And I ain't playing," she said looking hard at Raphaella. "Right, Raphaella?" Then she looked at me.

"Um, I'm just here to get my daughter," I said.

"But still, is you or is you ain't?"

"What?"

"Is you or is you ain't I said?"

"Is I or is I ain't a what?"

"See, now you did it. You already proved you a dog. A dumb, slow, ass-licking dog."

"Actually, I can't reach that far," I said. "My neck won't bend." No one laughed. No one except me. I let out a nervous *guhuh.*

Like Torquemada, Diamond Lee went on. "But, if it could you would right?"

"Lick it?" I asked exasperated. "Would I lick my butt?" I paused. "If I was a dog?" Right then, Raphaella calmly got up and with a slow, majestic stride filled the room with her presence. Each of the women, like myself, watched as she made her way towards Diamond Lee. She approached gently.

"More coffee, Diamond? Anyone else?" She had two other takers. "David, could you help me with the coffee?"

I trailed her into the kitchen, her inviting body clearing the way for my escape. In the kitchen, I leaned in and in a whisper said, "This can't be good for our daughter."

She looked at me kindly and spoke loudly over my shoulder. "Diamond, David's got the coffee." She then retired to Dana's room. I looked out over those women with three coffee cups in hand, wisps of steam gently ascending into the air. They all stared at me.

"Your coffee," I said, handing over the drinks like a waiter.

"Mine's black, I hope," Diamond Lee said dryly. The woman under the covers giggled again. I felt a twinge of nausea and a strong desire to drop the coffee, and then, thankfully, Dana appeared from her room. I kissed her on the cheek. Set against the refugee-camp living room, it felt like familial bliss.

***

It is the third day of questioning. I want to know why Raphaella was allowed to keep the homeless women in the apartment. I ask Mitkin if he knew about the flophouse. I ask him if he should have done anything.

"I knew. My family in Westchester knew too. They asked me to take care of it. They let me know I should threaten her."

"Did you?" I ask.

"I did."

CHAPTER XX

The Ostrich Bar

Mitkin decided to meet Raphaella at a place called the Ostrich Bar. If Mitkin were to spend time out on the town, this was the only place he'd ever go. The bar welcomed many lonely people, older lonely people mostly, but also a clientele of alternative college types, wannabe Raskolnikovs. The place was cramped and dingy, stretching no wider than four arms' lengths but running deep and long, like a cave, back to an area only slightly wider than the front. A dim lamp hung above four little dinner tables. There were nearly no signs of consumerism, no little blow up beer bottles. It was mostly just black—black steely chairs and black and white checkered floor tiles. A haggard woman, thin like a sick person, worked the long bar.

"One?" she asked as Mitkin entered.

"Two today," he said and went to the back. He looked at his watch and took a seat. He curled his head around the corner and looked for Raphaella. Nothing.

Sitting alone, Mitkin fought urges. One, and perhaps the strongest, was to simply leave. But he couldn't do that, his uncle had sent him to deal with her and the homeless issue. Another urge was to confront her, fight her over the same things they'd already discussed on that hill at The Cloisters. And yet another urge pushed him to reconcile, to open his soul to her one last time, even tell her about the movement. But more than anything, more than these temporary urges and conscious desires, everything boiled down to one thing for Mitchell Mitkin. Who loved him, and who didn't? That was it. And like an ingrown toenail or a sick little facial hair, he had burrowed deeply into his own self, creating a pain-filled man replete with suspicion and massive amounts of ego-inspired energy.

After the baptism, Mitkin stopped considering how far he'd come since his father's death. He stopped examining the past altogether. He tried to make his life simple; he slept, ate, read and planned. He planned day and night for Taughtauer, trying to be the perfect architect. He read Rousseau again and again, he read Marx, Bakunin and Malatesta. These anarchists espoused what Malatesta called *insurrectionary deeds*, deeds so monstrous that society would reject them, but deeds that, in the end, would change society forever. Mitkin began to regain his swagger and his self-assured mannerisms, but all of these externals came with a rebuilt engine, a new Mach 5 soul. "Now," Mitkin told himself, "I see it all plainly."

For Mitkin, society rejected its medicine. Like a dying drunk, society refused the stomach pump. But out of love, he imagined, Mitkin would force us. Mitkin would have his insurrectionary deed, one that would make the heart of each unwitting American sink, shudder, shimmy, and swoon, preferably over morning coffee while staring at CNN. "What have we done?" Mitkin would make us all ask. "Do our school children even hate us?" he'd force us to wonder. And we wouldn't be able to just write it off as *those people*, as *those poor black people,* he thought. The deed would be too big for that, too regimented, too daunting.

As crazy as it sounds, Mitkin wanted to be the leader of a revolution, and he didn't care if the whole world thought he was some sort of circus freak for wanting it. In fact, he became enraptured with rejection. He liked being stared at. He dressed more and more like an outcast, often wearing a heavy black rumpled fedora, sometimes coupling it with a ridiculous black cravat that he tucked into whatever dirty shirt he was wearing at the time. He favored tight jeans over his old mainstay, khaki Dockers. He bought some very pointy black boots that he would walk the street in, head and hat down, oblivious to the people who moved to and fro to avoid him. "They were Middle America," he thought to himself, "the status quo, the enemy." Like a machine, he studied every detail of that enemy, observing their sickening pragmatism, their knee-deep selfishness and petty materialism. He took notes on their penchant for waste, grumbling about their whorish women and remarking how effeminate American men had become. "They are filthy," he thought. "They pick up the shit of their dogs but put their grandmothers away in faceless facilities to be diaper changed by total strangers. Lazy, selfish bastards." Even their acts of mercy were done for the tax books. He hated buttoned down dress shirts and Velcro sandals, Lands' End jackets and digital watches with alarm clocks built in. He hated SAT tests and goddamned college fraternities, and he paid special attention to the gilded youth and their spacious, four-door Volvos equipped with the new, hip air bags designed to save a life not worth saving.

In one half of Mitkin's heart lived a raging man willing to give his life for the cause, while in the other half the rational man rotted away. Looking back on what I've written here, it is clear that I, like Mitkin, am unable to capture exactly what afflicted him. His thoughts were not concise, crisp, or cauterized. Nothing was. And maybe that is why, finally, he chose Taughtauer's path. It was succinct, it was simple, and it required only the most primeval response, rebellion. Of course there was pride, too. He had always been very proud, very sure that he was somebody of latent fame. He always believed himself destined for greatness. And now greatness had come in little acts of rebellion. He was proud of defying Borly and he was proud of his baptism into the movement. These were crucial for Mitkin, and whenever he became tired, or whenever doubt wailed in him, he remembered these events. He had been a hero in that hallway, a hero. He alone had willed meaning back into his life.

"Something cold, Mitchell?" scratched the bartender.

"Oh, sure. Yeah. Um, got a cold green piss?"

"One Rock coming up."

"Just leave it on the bar, Alice," he said.

He went lazily to the front door and peeked out. "Maybe," he thought, "she's not coming." He snatched his beer from the bar and returned to his darkened brig in the back, pulling out a notebook filled with plans for the revolution. It was a beautiful little notebook, bound in brown burnished leather. He had taken to carrying it everywhere. Inside, it was divided into four chapters or sections, each with a title: *Recruitment, Education, NY GO*, and *Monies*. He fingered through the first section containing a long list of names. Like a craftsman, he slowly passed his finger over the names.

Next he flipped to *Education*. There, on a blank page, he doodled. Back and forth he moved his pencil until he had created a cartoon image of a man with a fat mustache and pompous pinstriped suit. The character was holding a long piece of paper, one that almost went to the ground. On it, Mitkin had penciled in the title *To Enforce*. He then began to draw little heads, lots of them, situated far below the big mustachioed figure. They all looked up with their mouths agape and a sickly look in their eyes. He drew and drew these little figures until they resembled a horde of hungry babes all staring up at the parchment in the giant's hairy hand. Then on either side of the mustachioed man he drew two smaller, thinner versions of the same man. They, too, held very long scrolls entitled *To Cut*. The three men stood side by side, a hulking trio of admonition, while below the babes with shrunken heads and hollow eyes stared beseechingly. Then, tucked into the mass of hungry children, Mitkin drew the figure of a healthy boy. This boy held a gun in his hands, a big, sleek, powerful gun, a weapon the boy wielded with ease. Mitkin made the boy growl and point the gun at the mustachioed men, and then, hunched over and utterly entranced by his own work, Mitkin drew a T-shirt on the boy, its backside replete with the unique symbol of the movement.

"Am I too late?"

It was Raphaella. He closed his book quickly.

"A bit."

"I couldn't find the entrance to this place, man. There's no sign out front."

Mitkin thumbed the leather on the notebook cover. "They took it down to fix it, but never bothered putting it back."

Raphaella nodded. She stayed standing until Mitkin motioned her to sit down. She sat squarely in front of Mitkin and revealed again for him her beauty. The rant of first love returned instantly and he felt his limbs go tight and his palms perspire. He ran through his mind looking for the right topic, but forgot what he had come to say. He forgot everything, entirely. She stared and he felt his book again, remembering the movement. A sliver of cynicism shot through his stalled soul and he remembered his mission. Ugly pride welled in him.

"You know that you can't just keep beggars in your apartment the way you are," said Mitkin. "It's against the law."

"That's why I'm here?"

"Basically."

"Where will I take them?"

Mitkin again bogged down under the genuine disappointment of Raphaella's voice, and there was silence.

"Could I apply for some sort of waiver from the city and keep them that way?"

He looked away. "Just take them to a shelter."

"But they're friends, not puppies."

"Then go and work at the shelter," he said, waving his hand abruptly.

Raphaella was calm, studious. After a moment she pushed her chair back and slid it sideways so he sat facing her profile. She crossed her legs. "I heard you're not teaching anymore, is that true?"

"Substituting."

"Why?"

Mitkin slid the notebook under his thigh. "Teaching didn't live up to my expectations."

"Why haven't I seen you in the building? It's been almost four months, Mitch." The barkeep came and looked at Mitkin.

"Food?"

"I don't think so," he said.

Still looking at Mitkin, the barkeep nodded, "Her?"

Mitkin spoke, "Nothing, just two beers." She left.

"Okay, that was weird," said Raphaella. "What did you tell her about me?" He smirked.

Raphaella waited for Mitkin to say something, turning a bit in her chair. Then she turned again, this time back to where she had started, face-forward. She looked at Mitkin, her chin in her hands. "Busy, huh?"

He glanced at her, and then looked away. She just kept staring. He pawed the ground with his foot and she kept staring. The bartender brought the beers, and still Raphaella was staring. Finally she grinned, "Come on, Mitch, talk to me." Silence. "What's in the book, Mitchell?" And quick as a bird, she plucked it from between his legs. He blushed, and then flustered, tried to take it back. It was a weak attempt, and in fact, he felt relieved that she had his book, as if waiting the whole time for this moment. She thumbed the pages.

"It's my other job," he said.

She was having trouble reading his handwriting. "What kind of job is this?"

"A good kind." He leaned back. "The kind you'd like if you had the courage."

She sat up. "There he is, my Mitchell. Say it again Mitchell, say something half-mean again."

His face retreated into a cynical smile and he reached over the table for his book. With care, he put it back in his lap. They sat squarely across from each other now, as if playing chess. "Semi-mean?" he said. "How about this, you're a coward, Raphie. Is that mean enough?"

"I think so," she said.

"Here's some more for you. I'm not that person you got to know five years ago. I'm different now. I like warm fuzzy shit, and oh, I curse now, too. I also like people who tell the truth, but sadly, it seems that you aren't one of these people." He cocked his head primly. "See, I opened up a hardened heart and I used some sacred words, they went like this: *I. Love. You.* And I meant them. But what did I get in return? Lies."

"I didn't lie to you, Mitchell."

"Yes, you did. No one can say what you said and be telling the truth. 'I don't know what love is?' That's a fucking cop-out, Raphie. 'I love you as much as I know how to love?' What the hell is that? Why didn't you just tell the truth? Why didn't you just say, 'No Mitchell, I don't love you!' Why?"

"Because I do love you, as much as I know how to love."

"Enough!" he shouted. "You're all stopped up, Raphie! Constipated! Measured beyond belief!" His head shook as he yelled. He looked around and grabbed the saltshaker. He unscrewed the top and hurriedly poured salt onto the table. "Let it out like this, let it just flow out. Stop trying to measure it. Just let it out." He raised and lowered the shaker as if pouring a drink. Salt piled up below. Raphaella just watched. "Empty yourself, Raphie. You know you love. You do. I know you do." Like oily rubber burning itself out, he pushed a smoldering, "You fucking love me," between his clenched teeth. Then moving his hand as if polishing a car, he spread the salt all around the table. "Let it out and let it go everywhere," he said oddly, as if suddenly removed. His eyes followed his own hand. "Just let it go." The mood was thick.

The barkeep returned. Noticing Mitkin and his salt pile, she paused. "Everything alright?"

Raphaella looked at Mitkin who had now stopped his manic hand circles and, suddenly, as if taken by an idea, grabbed her half-empty beer. "Sure," she said, "I'd like another, just let me finish this one real quick." Raphaella poured her beer over her head. With her hair dripping suds everywhere she turned to the barkeep and smiled. "Make the next one a Guinness, okay?"

"Shoulda called home sick," the bartender muttered, walking away.

"How did I do?" said Raphaella.

Mitkin, his black hat nearly down and over his eyes said, "You're mocking me."

"Yes, yes I am. I am mocking you, and you're mocking me."

There was a long muted moment in which nothing moved, the silence keen and uncorrupt. Finally, Mitkin wiped his hands clean with a clap and said, "Just get rid of the bums."

"So you're kicking me out for real?"

"Not you, them."

"Really? Are you sure?"

"I'm not alone in this, it's the whole family. Just get them out. Over. Enough." She had never seen him so hard and rough as this.

"Mitchell," she said solemnly, "what were you drawing when I came in?" He was unmoved. "Where have you been, Mitchell? Please tell me, please."

"You can't handle where I've been," he said.

"You're in trouble, I can tell. Talk to me."

"Maybe one day, Raphie, just not yet." He got up and dropped a twenty-dollar bill on the table. "Have them out by the weekend or I call the cops."

CHAPTER XXI

Seever and the Date

It was about this time that I had begun to hang out with Andrew Seever, the young weightlifter and insurance broker from Wisconsin. We struck up a friendship in the throes of my disintegrating relationship with Raphaella. At first, I was suspicious of Seever. He seemed to always be prodding me about Raphaella, as if to test my level of devotion to her in anticipation of a big night out. That I could be jealous of such a match, Seever and Raphaella, informs the reader of the depth of my insecurity. But I did worry. Soon however, the worry gave way to utility. I found that Andrew Seever had something I wanted. He had friends. One of these friends was an attractive woman of twenty-three, a woman who had expressed interest in meeting someone her age and someone with whom she could, tritely, "spend quality time." I asked Seever if I could be that person. He was obliging and together we planned a double date, Seever and his friend Deb, me and the woman I had not yet met.

I dressed practically, but I remember a giddiness that urged me to dress more handsomely, even elegantly. I had not been out with another woman since returning from California, and in getting ready for my big date, all the drudgery and toil of maintaining ties with Raphaella took flight. I was free from the thought of her and our child for these few hours and I liked it. Well, I liked it as much as I could, because in going out I experienced a more profound toil and angst than I ever had with Raphaella.

The date started on the corner of 72nd Street and Columbus Avenue. Seever and I had met earlier in a bar and then made our way to the girls. They did something of the same downtown. Riding the subway on a Friday night, I felt surrounded by like-minded men and women, young people on their way to meet, movie, mingle, and if all went well, make love, or some safe sex approximation thereof.

Watching the prowlers on the train gave me a deep sense of departure. I was leaving one world and crossing into another, a land too enticing to ignore but too parched and meager to enjoy: the single life. Doing this, and doing life with Raphaella, were incompatible. But I kept on, telling myself all night, *she wants it this way. And besides, I'm a good-looking guy, unmarried, unattached and deserving of a little peace in my life.*

I got the feeling the other men and women on the subway were less conflicted. The train ride was jocose. The staid stares of the weekday rush disappeared, and in their place I saw wily faces filled with anticipation and appetite. I saw young lovers holding tight to one another and yearning inside to find a private place far away from the laws and regulations of a mechanistic work world. I did my best to join them in their joy.

I turned to Seever and began to share my thoughts but his countenance deterred me. It was flat, inert, dumb. It was kind, too. That was the thing that kept me there with Seever, that and his friend, of course. However, if I have given the impression that Seever was stupid I have misled. Seever was smart as a whip, a meticulous consumer of information. He loved the newspaper, loved the talk shows, did great at dinner tables and always worked hard at well, work. He was due for a promotion and would make more money by May than I would make in a year. No, Seever was not stupid, but there in the subway he was dumb, and I knew why. He, unlike Raphaella, was not willing to investigate every nook and cranny of his existence. He probably had never even asked himself the real hard existential questions that now ruled Raphaella. What am I? Where is the soul? Am I purely animal, or am I also divine? What is divine? See, these were all inconsequential for Seever. He just lived in pursuit of that which moved him, then, that moment, that day. And usually what moved him was money, and if not money then women. From there things got murky. He never thought of death, and if he did, he seemed never to think too hard. He was a big, muscular, well-dressed hunk of living flesh and, that night, he was my buddy.

Then, as if addicted or simply intellectually incontinent, I inexplicably asked, "Do you ever wonder what will come of us, how we'll die?" I was a goddamned recovering alcoholic.

"How we'll die?" he repeated cloyingly.

"Mmmhuh, you know. What will death be like?"

"Probably painful," he said. Then he stepped up to a newspaper kiosk and bought some Certs. "Want one?" We shared a mint as he sung the Certs theme song, loudly, as if alone in the shower. I cringed and scanned the street for others who might be cringing too. "Don't worry," he said, "no one cares. That's what I like about this town, you can just be who you are, no worries." Seever approved of himself with a series of nods, content with his cliché, happy with its accuracy. I nodded too, and smirked a bit, slightly happy to be with a guy who didn't recognize clichés. We walked briskly to the corner where the two girls stood waiting.

They were nice-looking. Both had florid, sensual, wavy hair. By the way Seever greeted the tallest, I knew the short one was for me. Thin but shapely, she had large green-gray eyes which invited behind heavy lids. I felt myself staring and in a rush held out my hand. We greeted, but stopped there. Her name was Allie. I smiled and shimmied out of view, under my skin, standing still while Seever made small talk. In my heart, there in that tiny sliver of time, I was regaled by soul-burps of guilt. They bubbled to the top of my consciousness and called me out for being here and feeling excitement in another woman's presence. My head fought against these recriminations. It was stupid, I thought, that I could feel guilt. It wasn't fair. I bit my lip to stave off the image of Raphaella's eyes in hers. I stuffed my hands in my pockets and smiled again. Allie smiled back. Finally Seever spoke to us.

"Dave, this is Allie. Allie, Dave."

"Yep, sure. Hi again," I said quickly. "How about dinner?"

Seever led us. He stopped at every crosswalk and waited for every light. Behind us, I could feel the impatient New Yorkers waiting for their moment to pass us on the left. And they did, flanking us whenever sidewalk traffic allowed, weaving around tree bowers, over rain-flattened humps of dog feces, tiptoeing gracefully to avoid tripping over our slow-moving heels. Allie and her friend Deb were transplants too, Californians from a San Diego suburb, queer bedfellows for Seever.

"Well, as artists you take any work you can get. That's how we met Andy, we were temping for his firm." Allie's voice flittered in the restaurant. We ate Chinese at a typical West Side joint, and sitting there our knees touched beneath the tiny table. Allie was across from me, leaning in to hear over the din. Deb was next to her. She, too, was leaning but impervious to our conversation. She was lost in Seever's muscles, ogling them and whinnying. Her shiny blond hair bounced as she laughed. I tried my best to watch Allie's mouth move but a part of me wanted to ogle Deb; her desire was contagious.

"What?" I asked, shaken.

"I said what are you doing?" Allie was speaking to me.

"Oh, I'm a teacher."

"That must be interesting," she said.

I said something like, "It is, the kids are real great," or "Sure, you are your own boss." But what I said inside was something like, "I don't think I can do this." I didn't want to feel this way, it was the old irritation again, the question of the deep hollow and I was tired of it. So I watched Allie's eyes and mouth as they moved on her ruddy face, I watched her hands articulate moot points, her bridled shoulders barely shake. I watched her try to get to know me. She was trying in vain.

"...that's when I met my first boyfriend. He was a senior in high school and I was just going off to college..." My food needed salt. "...he was training to repair electronic equipment and got a job at a bowling alley fixing the pin placers, that's where we spent all of our time..." And I needed to talk to the waiter.

"Could you bring some mustard, please?"

"It just wasn't right, he and I." She was about to tell me why when I got my mustard.

"Mustard?" I asked. She declined and I thought how she sure could use some, but I was being unfair. "So tell me more," I tried.

Then with a heavy, stumbling lilt, an offish Seever inexplicably interjected. He appeared to mistake Allie's story for mine, as if all old relationships were the same.

"Raphaella and you just seem like such a weird pair, Dave. Did you know she's got a whole bunch of bums living up in her apartment?" The word *bums* seemed to fix a spotlight on Seever, make him a man with an opinion, a man with something to say. The girls listened intently.

I nodded my head. It was all going to come out, spill all over like toilet water against shoeless feet.

"I spoke to her about it," Seever said. "Told her I didn't like them in the building. They could be dangerous, right?" He looked for and found nods of approval. "She was nice and all but she had this look, it was real serious, like she was listening to every word, but then she said the opposite, like no way. I wanted to clean out the cobwebs."

"What did she say?" I asked tentatively.

"She wanted me to take a few for a while."

"Take a few?" said Deb.

Seever scrunched up his face and threw up his hands. "Yeah, take some homeless people in! No kidding! I told her I've got Bose speakers in my place, and that you gotta be crazy." Seever was incredulous. "But she meant it, like she was serious about me taking some bum into my house." He hunched his shoulders. "I guess she's having problems with Mitkin on second. He's got some kind of legal action going against her, his uncle actually."

Allie turned to me. "That's your girlfriend?"

"Well, sort of," I said.

Seever went on. "I think you should talk to her, Dave. Your daughter's probably learning some bad lessons from those people and you never know who they're going to bring up to the apartment."

Seever's bouncy girlfriend chimed in. "You have a daughter with her and she stays there with the bums?"

Seever turned to Deb as a consoler and nearly in a whisper said, "It's only women as far as I can tell, so there's probably not any child molesters or anybody like that up there." He looked at me with dull, simple, blue eyes. "Still Dave, it seems like a bad situation to me. I called the city once, too, you know."

"You did?"

"Bad situation, Dave..."

I was feeling assailed, like a nerd at the bike racks after school. A part of me wanted to defend Raphaella, though in my head, I, like them, was convinced of Raphaella's naiveté. "Yeah, well, it is. But don't worry about the molesters and all that, please. She's a good mother."

"I'm sure she is," said Allie. And then it all began, again. She spoke more about her bad relationship, and this time I spoke of mine. I did. I kind of piled on, took it to Raphaella, I joined in on the fun by ridiculing her. I told Allie all about Raphaella and how we shared a child. I mentioned how much I loved my daughter and how *hard* it was dealing with her mother. She seemed to like this. My vulnerability sewed an unforeseen stitch between us and we trod the speed bump together, entering a new place. There we introduced ourselves to each other's image, the idea of ourselves. I met what she wanted me to meet, and she met the weak me, the person I'd wanted to be all along but couldn't be in the presence of Raphaella. In the back of our minds we planned the evening, and the plans were the same. It was decided, somewhere in the thing that was becoming us, that we were taking natural action, and speeding along a natural course. This, it was communicated, is how things are done. Eat, talk, vibe, soothe, cool, like and then, love; we were getting there and it was all real deep. We reached a very unspoken understanding about the night. It would end a certain way, and just in case there was any doubt about why it should end this way (dim, blue, and carnal), we let fly the grand grenade of lust, the one self-justifying argument of an injured ego: We were healing. This would heal us. Poor us. The soft tones and gentle whispers of a nameless night demanded so little and promised so much. I imagined a match because I wanted to. She wanted to as well. Seever got up and laid down some bills, and I watched as Allie did the same. My head jerked involuntarily.

"I've got it," I said reaching for my wallet. It was all part of my body's plan. "Please, let me get that." She followed her body's plan too; she picked up her money. We all smiled at one another and left. The rendezvous corner came at us and I jockeyed for position, the correct position for a proposal, a sorry substitute for *the* proposal, but one I'd settle for this night. We stood side by side with one block to go.

I didn't ask. I didn't have to; she beat me to it.

"We take the 1 Train. Our stop is 18th Street." That was easy, I thought, and assented.

Seever never flinched during all of this. All he said was, "Do you want to play ball tomorrow?"

"I don't really play ball, Andy."

"Okay then, see you guys." And he left, arm in arm with Deb. That's when I followed Allie into the underground and in my pocket, with my hand, searched for a token. Chivalrously, I found two.

The next day I wished there had been only one. It was morning, a bright, brittle morning filled with blinding slivers of crystalline sunlight, and I was standing above the 18th Street subway stop doing exactly what I'd done the night before, but this time I was empty. Huge rancid waves of regret poured through my soul as I stood in line to buy more tokens, the back of a tall man's head suffocating me from above. He wore a baseball cap and a ponytail, the kind that bounced around on his neck every time he moved his head in the slightest. That bounce irritated me. I peered at the overweight token clerk behind thick bulletproof glass, and again was irritated. I didn't like that this tightly uniformed lady was like a god, an enthroned, inviolable deity, a St. Peter of the Gates who wielded the power of subway absolution. I hated the subway suddenly. Daytime pissed me off too. It was too bright. And Allie was annoying as hell. She was right there with me, an unclouded vision of nakedness, lying beside me, pretending to moan or something, but right there, not leaving me, even when I closed my eyes. This, most of all, piqued me.

In the subway, I did not have any visions of love or lovers. It was Saturday morning now, a sober time, and the trains had a different job. They moved part-time workers mostly, and a few college kids in basketball shorts or sweats, some of them off for a bagel and a paper. I rode and waited and transferred until I finally reached my apartment where it dawned on me that I'd already lost Allie's phone number. I felt shallow. A palpable knowing raised itself in me and I came to realize the one true thing about my life—I was a slave. Somewhere, somehow, I had sold myself willingly to a woman named Raphaella, and now, try as I may, I could serve no other master but her. I couldn't even obey lust properly.

***

Mitkin is now asking me lots of questions. It is late in the day and Rocky is on the verge of sleep. The room is gray. Mitkin, however, is wide awake.

"Do you pray now?"

I have been waiting for him to ask me this. "I try."

"Why do you think it is difficult?"

"I don't believe."

He nods and nods. A kind silence separates us, and I see that he is happy with the answer and content to leave the conversation. But I am not.

"Do you?"

"I do now," he says, straight-faced.

"Not before, before coming here?"

"Never."

CHAPTER XXII

War of the Gods

The date was over and I was home—and what a home I kept. It was like a ferret had gotten loose inside. Piles of washed clothing lay wet and furrowed on the couch and a pizza box sat on the floor. Crumpled yellow stickies had been thrown at the garbage can, only to miss. I picked one up, and noted the three-digit prefix, the Bronx, I thought, but which number or whose, I had no idea. It wasn't Allie's, that much I knew. A red light blinked on the answering machine and I moved slowly to recover my messages.

The first was a hang-up, though the line stayed open for that very unsettling extra second before clicking off. The second message turned my stomach. It was Seever from the day before and he spoke glowingly of "the girls." I grimaced. The next message was from Raphaella. It was two days old. She spoke cautiously:

David, can you call me as soon as you get in? It's about Dana. I'm at her school right now. It's four o'clock.

At the school, for Dana?

I dialed and Raphaella answered.

"It's David. What's going on?" I hadn't spoken to her since the park incident and the image of me ranting at her all the way down Lexington Avenue issued a sick queasiness into my belly.

Raphaella was calm. "Did you get a call from the school yesterday?"

"No."

"Not even a message or anything?" She picked her way through her words.

"No, what's going on?"

"They told me they'd call you yesterday, I told them that they should."

"What the hell is going on?" She was being far too delicate and I wasn't in the mood. My nostrils flared. "Is she suspended or something?"

"It's not a bad thing," she said. "In a lot of ways, it's beautiful." I started to fume. "Hello?" she said.

"This is ridiculous," I said. "Just tell me what happened."

"She's been getting into arguments with other students."

I sighed. "Fights or arguments?"

"Well, arguments mostly, but this week she got into a pretty big fight. They called her names. And they want to test her, the psychiatrists."

"For fighting? This is crazy, whatever you do don't let them test her."

"That's why they want to 'brief you' or whatever."

The whole conversation was maddening.

"Okay, Raphie, here's what you need to do. You need to get to the point. What is going on?"

"David, before you yell at me, remember that Dana and I live together, so she's learning a lot from me, and for that, I want you to know, I'm not making any apologies." I waited. "It seems that Dana has been telling ghost stories at school, real ghost stories about demons and saints and death. The kids think she's weird, but she's not, she just tells her stories like they're real, really true, and like that, they come off differently than when other kids tell similar stories. Dana won't back down. She insists that demons are real."

Oh yeah, I thought, demons are real, and the chief demon is on the other end of the phone. The whole thing was like *The Exorcist* in reverse, and all I could do was laugh.

"So," I murmured, "Dana sees demons and they want to do tests on her? I don't know who's more crazy, them or you? Maybe this time," I smirked, "just maybe you went a little too damn far, Raphaella." I paused and then yelled, "Don't you think!"

"She's a reader, David."

"I'm a reader, too, but the frickin' white coats aren't coming for me."

She waited. "David, she reads the lives of the saints every day. She loves them."

"Get rid of the books. Tell the school you'll get rid of the books and they won't test her. I'm telling you, she'll end up in special ed if you're not careful. Tell them she'll stop."

"That's not an answer. Besides, I refuse to do that."

I huffed. "Well, what then?"

"They want to talk to you, they don't trust me." This must have hurt her, but I didn't hear it in her voice.

"What about Dana? What does she say about all of this?"

"She regrets the fight, but not the stories. I tell her to be quiet unless they ask, but she says they ask, and I believe her. Kids just like being mean sometimes, David. They call her possessed, the freak girl. You'd fight too, you would."

Sympathy started to break over me, and I mused aloud. "They shouldn't be talking tests for this. It's disturbing. Why tests?"

"I don't know. They say she's having trouble with her reading, but that doesn't make any sense. She reads very well. I don't understand it at all."

"What about her grades? Look, don't let them evaluate her for anything. The whole thing is a crock. I'll talk to them on Monday." I was nearly calm. "Put Dana on, please."

She did and we talked. Dana was absolutely unconcerned in a way that was very comforting. She spoke plainly. "I didn't hit anyone. I just kicked Tom and that other boy called Turtle."

"Turtle?" I said.

"He's slow, that's why." I smiled and imagined my little girl's face on the other end of the phone. Beautiful, I thought. I asked her about demons.

"They are smart, Daddy. They get you to believe things, like that hitting back is good. It seems good, right? But it's bad, right?" She waited for me to say yes, and I did. "But the kids think they look like *X-men* cartoons and I tell them that they can look like a mommy or a daddy, and sound like them too."

I couldn't hold back a groan. "Did the teacher hear you say that?"

"Yes, she told me demons aren't real."

"What did you say?" I asked.

"I told her to stop lying."

"You said that?"

"Yes, she sent me to Ms. Applegate."

"The principal?"

"No, a lady who asks questions about stuff."

"What kind of questions?" I asked.

"About demons. She was nice but I could tell she didn't believe me, too. I told her she better watch out." My head sunk and I laughed another groan. "Demons are like love, Daddy, you can't see love either."

I was being torn in two. My daughter was paying for the beliefs of her mother, struggling with people who marginalized her and believed she was a lunatic. My heart ached, and parts of it burned with anger. I asked Dana to put her mother back on the phone.

"This is on you, Raphie. Can't you just let her make her own decision about religion?"

"Sure, David," she said. "I'll do that. And then on other things, too, like my belief in homework, or eating right, how about that? I'll let her choose cartoons all day, I'll let her eat ten pieces of chocolate cake if she wants to, and at bedtime I'll say, eight or ten honey, or maybe you'd like to stay up 'til midnight? Good advice, Daddy, I'll let my child decide for herself on all the important things, God included." Her sarcasm bit hard. "Nobody who says kids should make up their own mind about God believes in God." Then, as if ending the whole conversation, she said, "So are you with me or against me?"

We had been on the phone for a long time and my ear was red-hot against the receiver. "What?" I said.

"When you go in there, David, that's all they're looking for, a wedge so they can reprogram her, make her a little more mainstream, not so superstitious." She sighed. "I'm sorry about raising my voice, but all of this talk kills me."

Me too, I thought.

"So, with me or against me?"

The creeping static of the phone line amplified itself in my silence. I felt caught in the wake of Raphaella's conversion.

"I'm with you," came blurting out.

The manacled silence relented and Raphaella signed off.

As things turned out, the school was not interested in testing Dana for special education. They wanted to ask me about abuse. They had overheard Dana talk of homeless people in the house and were suspicious. Their theory was that her fights were an expression of her fear. I could not really help them with that, after all, I was a victim of her new lifestyle too. I told them as much. The vice principal and I commiserated and that made me a little uncomfortable. The word *traitor* came to mind. Then they brought in the reading teacher, Mrs. Prudehome. She was very vocal about Dana's belief. She said it was ruining class discussion and that all the kids were transfixed by her stories and overwhelmed by her complete and total devotion to the "colorful characters" and "mythic figures." In a little room with a coffee pot, across the hall from the principal's main office, I asked her why this was so bad.

The teacher, a sallow-faced woman with stringy, flaxen hair said, "The kids all believe her stories, they don't see that the stories are made up." She bunched her eyebrows and nodded. "You should see the way she tells them, very intimidating and quite scary." She flicked the hem of her plain dress and it rustled softly just over her knees.

"But isn't that good, that she's so involved?"

"It's not only how you say it, Mr. Higgins, but what you say and where. My classroom is not a podium for evangelists, no matter how young and innocent. Church and state, as you know, are separate in this country. We respect your daughter's views but they are inappropriate in a school setting. Surely you can see that?"

I could, and I told her I could, but something pipped in my stomach telling me I should say more. I needed to defend Raphaella, and I needed to protect my daughter. "She's just five years old you know, the more she talks the more she'll grow and that's what school's for, right?"

"What about the children who must endure her offensive stories? Why do you think they punched her, sir?"

"I thought they were scared," I said. The coffee pot gurgled in the background.

"They're scared and offended. Look. I just want you to remember that religion belongs at home and education belongs here, in the schools. It's the only way anything can get accomplished. It's the only objective way to learn."

"But Mrs. Prudehome, the school's not mixing religion with education, just my daughter. Right?"

"I'm afraid not. She's teaching religion. Her stories are personal and faith-based and should be kept in the proper place."

I tried to add more but eventually the conversation petered out and I left. It was clear that for the sake of others she would have to stop talking about demons and gods. As I walked out from under the big building's rusty shadow, I was overcome by a sense of the absurd. We teachers, I thought, hold a power that has no boundaries, a power characterized by nothing if not its absolute discretion. We're like lords and the classroom is our manor. All good teachers realize this. Unfortunately, my daughter was an outcast in this classroom, and in truth, she was an outcast in every classroom I'd ever known. There, emerging from the shadow of the big brown school, I realized that this included even my own. There simply was no place for my daughter in this system, or, really, in this modern world. She would fight forever for her faith or give up the fight altogether. This, though I had never imagined it could, saddened me deeply. In a gushing moment I was made privy to Raphaella's struggle. I saw, if only for a second, that she was infected by a concept that goes counter to every idea fed to us in school, on TV and in the papers. Raphaella's infection was otherworldly and now, as if her own illness were not enough, she had to deal with the pain of her infected daughter. Who would choose such pain for loved ones? It couldn't be that she liked all of this, it had to be that she was a victim of it, the belief in demons and God and sacraments and all.

But then, I too was a victim, I thought. I was a slave, too. After all, I didn't freely choose to get up and trudge to my job every day. It was more like an order, a singular voice whispering to me as I lay in an early morning funk. *Obligation*, it said. *Obligation*. In fact, most of my life was commanded by this perennial voice. *Date the pretty ones, wear the latest things, get the highest degree, make the most money, serve the self*. The voices came to me all day long. And I followed and served up sacrifice at every pop altar, and yes, I quietly told myself, this *is* good, this *is* right, this is *the way*. I had religious accouterment, too. I reverenced the icon of individualism, the pure power of the market, the sanctity of democracy and the precepts of enlightened society. I supported public education, shelters for poor people, high enough taxes to secure a safety net but not too high to deter investment, I espoused pro-choice and fair prices for familiar products, and I venerated these neat clichés spoken into existence by society watchers who want to make sense of the world around them. Digging even deeper, maybe going back behind the holy curtain, I found that the core of my religion was *me*. I believed in *me*, period. The first and most important canon of me was my pursuit of comfort. So I got laid, I drank good beer, I bought downy couches and feathery beds, took longer lunch breaks and longer naps. I served my god well. And Raphaella served my god too, at least until this new one found her. What a god it was. He demanded her life, her ego, every jot and fragment, every passing thought, trite remark, gesture and breath. He demanded it all. She was asked to shoulder the truth, to accept the fact that she was made perfect and could be perfect like her God in Heaven. This God was opposed to mine, and now, under the roof of our most vaunted public institution and within the heart of my most beloved daughter, the two gods would collide. That I had gone to the school in an attempt to make it all better disguised my relationship with my daughter. I was not her protector. I was, in fact, the fox in the hen house.

One might say, just as I did standing on the steps of Dana's school, *Relax. Life goes on. Chill.* And yeah, most of the time I'd say sure, absolutely. But this time I couldn't. I came again and again to one word, *truth*. Either my shrines venerated truth, or they did not. Either there was truth and one of us was wrong, or we all were right, every one of us, and that goes for Mrs. Prudehome, Ms. Hurston, Mr. Higgins, the NAACP, the KKK, NOW, Fox News, MSNBC, ACT UP, and even good ole' child molesting members of NAMBLA. If we're all right, then there is only war, total and continuous war by any means necessary. If we're all right, then there is no peace. Heavy and swollen, my heart pounded in my chest. I looked up again at my culture's sacred temple as it swayed under the maundering clouds and blue sky. For a moment, I thought it might topple.

But the clouds stilled and my moment passed and I walked away under the flesh of two unsteady feet. At the corner, I tried to recall all of my thoughts, but they eluded me. By the subway I pondered my wallet, placing it in my front pocket to avoid the thieves, and soon I was back at school teaching the last of my two classes and asking myself nothing about truth or war or life. The gods sat quelled— I was once again in charge. I decided to see Raphaella that night and tell her we just had to gut out a bad situation. Mrs. Prudehome, I'd say, won't be there next year.

CHAPTER XXIII

Death Awaits Us All

The eviction notice came. It came in person, but oddly enough it came from a city council member, a high-profile man named Ray Carver. Somehow he'd come to know about Raphaella and her little shelter. It seems that he was an old friend of Mitkin's father, Martin, and that he owed the family a few leftover favors. This was one of them, requested by Mitkin on behalf of Raphaella, a genuine act of love.

Raphie and the councilman talked in the living room. Carver was forthright and his plan was simple. Raphaella could avoid eviction by moving her makeshift shelter into a new city building where she would work as chief coordinator. Ray Carver would receive credit for finding her and her boarders and saving them from the streets, not to mention rewarding her with a job she would surely love. It was a snug fit. I was stunned. It seemed that Raphaella's new god was shining on her. As if in biblical times, I told myself, the sea had parted, the lame walked. I was impressed, but she wasn't. She told me she wouldn't take the job, said it wasn't blessed. I was confused.

"It's everything you wanted," I told her as we stood in the foyer of her place, waiting for Dana to get ready for our weekly visit. "It makes perfect sense."

"It's too much. It's got too many dangers."

"For who?"

She was calm, but in her eyes was a look of loneliness. I could see that she thought I'd never understand, that it would just be more of the same silliness—demon talk, more demon talk. "Forget it," she said.

I shook my head and escorted Dana down the stairs muttering. "It just gets weirder and weirder." In typical fashion, Dana put on her mother's mood. She hung her head. She walked solemnly to the car, a barefoot tenderness in her stride. We kept silent all the way downtown, the sway and jog of the moving car the only thing between us. Finally I spoke up.

"Mom's real sad, huh?" She nodded, but still didn't look at me. "She doesn't want to quit her old job, huh?" She didn't respond. "Is that why she's so sad about the new job? She likes it, but wants to be nice to Doctor Ferrare?"

Dana furrowed her brow and looked at me sternly. "That's not it, Daddy. Father Seraphim says she shouldn't. That's why."

Of course, I thought. My knuckles whitened on the steering wheel. "He said she *can't* take the job?"

"Sort of, uh huh."

"Oh boy," I pined. "Why would he say that?"

"Mommy says she's too proud for the job."

"Mommy said that or the priest said that?"

"Mommy said that herself."

I slowed the car and pulled crookedly into a parking spot. We had come to the Lower East Side for a birthday party, though rage now blocked my ability to remember just whose. I went inside with Dana and she immediately fell headlong into the party, swallowed up by her friends, their mothers, and music. I simpered and thanked the hostess, got the pick-up time, and left.

The damn priest. I sped uptown. The freeway led me up the East Side where the city rose like iron cliffs to my left. Rows and rows of rust-brown buildings lined the freeway and pushed me against the steely East River. One by one, the fat, concrete viaducts passed overhead and marked my ascent. Fourteenth Street. Thirty-fourth Street. Forty-second Street. Midtown Tunnel. Seventy-second Street. I threw my car into the fast lane and fixed my eyes on the car ahead.

Like this, I slipped into conversation with the bearded bane of my existence. I shouted and he argued back, my tack wholly logical, foreseeable, clean, convincing. We battled over Raphaella. I told him to stop controlling her and he said he didn't. I told her he should let her take the job, and he said she could if she wanted. He looked into my eyes and saw my love for her. He saw how serious I was. It was easy, he'd understand. But then the shadows of Dana's school crept over me like a canopy of confusion. I remembered Raphaella as she was, an enslaved believer and one filled with an impractical conviction about right and wrong, good and bad, truth.

There was the real problem: truth. I couldn't avoid it. I'd have to battle the monk over truth. So I did, at top speed, in my head, in my car. He told me Raphaella needed to find truth on her own. I told him truth was happiness, and that she would be happy if he advised her to work at the shelter. He said perhaps, and then nodded, and I knew what he meant. He wanted *me* to convince her, he wanted *us* to work it out and then I realized that this was all part of his plan. He wanted us to be together, and hoped I would make it happen. Indeed, it was a stunning plan. He was an amazing man. I saw why she would love him and his ideas. Raphaella was right, he *was* wise. I envisioned it all. He would advise us to marry and run the shelter together. I would write about the lives of the women and we'd be in love and I'd love good things. That was what the monk wanted, and it was my insistence, my sheer devotion to her, this speeding car, this frenetic romantic energy that had convinced him that we should be together. I was a love bullet and I was going to be rewarded.

My conversation with the simulacrum ended just as I slipped onto the ramp of the 125th Street Bridge. Emotional, I pounded the gas pedal and the car jerked ahead. In and out of traffic I went, shoving my way back and forth, faster and slower until, finally, I dipped into blotchy Harlem traffic. A hollow, breezeless air enveloped me there and I rolled down the windows. I checked my watch and then surveyed the neighborhood. It was barren. A long, craggy, concrete parking lot sat astride a run-down and abandoned warehouse. Next to the warehouse was a school. The school blended in with the other buildings, all of them lifeless. A tall, yellow, revolving sign read LIQUOR. The monastery was just two blocks up and a few blocks north.

But I couldn't move. The only things moving in this jam were the waves of sound carrying bleating horns. I sighed and wagged my head in disgust and then, out of the corner of my eye I caught the illusive image of a man in black robes seemingly skimming along the sidewalk, hovering really, alongside my car. I focused and sure enough it was the old man, surreal and like a wraith in his robes, striding sternly beneath his black sauterne which covered his feet and dragged slightly on the ground. His beard blew in the wind and he held his round black hat to his head with his hand. I watched, ferociously interested and intensely amused. He walked ahead, moving faster than my car, until he came to a stop under a tree. There were two men there, disheveled men, both of them selling peanuts out of a big burlap bag. Their gaunt black faces told stories of despair. The priest bent over and slid a tiny stool beneath him, tucked his robe between his legs and sat. Together they cooled in the shade, three old men shelling peanuts, hawking peanuts and munching peanuts. I pulled slowly alongside and yelled out the window.

"Hello." I coughed to clear my throat and said again, "Yes, hello, it's David, Raphaella's friend. Do you have a minute?"

One of the old black men straightened his neck and strained to identify me. I smiled.

"Who's Raphaella?" he said. At that, the priest looked at him and then at me. I yelled again.

"Father Seraphim, it's me, David, Raphaella's friend. Do you have a minute?" He got up and came gently to the car. His mouth was full of peanuts. "I just wanted to talk to you about Raphaella and the homeless shelter."

He squinted. "David?" He leaned over into the driver's side window. "Oh yeah, hey. Hello. How are you?" I nodded my head. He paused and said, "She's got you thinking some more, huh?"

"Yeah, I guess. Can we talk?"

A horn blared behind us, and right away the priest straightened up and shouted with an outstretched hand, "How 'bout we all just relax, huh?" The horn blared again and Father Seraphim laughed an, "Ah, come on buddy," and then hopped into my car. "Wow, the mean streets, huh? Probably on his way to get an emergency coffee and donuts." He looked at me. "So, you want to talk?"

"Yes," I said. "I do. I've been thinking about something that I found out today. About Raphie and the shelter."

"What's that?"

"It's just that you told her she shouldn't take the job with the city, the shelter job."

"The shelter job?" he said. I nodded and then he pointed. "Here, take a right." The car moseyed up Madison Avenue. "Oh yeah, sure, the shelter job with the city." He shook his head. "That's no good for her. But she can take it if she wants it." We pulled in front of the monastery but there were no parking spots. We idled.

"She's not going to take it," I said, flatly.

"That's a good decision. But you don't think so, and that's why you're here. You zoomed up here to let me know, and you're angry, and I don't blame you really. I can see why you're angry, but you should know anger won't serve you. Ever." He reached out and drummed on the dashboard. "How about some focaccia? You like focaccia?" Before I could answer he opened the door and crawled out.

"You'll love this place. Great focaccia. Just double-park it, nobody'll bother you for a while. Here." He unlocked an old blue station wagon and pulled out a dashboard sign that read CLERGY. He flipped it onto my dash. "There you go. Focaccia."

We walked about a block and a half and found a busy pizza parlor. Everyone turned and stared at us as we came in, and then, as if hypnotized by his familiar presence, they all went back to their food. I stood uneasily at his side. "Hello, Liberty, could you give me that piece right there?" He got on his tiptoes and pointed. "Yep, perfect. Thanks, Liberty." As I ordered he turned to me and said, "Her name's Liberty, how about that? Great name, huh?" I nodded and thought that his name was Seraphim and how about *that*, but I didn't share my thoughts with him. Turns out I didn't need to. Still waiting for our order, he turned again and said, "She thinks my name is odd too. Don't worry, David. I'm a regular."

The pizza joint was small with little wooden parlor chairs and tiny, round, wooden tables. A few booths filled the back of the shop, but they were currently being used as storage for cases of soft drinks. We scrunched in and before I could even reach for a napkin, he had waved his hand over our food in the shape of a cross. He smiled at me and then took a hearty bite. While chewing, he rearranged his seat and tucked his robes up under him, out of the way. "Those two guys I was selling peanuts with, they are both dying. They sell peanuts for the monastery, and for themselves. I get the peanuts donated to me by some downtown vendors." He chewed. "They don't have long. Death is coming for them. It awaits us all."

Not another story, I thought.

"I knew this monk once, on Mount Athos. He slept in a box that had a lid on it. On the top of the lid there was a painting of a skeleton. Neat huh?" He wiped his mouth with a crumpled napkin. "He got into that thing every night after his evening prayers and went to sleep. Then, in the morning he'd get out, turn around and shut the lid, say his morning prayers and guess what? Even we monks thought he was crazy." He reached and shook some Parmesan cheese over his focaccia. "But he used to say to us, 'Who's really crazy? Each day I am resurrected and given the gift of life! Look,' he'd say, pounding his chest, 'I am alive, I can repent! One day the box will claim me and when that day comes, I am finished on this earth, Fathers, my soul will be all I have. This day, every day is for the preparation of my soul for death.' I used to say to myself, you sleep in a coffin, you crazy old coot! But of course, he wasn't so crazy was he?"

I hoped this was a rhetorical question.

"Remember death, David. Remember death."

I listened as best I could, but we were surrounded on all sides by Harlemites on lunch break, crammed together and eating pizza, subjected, I thought, to this priest's unbridled voice, and of course, to his beard. I searched his waterfall of whiskers for food bits, but found none. I stole glances side to side. A cement-faced man with a bandana chewed with his mouth open, surely grinning at me, snickering a little, intrigued. A woman with tight jeans and long beaded braids squeezed passed with her pizza on a plate and her hand high in the air like a waitress. She glanced at us and I mugged a smile of discomfort. She smiled back breezily. I had maybe a foot or two on either side of me, and there was Father Seraphim going on in a none-too-subtle way about death and naps in coffins. Suddenly, my wonderfully crafted car conversation about Raphaella and living together and marriage, well, it all sort of caved in like a bad angel food cake, crumpled up and sticky. I nodded to the "death awaits" comment, and I managed to realize that he was right, at least about death.

"But you didn't come here to hear about death did you, David?"

"No," I said.

"So?"

I paused, wearily. "So... I really don't see why Raphaella shouldn't take the city job. The job makes sense for her."

"To you, sure. But what about for Raphaella?"

"I think she thinks it's good too, at least until she spoke to you."

"Do you really think it's that easy, David? I just talk and she listens and then she marches off and delivers?"

"Well, it seems like it sometimes."

"Things aren't always what they seem, David." He leaned over, closer to me, and with a theatrical whisper said, "She has been invited to perfection, armed as it were with the truth, invited to live in Christ, in the Church, and not live for this world. See, she isn't living to get promotions anymore, David, she's not interested in choice apartments, job promotions and 401(k)s. She's living to acquire choice bits of humility, meekness, love." He smiled and still leaning, addressed the man with the bandana. "How's your slice, brother?"

The man grinned and chewed.

Soberly, Father Seraphim wiped his hands, finger by finger cleaning himself, neatly, patiently. "The reason she won't take the shelter job is because she fears pride and ego like you fear unemployment and life without sex."

"Unemployment and sex, huh?" I said angering, and on the verge of becoming rude. "That's what you think I care about?"

"Don't be angry, David, the glass you see through is not hers."

"Maybe, but her daughter doesn't see it her way either."

"I don't think so," he said. "Dana and Raphaella are growing together, seeing things together, just as mothers and daughters are prone to do. How could it be any different?"

The pizza shop, the pizza eaters, the close quarters, the girl named Liberty, the smell of pepperoni, the beard, all of it, faded into the background, away from us. I thought how nothing had come off as I had hoped, nothing was said that needed to be said, no one had heard me as I needed to be heard. Instead, I had been given death and coffins and worlds to come, and I had been given embarrassment and confusion and a sense of emptiness, no matter what he said about newness and joy. He had imparted nothing but a sense of emptiness, actually. The words *the end* came to mind. I was distraught.

"She loves you, David, at least she tells me she loves you. But you, you David, need to look into what love is. It's as profound a reality as we long for it to be. It is everything that we hope it is, and that means it doesn't come easy and it ain't about sex."

"Sex?" I said, my eyes narrowing. "Why do you keep bringing it up, sex, why!" I stopped and stared at my pizza, shaking my head. "You know what," I said slinging an open hand, "you can have her. Forget you and her and all this bullshit." I stood up. "Whatever. Go and get her killed with your otherworldly advice because that's what's going to happen. One of these bums is going to do something crazy." I pointed demonstratively to within an inch of his face. "And her blood will be on your hands."

The big priest remained seated in his chair, looking up at me, his blue eyes still and serious. "It looks like we've returned to the starting point, David. Death. Death awaits us all."

I left him, seething, and as I marched out I realized the entire pizza parlor was watching me go. I didn't care. I mean was this guy a frickin' lunatic? Sure death awaits us all, but what about a little fun along the way? I don't know, how 'bout a goddamned ball game or maybe a dance around the maypole, asshole. I wasn't some idiot, some hedonist sex addict who couldn't keep his pants on. Plus, I *had* been trying to figure this all out. I *had* made an effort. Hadn't I grown closer to her of late? Hadn't I started to see things as she did, spiritually, otherworldly? I'd had little revelations. I'd been trying. But now the monk spoke so candidly of death, death and the end of things, consumption and destruction. The end of all, end all to be all, end, over, darkness, death. I hit the accelerator.

Death awaits us all.

I couldn't shake it. His words were gummy and uncomfortable, and they got in the way of my driving. The copious rows of oaks which line 5th Avenue all along Central Park's east side were alive and well, but I imagined them withered and dead, leafless and hollow. The new sods of Bermuda grass, verdant and rich, beautified the park, but I imagined it pale and weak, sick and dying. The people on the lawn were dead too—on their backs, arms folded, staring vainly at a barren sky which wasn't a sky at all, but rather a putrid, beige-brown ceiling, the top of a rented funeral parlor where the carpet smelled like damp fruit and the people maundered beside decapitated flowers, the flowers themselves cut from their roots, suffocating and in the throes of death. A smutty film of despair covered me. Everything nettled and piqued me. I was physically uncomfortable.

I grew despondent about Raphaella. Pure, crystal-clear capitulation shuddered inside of me. There was simply nothing to do to get her back—nothing. I was overcome by the reality. Our relationship was over. All of my imagined needs, to be a father, to be a husband, to be a friend and mate, to be a teacher to my daughter, to be there, in the lives of the ones I thought I loved, all of these needs were needs no longer. They all got swallowed up in his words, "Death awaits us all." Life became meaningless and I drove on without sense. The skin on my jowls hung heavy on my face and I felt my lips sag into a frown. My eyes saw hazily, and my shoulders hunched. This was the end; I would leave again. Maybe this time I'd go down south and stay with my father's side of the family and I wouldn't send money, I wouldn't send pictures and I wouldn't feel guilty. I would feel nothing, simply nothing. We *were* dead. The monk had won.

I retrieved Dana and we drove in silence.

"Daddy, what's wrong?"

"Nothing, honey."

"You look sad."

We slowed gently at a stoplight and a big truck let out a hydraulic sigh. My hands sat limply on the steering wheel, and the smile on my face sagged.

"Everything is fine, Dana, really."

Raphaella was out on the stoop, sitting with Kitty, both of them wearing baking aprons. Kitty saw us first and smiled, then Raphaella. Dana smiled back. I got out and let Dana out of the car. She bounded to her mother and they embraced. Before much could be said, I got back in the car and put it into drive. As I drove off I turned to meet Raphaella's eyes. Staring like that, I drove slowly, saying nothing, just watching her watch me and wonder.

CHAPTER XXIV

A Million Strong

Two days later, Mitkin showed up at my school. He met me outside my classroom after the final bell, his expression all soft and sugary, his stride airy.

"David, you look good. How have you been?" I was wary. Mitchell Mitkin never greeted me like this before. "I'm not teaching full time anymore," he said. "Did you know that?"

"Yes, Raphaella told me."

"Yeah, we don't talk much anymore, me and her. I'm real busy now, got a job as a full-time substitute right next door."

"LaFollete?" I asked.

"Yes, exactly. See I'm up here for the rest of the year, just one more week now. I was wondering if I could come by one lunch and talk to some students of yours, your toughest students preferably. Maybe you'd like a day off, huh?" He stared directly into my eyes. "Maybe?"

"Maybe," I said. "But why?"

"Of course. I am involved with a citywide program for students. It's called the Student Coalition. We are a student advocacy group. We are into empowerment, like when you worked at The Plateau."

"You're the spokesperson?"

"See that's the most salient aspect of the entire program," he said sounding like the old Mitkin. "I just watch mostly. We have a small cadre of dedicated students who make presentations to other students. Students teaching students, like Stop the Violence."

"Oh yeah," I said simply.

"Yes, we are a bit like them, though more academic. You'd really like it."

I asked him if Raphaella had ever seen this new project of his and he grew dark. "No. She wouldn't get it. She wouldn't like it. She's too closed-minded." I nodded and suggested lunch, but really I just wanted him to leave.

"When exactly? You know, for lunch." Before I could answer he said straight-faced, "Tomorrow? We could have lunch tomorrow?"

"I…"

"Too soon? Day after tomorrow then, I'll meet you in front of LaFollete. Twelve sharp."

"Why don't you call me," I said. Becoming quiet and moving deliberately, he handed me a pen and the back of an old business card. I gave him my telephone number and left. I left him even though this was my school, *my* place of employment. I walked around the halls for ten minutes and thought that surely he would call.

And he did, that same night. I listened as he spoke commandingly to my answering machine. "Again, I think your students would truly benefit from our presentation and I think you would too. I hope that you won't be like other pig-headed teachers on this one, David. Pick up the phone please." He didn't hang up but stayed on listening. "Pick it up David, you're there, I know it, you said you'd be." He silently waited some more and then hung up with a clang. I never called him back, mostly because I loathed the idea of trying to deflect his sales job. He left another message on Thursday evening, the last Thursday of the school year, four days after he'd shown up at my classroom. An understated contemptuousness broke through an otherwise polite voice as he told me that his Student Coalition was holding a "campfire" at Luther High the very next day. "It doesn't matter that you never called back," he said. "Go. You must go."

I went this time, afraid not to.

The sun was high and bright and I was impressed by the turnout. There had been a buzz all day concerning the meeting, and three of my most combustible students had even urged me to go and "see this wild guy speak." I wondered if "this guy" could be Mitkin. I walked from the dingy school hallway into a courtyard gleaming white from the rays of a hot sun. A thin boy was speaking rhythmically into a microphone.

"You ever asked yourself why these buildings exist, yo? Look at 'em." The young man pointed at the school and shouted, "Why is this building here, why?" He pointed again, shading his eyes with his other hand like an army general in battle. "They here because the older generation needs us, they need us to be a certain way, to think a certain way, to act and believe a certain way. And if you look 'round, especially when you look 'round Manhattan, you see *the* way. They want us to buy things yo, consume some shit. Let me break it down for you." He surveyed his crowd. No less than fifty kids had come out to the meeting. I looked and found Mitkin sitting dispassionately and inconspicuously against the far wall. He was flanked by two students; one, a young man, was staid and serious, the other, a thin girl, sat content, a wry smile curling her lips. To the side sat a folding table with a sign affixed, reading MLHS STUDENT COALITION. The speaker, the boy I'd one day come to know as Richie Rovers, went on:

"I'll break it down like this, y'all. Everybody wants a piece of you. I mean everybody: teachers, parents, the po-po, politicians, moviemakers, advertisers, all of 'em, every one of 'em. They looking out for themselves by looking out for your desires. It's the same with the Board downtown, and it's the same with this administration right here." He pointed again. "They want a piece of you, the piece that makes you free." He paused for a spattering of applause. "You know what I'm saying?" He nodded big, heavy-chinned nods. "You know, you can feel it when you wanna take a class about something you love, African-American culture maybe, but it ain't on the list." He raised an angry eyebrow. "You can feel it while you stand in line to get scanned in the morning like common criminals."

Rover's nod kept pace with his words, up and down, louder and louder. "You can feel it when you are trapped in a class with a teacher who wants one damn thing, a paycheck. You can feel it! Why don't they get ridda that teacher, you wonder. Why don't they offer that class, you say. Why don't they care about you and what you want in life? And the answer is the same every damn time. Because they don't care about what you want, about what *you* want you to be. What this administration wants, what the chancellor of the schools wants, what society wants, is us acting like little robots yo, little bitty parts in the great big American machine. And am I lying?" He looked wildly around the courtyard as kids slowly made their way out of class and passed his raw voice. The crowd swelled and among them I saw three of my three students, three difficult kids whom on this day sat so still they appeared desperate to hear.

"Am I lying?" Rovers shouted, and then again, louder, as loud as I imagined he could: "Am I lying to y'all?" Then his voice grew soft, and the speaker system pushed out his whisper. "Why do we have bells at the end of class, ringing, all day long?" He turned up his palms and feigned not knowing. "Why bells?"

"Tell us," two thick girls yelled out.

"Because our school is a factory and guess who the product is, nigga?"

The girls yelled, "Us!"

He pointed and looked right at the lonely voices. "That's right. We go from room to room all day just like cars pass from spot to spot on an assembly line. At each station they add a part, here some math, there some English, here some bullshit history. One by one, bell by bell, we get fixed up 'til finally, after four years of fine-tuning we s'posed to be fine-oiled machines ready to enter the world and consume our little asses off, we s'posed to be ready to produce and consume until we drop. And that's exactly what we foolish people do. Drop. Dead. But death ain't the worst part, yo. The worst part is that we think that this cycle is good. That this is natural. We think that we need shit, the right shoes, the right jeans, Pampers, we programmed and we think it's all good. But that ain't living, I hate to say. That's slavery, yo, that's death. That ain't freedom." He wiped his brow. Like a Pentecostal preacher Richie Rovers was unaware of his silver tongue, but once he got started, it was like a geyser of words spilling wildly onto the courtyard and warmly into the ears of kids just like himself. Those who stayed watched him closely and those who passed by did too. Mitkin did not, however. He watched the watchers.

"So basically I just wanna say I'm tired of all this ramming in. I'm tired of shit being stuck onto me as if I didn't have no voice of my own. Millions and millions of dollars go every year so that they can ram shit down my throat, shit that I didn't even ask for. So," he took a big breath, a dramatic breath. "What to do?"

"Yeah, so what you gonna do about it?" came a voice. "What you gonna do, nigga?" shouted another.

"I'm gonna do what my teachers always tell me to do—I'm gonna rewrite this mother! Nobody says it has to be like this, yo, there is one million of us in this system. One million! Now that's power! We need to practice what was given to us, what belongs to each of us, what is our right. We need to act free to be free.

"Let's rewrite this system, totally, all of us, together. Let's have students choose teachers, and principals, and school boards. Hell, let's get rid of the school boards altogether. Let's write our own budgets, create our own classes, set our own standards, elect our own chancellor. And why not, yo? Why not? What, we don't know what's good for us? That's what the slave masters said about their slaves, yo! Niggers couldn't take care of themselves, they said. But that's a lie. Freedom, yo. That's the whole point of this country right? Getting yours, right?

Isn't that what they teach us? Hell, yes, look around. The only class of people who don't have equal rights is us young people, and forget about young black people. We ain't got shit. And by the way, I'm not talking about holding little mock elections where everybody smiles and acts real cute about 'what the little nigger kids want.' I'm talking about a system by the niggers, for the niggers, right here at nigger high! Isn't that the whole idea anyway? Isn't that what all the really slick principals say they want anyway? Isn't freedom for individuals what the old white men who founded this country wanted?"

Richie Rovers was sweating a great deal. He stopped and pulled a bandana out of his pocket and wiped his brow. "You *know* what I'm saying about being in charge because you live it. How many of you have to make decisions all day everyday about your life because you got parents who are all fucked up? Yeah," he slowed down, "that's right, moms that are all fucked up, I said that shit. Yep. And don't give me any of this 'don't talk about my momma' shit. It's true what I'm saying. They all messed up 'cause they just like we're gonna be; slaves to a system that deep down we know is wrong. See, that's why black and brown folks never seem to get it right in America, it's why they always think we acting crazy, it's why we poor and never run nothing. See, we deep down refuse to just give in and be a part of their corrupt system, their bankrupt ideas. We refuse to be their slaves, but that refusal comes unknown by us, it just happens in us because we understand deep down, see.

"But now I'm telling you that you can change everything, the system and your life included. See, your runaway pop was trying to get free, but he just did it all wrong. See, he didn't know how to fight correctly, he only sensed how fucked up everything was and didn't have any way to cope with it so he left you, out of anger and frustration, and like that, alone, it got worse for you and him. See, he left and made everything worse. But it doesn't have to be like this. There is another way to fight, another way to make things better. And so I ask you a question, is this system doing anything good for you?"

"No," came an earnest cry from the crowd. "Hell no!" A boy started to laugh at his friend's involuntary show of support but stopped when a crew of gangbangers stared him down. The crowd of malcontents waxed and waned between giddy and aggressive. With his wiry body and hairbrush voice, Rovers continued.

"Hell no, this system ain't helping us," he blared. "This system is out to destroy us. We gotta be responsible for ourselves now, we gotta create a system that we run, that we fix and that we like. And forget society out there somewhere." He waved his arms. "They don't care about us, haven't thought about us, provided for us in three hundred years, so stop calling on *society* or *government*, whatever that means. They don't care, they don't give a damn. So, I'm almost finished. But check it out. Take a flier. Think about why you get up every morning and come to this place." He pointed at the school again. "Just ask yourself that, and then come and help us get the monkey off your back, yo. Good things 'bout to happen y'all." Rovers pounded his chest twice and took a quick bow.

Cheers broke out in bunches as Richie Rovers made his way down from the podium. The thin girl at Mitkin's side got up and mounted the makeshift stage.

"My name is Alysha Cooper and I'm the presiding officer for the MLHS chapter of Students for Students." She proceeded to list a set of upcoming activities. In her hand she clutched a pamphlet and asked everyone to take one—many did including me. I flipped through it as I walked toward Mitkin and saw a cartoon with many childish faces and big mustachioed men holding long lists. Mitkin's art had been reworked by a student, and now the imposing gun became a flag with the slogan, OUR TURN.

I rolled the pamphlet in my hand like a morning newspaper and tapped Mitkin on the knee. He looked at me and held out a welcoming hand. As he did so, he laughed.

"Phone working yet?"

His grip was as gritty as his grin. I tried to ignore his gibe and said, "That kid's pretty good with words."

Mitkin glanced and winked. "Sure. Just like a preacher."

"Is he one of your students?"

"Yes."

"Is he like that in class?"

"Yep, yep, he's just like that."

"Does he get good grades?" I asked.

Richie Rovers was suddenly alongside me and I felt his breath. "When I want to," he said, and then looking sharply at Mitkin he asked, "Who this?"

"A friend of a former friend. He teaches here. He's the one I told you about, the one who was going to get us some class time." Mitkin slung a glance my way, even as he spoke to Richie. "He's no problem, Rich." Behind us all droned the proficient Alysha Cooper.

"So get involved. Be ready to commit. And thank you for coming." A smattering of applause went up.

"Is he with us?" asked Richie pointing at me. Mitkin did not respond but rather deftly allowed a blighted pall of silence to fall wholly on me. Apoplectic, I was unable to reply right away.

"So?" said Richie, "are you?"

"No, no, not me. I'm real busy," I said.

"Real busy doing what?"

"Teaching."

"Oh yeah? What do you teach?"

"History. I heard what you said up there about history. You've got some good things to say."

"And so?" he said suspiciously.

"And well, I don't think so. No, I'm not 'in.' It's not for me just yet."

"Change is a bitch, huh?" said Richie, while Mitkin just sat there on the ledge taking notes in his threshing-machine mind.

"How old are you?" I asked Rovers.

"Why do you ask?"

Like a dog owner calling off his hounds, Mitkin interrupted, "He's nineteen."

"Do you still go to school here?" I asked.

Mitkin again intervened. "Richie speaks for the students of New York City, that's all. But forget all of that, David," he said unwinding a bit, "I'm glad to see you here. I thought you'd find it interesting, maybe a bit of what he said could start a good discussion in your history class, huh? Rights and freedom are fuel for good discussion."

I did not move.

"We've got a lot of support here at Luther. Your kids are very active and bright. I could see them needing some guidance when the going gets real tough, you know, prepare them a little. Maybe try using this pamphlet as a starting point. Make some waves."

I nodded, but inside I stewed uncomfortably, afraid of the intensity of this so-called advocacy group. I also wondered how long it would be before this group found itself disbanded and outlawed. I blurted out, "You want our kids to give up everything and put their futures on the line? Might not go so well."

Richie spat in disgust and turned and walked away. Mitkin got up off the ledge. "Yes, David, you're right. Our coalition asks students to take a chance, we ask them to trade slavery for freedom. That much is absolutely true. It's a risk. So what?"

"Well, for one thing they might just get police attention."

"So?" said Alysha. She had finished packing up the podium and now stood alongside Mitkin, joined by a very quiet kid with exceptionally dark skin.

"So," I said, "the kids who want to get their education will have a harder time."

"You mean the five percent who actually want one of these bullshit diplomas," said Richie, again back in the mix. I noticed that there was no one left in the courtyard but Mitkin, his coalition, and me.

"That number's a little low, don't you think?"

"Not really. That's about all that actually believe in this place. The rest, and I'm talking about some good students, the rest have this crazy doubt way down deep just like I said. It keeps telling them they ain't getting what they deserve."

I almost groaned. "Nobody gets what they deserve, even in the suburbs. You have to work with what you've got. Starting a riot isn't going to help. Besides Mitchell, this doesn't sound like you at all. It's not what you believed in before, what's going on with you?"

From behind a wall of students the dark-skinned boy called out, "What you believe in, Mister?" He held his chin up and waited for me to answer. I looked at Mitkin who was doing the same.

"What do you mean?" I said.

"What do I mean? I believe in being free, what you believe in?" The thin girl snickered.

I thought how this whole conversation was dubious. Teenagers don't act like this. "You don't care what I believe, you just want me on your side. This whole thing is like a brainwashing, and you Mitchell, you should stop teaching them this. It won't serve them."

Mitkin did not render an emotion. He just looked at me and with a distinct arrogance said, "You didn't answer the question, David."

Just like the monastery, I thought. Here I was, with the abbot and his monks, life and death and the big ideas again. "This is ridiculous," I said between clenched teeth, barely audible. I frowned and looked back at the boy. "I believe in living a good life, okay, I don't hurt anybody and they don't hurt me. That's about it. Sorry, no big ideas from me, and besides, it doesn't matter what I believe, this is a school, a place for academics and that means we need order." I said what sounded right and then ended by unrolling the pamphlet in my hands and sticking it straight out. "Give it to someone who cares."

As I walked away I heard Mitkin saying, "You've bought their lies too, David. Don't bury your head in the sand." His words harried me as I ducked into the school.

***

"And that was the last time we spoke until this week?"

"Yep, think so," replies Mitkin.

"Do you remember what came next?"

He closes his eyes meditatively.

"I do."

I wait for him to elaborate, but he does not continue. He blushes a rose hue and looks down. He persists with his rope, turning it faster and faster through his fingers. I wonder if we are done for the day, so I ask.

"No," he says, "I think we should continue. It's early still."

I pick up my pen and press it to my dull yellow pad.

CHAPTER XXV

Seever's Cool Digs

Mitkin's little political rally had left me cheerless and but for a pounding headache, alone. I went uptown to see Raphaella but found no one home. A bit edgy, I waited. It was Seever, the lumbering Wisconsinite from the first floor, who found me there on the stoop, on a Friday night, alone, exasperated.

"You look like you could use a big couch and a remote," he said.

"And a beer."

"I got those. Have you ever had a bratwurst?"

We went inside and lounged all night. His television was wide and tall and sat on a finely carved stand almost in the center of the room. The stand swiveled and Seever showed me to what end.

"I can make it turn without touching it," he said. He held out his big blonde forearm and pressed a raised yellow button on the stout remote. The word *interstellar* came to mind. A humming sound escorted the TV as it pirouetted. "In case the sun is bad or you want to rearrange the room quickly, like for company. Pretty neat, heh?"

I fiddled with the yellow button and watched the television pivot. I stared glassy-eyed, not sure how to respond to such a mighty display of Japanese excellence. "Got 'em all right here," he said plopping down a cooler filled with beer and ice. "No need to make a kitchen run and miss the fight." We both popped open a can. I slid deep into the spongy couch.

He then wheeled out some snacks. They were neatly arranged in matching bowls and included chips with dip and pretzels. There was a bowl of popcorn too. We ate and drank and watched as the pre-fight ceremonies dragged on. Seever kept his hand on the remote and turned the channel with great regularity. We rode from station to station, image to image, and all of it while enjoying his super-furnished apartment and his super-cold cold beers.

I was as comfortable as contrivance can make a man, but above me, in my head, other images clicked on and off. Mitkin's students were there, gathered around a candle in Mitkin's apartment, discussing their day's work. I could not shake the wraith of the little preacher boy, Richie Rovers. His bony face and his silver tongue hovered there too, just beyond the pulp of my mind. And Raphaella. She was up there too, gliding back and forth, reminding me of my past and my inability to resurrect a relationship. I could see all of her idiosyncrasies, her stubborn faith and her genial dedication to the less fortunate, to bums. Our daughter, too, I saw her above me with her head on her mother's shoulder, reading a book and in love. And the priest. All of them crowded into my mind and nearly ruined my Friday night Wisconsin party. I concentrated on the TV.

It birthed ideas at an incredible rate. They were sensual ideas mostly, creative, enticing ideas that let me get away from the Mitkins and Seraphims of the world. I got lost in them, and who wouldn't? I was in Haiti one minute, working with UNICEF and feeding big-bellied babies and then, suddenly I was back at the fight, jumping gingerly up and down, my muscles bulging under dark skin, my mind prepared to bloody someone. Next, I was bombarded by a middle-aged fight commentator. So many words, words and more words, all of them tumbling out of his mouth: jabs, straight lefts, right hooks and cutting off the ring and use your strengths, and on and on. Then Seever was there with the bratwurst. These were obese hot dogs with acne, essentially, their tips charbroiled and crispy. He poured mustard all over them and I watched as he demonstrated what occurs when you bite in. They spray. I felt the hot, stinging tick of brat-grease on my cheek and then hurried to gobble down my own, forgetting about those chimerical things. It was good, and I smiled as Seever switched channels and we watched a team of college cheerleaders fling each other around a matted stage. They chucked and yelled at the same time, something about wildcats. Next I watched gritty black and white film of a great president delivering a speech, but that image lasted only a second— Seever nuked him in favor of a man with a tall white hat, puffy on top, who chopped away at some exotic vegetables. Again came the strong boxers and I popped another beer.

The front door to the building rattled and I ran to the front window to see. Whoever it was had already slipped inside so I ran quickly to the peephole of Seever's front door hoping to catch a glimpse. Through the peephole, I saw Mitchell Mitkin struggling with something heavy. I watched without breathing.

He produced a box, a weak-bottomed box which was about to give out. He pushed the door open with his buttocks and then dragged the box with his arms and took a break. I saw him wipe his brow. It was a long, deliberate wipe, and through the concave peephole it took on mammoth proportions. He disappeared suddenly, and then instantly was back in view, staring directly at me through the peephole, his nose sticking out elfishly. He turned and balanced the big box with his thighs, slowly ascending the stairs, step by step, breath by breath. Out of view, I heard his door open and then slam shut.

"Is it Mitkin?" asked Seever now standing behind me.

"Mmmhuh. He's carrying a big heavy box."

"I don't like that guy," said Seever. "He's crazy, heh?"

"Yeah." I wanted more channels and more beer.

"Have you noticed he stopped talking to everyone lately, even Raphaella? He's got some kind of crazy chip on his shoulder, I think he's got some kind of complex." He walked with me back to the sitting area with its soft couches and inviting rugs. I slumped again, but he was not finished. "Did you ever find out what his deal was with Raphaella?"

I reached for the bowl of chips.

"Because I mean when I first moved in here, remember, like, what, two years ago? They were real tight. Or at least it seemed that way. I'm not saying they were doing it or anything, it's just that he had this thing for her. You could tell." He chugged on his beer while awaiting my response, and as he did I saw his bicep flex snug against his T-shirt's rolled up sleeve.

I did not want this tired old conversation. I wanted what he had offered earlier, a respite.

"By the way, whatever happened with Allie?" he asked. I thought how he's gotta be drunk to keep at it like this. How could he miss the hints I dropped all around him; the languid droop of my eyelids and insouciant fold of my legs, how I rolled my eyes and sucked up a vexed breath. I looked at him and, finally giving in, answered.

"We got together."

"You nailed her, heh?"

"Yeah, sure, I nailed her."

"Excellent dude. She had a nice body, right?"

"Yeah, nice." What about the fight, I thought. I wanted him to shut up. "I think this is Holyfield's fight. He's too strong," I said.

Seever fumbled with his thoughts and turned toward the TV. "Yeah, he's real strong."

We watched silently. The fight plodded on. The room began to shrink under the weight of an awkward silence until finally Seever spoke.

"I made bonus this week. I've got an extra five grand coming around Christmas time." A grin spread wide under his Nordic cheeks. "New York is a great place."

I humored him and we spoke at length about his job and his choice to move here. He told me about his family and brothers, all of whom were successful in their fields. One was a lawyer, the other a doctor. He had been competing with them for years and now was finally able to say he'd made it too.

"I'm thinking about trading in my Camaro, I want something a little more classy."

I nodded and he continued, he said he was after a BMW or a Mercedes and he thought he'd like to drive back home for Christmas, pull into the driveway and honk the custom horn of his sinewy new success symbol. I went along. "That's a good plan, man," I said, remembering that Raphaella and I used to have similar plans and how, before her crazy conversion we could have been content with a BMW too. But that was before.

"My brother just bought his cruiser," he said. "It's a boss boat, rigged with a sweet Bose Cruiser Deluxe, I mean that music just cranks. His wife made him get lots of insurance on it but he says he's wasting his money. 'It's a waste,' he says, 'thing's unsinkable.'"

I imagined his brother as a big man, a square-jawed, square-bodied man with tight jeans. I imagined them all, in fact, around a robust Christmas tree, Seever describing New York for his family, using phrases like *mean streets* and *don't go uptown* and *bridge and tunnel crowd*. They would envy him, I thought.

"Do your brothers have plans to visit you in New York?"

"Oh heck, yeah. They think New York would be a great place to visit, just not great to live in. You ever heard somebody say that?" I nodded. "But my father, well, he just thinks I'm crazy all around. He's not mean about it or anything, he's just, well, he's proud to be from Wisconsin. He kids me now. Says I'm a big city kid that forgot about the little people. But he's not so little, you know. He's a judge, and he's tall too."

The door rattled again.

"Hey," said Seever, "that's got to be Raphaella." We both hopped up. I felt the beers rush to my head and the floor swirl beneath my feet. Still, I got to the peephole first.

I saw a deformed, exaggerated image of Raphaella dragging a sleeping Dana with one hand while fumbling through the door with the other. She was serious and strong and determined, her jaw was set and her beautiful green eyes. She wasted no motion, no time. Hypnotized by drink and hemmed in by a torpid soul, I could not move. She struggled with our child, step by step, upward.

"Is it her?" whispered Seever.

I stammered a silent, "No."

"Who is it?"

"Somebody for Mitkin I think."

"Really. That's a change," said Seever, scratching his head.

"Yeah."

I watched her go. Out of view, I could only hear her stomp, and then, soon enough, high overhead, I could only imagine her, living life up there, an angel of sorts, caring for our daughter and struggling.

"Are there anymore beers?" I asked.

Hopping up and with a smile Seever replied, "You bet there are, heh."

We drank them all. The last thing I remember is the image of two women in floral patterns holding court over two shiny earrings and quoting prices. They went on and on about how great it was to have such an opportunity as this. I think I was on the floor when I fell asleep, at least that's where I was in the morning. Seever was on the couch above me, and I pictured his big, cock-jawed face looking down on me as my eyelids closed and I passed out. That memory and the musty smell of my underarms put me in a bad mood as I emerged from the building and into the sunlight of the next day.

***

Mitkin looks exhausted. I have been telling him about Seever and he watches me closely, saying little. He has assumed a new posture, one hand holding his chin, elbow on the table, the other stuck beneath his bottom. He waits for me to finish.

"You were comfortable there?"

"Yes, very."

"And drunk."

"Yes."

"Did you wonder what I had in the box?"

I think back. At the time I chalked it up to eccentricity, but now I am curious.

"I had our first shipment," he says without prompting, "though I wasn't supposed to."

"Shipment of what?"

"Guns."

"You had guns in that box?"

I am amazed. Mitkin was in deep and I had no idea.

CHAPTER XXVI

Summertime Rebels

Mitkin took a job teaching summer school. He taught at a place called Clinton in the Mosholu Parkway neighborhood of the Bronx. Taughtauer hoped to consolidate support in the Bronx by recruiting the toughest summer school cases, the hard-core of the high schools. He had done this every summer for four years and it had worked. Three of the martyrs had come by way of Taughtauer's summer school classes and now, taking the summer off to plan the actual takeover, Taughtauer entrusted Mitkin with summer school recruitment. And it wasn't just in the Bronx. Mitkin was asked to throw a wide net over the entire summer school system, a large system filled with apathetic, indolent kids, kids who Taughtauer loved to "save."

Mitkin, as he had done since joining, worked hard for Taughtauer. He continued to produce his pamphlets, serializing them and keeping a story line running throughout each. He printed them on the Lower East Side, working closely with a cabal of underground anarchists who were well-versed in subversive publications. None of his tracts were ever accredited and none of them ever advocated outright violence, but each tract was very clever. They satirized public officials, including the Chancellor and they did it all in a student vernacular, each edition laden with glossy photos and busy covers and words like *whack* and *da bomb* and *fly*. The tracts became popular among the summer school students, and as his fame grew, Mitkin became an icon. He had learned how to teach, too. His lessons brimmed with confidence and swagger, and he deftly intertwined school curriculum and the philosophy of revolution. His classes were laced with controversy and youthful energy, and his reputation as a great teacher grew daily during that last summer. This was exactly how he knew it would be one day.

By the middle of July, he had found two new martyrs for the movement. They were baptized and Taughtauer was impressed. He asked Mitkin to find more and they were found, like clockwork, one by one. The movement was truly growing. Not only did the elite ranks grow, but the outer ranks too, with kids who were deemed trustworthy enough for basic initiation, "The Oath" as Taughtauer called it. It was in this vortex of activity that Taughtauer called a Sunday evening meeting of the martyrs. It was time for the assault on Livingston Street—the beginning of the end of the NYC Board of Education.

Standing in front of his televisions, the sounds of news muted but the images of death and destruction in full flower, Taughtauer began. "We need to act soon. September 6 is our target date, can we make it official?" One by one he questioned the martyrs, and each reported on the status of preparations. James Hunt reported that he now had a surplus of firearms and that the 6th was possible. His report was given in quiet tones and with a profound sense of humility. Hunt offered, "I can show you what we have tonight, if you'd like?"

Taughtauer nodded and then turned to Mitkin. "The lists? How are the numbers?"

"Higher than they've ever been, Ed."

Taughtauer stood up and turned to his compatriots. "This is the flag that I intend to fly in front of each coalition school once we've taken Livingston."

He held up the flag. It was half red and half white with a black line down the middle. The word FREEDOM was emblazoned in stern black letters across both halves.

"Our girl Alysha designed it. I like it."

"No flowers? asked Richie Rovers. "That girl loves drawin' her some flowers."

"Once this flag goes up," Taughtauer continued, "my kids will know what to do."

"And what's that?" asked Judy Strand.

"Go to the principal's office with our demands. At that point, the priests and deacons will be authorized to use force, and hopefully the laity will all follow their lead."

"I've got every name of every student at all levels, Ed," said Mitkin. "From laity all the way up to us, the martyrs. I'll sit with you after the meeting and show you where our strengths lie. But you already know that it's not Manhattan. Brooklyn and up here, that's where we are strongest."

Taughtauer nodded and then became very grave. He seemed to get emotional, rubbing his hands together as if to hold back a cry. He asked Judy Strand, Roger Nin and an old former principal with whom he'd been close for more than twenty years, Elvira Ramirez, to each stand up. With all four of the older martyrs with him in the front now, he turned to his cadre of students, about thirteen in all, and addressed them.

"And now I want to do something that I've waited fifteen years to do. Many times, yep, I never thought this day would come, but it's here, and well," he wiped a tear, "today we must assemble the Livingston team. I need six of you."

Immediately Richie Rovers stood up. "I'm one." Ricky Cuevas motioned Richie to sit down, but he wouldn't. "Naw, Rick, I ain't sittin' down on this one. I'm going into that bitch and I'm lighting that fire. I'm going."

"In time, bro. Right, Ed?" said Ricky.

"I want you to decide for yourselves who goes, all of you together, the only way I've ever imagined it. So now. Decide."

Taughtauer called the teachers out of the room and onto the back porch. "This is the meeting I've been waiting for, for fifteen years, this is it!" He looked wild-eyed at Mitkin and then, one by one, at the others. Finally he settled on his old friend Elvira. "We've done it. They will choose."

Judy Strand looked anxious. "I don't want Ricky to go, Ed. He's my baby. He's been telling me since the first day that he has to go, that he can't sell out, but I'm afraid—"

"If they want him, then he'll go," said Taughtauer. "It's not our decision."

"Then I'll go too," she said.

"None of you will go to Livingston. Only students, they are the ones, they are the masterminds, the victims. Each of you will stay in your schools and prepare to fight there. This is very important. We will take and hold the building for the night, and then, the next day, at the schools, you will organize your kids."

"You're going?" said Mitkin, sharply.

"I'm going," he said.

"But—"

"I'm going, period, the end. Now..."

As Taughtauer went on, Mitkin heard the voice of loneliness well up in him and he did not want to stay in his school during the assault. He wanted to join the kids and he wanted to be with Taughtauer. He felt compelled by a sudden unknown fear.

"Now I know Romero, he'll want his system to work," Taughtauer said. "He will tell the mayor to keep the schools open, and he'll be too proud to call school off that first day. I know it. He'll play right into our hands. That's why you must be at your schools, and the others too, the ones you've been organizing, Mitch. They must be there and you must make them aware of what's coming." He waved his index finger. "But never talk of violence, never, not until the exact moment… and then, pow."

Taughtauer put his hand on Mitkin's shoulder. "I need you, Mitch. I need you. You are magnificent, all of you." Mitkin's eyes were fixed. "And Roger, listen, your school is the jewel of this operation. If we can get King, well…" He smiled and went silent, thinking of just how perfect all of this could be. King High School was important not only because it was home to two thousand city students, but also because it housed all the offices for the Manhattan public schools.

"Which of them is going with you, Ed?" asked Judy Strand, her flaxen hair pale like the troubled countenance of her wrinkled face.

"I don't know, I told you, they will decide."

"Yes, excellent," peeped Roger, the sycophant from Manhattan.

Ricky Cuevas approached with paper in hand. "It's done."

Taughtauer took the paper and gave it to Mitkin, and they all returned to the room. They were greeted with a mix of hope and fear, but more palpable still was the glow of reverence visible on the face of each child in that room. Mitkin, filled with pride, looked out over the little gathering and read. "Richie Rovers. James Hunt. Nicole Harrison. Alysha Trotter. Jason Olivo. Ricky Cuevas. You all agree to go?" They nodded.

Taughtauer chimed in, "And that's the list, the end? Everyone in this room agrees that these six will go, according to their own free will?"

"The end," said the thin, dark-eyed Cuevas. "It's what we want."

"Good. Next up, you'll write a plan for the rest of you. Think hard. Maximize your presence in the city. We are not just taking a building here, we are overthrowing a regime."

CHAPTER XXVII

To the Rooftop

It was about this time that Raphaella received news that she had to vacate the premises. September 30 was the exact date. I remember her then, in that hot summer, scurrying all about town, looking for homes and good shelters for her women. She called old friends who, to the last, denied her, calling her kind but crazy. She spent every dollar she had on security deposits for the girls. She did manage to get Kitty and Diamond Lee into a small one-bedroom in West Harlem. "Better than the old Greystoke Motel, I guess," said Diamond Lee. "Roaches is better than rats."

Slowly Raphaella cleaned out her apartment and returned it to its previous elegance, a sparse simplicity being the appeal. She was so at peace now. Her decision to forego the shelter job and abide by the admonitions of her priest had settled softly in her soul. I asked her from time to time how he was and it was always the same, "Good, thank God."

Dana, too, seemed serene and happy. She had finished school without entering special education classes, and as for the demons, she had not backed down. If asked, she always asserted that they were there, right there with them in the classroom, watching and waiting for weak souls to invite them in. She simply learned to deal with the belittlement and ostracism, and her teachers learned to write her off as the odd one. They'd talk about her in the halls as "the one who'd one day turn out okay if only she'd be allowed to."

Life now was uncomplicated, at least as far as I could tell. During the day, Raphaella worked hard for Doctor Ferrare, and at night she and Dana would attend 6 p.m. Vespers. Afterwards, Raphaella would serve a small meal in the monastery while Dana played with a tough little girl named Anya. Anya was an orphan who had been adopted and brought back from Russia, a quick-witted, golden-haired girl who liked to spread food on things like jeans and the floor.

After Vespers, Raphaella and Dana would return home, bathe, then fix some tea and eat shortbread cookies. She'd read her daughter to sleep and then pray her nighttime prayers, unfailingly. She never asked me for money, never spoke anxiously of the future, never criticized me and always volunteered to help in any way she could.

During that summer, I sensed that all of this was natural, not forced or dictated by an external voice. This was a change. I became enthralled with the paradox in her; she was both more austere and, somehow, more kind. She was filled with an unbounded sweetness and I found myself craving her more than I'd ever craved her before. But my appetite was less carnal now. My longing was for what I've come to know as sovereign beauty. I was uncovering the tip of the truest, purest iceberg man can know, and I was being transformed (though I don't think I knew as much then—I simply called it settling down, or whatever other cliché came to mind in whatever other canned conversation I was having at the time).

I slept soundly every night, got up early in the morning and even started to exercise. I began to write, daily, persistently, and without too much pain. I wrote poems and simple short stories, not all of them filled with some deep-rooted message or dark, solitary mood ratcheted from the recesses of my mind. Sure, many of them were childish and light, puerile disclosures on life and the beauty of creation. But they were still mine, low art, but mine. I thanked Raphaella and she very predictably refused to take credit. She, in fact, apologized for the past and her brittleness, though she did not apologize for our broken relationship. No, that was still a proper thing, a deigned fact of fallen life, one that could not be transgressed until I had become what she was.

And what was she? Well, according to her she was a sinner. That was it. A sinner. She wanted me (though she never told me and never would) to see myself as a sinner too. Believing as much would be a type of first step toward truth. "Lord Jesus Christ, Son of God, have mercy on me, a sinner." That's what she said, all day, every day, and it was these archaic mantras that poured from her heart and shaped everything she did in life. It was what divided us still. Anthropology. I could not come to see myself as fallen, as a member in the body of created beings who once occupied a land called perfect, and now, due to the sins of our fathers, are stuck in this world as holy fish in a sea of sin, sipping it up and swimming in it so thoroughly that we cannot even recognize our inimitable perfection. We, her life testified, are divine creatures who don't know it, deluded spirits who choose to desecrate their sanctified selves and place passion before perfection. I didn't believe this, and because I did not, I would remain apart from Raphaella.

Still she loved me in her way, in that crucial, transcendent way. Practically, it meant being attentive to me and what I perceived as important. She always returned my calls and made sure to ask me about work, about writing. She would buy little gifts, thoughtful things like ink cartridges for the computer, or bulk boxes of my favorite cereal because she was at a discount warehouse and knew that I "love these sugary things." This love made the simple life possible again. It was okay to enjoy a movie alone, to eat a hearty meal with good friends and never think once of her. It was possible to hug her and not wonder when I'd bed her. That summer, life was okay and getting better.

Still, I can't say I ever really understood just how the gap was closing back then. I was oblivious and appropriately so. After all, this was her charge against me, and against herself, against us all. But now I see that I was trekking the divide, or rather that she was trekking it in me. It is so striking to realize now the catastrophic expanse of that divide. How far across to the other side we must go, and how tiring a walk we must all be ready to take.

These ideas come to me as images from the past. I see us in Central Park West strolling with Dana, under a darkening blue sky, the final rays of a humid sun crackling through the thick green trees above. I see us finally finding a restaurant we can afford (but just barely), wandering in wide-eyed and a little loud, happy to be out, thankful. We'd get our food and they would make the sign of the cross over it, unflinchingly, while I would steal little sideways glances at the booth next to us, the one with the twenty-somethings furtively glancing back.

I see me and how I would go at dusk to retrieve the girls from Vespers, sitting on the stoop and waiting until they tumbled out of the monastery, Dana loping down the steep steps and plunging into Daddy's arms. Though I still did not go in, I went without angst and accepted, at least in part, the thing that I had once fought and railed against. The specter of the church had lost its sting. Even the fasting became benign that summer. I bonded with my two forsaken women, who in so many ways were little caricatures of a bygone time; two diminutive souls mocked by modernity and alone but for their love of obedience, hierarchy, simplicity, humility and meekness. They were like mascots of antiquity, but I loved them that summer.

I say this now, of course, but then it was not them and their love that brought placid joy to my soul. It was more my actions, my acceptance and insouciance that brought me joy. After all, I said to myself, I sacrificed the truth according to my ego so that they might be left to their delusion. I had it all figured out. We all got along. Finally, we could just all get along.

And so it was like this, wispy, wonderstruck and deeply delighted, that I went to see her one day in early August.

MEET ME UPSTAIRS, YOU'LL LOVE THE SKY!

That's what the note on her door said.

When I reached the roof, I realized why she took the time to mention the sky; it was the richest, most extraordinary sapphire. She stood in the corner wearing a white sundress, and in the bright sun I could see the lines of her lithe body. Her hair was as long as I'd ever seen it, curly and thick as ever, black and brilliant. On her feet were simple two-dollar flip-flops. She stood over a hardy acacia bush with its crimson blossoms in full bloom. In her long brown hands she held a shallow watering can. She turned and noticed me, and I waved.

"Look at it." She pointed with her chin and eyes, upward. "Isn't it fantastic?"

"Most," I said, stepping up to her and laying a gentle kiss on her cheek.

"Look at the garden, David, hasn't it grown nicely? I thought it would all burn to death up here but nope. Look at this." She bent over and conscientiously held the plump bud of a lilac. "He's still waiting, just waiting and not dying." She shook her head with a naive innocence. "And look here, this patch of marigolds are all going strong, just growing like weeds." She smiled without looking up.

I couldn't disagree. The entire garden, a mishmash of planters woven together on top of thin pea-green artificial turf, had taken life.

"I brought you these," I said holding out a little bag of seeds.

She took them. "Morning Glories."

"I don't know much about them, just that they're strong and can live a long time."

"Thank you, David," she said, her hand out, gently extended. I looked at it, upturned and supple, and realized it was meant for mine. I took it and she led me to the other side of the garden where she bent down in front of two empty planters, and I felt her mood change. She became very earnest as she ran her hand through the dry soil, motioning to me to bend down too. "I never planted here, David." She looked at me. "Will you plant something here, you and Dana? Make it your spot?"

She watched me, and in my gut I wondered if this was less a question and more a celestial attempt to reunite us all as we were meant to be.

"We could plant corn," I said. Corn?

She reached out and touched my forearm. "Corn is good." And then she got up from her crouch. I followed her to the building's edge where she placed her hands on the retaining wall, a grimy thing covered with a thin film of soot. She wiped them, one against the other, and then put them behind her, clasping them. She waited like that, looking off, facing downtown, toward the city's giant steel towers and their glistening windows. I walked over to her and stood close. The sapphire sky had begun to fill up with afternoon storm clouds, or perhaps they had been there all along. I took her hand, but our intertwined fingers hung limp between us and I frowned.

"David, we're moving."

I went dry inside.

"I've been invited to a monastery in Alaska. They want me to come and help them with a school and a day care they've started for the needy. We're going to live in the monastery but separate from the nuns."

I met the news with an inexplicable calm, as if I had known this already. "Forever?" I asked.

"No, the whole thing will be about a year."

"Is that why you asked me to tend the garden? You want me to keep the place for you while you're gone? A gardener?"

She looked at me worried. "That's not why I asked you to tend the garden. I asked you because I want you near to us." With trouble she said, "I've made many mistakes in my life. Please be my good friend, our daddy?"

From behind us, a steam valve lurched and I was filled with the emotions of someone who has utterly failed. "I just always wanted to be more than that, you know?" I looked down and said, "I'm sorry." She shook her head.

"You are a good father, David, young, good. We love you, David."

And there it was, the end. Because it came with the quiet and soft tones of sadness I thought how unexpected it was. I hadn't imagined it this way, but this was it. It was over in my soul, in that very thing she had tried so hard to enliven— and that's funny, that's a funny and awful thing. I found my soul when she killed it. "When?" I asked.

"We'll go at the end of September."

"Gonna be cold."

"Yes, real cold."

"I hope you can find a way to stay warm, Kiwi. I'll miss Dana. I love her." She nodded. "I'll miss you too, somehow. Somehow Raphie, I'll miss you too, I know it."

CHAPTER XXVIII

Casing the Joint

A rented white cargo van stood double-parked in front of a pizza shop across the street from the Board of Education headquarters at Livingston Street. Three men, Mitchell Mitkin, Roger Nin and Ricky Cuevas sat crammed in the front passenger seat, while Ed Taughtauer rested comfortably in the driver's seat. They watched like crows on a wire as the pizza shop patrons, most of them employees of the Board, meandered in and out of the tiny pizza joint. Most emerged with little white paper bags saturated with red pizza grease, moving lazily in front of the long red counter, chatting and cheerily enjoying their very light workload. It was summer and school was still out.

"They sure smile a lot," said Nin. "It must be the lunch."

"Or a joke, a really funny inside joke," said Mitkin.

"Everybody just give your neck a rest, huh," said Taughtauer. "We're here to learn, not gawk."

"They really do have that look though," said Nin, breaking the silence. "That bureaucratic, 'I don't care about nothing but the clock' look, don't they?" He shot a glance at Taughtauer. "They haven't thought about the kids in months."

"Months?" said Ricky. "My aunt used to work here. She said besides me, she didn't never talk to one student in ten years. She sent all my cousins to Catholic school."

Taughtauer grumbled, "You're missing the point, gentlemen." He looked at Mitkin. "Could you please tell these two fine revolutionaries the point, Mr. Mitkin?"

Mitkin spoke, still watching the civil servants come and go. "We need two things, one to get inside, and two, to make sure we do so with enough swagger that they know we mean business." He nodded toward a police officer waiting inside for a slice. "He has to know we are dangerous so he doesn't just rush in and make a mess of the whole thing. If everything goes up too quickly, well, our message is just violence, and then it's as good as no message."

"Not bad, Mitch, you're close," said Taughtauer condescendingly. "But even six dead students is a message. What concerns me is getting to the next day. We must get to Friday, period. We need everyone in this city to know exactly what is going on that night as they go to sleep, yep. There's the point, 'ole Mitch, that's when the pressure shifts. Then Chancellor Romero must make his decision and that's when all of you come in, you and Roger and Judy and the hundreds of students." He pointed at his eyes with forked fingers. "That's what I want to see with these eyes, that's the point, Mitch."

He reached across the front seat and slapped Mitkin on the thigh, as if an old football buddy. "Don't worry, no more words. Soon, Mitch, three more weeks. As for right now, here's the deal. I know this building well. The Chancellor is on the fourth floor. His office is big enough to use as our operations center, our very own bunker. You," he pointed to Ricky, "will be with me. And we'll have a few guests too, mainly the Chancellor and his staff. All of them will be bound and will not be allowed to leave under any circumstances." He unrolled a long yellow piece of paper. "These are the blueprints. I had Alysha reconfigure them so each of us can carry a copy neatly in our pocket. Here's the Chancellor's office, and here, here is the front door." He pointed at the paper, and then out the window and across the street. Heavily mirrored doors opened and shut, and on each was written: 555 Livingston Street, NYC Board of Education.

Taughtauer's plans were neither difficult nor particularly creative. He and six martyrs would simply walk in the front door just as the business day ended, just one day before the official start of classes. Their first target would be the Chancellor, in his office, flanked by staff. Brandishing guns, the martyrs would clear out all non-essential staff. This big office would then become the headquarters for the siege. At the same time, two martyrs would be sweeping the entire building from the top floor to the bottom. They would be cleared to fire upon inanimate objects and basically scare people to death. Taughtauer wanted all non-hostages out of the building, and out with a palpable sense of fear. These everyday bureaucrats would be instrumental in spreading the word about just how dangerous it was inside.

With the building clear and the Chancellor in tow, Taughtauer would begin to negotiate with the NYPD, keeping them off balance and always a bit confused as to motive and membership. For Taughtauer, these hours immediately after the capture of Romero were crucial. He knew he needed to remain in charge and with his hostages until the second day, the first day of classes citywide. If so, Taughtauer believed he would have his rebellion; he would have begun a revolution.

"But how do we know the Chancellor will still be there at the end of the day?" asked Nin.

"Politics."

"How do you figure?" said Ricky.

"I've been watching him for five years. He's always there late the day before, trying to make it look like he cares. He'll be there."

Nin laughed. "He'll get his overtime alright. Right, Ed?"

Taughtauer nodded.

"What about the guards?" asked Mitkin.

"They don't have guns. They'll just go with the others."

"And then what?"

Taughtauer's eyes lit up. "Mitch, I'm glad you asked that question. I've written a detailed outline of the next three days. There's one copy and well, that's all there's gonna be until the day before, then Ricky you'll get one, too. Basically, here's what I see happening." He propped the outline against the steering wheel, and leaned forward to read.

"On Wednesday evening we will secure the building. Thursday morning, schools will open and we will be in negotiation. But they aren't negotiations at all, are they Ricky?" Ricky shook his head. "Nope, just a stall tactic. We need time for you, Mitchell, and you, Roger, and all of the other school leaders to organize and overrun your own schools. So, if all goes as it should, by Thursday afternoon the movement will have at least eight schools under its control. Eight schools, each with its middle finger right up the mayor's ass, each becoming historical markers and future references for the greater revolution to come."

As he spoke, Taughtauer became even more animated. "And that's exactly what will come. I want to see spontaneous student sit-ins, classroom strikes, anything that has the mark of the movement, and anywhere. Philly will follow, Chicago, and maybe even Los Angeles. The whole day will be spent rocking the system to its foundation. I want the world to see how bankrupt this system is, and I want them to see that it is our movement, the students, who care the most that it is changed. We decide. We determine what is good for us. That's what I want on the radio, on television, everywhere, it must ring out across the city!

"Now we should try to avoid violence on this first Thursday, we want to appear to be negotiating. But if violence comes, if we need to fight to keep our hostages, then so be it. Violence is part of dying anyway, and that is what the system is doing, dying. Thursday night the city will go to bed without a deal and the Chancellor will enter his second night as a hostage. We'll release two staffers that night, give them a sense that we can compromise."

Mitkin interrupted, "How much will you have told the media about the movement at this point?"

"Good, Mitch, excellent. I'll give them the manifesto Thursday morning, mid-morning, just about the time you're securing your schools. I've got Bob Blass' direct line over at the New York Times. He'll eat it up."

Nin repeated the plan slowly, as if repeating directions given to him at a gas station. "Wednesday is hush-hush, then Thursday—"

"What does it say exactly, Ed?" Mitkin was serious.

"The manifesto? You wrote it Mitch, you know."

"Has it been changed?"

Taughtauer smiled sarcastically. "I've got it right here." He held his forefinger to his head. "Want to hear it?"

They all nodded, all but Mitkin. He sat still.

"First I'll give them the basics. The Chancellor of the NYC Board of Education, the leader of all public education in this city, and the champion of the world's most bloated bureaucracy is being held hostage, here, at 555 Livingston Street, Brooklyn, New York. He is being held captive as he has held students captive. The students who bind him are the same students he has pledged to serve. He will be held until it is clear to all bureau-kings and bureau-queens around the city, state and nation, that students have rights, inalienable rights, rights inherited at birth and rights that no man may take with impunity. Students are not second-class citizens. They are children born free, born with dignity and grace, but sadly born into an adult system of living wrought with hate, greed, pettiness, injustice, and market-driven slavery. Today is a new day. Today students can walk with their heads up, their chins stuck out strong and proud. Today all students can proudly say, *Change! Change is here!*"

Taughtauer looked satisfied. Mitkin had not moved, and continued to watch without expression. Roger Nin spoke up, hurriedly, like a child waiting for his bedtime story.

"What about Friday, Ed? What's next?"

"Friday we burn it down. We push everyone out the front and we burn it down. I'll leave last, guns blazing, so the firemen aren't in too early. I want ashes." His eyes widened wildly. "Right, Mitch, there must be ashes." He seemed to purposely break the silence into which Mitkin had sunk.

"I want to go with you, Ed," said Mitkin. "I want to deliver the manifesto, I want to be the last one out."

Taughtauer shook his head.

"Why?"

"Students, Mitch. That's who started this and that's who's going to end it."

"But—"

"I appreciate your work, but you're better on the outside. You're pivotal there, right Roger?"

Nin passively nodded his head. "You're good with the kids, Mitch, and they'll need you on the outside." He stopped and looked at Taughtauer. "Will anyone die, Ed? In your heart, do you think anyone will die?"

Taughtauer began to roll his eyes, but refrained. He looked at Ricky and repeated Nin's question slowly. "Will anyone die?"

The young Ricky Cuevas smiled. "They already have. Lots."

"Yeah, I know," said Nin. "But in three weeks will anyone, here," he pointed across the street, "die?"

Mitkin snapped, "Maybe!" He looked up at Nin with piercing, unforgiving eyes. "So what if they do? What difference does it make? It would only make a difference to someone real invested in this corrupt life. You don't know anybody like that do you?" Nin shifted restively, looking to Taughtauer for help. Mitkin, still staring sharply, continued with a loud, accusatory tone. "I don't know anybody like that, Roger. And if I did, I think I'd quickly disassociate myself, wouldn't you?" Nin looked at Ricky then again at Taughtauer. His eyes dimmed.

"Nobody's going to die, Roger," said Taughtauer. "I'll see to it. Yep, everybody lives."

Nin fidgeted. "I think it would be better, but that's not to say I'm afraid of it." He glanced at Mitkin. "It's just it would help our case in court."

"And that brings me to the last of the plan," said a softening Taughtauer. "We will surrender and go to court. That's exactly where we want to go. I want this to be in the news for as many weeks, months and years as possible. The powers that be will work hard to forget us and all that we've worked for, but in court, day in and day out, they'll be forced to remember us. I want the headlines to remember us for years, and I want sellout liberal factions to give us their weak-hearted support. And they will, they'll use us as an instrument in their plan to get what they want, but it will be the same old political power play bullshit. As usual, they won't care a damn for the kids. They'll speak up so that later they can speak down to us. Yep, they will all run to our rescue, but this time *we* use them. This time we get what we want, a new system." He turned the ignition key and slid the van into drive. "We'll take the war into the courtrooms, and with so many of us," he looked at Ricky, "the trials will go on for years."

"Each year will be a reminder," said Nin.

"A sour little cyst."

Mitkin looked at Taughtauer as he drove. Mitkin saw a man who had no plans of being in a courtroom. He saw that Taughtauer had tacked on the stories of trials and judges, and all for the sake of the weak. In his mind brewed something greater than judicial infamy. He was planning something akin to eternal rest. A pang of excited fear sliced through Mitkin's belly and he longed to take Taughtauer's hand, not out of friendship or flattery, but because he had in Taughtauer a companion who, like himself, was ready to die, to make the ultimate sacrifice.

CHAPTER XXIX

An Insurrectionary Deed

It was Tuesday, September 6, the day had arrived. Mitkin woke with a start. He had slept poorly, yet, in his eyes darted a wild, reckless, reverent awe.

A dying summer breeze slid in through the window as Mitkin peeked out and met the sun. It was getting hot, and the sun burned away at the gray city haze. He could smell the pavement stew and warm. Mitkin watched as little children waited alone at a bus stop.

"Finally," he said aloud.

He slipped into the shower and washed. His soapy washrag darted across his lithe, pale body. A giddy smile rose to the surface. His stomach fluttered. He had not felt this way in years.

"There is only one thing needful now."

Then, as if from a Rolodex, he ran the day through the index cards of his mind.

"First LaFollete High. Get there and get into the classroom. LaFollete is the linchpin, the screw holding the second day together. Second. Get ahold of Rutledge and the other teacher martyrs at LaFollete. They need a briefing, as they'll be worthless without it. Go over rendezvous points and riot orders, and all the details they have not been privy to for the last six months. The key is for each teacher to get his kids into the streets by ten o'clock, the second day, Thursday. Then the second briefing with the student martyrs at LaFollete, no more than ten minutes together in one place, and nothing but a bare minimum of facts, and none of them damning. Don't chance a snitch. The key here is to vitalize them for the coming day when they all will raise their fists high, exalting their own will and themselves as the arbiters of their own destiny."

His detailed planning came slowly to a stop as he stepped out of the shower and patted himself dry. Looking into the mirror and rubbing his head dry, he found his own eyes and said, "Give the speech." Dropping the towel and exposing his nakedness, he stood up very straight, very proud. He began aloud, his voice formal, his frame officious.

"The worst thing that can happen tomorrow is that you collapse under the weight of doubt and fear. The worst thing that can happen is that you become a coward. You, every one of you, and I know you well, have nothing to lose. The worst thing is not arrest. All of you, hundreds, together in jail? How bad could that be? And what, by the way, would they arrest you for? Searching for truth? Resisting oppression? Refusing to obey an army of flunkies and the corrupt system they are obedient to? Would they arrest you for wanting to be free? And what if they did, again, how bad could it be? 'Hey Mom, I got arrested for standing up for my rights, like Martin Luther King and Malcolm X. Sorry. Am I on punishment?' Who wouldn't gladly accept punishment for that, and what good mother would dole it out? This is history, this is for us, the good, fighting them, the bad, and making history forever."

He ran his hands over his face, digging at his eyes like a man waking up, then, using his fingers as a comb he brushed back his wet hair and grinned. It was a good speech. All was just as it should be.

He dressed in cool linen pants and a blue suit jacket, clothes he had shunned for a full year. He looked in the mirror one more time and thought, "For the cause." He tightened the knot on a forest-green tie. At 8 a.m. he walked confidently out the door and into a humid morning. He reached LaFollete by 8:30, right on time. His first contact was with a school security officer. Mitkin knew him as Fred. Fred stood about six feet six inches tall with a short-cropped Afro and a fat mustache sitting squarely on top of his thick lip. He was very good friends with most of the students at LaFollete. Most of the teachers thought he was too close to them, too close to do his job. Mitkin approached the front door and made a note of Fred's mood. Jovial.

"Mr. Mitkin."

"Fred." Mitkin nodded.

Two other guards sat idly by. On any given day, LaFollete employed as many as ten guards. At least that many would be there tomorrow and Mitkin wanted to know which ones.

"Fred, how many students do we have coming tomorrow? How many you think?"

"More than usual this year. I hear we've got thirty-five hundred."

Mitkin nodded. "Wow, how many of you guys are required here by law? Isn't there some number?"

"I don't know about that, but we've got nine full-timers."

"And tomorrow?" asked Mitkin.

"I think twelve here. The Board wants a good tight start here, you know, after the craziness last year. Course there would be fewer problems if they let us throw some of these crazy mothers out of here for good. None of this fourteen strikes and you're out shit."

"Yeah, well," said Mitkin, "the law is," he tried to think of an appropriate phrase, one that would go along with the conversation, "a bitch."

"Ain't it, though," said Fred. Mitkin gave him a quick upward nod and left.

He passed the program office. A large, crooked line of older students snaked out and into the hall. Shouts could be heard coming from inside. Suddenly the whole line backed up. People piled into each other and onto one another's shoes and then a door slammed shut. On it hung the sign: COME BACK AFTER 1 PM. Curse words rattled through the hall. Mitkin snickered. "Tomorrow can't come soon enough."

One by one, he dutifully finished his administrative obligations, and as he did he encountered teachers he knew. A little woman, blonde and built like a lazy gymnast, careened by. He had taught her class for two weeks the previous spring, and she had been impressed. She yelled for him.

"Ms. Hill," he answered over his shoulder.

"How was your summer, Mitchell?" she asked in a tenor voice.

"Good." He affected a smile and even a gentle handshake. "And yours?"

"Good." She looked him up and down, head to toe. "I've never seen you in a jacket, Mitchell. You look like you're looking for a job."

"I am."

She smacked him amiably on the back. "You can have mine. Those kids loved you last year. I'll be honest with you, they said I should teach more like you." Then wagging her head from side to side, she said, "I told them we have something called a curriculum, something called state-mandated bodies of knowledge, things like learning to read, exams. Anyway, they weren't too happy that I was back. Thanks a lot, Mitchell." She smiled somewhere between friend and foe. "Hope you get a job."

"Thanks." His flat eyes wished her goodbye. "See ya around."

She turned and Mitkin pinched his lips with scorn. Another acquaintance fell on him, tapping him on one shoulder while standing behind the other. Mitkin turned the wrong way and was met with a giggle. "Over here, Mitkin."

A woman named Gloria beamed at him. Mitkin feigned excitement. "Gloria, you're back."

"Sure am. And for a while. I just got finished talking with the honcho and she tells me I'm in for at least the first semester, and she said I was lucky, said there is an overage of fifteen teachers right now."

"Fifteen?"

"Yep, she said she's got to excess some of them."

"Did she mention me?"

"No. But you teach science so you should be okay." She smiled at Mitkin even as he went white with worry. "You could always teach art like me, an art teacher with an English certification, go figure."

"Yeah," Mitkin said, "go figure." He simpered and with his eyes darting, asked, "Where is the principal right now? In the office?"

"Yeah, or at least she was ten minutes ago."

Mitkin dismissed himself and charged to see the principal, Rochelle Dandino. He had to have a job, a classroom, and tomorrow, people were counting on him. He nearly slammed into the principal's secretary who was bent over and fiddling with her stockings. Straightening up she met a wide-eyed Mitchell Mitkin.

"Yes, excuse me, how can I help you?"

"I need to see Ms. Dandino, it's about my full-time position."

"She's in a meeting right now, could I leave a message?" Mitkin looked around anxiously. The door to the principal's office remained open. He craned his neck to see in. He saw Dandino. An annoyed voice met him from behind. "Sir, she's in with someone right now, I can leave a message."

Mitkin got up and headed for the open door.

"Sir," she was yelling, "she's in a—"

He gently pushed the door open and Dandino looked at him directly. "Mitchell? Hello. Welcome back."

"Hello, Ms. Dandino, I'm sorry for interrupting but I just thought I could get some quick verification on my position and then not have to bother you anymore until the end of the week."

Mitkin took a quick peek around the room. Two men. One, a man with beefy thighs and a jacket too small for him smiled simply and nodded. Mitkin nodded back. In the chair across from Dandino the other man sat comfortably, his heavy body sinking deep into the beige, faux leather couch. Mitkin's stomach sank.

It was Borly.

He felt his throat tighten.

"So what is it then, Mitchell? What do you need?" Dandino was carefree.

"Ah," he stammered, "I want to know if I should report tomorrow?"

"Did you talk to Stone yet? He's got the final numbers. I think you're on the list."

Mitkin snapped a glance at Borly. He nodded politely, but in Borly's eyes, met a sweet satisfaction.

"Okay then, I'll check with Stone." Mitkin hurried along hoping Borly would not remember him. "I'll get back to you." He turned to leave.

"Hello Mr. Mitkin, we meet again, and again you seem to have found your way into an office not your own." Borly's voice was ridiculously baritone. "You're quite a character, Mr. Mitkin, quite a character. I could never forget you, son." He looked at Dandino. "I used to have Mr. Mitkin over in the Bronx."

"Really?" said Dandino. "Last year?"

"Yes, last year." Borly looked at Mitkin again. "He turned out to be a fairly good teacher."

"Fairly good indeed," said Dandino. "Kids love him." Mitkin nodded a thank you and smiled. He was pulsating with a resolute desire to leave, yet he found it in him to politely nod again.

"I'll check with Stone then, Ms. Dandino?"

"Yes, he'll have the numbers."

"Thanks again." Mitkin again turned to leave.

"Mr. Mitkin," came Borly's hale voice, "have you made any inroads with your student movement of late?"

With his back to the administrators, Mitkin's eyes darted side to side like an animal hunting safety. "We're going slowly," said Mitkin, turning around. "Still looking for good kids willing to work hard."

Borly nodded and turned to Dandino. "Have you heard of Mitkin's hard work with students?"

"Oh sure. He's involved with at-risk kids. I love it, not that I love all that ranting. Still, better to give the students a voice and the rights due them than coop them up, you know stymie them, don't you think, Rich?"

Mr. Borly grinned. "Sure." He looked at Mitkin. "Keep me up to date on your work, Mr. Mitkin. You're getting quite a following around the city. What's the little group called again?"

"Student Coalition."

"At every school it's called that?" asked Borly.

"Some schools are different. It's a loose alliance." He smirked slightly and fought back an urge to do again what he had done before. The images of that day, in Borly's office, the students and the cheers and the courage, it all simmered just below his calm exterior. "Students," he said calmly, "choose the names for themselves, it—"

"Goes with the philosophy of the group, yes, I know," said Borly sarcastically. "Good luck then, Mr. Mitkin. Goodbye." In silence, Borly waited for Mitkin to leave.

Dandino chimed in, "Stone, Mr. Mitkin. See him and for God's sake get me something official on this coalition please, a schedule of events, or a blotter of some kind, you know, a blurb with activities for the month."

"Okay," said Mitkin. "Tomorrow."

"Too soon, we're busy all week. Next week. I'll see you here next week."

Mitkin left. The secretary glared at him.

In the corridor he worried, "What the hell is Borly doing here?" He climbed the stairs to the fourth floor. "This is bad. I don't like his tone, he knows too much. I don't like this at all." He had not gotten rid of the tightness in his throat. "I think he knows something. I think that's why he's here. He was bluffing in there, something's not right." He turned the corner and entered a big room now made smaller by cluttered equipment and cardboard boxes. In the back, he saw Del Stone. Stone was the science department's assistant principal, and the only established black administrator in the building. As a substitute the previous year, Mitkin had seen him in the halls, but he had never worked for him. Stone looked up from his desk as Mitkin knocked ceremoniously on the open door. Stone waved him in.

"You're the coalition guy, Mitkin, right?" said Stone, getting up. He wore reading glasses and a graying black beard. "You're full-time, Mitkin. Welcome."

Mitkin shook Stone's hand exultingly. "Thank you."

Stone shrugged. "No, thank you. Finding science teachers for this school is like, well, it's one of my least favorite jobs, and I've got lots of least favorites." He put his hands on his hips. "Forgive the mess. We've finally received the equipment I ordered two years ago, and I bet we can't even use most of it anymore." He shook his head despondently. "Another year of confusion, I can feel it. It seems like we're in constant transition." His stare was blank. "Anyway," he snapped to attention, "here's your schedule." Stone handed Mitkin a pinkish piece of paper. "You've got an extra class for right now, but I'm looking to trim it down. Sorry."

"No problem. Thanks."

"As for class size, well, don't thank me. It's only gotten worse. Here are your lists, tentative." Mitkin glanced at the pink and gray sheets and counted the students on each, skimming in bunches of ten. Each was over forty. One was fifty-one.

"Fifty-one?" asked Mitkin.

"For now. It'll change."

"Before Christmas?"

"It's not me."

Mitkin relented. He remembered the day, what it meant, the great changes to come and he experienced a vindicating freedom, a contentment that surpassed joy. He didn't care that he had fifty-one students in his class. What difference did it make now? He wanted to tell Stone to give him more students as a sort of code word, a way of letting Stone rest, too. He wanted to stop all the madness of a lurching system, a system that nearly burst from ineptitude every fall. "And," he thought, "today we will stop it." Peace settled over him and he spoke aloud, "I know it's not your fault, Mr. Stone. I know. The whole system is a mess."

"Yes it is."

"What can be done?"

"Lots," said Stone. "We could start by lowering class size. But hey," he smiled sarcastically, "that takes money." He itched his cheek and sat back. "Anyway, forget about it. The worst part about this system is not that you can't make it any better, it's realizing that you can't even make it any worse."

Mitkin burped an airy laugh. "Yeah, you almost have to tear the whole thing down."

"Not almost, must. Tear it all down and start over. Clean out the roaches, you know?"

Mitkin nodded. He longed to tell this Mr. Stone of the day to come, the urge welled in him and he was sure it broke through and shone on his face. He looked at Stone hesitantly wondering if he sensed his secret. "Tell him," thought Mitkin, "he can help, he's in a position to help." Mitkin did not move. *Tell him, he seems like a tired warrior. Tell him.* Stone was flat-faced, his dark, purple-brown eyes staring out from a handsome brown face. They hinted of exhaustion and the experience of many difficult years. Mitkin noted the sagacious lines on Stone's face, and then, suddenly, Stone reminded him of his father. It was Stone's apparent wisdom that attracted Mitkin. Mitkin glared and then started.

"Mr. Stone, how long have you been working in the system here?"

"In New York City?"

Mitkin nodded.

"I've been here about two years. I came in the middle of the school year two years ago."

"From where?" Mitkin was surprised.

"From upstate, Albany."

"Why did you move here?"

"My wife got a job here, she's a pediatrician. We never would have moved here, ever. The money was good for her though, and it was her dream to work at Mount Sinai."

Mitkin felt his stomach sink. The mask he had constructed for Stone was peeling away. Stone continued.

"My boss from Albany knows Dandino's husband, Chuck. He got me the interview as soon as Kelly left. Did you know Harry Kelly?"

"No," said Mitkin, nearly under his breath. He paused, and with a transparent civility, waited.

Stone leaned all the way back in his swivel chair and motioned Mitkin to find a seat. Mitkin cornered a box with his buttocks.

"This system is clearly bankrupt, that's why I'm getting out, see. Between you and me," his voice lowered slightly, "two years is two years—"

"Too many, yeah, I've heard that before," said Mitkin. The mannerly respect Mitkin had afforded Stone receded and he began to manipulate the conversation. "Two years too many, but, you can leave, right? What about kids in the system? They're stuck here for at least four. Doesn't seem right, does it?"

"It's like anything," said Stone. "These kids get what they deserve, they chase the good people out, drive them crazy and eventually, well, their school system is a joke. That's what this boils down to. Teachers are like anybody; we're all out for self ultimately and who wants to work in this system when you can work in another and enjoy life. Hell, there are a hundred thousand public schools out there. Find one you like, I say."

"So then what about the kids?" Mitkin boiled.

"Fix the parents," said Stone.

"Schools don't do that." Mitkin began to hate this conversation.

"Sure seems like we try. Aren't we constantly trying to redo all the wrong the parents do, I mean nobody here trusts what these kids are being taught at home, face it. We all think we've got more to fix than to teach. It's like having thirty-five newborns all screaming for attention and you're the daddy and they need some real, never-ending attention, some moral education. Anyway," he waved a hand, "I don't know how I got started on all of this. I don't want to think about it. Like I said, the worst part is not knowing you can't fix it, it's knowing that you can't even make it worse."

Mitkin was silent.

"So let's try this again another time, huh? Over lunch maybe? But to tell you the truth, Mr. Mitkin, these things are better left unsaid. They just make you crazy, especially if you work here day in and day out. They make you want to snap, you know, shoot somebody. Better just to leave them alone." He smiled slightly. "You understand. Stick to the science. That's the easy part, the clearest part of all. No gray." Mitkin looked at Stone. His face had changed, his wise lines giving way to seasoned villainy. "Stick to the science," Stone repeated. "Stick to the science."

"Yeah, I'll try," replied Mitkin, a traitor to his soul. Stone stood up and politely escorted Mitkin to the door.

"Have a good year, I mean it, and don't forget the department meeting tomorrow after school. There's a memo in your box." Mitkin nodded and walked into the empty hall.

"I am stupid," thought Mitkin. "*This* is the enemy." He took drowsy steps toward nowhere. "I am too soft, too susceptible, still." He began to question himself, the doubt coming like a peep from his soul, quiet and small and then bigger, faster, infectious. He recalled how his life had been lived in delusion, how science was his god and how pompous and self-assured he had been, how unclouded life had been and how ridiculous he was for believing it all. He felt embarrassed and angry. He repeated Stone's words under his breath, "Just stick to the science. Stick to the science... asshole."

An anonymous teacher passed him in the hall, but he did not say hello. He grew onerous. Then thankfully, an enormous sense of superiority washed over it all like a savior and he thought, "At least I've done something to change it all. I've put my life on the line, today, right now." He swaggered into a stairwell and ran down the stairs. He was a time bomb.

Mitkin looked up and saw Dandino escorting the fat-thighed bureaucrat out of the building. They chatted smugly with a school guard as they went. Mitkin's eyes darkened. "F them," thought Mitkin. "Fuck 'em all."

Then he met with the other teacher martyrs. First there was Terry Rutledge, the young chin-whiskered Brooklynite who loved girls and the idea of being important. They met on the front steps of the school courtyard, the one through which students would pour after a day in school. Rutledge was sucking on a cigarette. His face was young, and in the sun his squinty eyes betrayed a childish innocence, a look of everlasting inquisitiveness. He had the appeal of a knave. He walked on the balls of his feet and wore baggy pants. He was nearly thirty years old and taught remedial math.

"So here we are," he said knuckling a cigarette and blowing a large plume of smoke. "Today's the day." He looked around mistrustfully. "Anybody been acting funny like they got ideas?"

"The Lip's here."

"Borly? The guy from your old school in the Bronx?"

"Him." Mitkin looked over Rutledge's shoulder and stayed staring.

"What," said Rutledge. "What is it?"

Mitkin did not respond immediately.

"What?"

"Turn around and see for yourself." Mitkin's voice was condescending.

"The bushy-faced guy? That's Borly," he said slowly, his body contorted but his face remaining still and dumb. "What is he doing here?"

"I have no idea."

Another of Mitkin's martyrs came out of the building and into the sun. He was a young teacher, younger than Rutledge even, but dressed nattily. Short and built low to the ground, his complexion was dark. With small glasses barely covering his eyes, he appeared adroit and learned. He held out a hand. His name was Sinclair Freeman. "Mitchell, did you get the note from Taughtauer?" Mitkin shook his head. "Judy Strand brought it by about an hour ago and gave me my copy." He furrowed his brow. "You sure she never found you?" Mitkin shook his head again, still looking past Rutledge toward Borly. "The note was clear. All is go. No hitches, Mitch. They'll be inside before nightfall."

"The Chancellor is still on site?" asked Mitkin.

"Yes. So is the Deputy. They'll get them both."

"Good," said Mitkin. Terry Rutledge sucked hard on his cigarette again. Mitkin looked at him. "Did they confirm your math position?"

"Sure did. Start tomorrow, as planned. Nine sharp."

"What about the literature and banners. Are they safe?"

"Yep," assured Rutledge.

"And the mace? Five cases?"

"In my car, ready to go."

"Where's your car?"

"At home."

"Nobody sees a thing until morning," said Mitkin. Rutledge nodded, smoke crawling out of his nose. "Remember we are the key to this whole operation. Six pissed off students and one crazy teacher is not a revolution. We must have at least two schools by day's end tomorrow. This must be one of them."

Freeman got closer to Mitkin. "Are you sure we can count on two hundred here? That's a big number, Mitch."

"It's an estimate. They can't know about the rebellion, so I can't know about the numbers yet. Tomorrow. Everything will be clear tomorrow. They're as prepared as they can be, at least here." He pointed to his head. "I just hope they have the courage here," he said, now pointing to his chest. "Now, let me see what Dandino's got you two doing tomorrow." They handed him their schedules.

He looked for the best time for the march, for victory. Kids in the streets meant victory. He would gladly rot in jail, a hero, if in return he saw kids in the streets. If the march failed, he failed, his movement failed and hope failed in him. So he doted, and dallied and decided finally that they'd go into the streets third period, during homeroom, when things were a bit crazy to start with. Mitkin would have a holdover class, a group of flunkies he knew well. Freeman was a special education teacher and was entirely confident about his troops. Rutledge had a giant group of freshmen in his homeroom and worried that he could not count on them. Mitkin held out his schedule and shook it.

"Don't worry about what this says for third period. Forget the freshmen. I've already arranged for you to be in the cafeteria. You'll have lots of real rambunctious company too, somewhere in the neighborhood of two hundred. And all of them will be outfitted with fliers. A few, maybe twenty, will have mace."

"For the cops?" asked Freeman.

"Yes," said Mitkin. "The fliers will get them out there, the mace, if they don't let us march, will make it a riot."

"I've seen the fliers, they're perfect," said Rutledge.

"What do they say?" asked Freeman.

Mitkin smiled a satisfied smile. "TAKE THE CITY HOSTAGE AND MARCH FOR FREEDOM, and then directions for where and when to march." He continued, deadpan, "It says that one million students are poised to march in ten minutes, and then it asks the question, DO YOU WANT TO BE THE ONLY ONE TO MISS THIS?" Mitkin feigned holding a piece of paper in his hands, pointing to it and pounding it with his forefinger. "Go march or miss the boat of salvation." He looked at Rutledge and then at Freeman and grinned, slightly. A stultified silence invited him to continue. "Look, they'll go. Besides, I know most of them personally and they'll go. I know it. They're waiting for this. I can feel it. They'll go." Mitkin pointed to Rutledge. "The key to big numbers will be the lunchroom kids. Get them into the courtyard quickly, Terry. No later than ten after ten. Tomorrow."

"And then all of us into the streets?" asked Rutledge.

"Yes. As many as possible, but don't go far. We must get back to help with the principal's office. Two martyrs, Melinda and Shakina, will already have secured it."

Freeman lowered his chin an inch. "Girls with guns, I love it. So our job is to return to the school after the march begins?"

"That's right," said Mitkin. "If we can, we come back here."

Rutledge finished his cigarette and threw the butt on the ground. "And then in Dandino's office for how long?"

Mitkin's nose flared and he sucked up a deep breath. "Until Taughtauer burns down Livingston Street."

They walked back into the school, apart and alone, carrying their secret, bursting to act, bursting to tell. Quietly they inched further and further toward fame, but Mitkin walked closer to his soul and nearer his spirit than the others. Again and again, he ran the whole thing through his mind. *Action. Cut. Action.* The day's significance revealed itself, shuddering and heaving inside a mind already filled with so many decaying hopes that barely any room could be made for happiness.

It was just after 2:30 p.m., two hours until Taughtauer was scheduled to lay siege to the building. One hundred and twenty minutes kept Mitkin from his dream. He checked every clock in every room as he moved from floor to floor, nervously doing nothing. Unable to concentrate on the little things he had been assigned to do on this day, the before the opening of school. He finally came to rest in the yearbook office across from his classroom, a place he went often in the latter months of the previous school year. There he picked up the phone and dialed.

"Hello." A dull-voiced girl answered the phone. "Who's this?"

"Mitkin. Where are we?"

"On schedule. The van is gone. They should arrive by four, no hitches." A pause and then a giddy, "All is go, that includes every TM at every school. No changes."

"Are you sure, Alysha?" asked Mitkin.

"It's all good."

"And the house? Is it cleared out entirely?"

"Almost. I should have it ready within the hour."

"Be meticulous, you know, thorough, take it all, leave nothing behind. Be smart, please. Please."

"I'll take care of it."

"Where will you stay tonight? You cannot stay there."

"I'm going to stay at Richie's, most of us are. We've got the whole place to ourselves. We'd love to see you there, Mitchell."

"What about his mother?"

"He says she's tripping," said Alysha. "Good thing for us too, I didn't know where we'd stay. You got the number, right? Please call."

Mitkin said that he would and hung up. Next he reached each of the teacher martyrs. One by one, each confirmed what the students had been telling him all day. Judy Strand sounded jubilant.

"It's gonna happen, Mitchell. They're on their way. Not one hitch all day, great. The police have never been a problem, the FBI is nowhere to be found and the schools themselves are clueless, even when kids like Rich scream at them from their own courtyard. Amazing, truly amazing. It's almost too easy."

"Don't get overconfident, Judy. It's been easy because nobody takes the system seriously, everybody figures it's such a waste that people like us could not exist. Well, we do, and the only ones who need to know about it for the next forty-five minutes are us. After that, the whole world."

"And they will..." Her voice trailed off. "Have you heard from Roger and Terry?"

"I saw Terry today and Sinclair Freeman too, I'm waiting for Roger to call back."

Judy Strand nearly screamed into the phone. "Who the hell is Sinclair Freeman?"

"A teacher martyr."

"Since when?"

"Since last week. Terry recruited him."

Judy Strand paused over the phone. "Does Ed know about him, I mean, I never heard about him getting baptized?"

Mitkin hadn't either. "Terry told me Ed knew about him, that Ed had given the go-ahead for him to be a martyr. I think he even said he's baptized. That's what Terry said." He tried to remember. "That's what he told me, he's legit, I'm sure."

"Then why wasn't he baptized properly? I wasn't there." Strand didn't wait for an answer. "Where is he now?"

"Still here I think," said Mitkin, glaring out over the phone at the empty room. "I'll find him, right now." He hung up. An image of Freeman's visage hung in the air, his little learned glasses and fickle eyes there in front of Mitkin. He spoke aloud to himself. "He's genuine, he's got to be." He balled his fists and flew into the hallway. Mitkin clacked down the stairs and into Terry Rutledge's burrow, the teachers' lounge. There he found Rutledge, alone, sipping on a cold can of fruit juice and playing solitaire.

"Where's Freeman?" asked Mitkin.

"I don't know, he may have gone home. What's up with you? You look crazy."

"Was he baptized?" asked Mitkin fiercely.

"Of course he was."

"Submersed? In the basement?" shouted Mitkin.

"Well, sort of, I mean he might have—"

"Who baptized him?"

"What's the big deal, Mitch? Geez. He was approved by Ed, what else do you need to know?" Rutledge's drawn temples betrayed resentment.

"I need to know everything, Terry. Now. We are thirty minutes away from D-Day, thirty minutes. Do you understand? I don't get the conflicting stories. Why wasn't he baptized like he was supposed to be?"

Rutledge smirked, "Because, we didn't have time. Come on Mitch, calm down. Ed felt like we needed another teacher martyr on the ground here, someone who could help us tomorrow. I mean come on Mitch, Ed okayed it all."

Mitkin ground his teeth. His stare was fierce. "Did he, or did he not go down and get baptized?"

"No. Damn, lighten up, Mitchell. So what? It's just water, Mitch, no, so what?" Rutledge was loud.

"So what?" repeated Mitkin through gritted teeth and red-hot lips. "How about this for one? Our lives are on the line today, Terry. Every one of us has been quiet for months, some of us years, and now, just like that, two weeks before D-Day I've got some uninitiated guy working close enough to ruin everything. It's not just water, Terry, it's deeper than that. Deeper."

"You're crazy man, relax. It's frickin' water, and it's not the point of this all. Relax, shit." Rutledge's young face fell flat, his eyes dimming as if losing power. He seemed unwilling to accept Mitkin's spontaneous analysis, content to just shrug his shoulders and raise an eyebrow. "C'mon Mitch. Freeman's legit. Someone in his family was killed in school, the Tom Jefferson case. You know about it. That was Freeman's baby brother."

Mitkin did not say a word.

"Don't worry, he'll be with us tomorrow and he'll kick some ass. Don't worry. Relax."

There was no relaxing, however. Things were getting dangerous. Mitchell jumped to the most lurid of conclusions, the conclusion that all of it would end without a peep, at the front door of Livingston Street, a huge army of helmeted policemen clubbing silly a bunch of half-crazed lunatics whose only goal was to kill the Chancellor. They'd probably even say something about special education and broken homes, and suddenly it wouldn't be the system at all, it would be them, the fixers, at fault. He cringed and then recalled the many months of preparation, months that for Taughtauer were years. He saw Taughtauer as a young man hatching the plan and now, this day, this momentous day was at hand. How terrible it would be if it all ended that way, unceremoniously, at the foot of the dragon's lair. Mitkin looked at Rutledge and wondered if he thought this way too. He wondered if it was *his life* that he had given. Because that is what it was for Mitkin. It was his life, his entire being, given in the service of an idea. He had come to worship at the altar of freedom and genuine love for children. The idea had rescued him. The ideas of freedom and service had made him great again and had given his life design. He had gone from hopeless animal to hopeful spirit and was grateful. Wasn't Rutledge grateful too?

"Is he genuine, Terry?" he asked one last time, tired from thought. "Tell me he's truly committed."

"I already told you, yes." Rutledge saw Mitkin's fervor and put his hand on Mitkin's shoulder. "He's not gonna ruin anything Mitch. It's good, don't worry."

Mitkin looked at him sternly. His fiery confidence returned. "Good then. I'm leaving now. Where will you spend the night?"

Rutledge looked calm. "At Sinclair's. We'll be there all night, call us."

"I will," said Mitkin. "I'll call you when I hear about the takeover. Listen to the radio, seven seventy. When it comes over, then I'll call."

As Mitkin turned to leave, Rutledge said, "You were made for tomorrow man. Cheer up."

Mitkin walked the two flights of stairs down to the main floor. He shook his head and rolled it around on his neck and then entered Dandino's office. Her secretary had gone for the day. Mitkin peered into the office.

Dandino was in a leather armchair reading. She had reading glasses shaped like cat's eyes and bejeweled with emerald studs of some sort. A long pearly chain attached to her glasses hung around her neck and swayed a U on either side of her face, just below her ears. She looked up and saw Mitkin. She stared for a moment and then invited him in. Her gray hair bounced slightly on her head. "You're still here? You're probably one of the last."

"Not quite," said Mitkin.

"What brings you back, Mr. Mitkin?"

"I wanted to talk to you about Mr. Borly, the gentlemen I saw here earlier. I wanted to give my side of the story." He mimicked meekness. "I really love this school and I don't want anything to be misunderstood, anything that might jeopardize my position here."

She nodded. "What is it then?"

"I was released from SBHSS after an altercation with Borly. He and I argued over his misuse of power. The kids, and I, felt he was unfair."

"Yes, I know. I already had that talk with him, long before today. He told me about your run-in. He said you were a trouble maker."

Mitkin nodded.

"He said you were inciting the students. Were you?"

"No."

"You were helping students express themselves then?"

"I was just trying to do what was right. Some students expressed dissatisfaction with Mr. Borly, so I told him about it. I tried to be polite, but if you knew the situation there you'd know he, well, runs a tight ship." Mitkin wanted to retract his last statement; it didn't go well with obsequiousness.

"Too tight perhaps?"

Mitkin nodded, confused. She seemed to lead him against Borly.

"You could say he did a disservice to his students by treating them like voiceless creatures, couldn't you?"

Mitkin hesitated. Then he nodded.

Dandino waved her reading glasses like a handkerchief and spoke up, "I couldn't agree more, Mitchell. That's partly why I hired you here. I'm not afraid to hire teachers who believe in students' rights. Children must have a voice in their education, a strong voice. I feel like every student gets an education when they get to know themselves and their inherent rights and responsibilities, and all the rest. You can't just treat them like empty vessels." Mitkin's lips parted. His chin fell. "And besides, between you and me, Borly's an old windbag."

Mitkin cocked his head. "So he didn't come to tell you about me?"

"Oh, don't be so presumptuous, Mr. Mitkin. He came for other reasons that have nothing to do with you whatsoever. In fact, it is safe to say he has forgotten your name already. He's like that, the system comes first for Mr. Borly, teachers second."

Mitkin stood up before it was time, propelled by his reprieve. But Dandino glared and he sat back down.

"Now, as for your Student Coalition thing, I have only one thing to say." She paused and then jerked with a malformed thought, her hand to her mouth. "Let me back up first." She flittered her fingers. "What is your position with this group again? If I remember right you're the coordinator for the whole city, and have been?" She paused and gathered her thoughts. "But you weren't even a full-time teacher, right?"

"I'm just a coordinator. I don't really do much but give them a little teacher credence, you know some legitimacy." He tried a smile.

"And what exactly do the kids do?"

"We, well, we are, uh… a group committed to…"

She interrupted, "To student politics and leadership, I hope. Isn't that it?"

"Yes, absolutely, yes."

"Well," she said quickly, "you are welcome to use the rear courtyard whenever you think it is necessary. However, I don't like the kids cursing on the loudspeaker. That was your group last spring, wasn't it?"

He nodded.

"Well, that must stop. And as for the message, I respect it, the underlying element that is, but I don't like the way it came out. It needs to be more constructive, as I am sure you will agree. I know these kids have lots of hang-ups and anger and I know that you are teaching them how to release some of it. But I don't think yelling curse words at just anybody counts as constructive. So, do what you can. Get the kids to be a little more subtle maybe, less political perhaps, but do it without taking away the sense that they are in control. It's a fine line, Mr. Mitkin, but that's what you're there for, it seems. You're a kind of rudder. Get them to hold the wheel while you do all of the driving, it's the way we learn." A Pollyanna smile oozed out. "Again, I am not saying I don't like their enthusiasm and passion, it actually reminds me of when I was young, with dreams. Still, keep it from being some crude display of rage, please. That is all. Now," she smiled, "you may leave."

Mitkin got up and shook hands, turned, and walked calmly toward the door.

"Oh, and by the way. One of my assistant principals tells me the kids are having some kind of march tomorrow. Is that true?"

Mitkin froze.

"If it is," she added, "why haven't I been told?"

Mitkin's lungs filled with air, his stomach with panicky pinpricks. "Ah, there's no march tomorrow." His head pulled back on his chin in feigned disbelief. "I haven't heard a thing about a march."

"Good, I just wanted to make sure." She stretched out her hands palms up, like an island despot receiving a guest. "Remember what I said now and have a good day."

He walked as fast as he could out of the building. An urgent voice called to him from behind.

"Mitch!" Terry Rutledge ran to catch him. "Did you hear?"

Mitkin stopped.

"It's on the radio. They're in. They're in, Mitch. They've got the Chancellor."

Mitkin took a step closer to Rutledge. "Who told you?"

"I was in Freeman's office upstairs. I heard it on the radio. They're in, I'm not bullshitting you, Mitch. They're really in. It's on!" Rutledge held Mitkin's shoulder, his grip a mix of fear and elation.

Mitkin became emotional. A wild loosening of everything rational overtook his soul. Triumph swelled. He grabbed Rutledge by the shoulders and together the two stood, neither particularly sure what to say but both wrought with a deep sense of mission. "Call me tonight," said Mitkin. "Be ready for anything." He turned and walked away, his hand high in the air, a fist to the sky. He lived a renaissance as he walked through the courtyard, a magnificent brightness hanging over him and following him like the halos of old, signaling his acceptance among an elite group of individuals who in the course of history have taken their cause beyond thought and words and into action, into reality. For it was, he knew now, true what Taughtauer continuously hymned: The only thing real is man's will, his will to action. Everything else is subjective and prey for the labyrinth of despair. It was true.

Mitkin came to the edge of the elevated courtyard and looked down on the traffic below. Like spit, cars shot past. They roared from one light to the next. Mitkin watched as pedestrians streamed unevenly through the crosswalks, scurrying from one side of the street to the other, some with, some against the light, but all endeavoring action, no matter how inconsequential. This was life, *Just Do It.* He plunged down the steps and onto the sidewalk. He too entered wildly into the street, dodging in and out of traffic and loving it. He yelled for no reason. He caught a glimpse of the big, digital clock hanging over 72nd Street, it read 4:00

p.m. A zephyr of raw emotion blew through him as he pictured Taughtauer calmly walking into the Board of Education and nimbly heading upstairs, his stealthy martyrs at his side, all ready to act in defense of the idea. They, like him must be feeling the joy of action, of being meaningful in the world. "It's perfection," he thought as he scampered to the bus stop, jostling playfully for a place in line.

The bus pulled in and settled with a high-pitched sigh. The straphangers swarmed and tangled together trying to get on the bus, and like this, Mitkin could feel the press of bone-backed flesh on all sides. It rubbed and stroked his spirit, his soul dancing freely among the crushing humanity. The breath, the sweat, the hair and the sweet aroma of the human body all saturated Mitkin as he lived, really lived, between them all. He shuffled on with an imbecile's smile, eyes half-open, cheeks high and tight and rosy. A woman mistook him for inebriated, another for a fool. He stared with perfect cheer at everyone on the bus, one by one. He was happy, rejuvenated and free from the pain of trying to know everything, of trying to plan life. "The planning was over now," he thought, "life begins now." A man, trying to pass Mitkin, stepped hard on his toes.

"So sorry, excuse me," said the big man.

Mitkin nearly yelled through his ebullient smile, "For what?"

"I stepped on your foot, I hope I didn't scuff your shoes," the giant said, gently.

"These?" Mitkin took off his shoes. "These are nothing." And he flung his shoes out the side window of the bus. "Thank you," he said and gave the man a Russian-style peck on the cheek. A woman snickered in the seat below and Mitkin looked at her with a beggar's smile before kissing her, too. She snickered some more, liking it. He made his way to the back of the bus and as he did, his thin black socks began to come off his shoeless feet. They flopped back and forth as he walked, yet he went on unfazed. His tie was undone around his neck and the sport jacket he wore to impress the administrators hung unevenly off his shoulders. Mirth was undressing him like a lover. The bus crossed Central Park and rolled onto Manhattan's Upper East Side.

A strong young teen wearing a Walkman stood near Mitkin on the bus. He stood taut, like a centurion. Mitkin looked at him with fascination, slowly making his way close to the boy and leaning in, conspicuously close now, his ear nearly against the big headphones and his cheek slightly rubbing the cheek of the tough boy. The boy jerked away.

"Yo, why you buggin' motherfucker?"

"Listen to the radio," said Mitkin softly.

The boy upped an angry lip.

"Listen to it, could you? Just a moment. Seven seventy."

The boy stared.

"Please? It could change your life."

"What white boy, President got took hostage? Get the hell outta here shocless fuckin' Joe."

"No, but Chancellor Romero did," said Mitkin flatly.

"Oh yeah? Really. And what makes you think I give a shit?"

"Because you should."

"And you 'bout to catch an ass whoopin'." The boy pushed Mitkin back very hard, by his forehead, wrenching his neck and clubbing his head against an alloy handrail. Everyone on the bus recoiled, one by one, like dominoes. A scream went up. The bus stopped and the big boy got off. Mitkin's head bled from a cut above his eye.

A woman offered an infant's handywipe. "You need this, baby." Mitkin grinned and wiped his face.

Another woman, this one with a West Indian accent, pointed and said, "There's some on your neck, here mon." Mitkin wiped his neck too.

"He's right, yo," came a squeaky voice from nearby. The bus lurched forward and Mitkin recoiled like a rag doll. "Yo, dude with the bloody head, you're right." It was a girl's voice, and now everyone was looking at her, a bag of bones draped in a heap of jeans and designer wear.

"They say some radical Puerto Ricans kidnapped the Chancellor, they got guns."

Mitkin laughed. "Puerto Ricans? Is that what they decided to say?" He looked at the girl and she looked back, blankly. Mitkin pointed slowly to his ear and rolled his finger as if asking for more.

"They cleared the building and they don't know how many perps. It all just now went down now." The girl was announcing it all as if calling a baseball game. "What a trip, yo."

The bus pulled to a stop and Mitkin ran off, his hand still pressed against his bloody forehead. Suddenly he stopped, just beneath the big back window of the city bus. He searched the tinted window intently and felt the eyes of the passengers looking out at him and imagined that they were waiting for him to say something, do something, and so he did, he raised his fist and then, comically, raised his thumb, a thumbs-up for all those on the bus. And he smiled again too, brightly, like a clown, just like a clown with floppy socks and a bloody head and an eyeful of hope. He ran down the block and onto the stoop of his home, flung the doors open and careened up to his second floor apartment. He got inside and turned on the radio. It blared the same news over and over again:

We think five hostages, but that remains unsubstantiated... Now we are hearing ten assailants and all of them apparently from a Puerto Rican nationalist movement. Quite a scene here, Vincent. We'll keep you up to the moment.

Mitkin grinned and then curled his lip. "Not quite," he said under his breath. "Try again, morons." He laughed wildly.

So everything *was* going according to plan. Taughtauer had gotten in without a hitch. The building had been cleared and all ten martyrs were safe and accounted for. Each, apparently, had taken up post and now, on the fourth floor, just like they had planned, Taughtauer and Ricky held the Chancellor and his deputy hostage. "Unprecedented," thought Mitkin. "Perfect." And the rest of the plan crystallized in his mind. Two things: Taughtauer could not give in until the fire. Secondly, he could not identify the students involved or the breadth of the movement. Not yet. But Mitkin knew Taughtauer would succeed, it was working. It would work.

CHAPTER XXX

Baptism by Fire

The radio prattled on and Mitkin turned to survey his apartment. It was clean, very clean, and spartan. Nothing was left but his little foam mattress, his radio and a telephone. Through the window poured the sun's heavy rays, deep warm evening rays lush like wet rivulets on polished hardwood. A great largeness swept the place, and it swept through his mind, too. With his jacket still crooked on his shoulders and his socks still dangling off his heels he began to laud his life.

"Finally the fool is vindicated. Free." He smiled broadly, dropped his wrinkled jacket and walked to the window where he snuggled up comfortably on the sill. Below, New York bustled, people came and went. A day-shifter with a lunch box shuffled past a night-shifter in a blue, mass transit uniform. A crying child met his parents on the stoop of a day care center and two idle teens slouched on a craggy service entrance stoop, savoring a single, cheap, ember-tipped cigarette. Mitkin wanted to shout out to them all like a prophet from ancient days, "Prepare yourselves people. Tomorrow is truly a new day!" He wished he could fly and set out over the city, into its dark alleyways, announcing the coming revolution with a clarion call of hope. He laughed at his own sentimentality, but he did not despise it now, he loved it. He loved that he could think this way, could imagine himself flying and announcing something joyous and wonderful, and he loved that he could be absolutely idealistic and not have to prove one word of anything. He loved that he had only to know in his own soul. He laughed so hard sitting there in the window that he began to cry. The tears streamed down a ruddy, resonant face.

"I was dead, it's amazing, I was dead, a pitiful person, a heap. One man dies and just like that, I go into the shithole, dead, but not quite, not totally, alive just enough to know it and hate it. Damn my father's religion was weak, so weak, so simple and ridiculously weak. But now it's clear. Clear." He looked across the street and saw an old man perched in a window, wearing a white fisherman's hat and smoking a cigar. Mitkin waved. The man waved back.

"He'll be in the grave soon," thought Mitkin. "And that's how it should be. Life is meaningless without death, it's all connected, one giving meaning to the other." His tears ran. "I don't fear death! Courage is the thing... it's uncontaminated, strong, life-giving. A god, I want to be courageous! Nothing else matters, and now I have, we have," he balled a friendly fist and pounded it on his knee. "We are perfect today. Hell yes!" he yelled out.

The old man looked at him.

"Hey, old man," he waved, "today we did it. We willed it! That's it, we wanted it and it is ours." He pumped a fist. "You *can* change the world, you can," he screamed.

The man worked a confused smile and said something in Spanish.

Mitkin laughed and turned back inside, nearly drunk with joy. "Just do it, man, that's right. Just overthrow the goddamned New York City Board of Education!"

From the corner of his eye he saw Raphaella. She was crossing the street with Dana, holding her hand. The wind blew Raphaella's thick hair, and her cotton sundress flittered behind her like the train of a wedding dress. Her gait was elegant as always, and she was beautiful.

He sighed to himself. "Look at this. I have to share." He got up, but then sat back down immediately. "If only she would have followed me." He watched them come up the block. "We were in love, but now," he sighed, "too far apart. It's a waste." He leaned out the window and shook his head. "God, I'd love to see her face when she finds out about Livingston Street. I'd love to see her when she finally puts two and two together and realizes it's me. What will she do? She'll be impressed, yes. She'll wonder how, she'll admire me, my devotion. That's what she loves, devotion. She's devoted too. She's in love, like me. Damn, I would love to see her face. Damn."

The front door clicked open below and the steps groaned as Raphaella and Dana made their way up the stairs. As if unable to control himself, he flew on the balls of his feet to his front door where he stuck his eye into the peephole. He breathed heavily but as silently as he could.

"Mitchell?" She had stopped in front of his door. "Is that you?"

In the peephole he saw her face, stretched round, distorted.

"Mitchell, are you there?"

He remained still, frozen by a wicked mix of admiration and disdain. Then out of his heart came a soft, bleating groan—it was loneliness and he desperately wanted her to knock on the door. She stared into the peephole. He stared back, glimpsing cloudily all that had made her so important to him; her hopeful green eyes and the winsome upturn of her thick lips, her manacled hair that spoke of an innocent recklessness, the perfect sorrow of her brow, all of it, in front of him, just on the other side of the distortion of the peephole.

"Mitchell?"

He stiffened with a hateful resolve to hide his self-pity. Lifeless, he waited for her to go, and for the loathing to pass.

She took Dana's hand. "Come on, honey. Up we go." Mitkin watched them ascend until they passed out of view. He turned and sucked his teeth.

"She's a waste anyway, stick to the mission, she'd only find something to ridicule, something *wrong* with the process. But that's just the problem with this world, isn't it? Too much upside-down morality, too much weakness, feeble people who can't stand up and fight. Sheep. Sheep, all of them sheep. The kind of person we must eliminate."

With heavy strides he marched into the kitchen and opened the refrigerator. It was nearly empty. He pulled a lone Guinness from the door and then dug out a half-wrapped piece of cheese. He looked for a knife to cut the hard, dark corners off the unexposed center. All he could find was a meat cleaver and it fell indiscriminately. A tough, ropy ball of cheese was all that was left as he flung the stiff corners out the window.

As he chewed the phone rang.

"Mitchell, have you heard? It's happening right down there in New York, some kind of revolution. Are you safe?"

Mitkin leered behind the phone. "I'm fine, Mother."

"It sounds like the Sixties, Son. I lived through that time remember, angry groups trying to start trouble. They say these are Puerto Ricans." She paused and then, as if to herself, said, "Your father would have been so interested."

"Is that the only reason you called, Mother?"

"Well, yes, sort of. You know we haven't spoken in nearly two months. I'm back and forth so much and you're so involved in teaching and everything, and, how's that working out? Are you still enjoying it? What class is it, the one you're teaching?" She spoke in a high voice as if rushing to make herself known to her wayward son.

"I'm teaching biology," said Mitkin, frowning into the phone. "Biology, Mother."

"And all goes well? It seems like you were really enjoying it last time we talked. I was glad to see you had some solid distractions after Martin's, well..."

Mitkin waited. She continued to fumble through less than fully formed thoughts.

"...and soon you'll be back in school, I would guess. I think about you and your dreams every day, Son. I want you to achieve everything you put your mind to. You can do anything in this world, Mitchell. You're so bright. I just worry about you, you've gotten so, so... serious." She paused. "Life is to be enjoyed, like your father enjoyed it."

"Yes, Mother, just like Father enjoyed it." He rolled his eyes and thought to himself how his father had spent his whole life trying to do what he would accomplish in one day. "How sorry," he thought, "how ironic."

"Your father loved his work. And he loved the schools and learning, and you, too. He would never have thought of doing what they are doing there today. It's so sad that people hate so much that they can ruin lives for the sake of, well, whatever it is they claim as, well, whatever. It's just a waste."

"The system is a waste, Mother. To try and change it, how is that a waste? Tell me please."

"Well there are other ways to fix it, Son."

"Like..." He waited. "Like, Mother?"

She stammered, "Like your father did."

Mitkin shook his head coarsely. "He didn't do anything. If he had we wouldn't need a revolution, I mean, what do you think? That these kids like to take guns and shoot people and go to jail just to make a statement? It's not like they're earning rewards, a new car or a big bank account. Nothing has gotten better for them."

There loomed a pent-up silence.

Mitkin continued, "But, Father knew all of this anyway. Trust me, he knew. He had all kinds of ideas like this stacked away in his head and on notepads, all over the place. He was closer to revolution than you think Mother."

"Why would you say such a thing?"

"Because, it's true," he said spitting disgust. "Because this was his idea."

A spattering laugh could be heard on the other end of the phone. It went on and on. Mitkin fumed.

"Are you laughing at me, Mother? Are you laughing at me?"

"Mitchell, your father could never have planned what's going on there. He was a scientist, honey, not a revolutionary. Please don't think he'd ever be involved with hostages and guns. There's too much danger in it for Martin." She chuckled again. "He was not like you, Mitchell. You're more tense."

Mitkin went blank with rage. His mother was in the Keys, or Palm Springs maybe, on a cruise ship, or at a steakhouse with friends, eating, gobbling, comfort-seeking and never thinking hard about the world and its cruelties. She had never known them.

"Look, I have to go, Mother. Don't call me here tonight." He hung up.

Speckled sunlight faded into a flat, low, cloudy gray. The capacious room grew darker, colder, more impersonal, and the empty walls and hard barren floors were suddenly too still. His mother's voice rained inside the room.

And the radio kept on in Mitkin's pale hand:

It is now the police's contention that somewhere between fifteen and twenty students occupy the building and most of them, they say, have guns. From where we are, Vin, across the street on top of a nearby building, some of the students can be seen passing in front of a stairwell window, carefully, as if knowingly under surveillance. It is an odd and really very terrifying scene down here Vin, and still, no definitive word on what the rebels want in exchange for their hostages, one of which remains Edwin Romero, the Public School Chancellor. Back to you, Vincent.

"Twenty?" Mitkin said to himself. "Good going, Ed. They won't try anything if they think twenty." Mitkin listened closely. A deep, rehearsed voice came on:

One thing is clear, some angry students have taken deliberate action to force some sort of change in our school system. Another thing, too, is clear. These are sophisticated students, not just street thugs. It looks like we have some very artistic young people here, kids who want to make a stand for the rights of African-American and Puerto Rican young people.

Another voice chimed over the rehearsed one. This voice was scratchy and female:

A part of me says, 'Hey, good for them,' like it's all a big class project. Wouldn't that be a great class project, Chuck? Abduct the Chancellor, teach him a lesson, test him, tie him up...

Laughs and a third voice peeled in, this one an Italian-American sing-song affair:

I think what all of New York City wants to know right now is, who is da mastermind? Is it simply some angry Puerto Rican kids, brown knife-wielders, Latin Kings with guns who decided to go out like Clint Eastwood, or is this the work of some evil, raving genius, a crackpot no doubt but one with real chutzpah, brains. A cult leader type, Doctor Moreau maybe, who has brainwashed regular old kids, kids with loving mothers at home, into doing something they will in the end regret? And all on the eve of the first day of school! What do you think? You, the people of Gotham, the mothers and fathers of school kids? Call us now at...

"Idiots," muttered Mitkin.

In the distance a police siren wailed, and Mitchell fluttered inside. He was a fugitive and it was only a matter of time before someone put it all together and his name surfaced as an accomplice. "Just not until tomorrow night," he said aloud in his empty apartment. "Nobody takes me until tomorrow night." The siren came closer and Mitkin craned to see from which direction. Then it was under him, the pitch unbearable and whirling from all directions at once. He slipped quickly off the ledge and down to his knees. His eyes peeked over the sill and out the window. The siren wailed beneath him, then forward, and then it was gone, down the block, hurtling through the crowded Harlem streets. Crazed, Mitkin popped up and watched. He waved.

"Tomorrow officer, sir, see you tomorrow!"

He smiled at his own bravado. From fear to courage, to loneliness, to an arrogant nonchalance and back again, that was how he went. He pictured the recent past, Taughtauer standing before him, one hand on Mitkin's shoulder: "You are made unlike anyone I have ever met, Mitchell. I would even venture to say that you are like no one in the whole world, no one now, no one ever." He bobbed a little and nodded affirmatively. In one enormous untamed moment he saw himself dying in a raging fire, surrounded by dead girls and boys, alone but for their memory, eyes beaming, heart pounding, teeth flashing under a vigilant grin. He saw millions watching him and admiring him, loving him and each changing within, each converted.

The doorbell broke in. It went off in loud spurts as if someone were in danger out on the stoop. He walked to his front door and listened. The buzz continued. No one was supposed to visit him today, nobody. Every martyr had clear directives—stay inside and out of the way, raise no suspicion and do not make unnecessary contact with anyone. The only one with license to change these orders was Mitkin himself. He stiffened. Another manic buzz electrified the room and then another, but this time the bell was much quieter, more distant. It came from upstairs; in fact, it came from within Raphaella's apartment. Mitkin listened to the buzzer scream on, then off, on then off, just as it had in his apartment. Then he heard it below, from Seever's apartment, and then again in his own. He looked out the peephole into the hall and saw nothing. He ran and hung his head out the window. Nothing. Then the buzz was back again, first his apartment and then hers above, and then below, in Seever's. Like a cornered animal, Mitkin searched his room for some suggestion. A spoke from a flatiron bed stood in the corner and Mitkin hurried to grab it. After one more look in the peephole, he opened his front door, inch by inch. At the foot of the stairs he saw a shadow. It was cast from a little ceiling lamp in the foyer between the front door and the building's second door, the entrance inside. Mitkin crept on. The shadow of a powerful man swayed to and fro. Mitkin strained, but could not see his face. He saw sneakers, big, black high-top sneakers. The door rattled violently.

"Come on!" came a cry.

Mitkin lurched and the iron cut his palm.

"Mitkin, what the hell are you doing, I can see you, man… It's me, Seever. I gotta get in and lay down…"

Dread sloughed off him. He sighed and lilted toward the door and as he went he heard a door open above. Little light footsteps. Looking up he saw Raphaella's hair dangling down, her sculpted face like a prize inside.

"Who is it, Mitchell?" she asked.

"Seever," said Mitkin, disgust in his voice.

Seever spilled into the hallway when Mitkin opened the door. He put one hand on Mitkin's shoulder, the other on a bulky radiator. "Oh no way, look at this dust, hey." He held his hand up. "Doesn't anybody dust anymore?" He smiled incongruously. "Isn't that your job, boss?"

"Where are your keys?"

"For the front door?"

Mitkin rolled his eyes.

"Right here are my keys," slurred Seever. He fumbled with his pocket and produced a broken key chain. Mitkin took it from him and held it at eye level.

"What happened?"

"Some big guy at happy hour." He faltered and then pointed at Mitkin. "Mitchell, you can't let someone pick on you just because you're from Wisconsin."

"What? He didn't like your accent?"

"How did you know?" Seever was puzzled. "How did you know he was making fun of me like that, wow." He blinked and tried to focus. His stout strong fingers dug into Mitkin's shoulder blade, his thumb into his collarbone. "He said I say O like an asshole. You should have heard how he said A. Caaaahr. Baaahr. What a Dick Tracy." Seever's head almost rolled off his neck. "I got a sore neck, Mitchell. Can you see a bruise? Hey?"

Raphaella approached Seever and examined his neck. "You're bruised all over your neck and back, Andy. You should lie down." Mitkin looked at Raphaella.

"Didn't you hear him buzzing like a madman?"

She nodded and hoisted a handful of her hair. "We were washing, I came as quick as I could. Sorry."

Seever dumped himself on the dusty radiator. It groaned under his heavy, muscular frame and Raphaella jumped forward to hold Seever steady. "Whoa there, you're going to break that," she said, but he didn't hear her. His eyes fluttered and began to close. Raphaella repeated herself. "You need to lie down, Andy. Where is the spare set of keys?"

"Here they are, can you let me into my room?" Seever held up the same, mangled key chain. "I can't get 'em into the lock. I've been drinking a little, ya know."

Raphaella glanced amicably at Mitkin but Mitkin did not return her amity. In fact, the whole scene was becoming irksome. He glared at the drunk.

"Raphie, have you spoken to David lately?" said Seever. "He loves you so much..." His words were slow and heavy. "I think you should think about living together again, heh? He still thinks you're hot." He nodded and there his chin stayed, on his chest. His eyes closed.

Mitkin sighed, gritted his teeth and looked at his wrist where there was no watch.

"Seven-fifteen," said Raphaella, still holding Seever in place.

"What are you going to do?" said Mitkin. "I don't really have time for all of this right now, just put him on the ground." He pointed. She raised an eyebrow. "What about your apartment then," he said. "He can sleep it off there."

Raphaella nodded. Without explanation she got under one of Seever's massive shoulders and motioned for Mitkin to do the same. Together they took a tiny step. All three fell to the ground. Raphaella laughed. Mitkin sighed.

"We can do it," said Raphaella. "One, two, three..."

They managed to get him upright and climb one step before stopping. Hunched over they caught their breath and their balance and continued, step by step. They fell two more times before reaching the second floor landing. Mitkin's door was wide open before them, just as he'd left it. Raphaella looked skeptically up toward her apartment.

Mitkin, too, looked up, and then at Raphaella who struggled to hold her half of the drunken Seever.

"Fine then, put him in my place. Drag him!" yelled Mitkin.

Raphaella moved quickly and they soon had Seever on the floor, on his side, a pillow under his head. Trying to be upbeat, Raphaella slapped her hands together, smiled and said, "Well, that's a job well done." She looked up and her face suddenly went still. Only her smile, curled so slightly at the corner, intimated the airy mood she'd brought into his apartment. "Wow," she said, "this place sure is cleared out. Are you moving, Mitch?"

"No. Are you?"

She stared and waited.

"I just wanted more space I guess," he said.

"I see that. Makes sense." Silence. "I got rid of my TV, too." Mitkin nodded. "Well, he should sleep just fine like that," she said, her tone straight and smooth, her mood airy again. "If you need any help with him, let me know. He's real drunk though, I can't imagine he'd be up any time soon." She turned to leave and took one more look at Mitkin. He still hadn't made voluntary eye contact, and under the weight of her stare, his limbs weakened and his lips trembled slightly. As if illuminated by lightning through a black night, clipped images of him in handcuffs flanked by police and her watching it all on television, flashed in his mind. Clammy with sweat, he looked directly at Raphaella.

"He'll be fine, just fine."

Raphaella peered back. "Thanks." She went upstairs.

Mitkin shut the door and cursed under his breath. "This is no good," he thought. He looked at Seever. The puffy body lay crooked on the floor. The chest heaved up and down and the mouth hung open, globs of spittle ensconced in the corners where his lips met. The sight turned Mitkin's stomach. "Absolutely empty," said Mitkin. He scowled.

The radio reminded him that the siege had been underway for a few hours. Nothing had changed. The reporters prattled on with various hosts missing the mark and perverting the purity of the siege. During it all, Seever slept. By twenty after eight, Mitkin was hungry so he ordered Chinese and paid the man with a fifty. He ate sitting on the kitchen floor, knees curled up against his stomach, a long fork in hand. He gobbled but did not get full. Promise was his sustenance now, the promise of a greater, nobler conflict. He sat still, imagining.

The phone rang again. Mitkin picked it up as fast as he could, expecting Rutledge.

"Mitchell?"

Mitkin stayed silent.

"Mitchell, it's your mother again. I've just had a terrible thought."

Mitkin looked at Seever's body and then around the room as if searching for an escape route.

"Mitchell, are you there?"

"Yes, Mother."

"Don't be mad at me, honey. I just had to call you. I've had the most terrible thought."

"Where are you, Mother?"

"With your uncle and his family, in Newport. Why?"

"What is it, Mother?"

"Mitchell, are you involved in this thing, this takeover? Something you said makes me afraid that you're involved."

Mitkin gripped the phone and saw his knuckles go white. "What did I say, Mother?"

"You said that Dad would have approved of this thing, and then you said *we*, you said *we* just now on the phone. We."

He closed his eyes, and began to lie through a smooth voice. "Mother, please." His whisper was kind. "Do you think Dad would really be in favor of something like this?"

"But you said he would."

"I was angry. I'm not involved. Guns and knives? It's just not me, Mother." He heard what he thought was squeaky leather and a sigh. "Mother, are you there?"

"Just sitting down."

"So don't worry, okay?"

"It's just that ever since your father's death, you've been a different son. You've become very erratic, Mitchell. I've been thinking about the things you must be going through, but I still just can't understand how you could be so angry, and so distant. Do you hate me, Mitchell? Do you hate your mother?"

It was difficult to keep his voice smooth and soft. Opposing emotions tore at him, scorn and pity, a remnant of love. "I don't hate you, Mom."

"Then why all this, this, odd behavior?"

"It's not odd," he snapped, but stopped. "It's not odd. I'm growing up."

"Then why did you get fired? Your father did wonders to get you that job. And what about your plans for medical school?"

His face grew small and his stomach tightened. "It's not odd. Mother."

"Well, it seems odd."

"Not everything is what it seems." Louder. "Not everything is simple. Shopping is not man's destiny, you know. You're the odd one, Mother. How can you watch a man wither and die and think nothing of it? Not look beyond yourself? Not investigate life? What have you learned about life in all your years? Didn't Dad teach you anything about life, Mother?"

She gasped. He wiped his mouth and continued. "Before he died, he taught me to swallow life up whole and use it as fuel for ideas. He taught me that life was a game of investigation, that man's intellect makes him free and special. But then he died and taught me the truth." He took in a gulp of air. "Are you ready for what I really learned from Father, are you ready, Mother?" There was silence. "Nothing is quite what it seems. Life is an illusion, Mother, and the only thing that rescues us from complete annihilation is action, a will to power."

His mother coughed timidly, and whined, "But he didn't teach that at all."

"His dead body did. Death exposed him."

"Because of one thing? Because you saw one thing a different way, you act like this?"

"That one thing was everything," he growled. "If you woke up one day and your breakfast looked like feces—wet, stinking fucking feces—what would you do, Mother? You'd eat it, and then continue to eat it day after day, like a machine?"

There was a long looping silence.

"I've changed my life, Mother, and now, I have a new father."

She was crying. "What is that supposed to mean?"

"I'm free."

"But—"

"Do not call back tonight. Have fun in good ole Newport. I'll call you tomorrow. Tomorrow. Wait until tomorrow."

"Please, Son," she screamed. "Tell me you're not involved in this thing."

"Hang up the phone," he screamed, and they screamed at each other. "No, stop, hang it up… goodbye!" He tossed the receiver away and threw his head back. Little bleating words frantically spilled from the still-connected phone and he wished she had never called. With the care of an executioner lining up his axe blow, he placed the phone back on the hook. It rang only seconds later. In a high, egregious pitch it went on and on, ringing and ringing. He looked at Seever, still dead to the world, then, calmly, he walked to the phone, lifted the receiver and put it back down again. And when she called back, he did it again. And again. Finally it stopped and he returned to the kitchen.

There he met a new voice. It was a workingman's bass with a Brooklyn brogue:

The fire looks like it started on the fourth floor, the same place where police told us the sounds of gunshots came from a couple of minutes ago. Our men are not allowed into the building until we know it's safe, we start with that, their safety. As it goes right now, SWAT has not cleared us to put the whole thing out.

Mitkin leaned closer, his toes knuckling under, palms beginning to sweat. Another voice, this one loud and anxious:

We've got a SWAT rep right here, I believe a Mister Antonio Tolido. Mr. Tolido, can you tell us exactly what is going on inside?

Well I don't know. What I can tell you is, well, someone has put fire to the place, and as far as I can tell that fire has enveloped all the floors above the fourth. Our men are trying to assess what to do next. Shots have been reported yet again.

This is truly a crisis.

Yes, it is. I haven't seen anything like this in all my years with SWAT.

Can you confirm that the shooter or shooters are indeed children?

Sirens wailed in the background.

Again, I am not sure, though it does appear that the gunmen previously at the front entrance were young men, somewhere in their late teens. That is all I can say and to say more is to speculate.

Can we expect more information soon?

Again, I can only speculate.

Mitkin swiped the radio and it crashed to the floor. He ran to the phone.

"Terry?"

"Mitch, you've heard?"

"It's way too early. What's going on?"

"Something's wrong, Mitch. Something's really wrong." Rutledge was raving.

"Stay where you are. Keep listening. Is Freeman still with you?"

"He's right here."

"Keep an eye on him. We must stay together. Whatever happens next, stay calm. We can still get through the night. Don't panic Rutledge, don't fuck this up now." A voice wept in the background. "Keep an eye on Freeman."

"But the place is on fire. Everybody's going to die or get captured. Call it off, Mitch," Rutledge clamored. "Call tomorrow off."

"Calm down. As far as you know we are on for tomorrow, all of us. If plans change I'll let you know. I'm calling Strand and Nin right now. Rev plans are on. Do you hear me? *Rev plans are on.*"

Rutledge was yelling at someone in his apartment.

"Rutledge!" cried Mitkin. "Do you hear me?"

"Yes."

Mitkin hung up the phone. He looked again at Seever and cursed. He dialed.
"Judy, it's Mitchell."

"Mitchell, everything's off right? Call it all off. Please, now."

"Not yet, Judy." His voice was forceful.

"Not yet? When then, Mitch, the end of the month, Christmas maybe?" cried
a sardonic Strand.

"We don't even know if Taughtauer's dead or alive."

"He told me he'd call in case of a disaster, break silence, he told me that,"
Strand said. Mitkin was surprised. "He said that, but he hasn't called and now the
building is burning down. It's over, Mitch."

"How do we know?" asked Mitkin.

"How do we know?" He could hear her heaving on the other end of the phone,
an unpleasant breathing sound filled with fear and anger. "We know, Mitchell,
because it's on the goddamned television! Guess what, there's no giant media
conspiracy to nab us, to fake out the rev-roaches. Come on Mitchell, it's over."

"Wait."

"For what? They'll be after us soon. It only takes one martyr to spill the beans.
I'm telling you, the minute I see one of ours in custody I'm done, I'm on my way
out of town."

"I thought you'd fight until the end?" Mitkin's voice was filling with a
seething sorrow.

"This *is* the end."

Mitkin looked into a half-eaten box of lo mein. The peas and onions sat limply
on the dark yellow noodles. Yep, feces. "It's not the end!" he yelled. "It's not over,
you can't just give up on the only thing that matters in life. Judy. Don't be a
coward."

"So now I'm a coward?" she cried like a shot.

"You won't be free on the run. Stay and fight. Judy, stay."

The phone clicked dead. Mitkin turned in all directions and dialed furiously
to Roger Nin.

"You're kidding me, right?" Nin pleaded.

Mitkin said nothing.

"Let them go, Mitch, let everybody get out of here. I talked to Nicole and James just now. They actually want to hear it from you. They're so good. Let them get out of town."

"And go where?"

"Anywhere. There will be dead people in there—you know that, Mitch. Taughtauer had every intention of killing people."

"I thought you had the same intention, that's what you said. Remember?"

"Life, Mitchell. It's natural to want to live."

"You're all cowards."

"No, Mitchell. No. Check your motives. The fire is enough now, we win with the fire. I'm telling them all that you called it off, Mitchell. Say it for yourself, say it and save the kids."

Mitkin could not speak.

"Say it, Mitchell!"

Still he seized. The phone clicked off and but for the heaping body and stinking food, Mitkin was alone.

And then Seever sputtered. Mitkin ran and saw the burly blond roll slightly to one side. Fury fueled latent strength and he yanked him by the arm and dragged him into the hall. There, with his foot he shoved the big body onto the landing, all as Seever mumbled and bled from his mouth. Mitkin gave one last look and slammed the door.

Click.

Clack.

Cluck.

Bolted in, he raged. He charged from one end of the apartment to the other, tearing at whatever was left on the walls. But so little hung there, and he found himself digging his fingernails into the shoddy sheet rock. He careened into the bathroom and put his fist through the back window, thick panes falling in big pieces to the ground below. He stroked his hair and cried out with wild wide eyes. "They'll be here soon." He marched to the radio and listened.

It's new, it's ranch, it's chicken! Burger King's Chicken Ranch Sandwich only one dollar when you buy another at...

Raising the back of his hand he slapped the little battery-powered radio off the nightstand. The batteries belly-slid across the floor, the radio itself skidding along only inches behind. He stood up straight and flexed his hand. Blood rolled over a knuckle.

The phone rang. It rang and rang and Mitkin ignored it. Slowly, he lowered himself into an Indian style squat on the barren floor. His hands began to shake.

"This can't be. It can't be happening. Tomorrow. Tomorrow is the day, not today." On his hands and knees he fumbled for the radio and then the batteries. As if suffering from a nervous disorder, he struggled to shove the batteries back in their skinny little slots. Crimson blood kept dripping onto the radio. Shuddering, he dropped a battery and it rolled away, on its own, alone. He held his hands to his face and cried, "not yet!" before slumping against the wall.

On the floor he became dizzy, as if he were drunk. His head pounded and a gourd of pity exploded in his belly. He clutched his face, branding to it a bloody palm. Alarmed, he fingered the open gash, holding it hard to stop the bleeding and thought, "They're coming." He whipped a glance at the front door. "They'll beat it down, in an hour, maybe less. And not just me." He picked up the phone and dialed. A brusque voice answered.

"Yeah."

"Is Phillip there?"

"Who's this?"

Mitkin shrunk.

"Who the fuck is this?"

"I am looking for Phillip."

"Well, you can tell Phillip I know where he went, and I know he deep in that fire shit and the dead people, and tell him that if I see him 'round here he's gonna get an ass whoopin' before I send his black ass back to prison where he belongs. You hear me? Tell him that."

Mitkin hung up.

"He is there," thought Mitkin, "with Taughtauer. Everyone who matters is there." Trying again he tracked down the battery and got the radio working. For the first time all night it spit out the truth:

Confirming what we suspected, the dead boy was with the terrorists and has been identified as a John Phillip Carr, of Brooklyn.

Mitkin saw Phillip's face, clear and beautiful, and then all of the other students who had gone to fight that night. Each lay in the emergency room and he at their feet, in a chair, waiting for them to be revived by pumping nurses and frantic doctors but knowing they would not. They were cold, and still, and empty, and their inert bodies made no sense except that they were dead. He saw his father in his final moments. He saw Taughtauer too, a rotund, bloated heap under a hospital-green blanket, his big, bulging eyes and expressive mouth resting limp and torpid, unlike they'd ever been, ever. Mitkin got a strong sense that he was supposed to be proud of their struggle, but he was not. He felt nothing. Another deathbed.

We are now reporting that three bodies have been recovered, all of them on the same floor and all of them apparently members of the same movement. Which movement, however, remains a mystery. Apparently the command center for the terrorists has been overrun and taken by a SWAT team. In it are the bodies, again at least four. As for the city's School Chancellor, Edwin Romero, his whereabouts are unknown. He, according to an unofficial count, is the only hostage still missing.

"I'll go," he murmured. He walked mechanically to the bedroom and began to sort clothes. "I'll go to Canada." He found his passport in a drawer. Rather than push the drawer back in, he pulled it out and let it fall in a heap to the ground. Then with his forearm, he calmly swept the top of the bureau clean, pushing without discretion, like a bulldozer into a landfill. A mirror splintered. A bottle of dusty cologne exploded. Oblivious, he stooped to examine a picture of his father which looked back at him from the hardwood, alongside a nail clipper and a faded receipt. His father sat in a boat, casting for fish in a deep blue lake. "There's nothing down there," he thought. "Nothing."

He slouched slowly to the ground, buttocks slowly to flank. He pulled himself to himself, like a child at bedtime. There, his cheek to the floor, he noticed an old mousetrap tucked under a dusty radiator, the cheese bait still in it. He squinted at the trap, staring for a very, very long time.

At the end of an empty stare, he pulled himself along the ground toward the radiator. Stretching out an arm, he watched as his forefinger got closer and closer to the mousetrap. Without hesitation he pressed on the cheese and winced as the trap buckled and fell with a whir. A cold sizzle ran through his body but he did not scream, and he did not get up. With the trap stuck to his finger he rolled onto his back and there he examined it at his leisure. A swath of tattered skin had been torn from the top of his finger. Slowly, decidedly, he pulled his finger out of the steel trap, blood dripping onto his chest. At its deepest, the empty gash was bluish with resplendent rivulets of crimson blood. A hint of white, his bone, peeked out from beneath the carnage. Drip by drip, blood fell onto Mitkin's belly. He watched it all and sniggered.

"I stay."

He got up. He went straight out the front door, stepping over Seever and down the steps. He moved deftly through the two doors and into the mild evening air of early September. He walked through a hole in the fence that surrounded the property and began to peruse the refuse pile in the tiny backyard. The place was a jungle. For a long time, it had been overrun by weeds and abandoned furniture: a beat-up microwave, rotting lumber and old rusty hubcaps. When Mitkin's father bought the property he planned to clean it up and use it to raise the rent, but he never did. Now his beloved son scrounged through it, head down, shoulders hunched, with a finger dripping blood, eyes afire. He pulled a piece of wood from underneath a pile and then another. He continued like this for about ten minutes until his foraging produced a bushel of old, ratty wood. Tucking it all under his arm, he walked back toward the front of the house. He returned for a soiled recliner and put it on his back. A horde of roaches scurried out and onto Mitkin's neck. He did not flinch.

Little by little, he amassed a stocky pile of garbage near the building's entrance. He did this and never stopped to look at his work or at the passersby who began to take notice. His head was always down. He then hinged open both front doors and began to bring in the refuse. When everything had been piled inside he shut the front door and went back upstairs to his apartment to retrieve his wallet. Stepping back out, over Seever, and then over his cache of debris, he walked like a soldier to the corner hardware store. He bought a giant bundle of heavy-duty utility cord, scissors, matches and a hefty can of gasoline. His bloody hand was all the talk, only Mitkin didn't understand enough uptown Spanish to realize it, nor did he really care what anyone said or thought during these manic moments.

Returning to the three-story brownstone, he began to construct a barricade. He pushed the recliner behind the front door (which opened out), and with the utility cord tied a door stop, fastening one end of the cord to the first door and then looping a knot around the handle of the inside door (which opened in). Squeezing himself inside and pulling the cord tight, he wrapped more utility cord around the fat base of the oak banister and tied an ugly knot. When he tightened the slack on his creation the whole thing creaked and reminded him of a giant tug of war, the banister versus the doors. Quickly, he buttressed all of this with wooden door jams fixed hard under the inside door's handle, a locking device he'd seen used effectively in many Manhattan apartments. The entire process took twenty minutes, but when it was finished Mitkin was assured of his fortress. He grabbed the gasoline and matches and weaved his way through the maze of cord and debris. He mounted the stairs. In front of his door, standing over Seever, he looked up and thought for a moment about Raphaella. Had she heard him? Would she get involved?

He toed Seever's mid-section and saw that the big drunk was still asleep, or not moving at least. He hopped over him into his apartment looking back and muttering the word "fool" before slamming his door shut. He dialed 411.

"I want the Channel Seven newsroom." The operator gave him the number and he dialed again.

The person on the other end spoke quickly and plainly, her voice disinterested and afar, her manner dismissive. Mitkin asked for a supervisor.

"He's very busy, sir, you've called at a bad time." She snapped some chewing gum between her teeth. "Can I take a message?"

Mitkin spoke flatly, "I am holding two hostages at 102 E. 103rd Street. I will kill one in ten minutes if I do not have the ear of every news crew in this city. I am a member of the Student Coalition, the same coalition that has taken Livingston Street and has killed the Chancellor. You have ten minutes." He hung up the phone and called 911, repeating his message. Next he went to the bedroom and retrieved the pistol, and then to the kitchen for the butcher's cleaver. The handles of each invited caress. They were thick, stout, smooth handles with finger notches that braced heavy steel and invoked power. With his hands at his side he stroked the handles with his thumbs, rubbing each up and down, back and forth, round and round. He held out his hands and felt the weight of his weapons, bobbing them twice like an equestrian preparing his reins. The steel of one chimed against the steel of the other. With his head down and his fists firm, he kicked open the door and hiked up the stairs. He pounded Raphaella's door with the underside of his fist and the butt of the butcher's cleaver. It shook violently as if against the gale of a hateful storm. Then gaining his wits, he tucked the gun into his waistband and slid the cleaver into his belt. He heard Raphaella move toward the door.

"Who is it?" she said anxiously.

"Mitchell."

He imagined her leaning closer and then saw the little dim light go dark in the peephole. She opened the door, and like a tempest all at once he grabbed her by the hair and pulled her, head wrenched to her knees, down the stairs. They plunged headlong, nearly falling, skipping stairs two at a time, wildly on, forward. They leapt over the drunk Seever and into Mitkin's apartment. A siren in the distance came wailing.

All the while Raphaella did not scream. At one point she said, "Why?" and at that he pressed the cold muzzle deep into her cheek. Inside his apartment, he let her go, pushed her forward, and pointed the gun at her.

"Sit down," he screamed.

He took her by the arm before she could move, and with a heavy hand threw her onto the hardwood. He kept the muzzle of the gun trained on her head, close enough that she could smell the sweat in his armpits.

"Is Seever dead?" she asked.

"Seever? Fuck him. In fact," he got up and opened the front door, "pull him in here now!" He pointed the gun at Seever and then at her. It trembled. Raphaella darted toward the door as Mitkin screamed, "Pull him!" With all of her might, she tugged at Seever. He groaned and she tugged again until finally the big body was in. The sirens were very loud now.

"They've come for you, Mitchell."

"No," he said, "I called them. It's what is supposed to happen. It's what I want to happen."

"Why?"

"I'm in charge here, goddammit! You don't care why, nobody cares why. Not one person on this earth cares why, not you, not anybody, there is no answer to why!"

The door rattled below.

"They won't get in right away," he said snatching the ball of utility cord and tying Raphaella's hands tight to the chubby radiator post. He pulled on her arms to test the knot and she winced in pain. Next he tied Seever.

The sound of steel in motion from outside the back window snapped Mitkin to attention. "The fire escape!" he shouted, bolting toward the window. Raphaella watched as he fired a shot toward the ground.

"I'll kill them!" he shouted out the window. "Don't come this way! I'll kill them!" Coming back inside, he locked the window and rushed back to the kitchen where he spoke quickly to his hostages.

"I won't kill you if they listen to me." And then, like a soldier he marched back to the front of the apartment. There he curled his head around and looked outside. Three police cars sat cockeyed in the street, their emergency lights dancing from building to building in the night, red and blue and glaring white, all of it oddly inviting, fantastic, fated. He fired a shot into the air and two policemen ducked behind their cars. "I don't see a news crew," he yelled. "Where are the talking heads?" A crackly voice shot back through a police bullhorn.

"Clear the streets. Get clear of the street."

Mitkin watched as pedestrians ducked, too, some behind garbage cans, others in stairwells, one entirely beneath a car. He fired another shot and watched as still others did the same. A wild rush of adrenaline made him smile like a joker. Then, in a second, that joker's smile turned wry, and he wheeled around, heading back into the foyer where Raphaella and Seever were bound. He fumbled in the kitchen for a piece of paper and a pen. He wrote furiously.

"What are you writing?" she asked.

"Not what am I writing, what am I willing. I'm willing the end, the one I've wanted all along."

He stuffed the note into a drinking cup and stepped over his human haul toward the big bay window. Ducking down, he reached over the sill and dropped the cup, listening as it clipped a windowsill and banged its way to the concrete below. Next he was on the phone. Everything was done precisely and unencumbered, as if already there, in his head, planned and prepared and now, finally, at liberty to explode into the world just as he orchestrated. He spoke clearly.

"I said I want a news crew. If I don't see a news crew in four minutes then I shoot the man from Wisconsin, his name is Andrew Seever. Then, well, then you'll have to report that New York is a dangerous place for people from Wisconsin." He simpered. "You now have three minutes."

Around and around he went, pacing and talking to himself and to Raphaella.

"The fire comes after I'm dead, really just as I'm dying, at the same time." He took the container of gasoline in his hand and unknowingly knocked the matches off and to the ground. "Start it at the door, right here," he mumbled. He splashed some of the clear liquid under the door and the whole apartment quickly filled with noxious fumes.

"Are we all going to die, Mitchell? Even Dana? Even little Dana?" said Raphaella.

"Not the plan! The plan is I die, but not before everyone in this city knows who we are and why we've done what we've done. They'll know how deep in shit they all are, how incredibly bankrupt their whole system is and how there is no meaning in any of their little schemes, in any of their tiny lives, and in all of this..." he pointed wildly in a circle with the gun. "When they know, you go."

"But for what, Mitchell?"

"Our will."

"That's all?"

"That's everything."

Seever moved. He rolled onto his back and unwittingly onto Mitkin's little book of matches. There, with his hands tied behind him, he instinctively held the matchbook in his hand, clutching it because he had nothing else to clutch for. He opened his eyes and moaned again, trying to sit up. Because his arms had been tied he could not and so, confused, he shook his head and stared at Raphaella.

"What are you doing here? What's with the—"

"Shut up, Seever," Mitkin hissed.

"Mitkin?"

Mitkin moved close to Seever and with the muzzle of his pistol flicked the underside of Seever's nose. "Yes, it's Mitkin."

"What's going on now, hey?" He glanced at Raphaella for answers. "Raphaella, what's going on with him?"

The phone rang.

"Mitchell Mitkin?" asked the deep voice.

"Who is this?"

"My name is Sergeant Wickus. I want to talk to you. I want to know what you want."

"I want a news crew, now."

"We have one here."

"Where?"

Mitkin walked with the phone to the front of the building. With his back to the wall, he peered gingerly out the window and could see a van sporting a television logo. He moved sprightly out of the room. "Put them on the phone," he said.

"I can't do that. I need to know what else you want. I want to help you."

"Then put them on the phone."

A slice of silence was followed by a new voice. This voice was far less calm. "Hello, who is this?"

"This is Mitchell Mitkin. Who is this?"

"My name is Albert Tucker. I'm a reporter with Channel Seven."

"The black one?"

"Yes."

"Are you ready to write?"

"I'm recording."

"Then record this: Today thousands of students are ready to change the NYC public school system by a sheer act of will. Record that they have lived with the thought of death and deception too long, and that they want to know something else, something they can call life, something that has meaning, something that rings of victory and smells like freedom and truth. Record that these students are ready to make something meaningful of their lives and they don't give a damn what anybody thinks about it, they don't give a damn if it's all good, or right, or true. Write that they are tired of nothingness and a world gone mad. They have changed their lives today."

"Who is in charge, are you in charge?"

"They are in charge." Mitkin was speaking loudly.

"Just them?"

"What, you don't believe it could be just them? Is that an impossibility, sir? Can't kids have valid ideas, too?"

"Then who are you?"

"I am one of their servants. Someone, who like them, is tired of the emptiness."

"Then which students are involved, who are the leaders?"

"All the students in the system are involved, every one of them knows the emptiness well. Not one student in this city is unaware of it, but I can assure you all of them are learning how to fill it. Action sir, this action is just the beginning. You're lucky, you get to record it for posterity."

"Where is the Chancellor?"

"He's dead."

"How many are at Livingston Street?"

"Thousands. Millions."

Mitkin became aware of a sawing sound coming from the foyer. He jumped up and lunged toward the door, his eyes meeting Seever's. Wild and flush-red, Seever's fear-filled stare stopped Mitkin momentarily, long enough to notice Seever's big hands out in front of him, free now, pulling hard at the front door. Mitkin fired his pistol. Seever, seemingly unhurt, kept pulling until the door opened and then tumbled out. Face first he went onto the stoop, his head hanging slightly over the top stair, his eyes now blank.

Mitkin rushed out after him only to sense movement over his left shoulder. He wheeled and saw Raphaella, standing untied, her palms up, her arms stretched toward him, entreating, soothing, freeing him, loving him. Instantaneously Mitkin visioned her martyrdom, their martyrdom, the validation of his cause, the perfection of their deaths in the same moment of time, an unforeseen blood pact that finally, perfectly consummated their relationship. Without thought and without consciousness, Mitkin fired twice. A sooty hole appeared on Raphaella's forehead, and a dash of crimson just above her belly button. She teetered backward and crumpled to the ground.

Now, Mitkin stood still, mesmerized as blood pooled and crimson fingers crept through the foyer, into the kitchen and onto the smooth linoleum floor. There they made their way under the refrigerator and out of sight. A wisp of smoke travelled upwards, mirroring the rivulets of Raphaella's blood and her blameless soul. He turned and looked at Seever who remained motionless in front of the door, carrying a bullet in his back. Like a grinding headache, reality crashed in and the sawing sound intensified below. Mitkin felt himself wobble and sway. The sounds of a little boy playing in the park came magically to him, carried from far away, laughter and quiet crying mixed sadly in a mist of memory that would stay with him forever, a reminder of what he had done this day. He listened to the little voice and in it, he heard his own.

"Mommy?" it said, a knock and then again, "Mommy, I'm afraid." Into the darkness of his mind came a sliver of reality and the high soprano of a terrified girl. "Mommy? Mitchell? Is Mommy there?"

Dana's bright eyes peeked around the door and into the blood-filled apartment. As Mitkin ran to shut the door, her innocent stare met his and she was suddenly ashen. He slammed the door before she could see her mother, or at least that was the thought he had in that eternal instant. Turning, he spotted the gas can and with a maniacal self-pity, fired into it. Gas spilled and sprayed all around him. From below he could hear more smashing, the sounds of breaking glass, and little Dana's terrified murmur.

"They'll rescue her in time," he rationalized. "They'll get her," he mumbled. He rushed to find a match. From room to room he ran, searching every corner for fire. He slipped on Raphaella's blood and fell to the ground as he entered the kitchen. His hands slithered forward and he dropped to his chest. Hurrying to get up he heard shouts from below and a giant crackling blast.

"Matches!" he screamed. "Fire!"

From his knees he twisted the knob on the stove in hopes of finding a spark, but the electric stove only stared back coldly.

It would be a while.

Slowing, he sat on the floor against the kitchen cabinet and surveyed his slaughter. It had come to this. In a void of resignation came together all of his failures and losses; his father's death, the defeat of science, unrequited love and unrealized dreams. It was out of control now, he had created chaos, with no saving grace. Fighting off one final urge to weep, he put the gun to his temple, looked one more time at Raphaella, closed his eyes, and fired.

***

I don't like looking at him sitting there, not smug but not dead either, like my Raphaella. I don't like to see him point out the scar, the place the bullet entered and where it grazed his skull. He is telling my story as his own, the only one I've ever wanted to truly tell. But this dislike is not hate or rage like it was only a week ago. This is something else, something different that brings me to tears. And I am crying all right, a stream of tears wets my face and he sees them, my first tears since that day. Suddenly, he gets up and leaves without a word and the door shuts behind him with a whoosh and I wonder where he has gone. I gather myself and wait. It's not a short wait, either. I sense that he has left the visiting area altogether. I look up at Rocky who looks back kindly and says, "I'll call." I wipe my eyes one last time and then, on cue, Mitkin walks back through the visiting room doors.

Rocky nods and goes back to his crossword puzzle. I notice the size of his taut forearms as he holds the pen, and everything suddenly seems normal, just as it has been for the last week; normal except that Mitkin is carrying something, a picture it seems. His face is pale, as pale as I've ever seen it. He approaches the table and takes a seat, and then, with a slow hand slides the picture across the table, like an informant handing over precious documents or a wad of cash. The sound of paper sliding over wood is the last thing I think of before I realize that the picture is of Raphaella, alive, in white, her long hair wet and over her face, her head bowed meekly. I don't recognize the picture, but I know what is happening. It is Raphaella's baptism, the day she truly left me, and the day she cherished above all others.

"It's all I have of her," he says, softly. "It's the only thing I've kept from then, from when I was with her."

I nod, but I can't entirely focus on the picture. It sits on the table between us, exactly in the middle, dividing us and uniting us at the same time. I look at him and feel a profound sorrow, one that is unlike any sorrow I've ever known because it comes with a hint of joy. A hint of joy! I feel it as if she had experienced it in me, as if she were with me now.

"Were you there?" he asks.

"No," I reply, "I went to a film festival that weekend."

"A film festival." He just nods knowingly, continuing like that for more than a moment, content to just move his head up and down, slowly. Then, finally, he says, "I was there. I took the picture."

"Did she invite you?"

"She did, but I told her I wouldn't go, that I hated her because she wouldn't love me." I wait as he pauses. "But then I showed up, I just showed up with my camera and I didn't really understand why. I watched it all from far away in the church, I don't even know if she saw me. I was off in a corner, like a voyeur. Do you see? Do you get it now?"

I look at him suspiciously, as if he is hiding something from me. He stares back and continues.

"Day by day I died trying to get her to love me, to fill in for my father and love me as I wanted to be loved. That was how I was living back then, David. I was living for her. Up at The Cloisters I felt that she ended my life as it was, ended me, and my hopes for love. I was so lonely, so alone then and she was so beautiful, so wonderful and I felt we could make it together. But, of course, this would never happen. She wanted something else, something that I could never have understood without," he pauses and looks right at me, "without there being a change, a renewal." His eyes well up. "She gave it to me, David. She gave me love." He stops, his eyes fill with embarrassment and regret but also a peace that goes beyond my understanding. "Selfish to the end, I was selfish right to the end and she knew it, standing there, her hands out, forgiving me, hoping for me, loving me. And I killed her." That is too much to say. He begins to cry in earnest, the tears coming like torrents. "Don't you see?" He wipes his cheeks with the back of his cuff.

I wait and then I ask, "Why the picture?"

Gently he picks the picture off the table and holds it like a placard in front of me. "I was there when she died to this world, but I refused to accept it, and this is that moment." He shakes the picture for punctuation. "This is the moment that I knew I would kill her, and I keep it because it reminds me that I am a proud, proud, sad man." I look right by him but not because I don't understand, it's more because I am in the process of understanding, sorting it out, making sense of it. I think he recognizes this as he continues. "She wanted what Christ wanted David, it's crazy to think about, but your Raphaella wanted to save the world the same exact way Christ wanted to save the world. She wanted what He wanted, exactly how He wanted it. No difference."

Could it have really been for this? I think to myself. "She's all wet," I say, pointing at the picture.

"She'd just come out of the font, out of the depths. She used to tell me that, tell me that the water was her tomb, and that it was in the tomb that she learned about life. Oh damn David, if only I'd had the ears to hear." He begins to cry again.

His tears would have been the most hateful things ever only ten days ago, but now they are like perfection rolling down his cheeks. I understand so much and I say, "Dana taught you this, didn't she?"

"She didn't teach me, David, I learned it in flashes, brilliant flashes even on that terrible day at 103rd Street, with the police and Seever and poor little Dana, I learned it all then. But Dana made me aware of it, she held the wax paper and ran the crayon over my tomb. By loving the man who killed her mother, she raised the words and made me see why I am here, and you too."

"Me too?" I ask.

"Raphaella has taken us both as lovers now David, and Dana too, all of us." He looks around as if coming back from a faraway place, looking up at Rocky who is oblivious. "She has assumed all of us and made it as it should be, everything, just as it should be, because of her." Incredibly, he smiles that ineffable smile.

I must admit that now, here, in this mud-brown hotel where I am holed up, writing this, this thing, I don't totally understand that profoundly peaceful and wise smile of his. But I can say I didn't flinch at it, I didn't want to wipe it off his face. I only know that it was absurd and that I wanted it somehow, and that I am in the process of finding that smile every day, each morning, each night before bed. In a very cliché kind of way it haunts me, and follows me, and I wonder if I will ever fully understand it. Mitkin, of course, was baptized long ago in this prison in the same manner as Raphaella, and Dana too. I remain uninitiated, but I don't think I am truly dead as if without knowledge. It's only that I don't get the smile yet, it hasn't washed over me entirely, entombed me, and that is okay I think, okay if only for the moment.

Alone here, I have been leafing through the folder that I put together around the time of Raphaella's death. It is filled with her letters to me, and her most precious items, things like her prayer rope, her favorite icon of St. Mary of Egypt, the business card her long-lost father gave to her mother, and her beloved art history book. In it, just today, I found a passage in a letter she wrote to me. It says that one day I will know the things that separate us, and then I will only have to choose. I think that day has come. I think that, at least now, I know what I must do, and why I have come into this prison, and why I have been given the gift of fatherhood. How difficult is the knowing though! In that same folder I found a little laminated copy of Raphie's favorite Psalm, the one that was said at her baptism, and the one she loved to sing in the car on the way to Vespers during those last days before her death:

Blessed is he whose unrighteousness is forgiven, and whose sin is covered. Blessed is the man unto whom the Lord imputeth no sin, and in whose spirit there is no guile…

ABOUT THE AUTHOR

John Heers is the founder and director of First Things Foundation. Heers worked overseas as a social entrepreneur and foreign aid project manager in the Georgian Republic, Guatemala, Sierra Leone, Haiti, Ethiopia and Mali. He speaks four languages and is a deep admirer of Fyodor Dostoevsky. His work as an educator includes eight years teaching in Harlem and the South Bronx, and ten years in Naples, Florida where he co-created the Seacrest High School. Heers has written numerous short stories and is the author of the podcast, *Why Are We Talking About Rabbits?* He and his wife Helen have four daughters and currently live in Greenville, South Carolina.

Learn more about the author and First Things Foundation at first-things.org.

Made in United States
North Haven, CT
22 February 2025

66073729R00198